HITCHED!
BY
B.J. DANIELS

AND

CLASSIFIED
COWBOY
BY
MALLORY KANE

D0833006

9030 00001 7300 7

MILLS

HITCHED!

BY
B.J. DANIELS

DID YOU PURCHASE THIS BOOK WITHOUT A COVER?

If you did, you should be aware it is **stolen property** as it was reported *unsold and destroyed* by a retailer. Neither the author nor the publisher has received any payment for this book.

All the characters in this book have no existence outside the imagination of the author, and have no relation whatsoever to anyone bearing the same name or names. They are not even distantly inspired by any individual known or unknown to the author, and all the incidents are pure invention.

All Rights Reserved including the right of reproduction in whole or in part in any form. This edition is published by arrangement with Harlequin Enterprises II B.V./S.à.r.l. The text of this publication or any part thereof may not be reproduced or transmitted in any form or by any means, electronic or mechanical, including photocopying, recording, storage in an information retrieval system, or otherwise, without the written permission of the publisher.

This book is sold subject to the condition that it shall not, by way of trade or otherwise, be lent, resold, hired out or otherwise circulated without the prior consent of the publisher in any form of binding or cover other than that in which it is published and without a similar condition including this condition being imposed on the subsequent purchaser.

® and ™ are trademarks owned and used by the trademark owner and/or its licensee. Trademarks marked with ® are registered with the United Kingdom Patent Office and/or the Office for Harmonisation in the Internal Market and in other countries.

First published in Great Britain 2011
by Mills & Boon, an imprint of Harlequin (UK) Limited,
Eton House, 18-24 Paradise Road, Richmond, Surrey TW9 1SR

© Barbara Heinlein 2010

ISBN: 978 0 263 88530 9

46-0611

Harlequin (UK) policy is to use papers that are natural, renewable and recyclable products and made from wood grown in sustainable forests. The logging and manufacturing processes conform to the legal environmental regulations of the country of origin.

Printed and bound in Spain
by Blackprint CPI, Barcelona

B.J. Daniels wrote her first book after a career as an award-winning newspaper journalist and author of thirty-seven published short stories. Since then she has won numerous awards, including a career achievement award for romantic suspense and many nominations and awards for best book.

Daniels lives in Montana with her husband, Parker, and two springer spaniels, Spot and Jem. When she isn't writing, she snowboards, camps, boats and plays tennis. Daniels is a member of Mystery Writers of America, Sisters in Crime, International Thriller Writers, Kiss of Death and Romance Writers of America.

To contact her, write to B.J. Daniels, PO Box 1173, Malta, MT 59538 or e-mail her at bjdaniels@mtintouch. net. Check out her webpage at www.bjdaniels.com.

LONDON BOROUGH OF WANDSWORTH	
9030 00001 7300 7	
Askews & Holts	19-May-2011
AF DANI	£5.30

This one is for E-Dub.
You are always an inspiration!

Chapter One

Jack hadn't seen another person in miles when he spotted the woman beside the road. He was cruising along Highway 191, headed north through the most unpopulated part of Montana, when he saw her.

At first he blinked, convinced she had to be a mirage, since he hadn't even seen another car in hours. But there she was, standing beside the road, hip cocked, thumb out, a mane of long, ginger hair falling past her shoulders, blue jeans snug-fitting from her perfect behind down her impossibly long legs.

Jack slowed, already having doubts before he stopped next to her in his vintage, pale yellow Cadillac convertible. Just the sight of her kicked up the heat on an already warm May day.

She had a face that would make any man look twice. He watched her take in the restored convertible first then sweep her green-eyed gaze over him. He thought of warm, tropical sea breezes.

Until he looked closer. As warm as the day was, she wore a jean jacket, the collar turned up. He caught a glimpse of a stained T-shirt underneath. Her sneakers looked wet, like her hair. Her clothes were dusty and the cuffs of her jeans wet and muddy.

He'd seen an empty campground in the cottonwoods as he passed the Missouri River, but it was still early in this part of Montana to be camping, since the nights would be cold. It was especially too early to be bathing in the river, but he had to assume that was exactly what she'd done.

"Going any place in particular?" he asked, worried what she was doing out here in the middle of nowhere all alone. Assuming that was the case. He glanced toward the silky-green pine trees lining the road, half-expecting her boyfriend to come barreling out of them at any minute. But then, that was the way his suspicious mind worked.

"Up the highway." She leaned down to pick up the dirty backpack at her feet. It appeared as road worn as she was.

All Jack's instincts told him he'd regret giving this woman a ride. But it was what he glimpsed in her eyes that made up his mind. A little fear was normal for a woman traveling alone in the middle of nowhere. This woman was terrified of something.

He saw her glance back down the highway toward the river, that terror glittering in all that green.

"Then I guess you're going my way." He smiled, wondering what the hell this woman was running from and why he was opening himself up to it. Any fool knew that a woman on the run had trouble close at her heels. "Hop in."

She swung the backpack to her shoulder, straightened the collar of her jean jacket and shot another look back down the lonesome highway.

Jack glanced in his rearview, half-afraid of what had her so scared. Heat rose from the empty two-lane blacktop. He caught a glimpse of the river below them, the dark surface glistening in the morning sunlight. A hawk squawked as it soared on a current coming up out of the river. A cloud passed overhead, throwing the rugged ravines and gullies choked with scrub juniper and pine into shadow.

As he turned back, she was apologizing for her muddy sneakers.

"Don't worry about that," he said, figuring this woman had a lot more to worry about than getting his car dirty.

As he reached across to open her door, she dropped her backpack onto the passenger-side floorboard and slid into the seat, closing the door behind her.

Jack tried to shove off his second thoughts about picking up a total stranger on the run from beside the road in such a remote, isolated place as he watched her settle into the soft leather.

He couldn't miss the way she pulled her bulging backpack protectively between her feet. The backpack, like her T-shirt, was stained with dirt and splattered with something dark the color of dried blood.

"Name's Jack. Jack Winchester." Then he asked, "I'm on my way to the Winchester Ranch. You don't happen to know the Winchesters, do you?"

"I don't know a living soul in Montana." She took his outstretched hand. Her skin was silky smooth and just as cool. "Josey." Her eyes widened a little, as if that had just slipped out. "Josey Smith."

She'd stumbled on the last name, a clear lie. It made him wonder again who or what was after her. "Nice to meet you, Josey." He told himself he was just giving her a ride up the road as far as the turnoff to the ranch.

Shifting the Caddie into gear, he took off. As they

topped the mountain and left the river and wild country of the Breaks behind, he saw her take one last look back. But the fear didn't leave her eyes as they roared down the long, empty highway.

JOSEY FOUGHT to still the frantic pounding of her heart. She didn't want this man to see how desperate she was. She was still shaking inside as she turned up the collar on her jean jacket and lay back against the seat.

She needed time to think. It still wasn't clear to her what had happened back there on the river.

Liar. She closed her eyes, trying to block it all out. But the memory was too fresh. Just like the pain. She could still see the car breaking the dark green surface and sinking, hear the gurgling sound as water rushed in, see the huge bubbles that boiled to the surface.

She'd stumbled and fallen as she scaled the rocky bluff over the river, then worked her way through the pines, not daring to look back. She'd only just broken out of the trees and onto the highway when she'd heard the growl of an engine and spotted the Cadillac coming up the hill. It was the first vehicle she'd seen or heard in hours.

Holding her breath and reining in her urge to run, she'd stuck out her thumb—and prayed. Her only hope was to get as far away as she could. She'd been scared the driver of the Cadillac wouldn't stop for her. She could just imagine the way she looked.

But he had stopped, she thought. That alone made her wary. She tried to concentrate on the warm spring breeze on her face, telling herself she was alive. It seemed a miracle. She'd gotten away. She was still shaking, though, still terrified after the horror of the past two days.

She opened her eyes, fighting the urge to look back down the highway again, and glanced over at the man who'd picked her up. Under normal circumstances she would have thought twice about getting into a car with a complete stranger, especially out here where there were no houses, no people, nothing but miles and miles of nothing.

Jack Winchester looked like a rancher in his jeans, boots, and fancy Western shirt. His dark blond hair curled at his nape under the black Stetson. She glanced down at her own clothing and cringed. She looked as if she'd been wallowing in the dirt. She had.

Furtively, she brushed at her jeans and, unable to refrain any longer, turned to look back down the highway.

Empty.

She felt tears sting her eyes. He wasn't coming after her. He couldn't ever hurt her again. She shuddered at the thought.

Not that it was over. By now California criminal investigators would have put out an all-points bulletin on her. Before long she'd be wanted in all fifty states for murder—and they didn't know the half of it.

AHEAD, THE LITTLE ROCKIES were etched purple against the clear blue sky of the spring day. As the land changed from the deep ravines and rocky ridges of the Missouri Breaks to the rolling prairie, Jack watched his passenger out of the corner of his eye. She chewed at her lower lip, stealing glances in the side mirror at the highway behind them. She had him looking back, as well.

Fortunately, the two-lane was empty.

As he neared the turnoff to the ranch, Jack realized he couldn't just put her out beside the road. He couldn't imagine how she came to be hitchhiking, but his every instinct told him she was in danger.

He could only assume it was from some man she'd hooked up with and later regretted. Whoever was after her, Jack didn't want him or her to catch up with his passenger.

He knew it was crazy. The last thing he needed was to get involved in this woman's problems. But he also didn't want her blood on his hands.

A thought crossed his mind. He prided himself at thinking on his feet. Also at using situations to his advantage.

And it appeared fate had literally dropped this woman into his lap. Or at least dropped her into his Caddie. Josey couldn't have been more perfect if he'd ordered her from a catalog. The more he thought about it, the more he liked his idea, and he wondered why he hadn't thought of it before he'd agreed to this visit to the "family" ranch.

He glanced over at her. She had her eyes closed again, her head back, her hair blowing behind her in a tangled wave of sun-kissed copper. She was stunning, but beyond that his instincts told him that this woman wasn't the type who normally found herself in this kind of position beside a road, and possibly running for her life.

Jack reminded himself that his instincts had also warned him not to pick her up back there.

He smiled to himself. Taking chances was nothing new to him, nor was charming his way to what he wanted. He'd been told that he could talk a rattlesnake out of its venom without even a bite. He knew he could talk this woman into what he had in mind or his name wasn't Jack Winchester.

But he didn't figure it would take much charming. He had a feeling she'd go for his proposal because she needed this more than he did.

"So, Josey, how do you feel about marriage?" he asked as they cruised down the vacant two-lane headed toward Whitehorse, Montana.

"Marriage?" she asked, opening one eye.

Jack grinned. "I have a proposition for you."

Chapter Two

Josey had been taken aback, instantly suspicious until he explained that he was on his way to see his grandmother, who was in her seventies.

"She has more money than she knows what to do with and lives on a huge ranch to the east of here," Jack said. "You'd be doing me a huge favor, and I'd make it worth your while. The ranch is sixty miles from the nearest town and a good ten from the nearest neighbor."

A remote ranch. Could she really get this lucky? He was offering her exactly what she needed, as if he knew how desperate she was. Was it that obvious?

"What do you get out of it?" she asked, wary.

"Your company as well as a diversion. Since we're on our honeymoon I have the perfect excuse to spend less time at my grandmother's bedside."

"I take it you aren't close."

He laughed at that. "You have no idea."

Still, she made him work for it. This wasn't her first rodeo, as they said out here in the West, and Jack Winchester was definitely not the first con man she'd come across in her twenty-eight years.

He was good, though, smooth, sexy and charming as the devil, with a grin that would have had her naked—had she still been young and naive.

She was neither. She'd learned the hard way about men like Jack Winchester back in her wild days.

But she also knew he would be suspicious if she gave in right away.

"One week," she said, hoping she wasn't making a huge mistake. Jack had showed up just when she needed him and this marriage charade. No wonder she was feeling this was too good to be true.

But given her lack of options…

He flashed her a sexy grin, and she told herself all she had to do was resist his cowboy charm for a week. No problem.

She closed her eyes and dozed until she felt him slowing down on the outskirts of what appeared to be a small Western town nestled in a river bottom.

"Welcome to Whitehorse," Jack said with a laugh as they crossed a narrow bridge. "I thought we'd buy a few things for you to wear this week. I'm guessing you don't have a lot of clothing in that backpack."

That almost made her laugh as she pulled the backpack closer. "I definitely could use some clothes and a shower before I meet your grandmother."

"No problem. Just tell me what you need. I'm sure there's a truck stop at one end of this town or another. It's the only town for miles up here."

She looked over at him. He was making this too easy. Was he thinking that with a wife his grandmother would give him twice the inheritance? "You're sure about this? Because I'm really not dressed to go into a clothing store," she said, sliding down in the seat as they entered town.

JACK FELT A CHILL as Josey turned up the collar on her jean jacket and slid down in her seat. *Who the hell is after her? And what the hell have I got myself into?*

Still, the gambler in him told him to stick to his plan. He couldn't throw this woman to the wolves. "My wife can have anything she wants or needs," he said. "Just name it."

And she did, including hair dye and a pair of sharp scissors. He hadn't even lifted a brow, but he'd hated the thought of what she planned to do to that beautiful hair of hers.

It definitely brought home the realization that he'd underestimated just how much trouble this woman was in. "I'll tell you what. Why don't I drop you at the truck stop? You can get a hot shower, get out of those clothes and I'll come by with everything else you need."

"You don't know my size."

"I'm good at guessing." He saw her hesitate. "Trust me."

Like a dog that'd been kicked too many times, her look said, *When hell freezes over.*

She told him what else she needed, which turned out to be just about everything. He had to wonder what *was* in that backpack. It looked full. But apparently there wasn't much clothing in it.

Whatever was in the backpack, it was something she wasn't letting out of her sight. She kept the backpack close, taking it with her when he dropped her at the truck stop.

Jack watched her walk away, her head down as if trying to go unnoticed, and told himself he was going to regret this.

JOSEY DIDN'T EXPECT to see Jack Winchester again as he drove away from the truck stop. She wouldn't have blamed him. She'd caught the look that crossed his handsome face when she'd asked for the dark hair dye and scissors.

Only a fool wouldn't get the implication of that and Jack, she suspected, was no fool. By the time she'd showered, she'd found the items she'd asked for waiting for her just outside the shower door.

She took the scissors to her hair, surprised by how painful it was. It was just hair. It would grow back. But she knew she wasn't upset about her hair. It was all the other losses in her life.

She let the dye set in her short hair as she avoided looking in the mirror, then took another shower, wondering if she would ever feel truly clean again. In the bags he'd left for her, she found jeans, shirts, a couple of summer dresses, sandals, undergarments, a robe and nightgown, and even a pair of cowboy boots.

Josey shook her head, amazed that he would make so many purchases including the two scarves she'd asked for. He really was good at guessing. He'd not only guessed her sizes right down to her shoe size, but he'd chosen colors and styles that she might have chosen for herself.

She'd been so touched, it had choked her up, and she realized how long it had been since someone had been nice to her.

Jack was waiting for her in the shade outside beside the Cadillac. It surprised her that she'd been dreading his reaction to the change in her appearance. She'd worn the boots, jeans and Western shirt he'd bought her, as well as a scarf tied around her neck that went with the shirt.

He smiled when he saw her. His gaze took in her hair first, then the rest of her. "I see the clothes fit."

"Yes, thank you." She felt strangely shy.

"I like your new look," he said, nodding, as they climbed into the car.

"You do?" she asked, and braved checking herself in the vanity mirror. It startled her, seeing herself as a brunette with short curly hair that framed her face. Her green eyes appeared huge to her. Or maybe it was the dark shadows under them. She didn't even recognize herself.

"It suits you," he said.

"Thank you." She snapped the visor up. Who was she kidding? Changing her hairstyle wasn't going to save her. Nothing would. It was just a matter of time before the rest of her world came crashing down.

She saw Jack looking at her backpack again, even more curious. She'd put her dirty clothing and sneakers into one of the shopping bags, and had to stuff the second bag with the new clothing.

She'd have to watch him closely until she had an opportunity to hide the backpack's contents for safekeeping during the week at the ranch.

If she lasted the week. If there was even a ranch, she thought, as Jack drove south on a highway even less traveled than the last one they'd been on.

She no longer trusted herself to separate the good guys from the bad.

JACK STUDIED JOSEY as they left town. The new hairstyle and color only made her more striking. A woman like her couldn't go unnoticed, if that was what she was hoping. So far, he thought she was safe. The truck stop hadn't been busy, and the clerk there hadn't given either of them a second glance. She'd been too busy watching the small television behind the counter.

Jack had noticed that when Josey came out to the car she'd carried both bags of clothing he'd purchased for her as well as that backpack she refused to let out of her sight. With her dirty clothes in one bag and the other bag overstuffed with her new clothes, he was even more concerned about what was in her backpack.

"You didn't have to buy me so much," Josey said now as he drove east out of town.

"I wouldn't want my grandmother to think that I'm cheap when it comes to my wife and her wardrobe."

His expression sobered at the thought of his grandmother, Pepper Winchester. He didn't give a damn what she thought, but he *did* want her to believe this marriage was real. It hadn't crossed his mind to bring a "wife" along. Not until he'd picked up Josey beside the road and had this overwhelming desire to help her. *No good deed goes unpunished,* he could hear his father say.

Jack admitted that his motives hadn't been completely selfless. Having a wife would allow him more freedom on the ranch, freedom he would need.

He thought of his mother and told himself he was doing this for her. It wasn't about revenge. It was about justice.

As he glanced over at Josey, he knew he would have to be careful, though. Josey was a beautiful woman. He couldn't afford to get involved in her trouble and lose sight of why he was really going to the ranch.

He reminded himself Josey had gone along with the

"marriage" because she needed to hide out somewhere safe for a week—just as he'd suspected. What was there to worry about?

"I hope we've got everything we need," he said, glancing back at Whitehorse in his rearview mirror. The tiny Western town was only about ten blocks square with more churches than bars, one of the many small towns that had spouted up beside the tracks when the railroad had come through.

"A few more miles and it will be the end of civilization as we know it," Jack said. "There are no convenience stores out here, nothing but rolling prairie as far as the eye can see."

"It sounds wonderful," she said.

"I should probably fill you in on my grandmother," Jack said, as the road turned to gravel and angled to the southeast. "She's been a recluse for the past twenty-seven years and now, according to her attorney, she wants to see her family. The letter I received made it sound as if she is dying."

Josey looked sympathetic. "I'm sorry. A recluse for twenty-seven years? I can understand why you might not have been close."

"I was six the last time I saw her." But he remembered her only too well. Her and the ranch and those long summer days with his mother, all of them living a lie.

As Jack drove out of Whitehorse, Josey felt a little better. She'd been nervous in town, trying hard not to look over her shoulder the whole time. At the truck stop, she'd just about changed her mind. She desperately needed to put more distance between her and her past. But the only other option was hooking a ride with a trucker passing through, since there appeared to be no place in this town that she could rent a car or even buy one.

Also, why chance it when she could hide out for a week at some remote ranch? She was anxious to do the one thing she needed to do, but it would have to wait just a little longer. She certainly couldn't chance walking into a bank in this town. It was too risky.

But then again, how risky was it pretending to be a stranger's wife? Even as desperate as she was. Even as good-looking and normal as Jack Winchester appeared.

Who was this man? And what was the deal with his reclusive grandmother? She reminded herself how bad her judgment had been lately, her hand going to her neck beneath the scarf and making her wince with pain. She hoped she hadn't just jumped from the frying pan into the fire.

As the Cadillac roared down the fairly wide gravel road through rolling grasslands and rocky knolls, she tried to relax. But Jack Winchester had her confused. He seemed like a nice guy, but nice guys didn't fool their grandmothers with fake wives.

Even though she'd fought it, Josey must have dozed off. She woke as the Cadillac hit a bump and sat up, surprised to see that the road they were on had narrowed to a dirt track. The land had changed, becoming more rough, more desolate.

There were no buildings, nothing but wild country, and she had the feeling there hadn't been for miles.

"Is the ranch much farther?" she asked, afraid she'd been duped. Again.

Sagebrush dotted the arid hills and gullies, and

stunted junipers grew along rocky breaks. Dust boiled
up behind the Cadillac, the road ahead more of the
same.

"It's a bit farther," Jack said. "The ranch isn't far from
a paved highway—as the crow flies. But the only way
to get there is this road, I'm afraid."

Josey felt a prickle of fear skitter over her skin. *But
come on, what man would buy you clothes just to take
you out in the middle of nowhere and kill you?* She
shuddered, thinking she knew a man exactly like that.

"You thought I was kidding about the Winchester
Ranch being remote?" Jack asked with a laugh.

When he had told her about where they would be
spending the week, she had thought it perfect. But now
she doubted there was even a ranch at the end of this
road. It wouldn't be the first time she'd been played for
a fool, but it could be the last. Josey had a bad feeling
that she'd used up any luck she'd ever had a long time
ago.

She shifted in her seat and drew the backpack closer,
considering what she was going to do if this turned
out to be another trap. Jack didn't look like a deranged
madman who was driving all this way to torture and kill
her. But then RJ hadn't looked like a deranged madman,
either, had he?

She stared at the road ahead as Jack drove deeper into
the wild, uninhabited country. Occasionally she would
see a wheat field, but no sign of a house or another
person.

As the convertible came over a rise in the road,
Jack touched his brakes, even though all she could see
was more of the same wild landscape. He turned onto

an even less used road, the land suddenly dropping precariously.

"Are you sure you're on the right road?" Her hand went to her backpack, heart hammering in her chest as she eased open the drawstring and closed her hand around the gun handle, realizing she had only four shots left.

"I'm beginning to wonder about that myself. I asked for directions back at a gas station in town before I picked you up, so I'm pretty sure I'm on the right road." The car bumped down the uneven track, then turned sharply to the right. "There it is." He sounded as relieved as she felt.

Josey looked up in surprise to see a cluster of log buildings at the base of the rugged hills behind it. A little farther down the road Jack turned under a huge weathered wooden arch, with the words *Winchester Ranch* carved in it.

Her relief was almost palpable. Josey released her hold on the pistol, trying to still her thundering heart as the Cadillac bumped down the narrow dirt road toward the ranch buildings.

She frowned, noting suddenly how the grass had grown between the two tracks in the road, as if it hadn't had much use. As they grew closer, she saw that the cluster of log buildings looked old and…deserted.

Josey reminded herself that the grandmother had been a recluse for the past twenty-seven years. At least that was what Jack had said. So she probably hadn't had a lot of company or use on the road.

After what she'd been through, Josey thought she could handle anything. But she suddenly feared that wasn't true. She didn't feel strong enough yet to be tested again. She wasn't sure how much more she could take before she broke.

As they rounded a bend in the road, her pulse quickened. This place was huge and creepy-looking. Sun glinted off a line of bleached white antlers piled in the middle of a rock garden. She noticed other heads of dead animals, the bones picked clean and hanging on the wood fence under a row of huge cottonwoods. As she looked at the house, she thought of the "big bad wolf" fairy tale and wondered if a kindly grandmother—or something a lot more dangerous—was waiting inside.

Jack parked in front and killed the engine. A breathless silence seemed to fill the air. Nothing moved. A horse whinnied from a log barn in the distance, startling Josey. Closer a bug buzzed, sounding like a rattlesnake. She felt jumpy and wondered if she'd lost her mind going along with this.

"Are you all right?" he asked. He looked worried.

She nodded, realizing she was here now and had little choice but to go through with it. But this ranch certainly wasn't what she'd expected. Not this huge, eerie-looking place, that was for sure.

"I know it doesn't look like much," Jack said, as if reading her mind.

The house was a massive, sprawling log structure with wings running off from the main section and two stories on all but one wing that had an odd third story added toward the back. The place reminded her of a smaller version of Old Faithful Lodge in Yellowstone Park.

At one time, the building must have been amazing. But it had seen better days and now just looked dark and deserted, the grimy windows like blind eyes staring blankly out at them.

"Don't look so scared," Jack said under his breath. "My grandmother isn't that bad. Really." He made it sound like a joke, but his words only unnerved her further.

As the front door opened, an elderly woman with long, plaited salt-and-pepper hair filled the doorway. Her braid hung over one shoulder of the black caftan she wore, her face in shadow.

"Showtime," Jack said as he put his arm around Josey and drew her close. She fit against him, and for a moment Josey could almost pretend this wasn't a charade, she was so relieved that at least part of Jack's story had been true. An old woman lived here. Was this the grandmother?

Jack planted a kiss in her hair and whispered, "We're newlyweds, remember." There was a teasing glint in his blue gaze as he dropped his mouth to hers.

The kiss was brief, but unnervingly powerful. As Jack pulled back he frowned. "I can see why we eloped so quickly after meeting each other," he said, his voice rough with a desire that fired his gaze. This handsome man was much more dangerous than she'd thought. In at least one way, she had definitely jumped from the skillet into the fire.

She gave Jack a playful shove as if she'd just seen the woman in the doorway and was embarrassed, then checked to make sure the scarf around her neck was in place before opening her door and stepping out, taking the backpack with her. *Showtime,* she thought, echoing Jack's words.

No one would ever find her here, wherever she was.

She had to pull this off. She was safe. That was all she had to think about right now, and as long as she was safe her mother would be, as well. One week. She could do this.

Jack was by her side in a flash, his arm around her, as they walked toward the house. An ugly old dog came out growling, but the elderly woman shooed him away with her cane.

Josey studied the woman in the doorway as she drew closer. Jack's grandmother? She didn't have his coloring. While he was blond and blue-eyed, she was dark from her hair to her eyes, a striking, statuesque woman with a face that could have been chiseled from marble, it was so cold.

"Hello, Grandmother," Jack said, giving the woman a kiss on her cheek. "This is my wife—"

"Josey Winchester," Josey said, stepping forward and extending her hand. The woman took it with obvious surprise—and irritation. Her hand was ice-cold, and her vapid touch sent a chill through Josey.

"I didn't realize you were married, let alone that you'd be bringing a wife," his grandmother said.

Jack hadn't planned on bringing a wife. So why had he? Josey wondered. It certainly hadn't ingratiated his grandmother to him. And as for money…was there any? This place didn't suggest it.

"This is my grandmother, Pepper Winchester," Jack said, an edge to his voice.

The elderly woman leaned on her cane, her gaze skimming over Josey before shifting back to Jack. "So, you're my son Angus's boy."

Wouldn't she *know* he was her son's child? The

woman must be senile, Josie thought. Or was there some reason to question his paternity?

"I remember the day your mother showed up at the door with you," Pepper said. "What were you then?"

"Two," Jack said, clearly uncomfortable.

His grandmother nodded. "Yes. I should have been suspicious when Angus involved himself in the hiring of the nanny," Pepper said.

So Jack was the bastard grandson. That explained this less than warm reception.

Jack's jaw muscle tensed, but his anger didn't show in his handsome face. He put his arm around Josey's waist and pulled her closer, as if he needed her as a buffer between him and his grandmother. Another reason he'd made her this phony marriage offer?

When he'd told her about his grandmother and this visit, Josey had pictured an elderly woman lying in bed hooked up to machines, about to take her final gasp.

This woman standing before them didn't look anywhere near death's door. Josey had speculated that this was about money. What else? But if she was right, then Jack had underestimated his grandmother. This woman looked like someone who planned to live forever and take whatever she had with her.

"Since I didn't realize you had a wife," Pepper Winchester was saying, "I'll have to instruct my housekeeper to make up a different room for you."

"Please don't go to any trouble on my account," Jack said.

The grandmother smiled at this, cutting her dark gaze to him, eyes narrowing.

Be careful, Josie thought. *This woman is sharp.*

JACK HESITATED at the door to the huge ranch lodge. This place had once been filled with happy memories for him, because he'd lived here oblivious to what was really going on. Ignorance had been bliss. He'd played with the other grandchildren, ridden horses, felt like a Winchester even before his mother had confessed that he was one and he realized so much of their lives had been lies.

"Coming, dear?" Josey called from the open front doorway.

He looked at his beautiful wife and was more than grateful she'd agreed to this. He wasn't sure he could have done it alone. Josey, so far, was a godsend. His grandmother was a lot more on the ball than he'd thought she would be at this age.

Grandma had disappeared into the musty maze of the lodge, leaving them in the entryway. Jack was surprised that he still felt awe, just as he had the first time he'd seen it. This place had been built back in the nineteen forties and had the feel of another era in Western history.

He stared at the varnished log stairway that climbed to the upper floors, remembering all the times he'd seen his mother coming down those stairs.

"Mrs. Winchester said you are to wait down here." Jack swung around, surprised to see the gnarled, petite elderly woman who had managed to sneak up on them. To his shock, he recognized her. "Enid?" She was still alive?

If she recognized him, she gave no indication as she pointed down the hallway then left, saying she had to get their room ready. She left grumbling to herself.

Behind them, the front door opened, and an elderly

man came in carrying Jack's two pieces of luggage from the trunk of the Cadillac. Alfred, Enid's husband. Amazing.

He noticed that Josey still had her backpack slung over one shoulder.

Alfred noticed, as well. "I'll take that," the old man said, pointing to it.

She shook her head, her hand tightening around the strap. "I'll keep it with me, thank you."

Alfred scowled at her before heading up the stairs, his footsteps labored under the weight of the bags and his disapproval.

"I can't believe those two are still alive," Jack whispered to Josey, as he led her down the hallway. "I remember them both being old when I was a kid. I guess they weren't that old, but they sure seemed it." He wondered if his grandmother would be joining them and was relieved to find the parlor empty.

Josey took a seat, setting her backpack on the floor next to her, always within reach. Jack didn't even want to speculate on what might be in it. He had a bad feeling it was something he'd be better off not knowing.

Chapter Three

Deputy Sheriff McCall Winchester had been back to work for only a day when she got a call from a fisherman down at the Fred Robinson Bridge on the Missouri River. Paddlefish season hadn't opened yet. In a few weeks the campground would be full with fishermen lined up along the banks dragging huge hooks through the water in the hopes of snagging one of the incredibly ugly monstrous fish.

This fisherman had been on his way up to Nelson Reservoir, where he'd heard the walleye were biting, but he'd stopped to make a few casts in the Missouri as a break in the long drive, thinking he might hook into a catfish.

Instead he'd snagged a piece of clothing—attached to a body.

"It's a woman," he'd said, clearly shaken. "And she's got a rope around her neck. I'm telling you, it's a damned noose. Someone hung her!"

Now, as McCall squatted next to the body lying on a tarp at the edge of the water, she saw that the victim looked to be in her mid-twenties. She wore a thin cotton top, no bra and a pair of cutoff jeans over a bright red thong that showed above the waist of the cutoffs. Her hair was dyed blond, her eyes were brown and as empty as the sky overhead, and around her neck was a crude noose of sisal rope. A dozen yards of the rope were coiled next to her.

McCall studied the ligature marks around the dead woman's neck as the coroner loosened the noose. "Can you tell if she was dead before she went into the water?"

Coroner George Murphy shook his head. "But I can tell you that someone abused the hell out of her for some time before she went into the water." He pointed to what appeared to be cigarette burns on her thin arms and legs.

"Before he *hung* her."

"What kind of monster does stuff like that?" George, a big, florid-faced man in his early thirties, single and shy, was new to this. As an EMT, he'd gotten the coroner job because Frank Brown had retired and no one else wanted it.

"Sheriff?"

McCall didn't respond at first. She hadn't gotten used to being acting sheriff. Probably because she hadn't wanted the job and suspected there was only one reason she had it—Pepper Winchester.

But when the position opened, no one wanted to fill in until a sheriff could be elected. The other deputies all had families and young children and didn't want the added responsibility.

McCall could appreciate that.

"Sheriff, we found something I think you'd better see."

"Don't tell me you found another body," the coroner said.

McCall turned to see what the deputy was holding. Another noose. Only this one was wrapped around a large tree trunk that the deputies had pulled up onto the riverbank.

As McCall walked over to it, she saw two distinct grooves in the limb where two ropes had been tied. Two ropes. Two nooses. The thick end of the dead branch had recently broken off.

She looked upriver. If the limb had snapped off under the weight of two people hanging from it, then there was a good chance it had fallen into the river and floated down to where the deputy had found it dragging the second noose behind it.

"Better go upriver and see if you can find the spot where our victim was hung," McCall said. "And we better start looking for a second body in the river."

PEPPER WINCHESTER RUBBED her temples as she paced the worn carpet of her bedroom, her cane punctuating her frustration.

The first of her grandchildren had arrived—with a new wife. She shouldn't have been surprised, given Jack's lineage. None of her sons had a lick of sense when it came to women. They were all too much like their father, suffer his soul in hell. So why should her grandsons be any different?

Her oldest son Worth—or Worthless, as his father had called him—had taken off with some tramp he met in town after Pepper had kicked him out. She would imagine he'd been through a rash of ill-conceived relationships since then.

Brand had married another questionable woman and

had two sons, Cordell and Cyrus, before she'd taken off, never to be seen again.

Angus had knocked up the nanny and produced Jack. She shuddered to think how that had all ended.

Trace, her beloved youngest son, had gotten murdered after marrying Ruby Bates and producing McCall, her only granddaughter that she knew of.

Pepper stepped to the window, too restless to sit. When she'd conceived this plan to bring her family back to the ranch, she wasn't sure who would come. She'd thought the bunch of them would be greedy enough or at least curious enough to return to the ranch. She didn't kid herself that none of them gave two cents for her. She didn't blame them, given the way she'd kicked them all off the ranch twenty-seven years ago and hadn't seen one of them since.

So why was she surprised that Jack wasn't what she'd expected? The same could be said for his wife. She wasn't sure what to make of either of them yet.

She pulled back the curtain and stared out at the land. *Her* land. She remembered the first time she'd seen it. She'd been so young and so in love when Call had brought her back here after their whirlwind love affair and impromptu marriage.

He hadn't known any more about her than she had him.

How foolish they both had been.

It had been hard at first, living on such an isolated, remote ranch. Call had hired a staff to do everything and insisted no wife of his would have to lift a finger.

Pepper had been restless. She'd learned to ride a horse and spent most of her days exploring the ranch. That was how she'd met neighboring rancher Hunt McCormick.

She shivered at the memory as she spotted movement in the shadows next to the barn. Squinting, she saw that it was Enid and her husband, Alfred. They had their heads together and their conversation looked serious. It wasn't the first time she'd caught them like that recently.

What were they up to? Pepper felt her stomach roil. As if her family wasn't worry enough.

JOSEY STUDIED JACK. He seemed nervous now that they were here at the ranch. Was he realizing, like her, that his grandmother had gotten him here under false pretenses?

"As you've probably gathered, my mother was the nanny here as well as the mistress of Angus Winchester, my father," Jack said distractedly, as he moved to look out the window. "According to my mother, they had to keep their affair secret because my grandmother didn't approve and would have cut Angus off without a cent." He turned to look at her. "As it was, Pepper cut him and the rest of her family off twenty-seven years ago without a cent, saying she didn't give a damn what they did. When my father died, my grandmother didn't even bother to come to his funeral or send flowers or even a card."

"Why would you come back here to see your grandmother after that?" Josey had to ask.

He laughed at her outraged expression. "There is no one quite like Pepper Winchester. It wasn't just me, the bastard grandson, she washed her hands of after her youngest son disappeared. Trace Winchester was her life. She couldn't have cared less about the rest of her offspring, so I try not to take it personally."

Shocked, she watched Jack study an old photograph on the wall. "If the only reason you came here is because you thought she was dying—"

"It isn't the only reason, although I've been hearing about the Winchester fortune as far back as I can remember." Jack smiled as he glanced at her over his shoulder. "She looks healthy as a horse, huh? I wonder what she's up to and where the others are."

"The others?" she asked.

"My grandmother had five children. Virginia, the oldest, then Worth, Angus, Brand and Trace."

"You haven't mentioned your grandfather."

"Call Winchester? According to the story Pepper told, he rode off on a horse about forty years ago. His horse came back but Call never did. There was speculation he'd just kept riding, taking the opportunity to get away from my grandmother."

Josey could see how that might be possible.

"When Trace disappeared twenty-seven years ago, it looked like he was taking a powder just like his father," Jack said. "I would imagine that's what pushed my grandmother over the edge, and why she locked herself up in this place all the years since."

"So what changed?"

"Trace Winchester's remains were found buried not far from here. Apparently he was murdered, and that's why no one had seen him the past twenty-seven years."

"Murdered?"

"Not long after his remains were found I got a letter from my grandmother's attorney saying my grandmother wanted to see me." Jack walked over to the window again and pushed aside the dark, thick drape. Dust motes danced in the air. "It was more of a summons than an invitation. I guess I wanted to see what the old gal was up to. Pepper Winchester never does anything without a motive."

His grandmother had suffered such loss in her lifetime. To lose her husband, then her youngest son? Josey couldn't even imagine what that would do to a person. She could also understand how Jack would be bitter and angry, but it was the underlying pain in Jack that made her hurt for him. She knew only too well the pain family could inflict.

The last thing she wanted, though, was to feel anything for Jack Winchester.

Nor did she want to get involved in his family drama. She had her own problems, she reminded herself. She pulled her backpack closer, then with a start realized there was someone standing in the doorway.

The housekeeper Jack had called Enid. Josey wondered how long the woman had been standing there listening. She was one of those wiry old women with a scornful face and small, close-set, resentful eyes.

Enid cleared her throat. "If you'll come with me." She let out a put-upon sigh before leading them back to the staircase.

As they climbed, Josey took in the antique furniture, the rich tapestries, the thick oriental rugs and the expensive light fixtures. She tried to estimate what some of the pieces might be worth. Maybe there was money here—if the ranch wasn't mortgaged to the hilt. She feared that whatever had brought Jack here, he was going to be disappointed.

Jack looked around as they climbed the stairs, his face softening as if he was remembering being a boy in this place. There must be good memories along with bittersweet ones during his four years here.

Josey felt a sudden chill along with a premonition. She tried to shake it off. Why would there be any reason to be afraid for Jack?

They were led down a long, dark hallway to an end room. "Since you're newlyweds," Enid said. "This way you won't disturb the rest of the household."

Jack arched a brow at the old woman behind her back.

"I'm sure you'll ring me on the intercom if you need anything." Enid let out an irritated snort. "Dinner is served at seven on the dot. I wouldn't be late if I were you." With that she left them standing outside the room and disappeared into the dim light of the hallway, her footfalls silent as snowfall.

"That woman is scary," Josey whispered, making Jack chuckle.

"Let's do this right," he said, surprising her as he swung her up into his arms. "In case anyone is watching," he added in a whisper.

She let out a squeal as he carried her over the threshold, making him laugh. His laughter was contagious and she found herself caught up in the moment as he kicked the door shut and carried her into the bedroom.

The room was huge, with a sitting area furnished with two chintz-covered chairs in front of a stone fireplace. Josey caught a glimpse of a large bathroom done in black-and-white tile, sheer white drapes at the open French doors to a small balcony and, at the heart of the room, a large canopied bed.

Jack slowed at the bed, and as he gently lowered her to the cool, white brocade spread his gaze met hers. The sheer white curtains billowed in, bringing with them the sweet scent of clover and pine.

She felt as if she'd been saved by a white knight and brought to the palace for safekeeping. It would have been so easy to lose herself in the deep sea-blue of his eyes as he leaned over her. Jack was incredibly handsome and charming. Everything seemed intensified after what she'd been through. The hard feel of his chest against her breasts, the slight brush of his designer stubble against her cheek, the oh-so-lusty male scent of him as he lowered her to the soft bed.

She wanted desperately to blot out everything but this. It would have been so easy, with her gaze on his sensual, full mouth, to bury her fingers in his a-little-too-long blond hair and drag him down until his lips, now just a breath away from hers, were—

"You're not thinking about kissing me, are you?" he asked, sounding as breathless as she felt. "Because that wasn't part of the bargain. Unless you want to renegotiate?"

Josey realized that he'd been about to lose himself as well, and, for whatever reason, he'd stopped himself. And her. She shouldn't be feeling safe. She should be thinking of the consequences of losing herself even for a little while in the arms of this man. Jack was making it clear what was going to happen if she opened that door.

She squeezed her hands between their bodies, pressing her palms to his muscular chest, but she didn't have to push. Jack eased slowly back to a safer distance, though it seemed to take all of his effort.

"Didn't Enid say something about dinner at seven?"

she asked, her voice sounding strange even to her ears. "I have just enough time to take a bath first."

Jack glanced toward the bathroom. He must have been wondering why she needed another bath since she'd had a shower in town.

"I can't resist that tub." A huge clawfoot tub sat in the middle of the black-and-white tiled floor.

His blue eyes darkened again with desire, and she saw both challenge and warning as he glanced from the tub to her. They were alone at this end of an empty wing pretending to be husband and wife. Unless she wanted the marriage *consummated,* she'd better be careful what signals she sent out.

Josey slid from the bed, grabbed her backpack and stepped into the bathroom, closing and locking the door behind her. The room was large. Along with the tub there was an old-fashioned sink and dressing table, and enough room to dance in front of a full-length old-fashioned mirror.

Josey set down her backpack and stepped to the tub to turn on the faucet. Enid had left her a bottle of bubble bath, bath soap and a stack of towels. As the tub filled, bubbles moved in the warm breeze that blew in from an open window in the corner and billowed the sheer white curtains.

She stripped off her clothing and, with a start, caught her reflection in the full-length mirror behind her. She looked so different. Slowly, her heart in her throat, she studied her face, then the bruises she'd been able to hide under her clothing. The raw rope burn on her neck made her wince at just the sight of it. What had she been thinking earlier with Jack? Had she lost herself in him, he would have seen—

She shuddered at the thought. She couldn't let that happen. It wouldn't be easy to keep her injuries covered so no one saw them until she had a chance to heal. But that would be easier than trying to explain them if she got caught.

Josey turned away from her unfamiliar image, anxious to climb into the tub of warm, scented water. She knew she couldn't wash away her shame any more than she could wash away the memory of what had happened.

As she stepped into the tub and slowly lowered herself into the bubbles and wonderfully warm, soothing water, she listened for Jack. Had he left the room? Or was he just on the other side of the door?

Against her will, her nipples hardened at the thought. She reminded herself that Jack was just a means to an end. A safe place to hide out until she could decide what to do. As Jack had said, the Winchester Ranch was in the middle of nowhere. Her past couldn't find her here.

Once she knew her mother was safe…

She lay back in the tub, the breeze from the window nearby stirring the bubbles, but the chill Josey felt had nothing to do with the warm spring air coming through the window.

Was she really safe here? There was something about this place, something about Jack's grandmother, definitely something about the Hoaglands, that gave her the creeps.

Josey shivered and sank deeper in the tub, realizing the most dangerous person in this house could be the man she'd be sleeping in the same room with tonight.

VIRGINIA WINCHESTER STOOD at the window where she'd watched the Cadillac convertible drive up earlier.

She hadn't been sure which nephew it was and hadn't cared. All she knew, and this she'd had to get from Enid since her mother wasn't apt to tell her, was that three nephews had confirmed that they would be arriving over the next few weeks.

She wouldn't have recognized any of them. The last time she'd seen them they'd been sniveling little boys. She'd had no more interest then than she did now.

By now there could be more. She shuddered at the thought.

She did, however, wonder why her mother hadn't just invited everyone back at the same time. Pepper had her reasons, Virginia was sure of that.

She herself was the fly in the ointment, so to speak. The letter had specified the time her mother wanted to see her. She assumed everyone else had also been given a specific time to arrive.

Virginia wasn't about to wait. She wasn't having it where her mother invited her favorites first. Virginia planned to be here to make sure she wasn't left out. So she'd come right away—to her mother's obvious irritation.

Growing up on the ranch, she'd felt as if their mother had pitted them all against each other. The only time she'd felt any kind of bond with her siblings had been their mutual jealousy, distrust and dislike of their younger brother Trace—their mother's unequivocal favorite.

Now Virginia worried that just because two of her brothers had produced offspring—at least that she knew of—the Winchester fortune would be divided to include them.

As the only daughter and oldest of Call and Pepper

Winchester's children, she deserved her fair share, and she said as much now to her mother.

Pepper sighed from her chair nearby. "You always were the generous one. Of course you would be the first to arrive and completely ignore my instructions."

"I came at once because…" Her voice trailed off as she caught herself.

"Because you thought I was dying."

The letter had clearly been a ruse to get them all back to the ranch. Virginia saw that now. Pepper Winchester didn't even look ill. "The letter from the attorney…" She floundered. There had never been anything she could say that had pleased her mother.

She'd been torn when she'd received the letter from the attorney on her mother's behalf. Her mother was dying?

The thought had come with mixed emotions. It was her *mother*. She should feel something other than contempt. Pepper had been a terrible mother: cold, unfeeling, unreachable. Virginia hadn't heard a word from her in twenty-seven years. What was she supposed to feel for her mother?

"I'm just asking that you be fair," Virginia said.

"I suppose you'd like me to cut out my grandchildren?"

Like her mother had ever been a loving grandmother. "Those of us without children shouldn't be penalized for it. It's not like you would even recognize your grandsons if you passed them on the street," Virginia pointed out.

"I also have a *granddaughter*."

Virginia turned from the window to stare at her mother.

"McCall. Trace's daughter. She's with the sheriff's department. She's the one who solved your brother's murder and was almost killed doing so."

"McCall?" That bitch Ruby had named her kid after Virginia's father? Why wasn't Pepper having a conniption fit about this? She should have been livid. "Surely you aren't going to take the word of that tramp that this young woman is a Winchester."

Her mother's smile had a knife edge to it. "Oh, believe me, she's a Winchester. But I knew the rest of you would require more than my word on it. I have the DNA test results, if you'd like to see them."

Virginia was furious. Another person after the Winchester fortune. No, not just another person. *Trace's* daughter. Virginia felt sick.

"So I have four grandchildren I don't know," her mother corrected with sarcasm. "And there could be more, couldn't there?"

Virginia swore silently. "Why did you even bother to get the rest of us home?"

Pepper raised a brow. "I knew you'd want to see me one last time. Also I was sure you'd want to know the whole story about your brother Trace. You haven't asked."

"What is there to ask?" Virginia shot back. "His killer is dead. It was in all the papers." Trace was dead and buried. "I would think that you wouldn't want to relive any of that awfulness."

She didn't mention that Pepper had kept her other children away from Trace when he was young, as if afraid they might hurt him. Her protectiveness, along with her favoritism and love for Trace, was why they had no great love for their little brother. He'd come into their lives after they'd heard their mother couldn't have anymore children. Trace became the miracle child.

"You weren't at his memorial service," her mother said.

Virginia couldn't hold back the laugh. "Are you kidding? I didn't think I was invited." She started for the door, unable to take any more of this. "You should have warned us in the letter from your lawyer that this visit was really about Trace."

"Your brother was *murdered!* I would think something like that would give even you pause," her mother said, making Virginia stop in midstep on the way to the door.

Even her? As if she had no feelings. Her mother didn't know. Her mother knew nothing about what she'd been through. As if Pepper was the only one who'd lost a child.

"I was sorry to hear about it," Virginia said, turning again to face her mother. "I already told you that, Mother. What about your children who are still alive? The ones you *didn't* protect when they were young? Aren't we deserving of your attention for once, given what you let happen to us?"

The accusation hung in the air between them, never before spoken. Pepper's expression didn't change as she got to her feet. If Virginia hadn't seen the slight trembling in her mother's hand as she reached for her cane, she would have thought her words had fallen on deaf ears.

"You are so transparent, Virginia," her mother said, as she brushed past. "Don't worry, dear. Your trip won't be wasted."

MCCALL STOOD IN THE DUST, staring at the makeshift camp, hating the feeling this place gave her. Her deputies had gone only a few miles along the riverbank before they'd come across it and the tree where the limb had broken off and fallen into the water.

This was where they had camped. From the footprints in the mud and dirt around the area, there'd been three of them. One man, two women.

A breeze blew down the river, ruffling the dark green water. She caught the putrid odor of burned grease rising from the makeshift fire pit ringed in stones. Someone had recently cooked over the fire. A pile of crumpled, charred beer cans had been discarded in the flames and now lay charred black in the ash. Little chance of getting any prints off the cans, but still a deputy was preparing to bag them for the lab.

"We followed the tire tracks up from the river through the trees," one of the other deputies said, pointing to the way the campers had driven down the mountainside to the river. "They came in through a farmer's posted gate on a road that hadn't been used in some time."

"You think they lucked onto it or knew where they were going?" she asked. The narrow dirt road had led to this secluded spot, as if the driver of the vehicle had wanted privacy for what he had planned. If he'd just wanted to camp, he would have gone to the campground down by the bridge.

"If he knew about the road, then that would mean he could be a local," the deputy said. "I say he lucked onto the road, figuring it ended up at the river."

Like him, she didn't want to believe whoever had hung two people was from the Whitehorse area. Or worse, someone they knew. Who really knew their neighbors and what went on behind closed doors?

McCall had learned that there were people who lived hidden lives and would do anything to protect those secrets.

She watched as a deputy took photographs of the dead tree with the broken branch at the edge of the bank, watched as another made plaster casts of both the tire prints and the footprints in the camp.

"Sheriff?"

She was starting to hate hearing that word. She turned to see the deputy with the camera pointing into the river just feet off the bank.

"I think we found the missing car."

Chapter Four

Jack listened to the soft lap of water, fighting the image of his "wife" neck deep in that big old tub just beyond the bathroom door.

This definitely could have been a mistake. He felt a surge of warring emotions. A very male part of him wanted to protect her and had from the moment he'd stopped to pick her up on the highway.

But an equally male part of him was stirred by a growing desire for her. Josey was sexy as hell. To make matters worse, there was a vulnerability in her beautiful green eyes that suckered him in.

His taking a "wife" had been both brilliant and dangerous. The truth was he didn't have any idea who this woman in the next room was. All he knew was that she was running from something. Why else agree to pretend to be his wife for a week? The thought worried him a little as he glanced toward the bathroom door.

The sweet scent of lilac drifted out from behind the closed and locked door. But nothing could shut out the thought of her. After having her in his arms, it wasn't that hard to picture her lush, lanky body in the steamy bathroom: the full breasts, the slim waist and hips, the long, sensual legs.

The provocative image was almost his undoing. He groaned and headed for the door. He couldn't let her distract him from his real reason for coming back to Montana and the Winchester Ranch—and that was impossible with her just feet away covered in bubbles.

Opening their bedroom door, he headed down the hallway toward the opposite wing—the wing where he and his mother had lived twenty-seven years ago.

Jack had expected to find his mother's room changed. As he opened the door, he saw that it looked exactly as he remembered. The only new addition was the dust. His boots left prints as he crossed the floor and opened the window, needing to let some air into the room.

The fresh air helped. He stood breathing it in, thinking of his mother. She'd been a small, blond woman who'd mistakenly fallen in love with a Winchester. She'd been happy here—and miserable. He hadn't understood why until later, when he'd found out that Angus Winchester was his father.

His jaw tightened as he considered the part his grandmother had played in destroying Angus Winchester, and that reminded him of the reception she'd given him earlier when he and Josey had arrived.

He shouldn't have been surprised. When he was a boy, Pepper hadn't paid him any mind, as if he were invisible. They'd all lived in some part of the huge old lodge, but seldom crossed paths except at meals.

It wasn't that she'd disliked him. She just hadn't cared one way or the other, and finding out he was Angus's child hadn't changed that.

He stood for a moment in the room, promising his mother's memory that he'd see that Pepper Winchester paid for all of it, every miserable day she'd spent in this house or on Earth. Then he closed the window and left the room, anxious to get back to Josey.

Who knew what a woman on the run with a trail of secrets shadowing her might do.

FROM THE TUB, Josey glanced over at her backpack resting on the floor of the bathroom. Just the sight of it turned her stomach, but she was pretty sure she'd heard Jack leave and she had no idea how long he might be gone.

She quickly climbed from the tub and didn't bother to towel off. Instead, she grabbed the robe he'd bought her and avoided looking in the mirror at her battered body. She also avoided thinking about how she'd gotten herself into such a mess. She was sick to death of all the "if only" thoughts.

As the saying went, the die was cast.

All she knew was that she couldn't keep carrying her backpack around like a second skin. She'd seen the way Jack had eyed it. He was more than a little curious about what was so important in it that she wouldn't let it out of her sight, and he'd eventually have a look.

Which meant she had to find a safe place for its contents.

She listened. No sound outside the bathroom door. Hefting the backpack, she cautiously opened the door a crack. The room appeared to be empty.

She shoved the door open a little wider, not trusting that he hadn't returned.

No Jack. She wondered where he'd gone. She wondered a lot of things about him, but mostly why he'd wanted her to masquerade as his wife. He'd have to have seen she was in bad shape when he'd picked her up on the highway.

So what was in it for him? After meeting his grandmother, Josey was pretty sure it couldn't be money. She just hadn't figured out what Jack was really after.

Josey reminded herself it had nothing to do with her. All she had to do was play her part, hide out here on this isolated ranch until the heat died down. No one could find her here, right?

She quickly surveyed the room. She couldn't chance a hiding place outside this room for fear someone would find it.

Across the room, she spotted the old armoire. The wardrobe was deep, and when she opened it she saw that it was filled with old clothing.

Strange. Just like this huge master suite. Who had it belonged to? she wondered, as she dug out a space at the back, then opened her backpack.

The gun lay on top. She grimaced at the sight of it. Picking it up, she stuck the weapon in the robe pocket. What lay beneath it was even more distressing. The money was in crisp new bills, bundled in stacks of hundreds. Over a million dollars splattered with blood.

Hurriedly she dumped the bundles of cash into the back of the wardrobe, hating that she had to touch it. Blood money, she thought. But the only way to save her mother. And ultimately, maybe herself.

She quickly covered it with some old clothing. Then, grabbing some of the clothing still on hangers, she stuffed the clothes into the backpack until it looked as it had.

Straightening, she closed the wardrobe and looked

around to make sure Jack wouldn't notice anything amiss when he returned.

Footsteps in the hallway. She started. Jack? Or someone else?

As she rushed back into the bathroom, closed and locked the door, she stood for a moment trying to catch her breath and not cry. Seeing the gun and the bloody money had brought it all back.

She heard the bedroom door open and close.

"You all right in there?" Jack asked. Her heart pounded at how close a call that had been.

Discarding the robe, she quickly stepped back into the tub. "Fine," she called back, hating that she sounded breathless.

"We're going to be late for supper if you don't move it."

The water was now lukewarm, the bubbles gone. She slid down into it anyway and picked up the soap. Her hands felt dirty after touching the money. Her whole body did. She scrubbed her hands, thinking of Lady Macbeth. *Out, damned spots.*

Suddenly she remembered the gun she'd stuffed into the robe pocket. She rinsed, stepped from the tub and pulled the plug. The water began to drain noisily as she looked around for a good place to hide the weapon.

There were few options. Opening a cabinet next to the sink, she shoved the gun behind a stack of towels on the bottom shelf. It would have to do for now until she could find a better place to hide it.

She intended to keep the weapon where she could get to it—just in case she needed it. That, unfortunately, was a real possibility.

WHEN JOSEY CAME OUT of the bathroom, she wore another of the Western shirts he'd bought her in town and the new pair of jeans that fit her curves to perfection. Jack had also picked her out a pair of Western boots, knowing she would need them to horseback-ride during their week on the ranch.

Jack grinned, pleased with himself but wondering why she hadn't worn the two sexy sundresses he'd picked out for her. He'd been looking forward to seeing her in one of them, and he said as much.

"Maybe I'm a jeans and boots kind of girl," she said.

She looked more like a corporate kind of girl who wore business suits and high heels, he thought, and wondered where that had come from. "You look damned fine in whatever you wear."

She appeared embarrassed, which surprised him. The woman was beautiful. She must have had her share of compliments from men before.

As he smiled at her, he couldn't help wondering who she was—just as he had from the moment he'd spotted her on the highway with her thumb out. Josey carried herself in a way that said she wasn't just smart and savvy, she was confident in who she was. This woman was the kind who would be missed.

Someone would be looking for her. If they weren't already.

Jack warned himself not to get involved, then laughed to himself at how foolish that was. He could have just dropped her off beside the road. Or taken her as far as the town of Whitehorse, given her some money and washed his hands of her and her troubles. He should have.

But something about her…

Jack shook his head. He'd played hero and sold himself on the idea of a wife for this visit with his grandmother, and now he worried he'd bought himself more than he could handle as he looked at her.

Her face was flushed from her bath, the scent of lilac wafting through the large bedroom. The Western shirt she'd chosen was a pale green check that was perfect for her coloring and went well with the scarf that she'd tied around her neck. The two scarves had been her idea.

She looked sweet enough to eat and smelled heavenly. It was going to be hell being around her 24/7 without wanting more than a pretend marriage.

Worse, their charade required a modicum of intimacy with her. As he led her down to dinner, he put his hand against the flat of her back and felt the heat of her skin through the thin cotton of her shirt. The touch burned him like a brand.

She looked over at him. Her smile said she knew what he was up to. He smiled back. She had no idea.

"Finally," said a woman impatiently from the parlor where they'd been shown in earlier.

Jack looked in to see his aunt Virginia, a glass of wine in her hand and a frown on her less than comely face. The years hadn't been kind to her. The alcohol she'd apparently already consumed added to her overall disheveled look.

Her lipstick was smeared, her linen dress was wrinkled from where she'd been perched on the arm of one of the leather chairs and there was a run in her stockings.

"We eat at seven sharp," she snapped, and pointed to the clock on the wall, which read several minutes after.

Josey started to apologize, since it was her fault for staying in the tub so long, but the other woman in the room cut her off.

"You remember Virginia," Pepper Winchester said drily.

"Of course, Virginia," Jack said, extending his hand.

His aunt gave him the weakest of handshakes. "Mother says you're Angus's son?" Like his grandmother, Virginia had also missed her brother's funeral. *Nothing like a close-knit family,* Jack thought.

Virginia was studying him as if under a microscope. Her sour expression said she saw no Winchester resemblance. "The nanny's child." She crinkled her nose in distaste. "Dear Angus," she said, as if that explained it.

Jack tried not to take offense, but it was hard given the reception he and his pretend wife were getting here. He reminded himself that this wasn't a social visit. Once he got what he'd come for, he would never see any of them again.

"This is my wife, Josey," he said, glad as hell he hadn't come here alone. All his misgivings earlier about bringing her were forgotten as he slipped his arm around her slim waist and pulled her close.

JOSEY FELT JACK'S ARM tighten around her as Virginia gave her a barely perceptible handshake.

It was hard not to see the resemblance between mother and daughter, Josey thought. Both women were tall, dark-haired and wore their bitterness on their faces. Virginia was broader, more matronly and perhaps more embittered as she narrowed her gaze at Josey, measuring her for a moment before dismissing her entirely.

"Can we please eat now?" Virginia demanded. "I'm famished. Little more than crumbs were served for lunch. I hope dinner will prove more filling." She turned on her heel and headed down the hall.

Josey turned to Pepper, who was reaching for her cane. "I do apologize. I'm afraid I enjoyed your wonderful tub longer than I'd meant to. That is such a beautiful bathroom. I especially like the black-and-white tiles."

Pepper seemed startled. "Enid put you in the room at the end of the south wing?" She quickly waved the question away. "Of course she would. Never mind."

Grabbing her cane, she followed her daughter down the hallway. Josey noted that Pepper Winchester was more feeble than she let on. Maybe she really was dying. Or maybe just upset.

"I knew it," Josey whispered to Jack, as they followed Pepper at a distance toward the dining room. "That room must have been your grandmother's and grandfather's. Wouldn't Enid know that putting us in there would upset your grandmother?"

"I would bet on it," he said.

Josey followed his gaze to where Enid stood in the kitchen doorway, looking like the cat who ate the canary. "She must have shared that room with your grandfather. I wonder why she moved out of it?"

Jack chuckled and slowed, lowering his voice as they neared the dining room. "I doubt it was for sentimental reasons. My mother told me that according to Winchester lore, Pepper didn't shed a tear when my grandfather rode off and was never seen again. She just went on running the ranch as if Call Winchester had never existed—until her youngest son Trace vanished."

DINNER WAS A TORTUROUS AFFAIR. Jack had known it wouldn't be easy returning to the ranch, but he hadn't anticipated the wellspring of emotions it brought to the surface. As he sat at the dining room table, he half expected to see his mother through the open kitchen doorway.

It was at that scarred kitchen table that he and his mother had eaten with the Winchester grandchildren and the staff. In the old days, he'd been told, Pepper and Call had eaten alone in the dining room while their young children had eaten in the kitchen.

But Call had been gone when his mother came to work here, and Pepper had eaten with her then-grown children in the dining room. When Trace was home, his mother had heard Pepper laughing. After Trace eloped with that woman in town and moved in with her, the laughter stopped. Jack's mother said she often didn't hear a peep out of the dining room the entire meal with Pepper and her other children.

"The animosity was so thick in the air you could choke on it," his mother had told him. "Mrs. Winchester took to having her meals in her room."

"Well, Mother, when are you planning to tell us what is really going on?" Virginia demanded now, slicing through the tense silence that had fallen around the table. She sat on her mother's right, Jack and Josey across from her. Her face was flushed; she'd clearly drunk too much wine. Most of dinner she'd complained under her breath about Enid's cooking.

Jack had hardly tasted his meal. He'd pushed his food

around his plate, lost in the past. Josey had seemed to have no such problem. She'd eaten as if she hadn't had a meal for sometime. He wondered how long it had been.

Pepper had also seemed starved, cleaning her plate with a gusto that didn't go unnoticed. For a dying woman, she had a healthy appetite. Almost everyone commented on it, including Enid when she'd cleared away the dishes before bringing in dessert.

"Well, Mother?" Virginia repeated her demand.

Enid had stopped in midmotion and looked at Pepper, as if as anxious as any of them to hear why the family had been invited back to the ranch.

"Isn't it possible that I wanted my family around me after receiving such horrible news about your brother?" Pepper asked, motioning for Enid to put down the cake and leave the room.

Virginia scoffed at the idea. "After twenty-seven years you suddenly remembered that you had other family?"

"Does it matter what brought us together?" Jack spoke up. "We're here now. I assume some of the others will be arriving, as well?" he asked his grandmother.

She gave him a small smile. "A few have responded to my invitation. I knew it would be too much to have everyone here at the same time, so the others will be coming later."

"Well, I know for a fact that my brother Brand isn't coming," Virginia said unkindly. "He's made it perfectly clear he couldn't care less about you or your money." She poured herself the last of the red wine, splashing some onto the white tablecloth. "In fact, he said he wouldn't come back here even if someone held a gun to his head."

"How nice of you to point that out," Pepper said.

Enid had left, but returned with a serving knife, and saw the mess Virginia had made. She set the knife beside the cake and began to complain under her breath about how overworked she already was without having to remove wine stains from the linens.

"That will be enough," Pepper said to the cook-housekeeper. "Please close the kitchen door on your way out."

Enid gave her a dirty look, but left the room, slamming the door behind her. But Jack saw through the gap under the door that Enid had stopped just on the other side and was now hovering there, listening.

"I only mention Brand to point out that not everyone is so forgiving as I am," Virginia said. She glanced at her mother, tears welling in her eyes. "You hurt us all, Mother. Some of us are trying our best to forgive and forget."

"Let's not get maudlin. You're too old, Virginia, to keep blaming me for the way your life turned out."

"Am I? Who do *you* blame, Mother?"

A gasp came from behind the kitchen door.

Pepper ignored both the gasp and her daughter's question as she began to dish up the cake. "I've always been fond of lemon. What about you, Josey?" she asked, as she passed her a slice.

Josey seemed surprised at the sudden turn in conversation. "I like lemon."

Pepper graced her with a rare smile that actually reached the older woman's eyes. "I don't believe you told me how you and my grandson met."

"I was hitchhiking and he picked me up," Josey said.

Jack laughed, as he saw Josey flush at her own honesty. "It was love at first sight." He shot her a look that could have melted the icing on her cake.

Her flush deepened.

"She climbed into my car and, as they say, the rest is history," Jack said.

Pepper was studying Josey with an intensity that worried him. The elderly woman seemed to see more than he had originally given her credit for. Did his grandmother suspect the marriage was a ruse?

"Well, how fortunate," Pepper said, shifting her gaze to Jack. "You're a lucky man." Her smile for him had a little more bite in it. "You have definitely proven that you're a Winchester."

Jack chuckled, afraid that was no compliment. It didn't matter. He could tell that his grandmother liked Josey and he would use that to his advantage. But it wouldn't change the way he felt about his grandmother.

He'd spent most of dinner secretly studying his beautiful "wife." Josey continued to surprise him. Her manners and the way she carried herself made him realize she must have come from money—probably attended a boarding school, then some Ivy League college. She seemed to fit in here in a way that made her seem more like a Winchester than he ever could. So how did she end up on the side of the road with nothing more than a backpack? And more importantly, why would a woman with her obvious pedigree be sitting here now, pretending to be his wife?

"You've hardly touched your food."

Jack dragged his gaze away from Josey as he realized

his grandmother was talking to *him*. "I guess I'm not really hungry."

Pepper nodded. "You probably have other things on your mind."

"Yes. I should apologize for making this trip into a honeymoon. It wasn't my intention when I answered your letter."

"No, I'm sure it wasn't," his grandmother said with a wry smile. "But what better place than the family ranch? I assume you remember growing up here. You loved to ride horses. Surely you'll want to ride while you're here and show Josey the ranch. You were old enough to remember your uncle Trace, weren't you?"

Virginia didn't bother to stifle a groan.

Her mother ignored her. "You must have been—"

"Six," Jack said, and felt all eyes at the table on him. Beside him, he sensed that even Josey had tensed.

"Then you remember the birthday party I threw for him?"

Jack nodded slowly. It wasn't likely he would forget that day. His mother told him years later that Pepper had been making plans for weeks. Everything had to be perfect.

"I think she really thought that if she threw him an amazing birthday party, Trace would come back to the ranch," his mother had told him. "Of course the only way he was welcome back was without the woman he'd eloped with, the woman who was carrying his child. Or at least he thought was carrying his child. Pepper didn't believe it for a moment. Or didn't want to."

"I had a cake flown in," Pepper said, her eyes bright with memory. "I wanted it to be a birthday he would never forget." Her voice trailed off, now thick with emotion.

Instead it had been a birthday that none of the rest of them had ever forgotten. His grandmother, hysterical with grief and disappointment when Trace hadn't shown for the party, had thrown everyone off the ranch, except for Enid and Alfred Hoagland.

"I bought all the children little party hats," she was saying. "Do you remember?"

From the moment he'd received the letter from his grandmother's attorney, Jack had known she wanted something from him. He just hadn't been sure what. But he had an inkling he was about to find out.

"I recall sending all of you upstairs so you wouldn't be underfoot," Pepper said. "I believe you were playing with my other grandchildren at the time." Her gaze locked with his, and he felt an icy chill climb up his spine and settle around his neck. "Whose idea was it to go up to the room on the third floor? The one you were all forbidden to enter?"

THIS FAR NORTH it was still light out, but it would be getting dark soon. Deputy Sheriff McCall Winchester listened to the whine of the tow truck cable, her focus on the dark green water of the Missouri River.

Déjà vu. Just last month, she'd watched another vehicle being pulled from deep water. Like now she'd feared they'd find a body inside it.

A car bumper broke the surface. The moment the windshield came into view, McCall felt a wave of relief not to see a face behind the glass. Which didn't mean there still wasn't someone in the car, but she was hoping

Hitched!

that bizarre as this case was so far, it wouldn't get any worse.

The tow truck pulled the newer-model luxury car from the water to the riverbank, then shut off the cable motor and truck engine. Silence swept in. Fortunately they were far enough upriver on a stretch of private ranch land away from the highway, so they hadn't attracted any attention.

McCall stepped over to the car as water continued to run out from the cracks around the doors. She peered in, again thankful to find the car empty of bodies. Snapping on latex gloves, she opened the driver side door and let the rest of the water rush out.

Along with river water, there were numerous fast food containers, pop cans, empty potato chip bags.

"Looks like they were living in the car," a deputy said.

McCall noticed something lodged under the brake pedal.

"Get me an evidence bag," she ordered, and reached in to pull out a brand-new, expensive-looking loafer size 10½.

"The driver got out but left behind his shoe?" a deputy said as he opened the passenger-side door. "But did he make it out of the water?"

"See if you can find any tracks downstream," McCall said. "The current is strong enough here that he would have been washed downriver a ways."

"Should be easy to track him since he is wearing only one shoe," the deputy said.

"Let's try to find out before it gets dark," McCall said. Otherwise they would be dragging the river come morning for a third body.

On the other side of the car, a deputy pulled on a pair of latex gloves and opened the passenger-side door to get into the glove box. McCall watched him carefully check the soaking wet registration.

"The car is registered to a Ray Allan Evans Jr., age thirty-five, of Palm City, California. Looks like he just purchased the car three days ago."

Chapter Five

Josey felt the air in the dining room tremble with expectation as she waited for Jack to answer his grandmother. What was this about a room that he'd been forbidden to enter?

"What would make you think I've been in that room?" Jack said, meeting his grandmother's gaze with his cold blue one.

His grandmother's look was sharp as an ice pick. She knew, just as Josey sensed, that he was evading the question. But why would he care about something that happened when he was six?

And why would his grandmother care after all these years?

"Those cute little party hats you were all wearing when you went upstairs," his grandmother said. "I found them in the room."

"Really?" Jack said, forking the piece of the cake Pepper had passed him. "I'm afraid I don't remember anything about some party hats."

"Is that right?" His grandmother's tone called him a liar. "Are you going to also tell me you don't remember that day?"

"Oh, I remember that day. I remember my mother

losing her job and us having to leave the ranch, the only home I'd ever known," Jack said in a voice Josey barely recognized. "I remember my mother being terrified that she wouldn't be able to support us since Angus had been cut off without a cent and didn't have the skills or the desire to find a job. I remember looking at the Winchester Ranch in the rearview mirror and you standing there, making sure we all left and didn't come back."

"Oh, my," Virginia said, clearly enjoying Jack's rancor at her mother.

"I remember Angus losing himself in the bottle and my mother struggling to take care of us while she tried to make us a family," Jack said, his voice flat and cold. "I remember the toll it took on her. But nothing like the toll being exiled from here took on Angus."

"Your mother. Is she...?" Virginia asked.

"She died a year before Angus drank himself to death."

Pepper looked down at her untouched cake. "I didn't know."

"Really? Then you didn't know he left a note?" Jack reached into his pocket and took out a piece of folded, yellowed paper. Josey saw that it was splattered with something dark and felt her stomach roil.

Jack tossed the note to his grandmother. "It's made out to you." With that he got to his feet, throwing down his cloth napkin. "If you'll excuse me."

McCALL SAT in her patrol car, studying the screen. The moment she'd typed in Ray Allan Evans Jr.'s name, it had come up. Ray Jr. was a person of interest in a homicide in Palm City, California. The murder victim was his father, Ray Allan Evans Sr. He'd been killed two days ago—just a day after his son had purchased a very expensive luxury automobile.

She put through a call to the detective in charge of the case in the Palm City homicide department, Detective Carlos Diaz. She told him that she'd found Ray Jr.'s car and that he was wanted in Montana for questioning in another homicide case.

She asked what they had on the Evans murder so far.

"A neighbor can place Ray Jr. at the house at the time of the murder. But he wasn't alone. His stepsister was also there. Her car was found on the property. No staff on the premises, apparently, which in itself is unusual. This place is a mansion with a full staff, at least a couple of them live-in."

"I'm sorry, did you say his *stepsister?*" McCall asked, thinking of the young Jane Doe the fisherman had hooked into.

"Josephine Vanderliner, twenty-eight, daughter of Harry Vanderliner, the founder of Vanderliner Oil. The father is deceased. The mother married Evans two years ago, was in a car accident shortly afterward, suffered brain damage and is now in a nursing home. The step-daughter had been in a legal battle over money with Evans Sr. Her fingerprints were found on the murder weapon. Neither Vanderliner or Evans Jr. has been seen since the night of the murder."

"What's the story on Ray Jr.?"

"Goes by RJ. Thirty-four, no visible means of support, lives with his father."

And yet he'd purchased himself a new expensive car on the day his father was murdered?

"The housekeeper found Ray Sr.'s body—and the

safe—wide-open. She says she saw Ray Sr. putting a large amount of cash into the safe just that morning. According to the eyewitness, RJ and his stepsister left together in a large, newer-model black car at around the time of death estimated by the coroner. Didn't get a make and model on the car."

"Sounds like the one we just pulled from the Missouri River."

McCall filled him in on what they had so far—one female victim in the same age range as Josephine Vanderliner and a car registered to Ray Allan Evans Jr., driver missing and suspected drowned. "We're dragging the river now for a possible third body," she told him.

Detective Diaz sent her photographs of both Ray Jr. and Vanderliner.

McCall watched them come up on her screen. Ray Evans Jr. first. A good-looking, obviously rich kid from the sneer on his face. She thought of the abuse her Jane Doe had suffered before being hanged and drowned. Did he look like a man capable of that? Or was he also a victim of foul play?

McCall held her breath as she clicked on the photograph of Josephine Vanderliner.

JOSEY TOUCHED HER NAPKIN to the corner of her mouth, then carefully placed it beside her dessert dish before rising to follow her "husband" outside.

"That was awkward," she heard Aunt Virginia say, as Josey left the dining room. "So what does the note say?"

"Not now, Virginia."

"He killed himself because of you, didn't he?"

As Josey reached the front door she heard what

sounded like a slap followed by a cry and glass breaking. She didn't look back as she pushed open the door
and stepped out into the fresh air.

Spotting Jack down by the barn, she walked in that
direction, just glad to be out of the house. She figured
Jack wanted to be alone and certainly wouldn't want her
company. For appearance's sake, she had needed to go
after her husband. She hadn't wanted to feel his pain,
but her own emotional pain was so near the surface and
had been for too long. She knew family drama and how
it could tear you apart from the inside out.

Josey slowed as she neared. He stood with his back
to her, his head high as if he were gazing out across the
ranch. The sun hung over the Little Rockies in the far
distance, the sky ran from horizon to horizon, so wide
and deep blue, she could understand why Montana was
called Big Sky Country.

Jack didn't look at her as she joined him at the corral
fence. He'd opened himself up back there at dinner, and
even though she hadn't known him long, she was sure he
regretted it. He'd exposed how vulnerable he'd been, still
was, when it came to his grandmother and the past.

Against her will, Josey felt a kinship with him. Life
hadn't been kind to him, and yet she sensed a strength
in him born of hard times. Jack might have taken a beating, but he wasn't down for the count, she would bet on
that.

"Did you enjoy my sad tale?" he asked, still without
looking at her.

She sensed the last thing he needed right now was
her sympathy. "It was a real heartbreaker. Was any of
it true?"

He looked over at her and grinned. "It almost brought a tear to the old bat's eye, don't you think?"

"I could tell it broke your aunt Virginia's heart."

He laughed and slipped his arm around her, his gaze going back to the sunset. "I can't believe how lucky I was to find you."

She might have argued that, but she was smart enough to keep those thoughts to herself. As long as no one discovered where she'd gone, they were both lucky.

"Have you ever seen anything more beautiful?" he asked, looking toward the horizon.

"No." She studied the wild landscape, broken only by a few outcroppings of rock and the dark tops of the cottonwoods. Between the ranch and horizon was a deep ravine that seemed to cut the place off from the world.

"The Winchester Ranch is the largest ranch in three counties," Jack said.

"So it's the money you're after?"

He smiled. "Who says I'm after anything?" He pulled her closer as he turned them back toward the ranch lodge.

Josey had seen how upset he'd been at dinner. Maybe he wasn't after his grandmother's money, which was just as well because Josey doubted he would be getting any. But he was after something, and that something felt more like settling a score with his grandmother.

She felt a chill as they walked arm in arm back to the lodge, wondering what his grandmother was after and why she was bringing the family back to the ranch.

Whatever Jack was up to, his grandmother had her own agenda, Josey thought. Out of the corner of her eye she saw a face at one of the lodge windows.

Pepper Winchester's face appeared for an instant before the curtain fell back into place.

THE PHOTOGRAPH OF VANDERLINER was several years old, but there was no mistake. She wasn't the Jane Doe now lying in the county morgue.

So who was the victim they'd pulled from the river?

"Our Jane Doe isn't Vanderliner," McCall told Detective Diaz. She promised to get back to him as soon as they were able to run the dead woman's prints.

Back down at the river, the surface golden with the last of the sun's rays, McCall listened to the sound of the boat motor as her fiancé, Game Warden Luke Crawford, helped drag the river for the bodies.

Because of the lack of manpower in a county sheriff's department, game wardens were often called in, since they had the same training as other law enforcement in the state.

Normally crime in and around Whitehorse was mostly calls involving barking dogs, noisy neighbors or drunk and disorderlies. Occasionally there would be a domestic dispute or a call to check on an elderly person who wasn't answering her phone.

Murder was rare, but not unheard of. McCall knew that firsthand. She'd had more than her share of bloodshed recently. The last thing she wanted was another homicide.

"So if the driver of the vehicle was able to swim to safety, he's on foot," George said.

McCall nodded, glancing down river toward Highway 191.

"You're thinking someone picked him up," George

said with a nod. He sounded exhausted. "Makes sense. He would probably need medical attention. I'll call the hospital emergency rooms." He headed for his vehicle.

"You don't have to stick around. I can call you if we find another body."

He shook his head. "I want to be here."

"Thanks." McCall turned back to the river. If RJ wasn't in the river, he'd be on the hunt for shoes, dry clothing, a vehicle and possibly medical attention, as George had said.

So what would he do? Head for the highway. The nearest town was Whitehorse to the north, but she doubted he'd be picky if he could catch a ride. If he was headed south he'd probably have to go clear to Billings to get what he needed. Or cut over to Lewistown, which was closer.

George came back to tell her that a man matching RJ's description or a woman matching Josephine Vanderliner's hadn't come into emergency rooms in Whitehorse or Lewistown.

"So either he wasn't hurt that badly or he hasn't gotten to a place where he can get medical attention," McCall said, glancing behind her into the tall pines. Vanderliner, she could only assume, was in the river.

She heard one of the search-and-rescue volunteers call her name. "Got something down here," the volunteer called.

McCall worked her way down the river to where the volunteer stood next to something caught in a limb beside the water. She shone her flashlight on the object. A leather shoulder bag.

Squatting down and pulling on her latex gloves,

she dragged the bag to her and opened it. A wallet. She focused her flashlight beam on the driver's license inside—and the photograph of a pretty, ginger-haired young woman. The name was Josephine Vanderliner.

PEPPER STEPPED BACK from the window, trembling inside with rage and embarrassment. How dare they condemn her? Couldn't they understand how devastated she'd been to lose Trace?

She brushed angrily at her tears. She wasn't looking for their sympathy. Nor their understanding. And it was a damned good thing, because clearly she would get neither.

She felt the note she'd stuffed into her pocket and eased it out. The paper was yellowed. The dark splatters made her recoil. Angus's suicide note. She didn't have to open it to know that he was blaming her even from the grave.

What about the failings of his father? Where was their anger toward the man who had gone to such extremes, spoiling them rotten one moment and then punishing them by locking them in that third-floor room?

She thought of the young wife she'd been. The foolish young woman who'd let Call Winchester rule all their lives for way too long.

Funny, she was still acutely disappointed in him even after all these years. Her anger had eased as did her fear of him, she thought with no small amount of irony, but not her disappointment.

Was it any wonder that she had never trusted another man? Even Hunt McCormick. How different her life would have been if she'd run off with him like he'd wanted her to.

She shook her head at the very thought. She hadn't been able to leave because of her children, children she should have protected from Call. All her children, not just Trace. But the older ones had always been Call's children from the time they were born, and she'd felt so helpless against him back then.

The truth was she'd loved Call, trusted him to do what was best for all of them, even when it came to how their children should be raised.

She'd been blinded by that love.

Until Trace was born.

Pepper would never know what had changed. Maybe she'd finally seen Call for what he was, a bully. Or maybe she'd finally fallen out of love with him.

Either way, she'd been determined to save Trace from him. That struggle had definitely killed any love she had for her husband and had cost her the rest of her children.

Pepper knew that some people thought she was cold and heartless. They pointed to her reaction when Call hadn't come back from his horseback ride more than forty years ago. She hadn't been able to hide her relief that he was gone.

But her secret shame was that a part of her still loved the Call she thought she'd married. Just as a part of her still loved Hunt McCormick.

She started to unfold the note, bracing herself, but changed her mind and dropped the paper into the wastebasket. For a long moment she stood there, staring down at Angus's last cry for help. The one thing she'd never been was a coward. At seventy-two, she couldn't start now. She bent down to retrieve the note and carefully eased the paper open.

The words were scrawled and almost illegible. The handwriting of a child. Or a terrified, sick man.

I'm so sorry, Mother. Forgive me. I forgive you.
Angus.

She crumpled the note in her fist, suddenly unable to catch her breath or stem the flow of tears. Her body jerked with the shuddering sobs that rose up in her. It was all she could do not to scream out her anguish.

Pepper didn't hear the door open behind her.

"I thought you might need something," Enid said, making her spin around in surprise. Enid held a teacup and saucer.

Pepper could smell the strong tea, strong to cover up the drugs her housekeeper had been systematically and surreptitiously giving her for years. At first Pepper hadn't noticed, she'd been so grateful for the oblivion. She assumed it made Enid's job easier having Pepper either out like a light or so docile she wasn't any trouble.

But after learning about Trace, things had to change. She needed her wits about her. She also needed to be more careful when it came to Enid.

She quickly turned her back to Enid, stepping to the window to hastily dry her tears and pull herself together. Enid was the last person she wanted seeing her like this.

She heard the elderly housekeeper set down the cup and saucer on the end table by the bed and move to join her at the window. Enid pulled back the curtain wider to see what Pepper had been looking at out the window.

She smiled smugly as she saw what Pepper did—Jack and Josey walking arm in arm toward the house.

"I brought you up some chamomile tea to help you sleep." Enid motioned toward the cup she'd put down beside Pepper's bed.

"You are so thoughtful," Pepper said, not bothering to hide the sarcasm in her tone.

"Yes, aren't I," Enid said and turned to leave. "Good night."

"Good night," Pepper repeated, just wanting the woman to leave her room.

"Drink your tea while it's hot."

She bristled. "Please close the door behind you." Pepper didn't turn until she heard the door close.

The smell of the strong tea made her nauseous as she stepped to the door and locked it, then she picked up the cup of tea and carried it into the bathroom, where she paused before pouring it down the drain.

Tonight she could have used the mind-numbing effect of whatever drug Enid had put in it. But she could no longer allow herself that escape.

She dumped the tea and rinsed out the sink. The cup she left by her bed before going to the window to look out across the deep ravine to the rocky point in the distance.

It was over there, just across from the ranch, that her precious son had been murdered. Pepper thought of the third-floor room, the binoculars she'd found, and the feeling lodged deep in her heart that someone in her own family was involved.

Nothing else mattered but finding out the truth. It was why she'd made sure her granddaughter McCall had become acting sheriff. While they had never discussed it, Pepper had seen something in McCall's expression.

She didn't believe, any more than Pepper did, that the alleged, now-deceased killer had acted alone.

And McCall, who was so like her grandmother, would never let a killer go free. Pepper was counting on her.

AS THEY ENTERED THE HOUSE, Jack discovered his aunt Virginia had been waiting for them.

"I'd like to speak to my nephew," she said, looking pointedly at Josey. *"Alone."*

"Anything you have to say, you can say in front of my wife," he said indignantly.

"It's okay," Josey said, touching his arm. "I'd like to take a look around the ranch."

"Don't go far," Jack said.

Josey looked amused.

"I'm just saying this is wild country and you can get turned around out there in the dark."

"Yes," Virginia agreed with a tight smile. "My father disappeared out there on a night a lot like this one."

"I don't want you disappearing, too," Jack said, only half-joking. "Also, there are rattlesnakes out there."

Josey glanced at his aunt as if to say, *And in here, too.*

"What is this about?" Jack asked his aunt, as Josey left.

"Why don't we step down the hall?" she said. "That awful woman might be listening. Both awful women," she added under her breath.

They stepped into the parlor. Virginia closed the door and spun around, clearly angry. "Okay, you can knock off the act."

"I beg your pardon?"

"You aren't Angus's son, and even if you are, you're not getting this ranch."

Jack had to smile. "Isn't it possible I'm just here to see my grandmother?"

His aunt scoffed. "You don't have to pretend with me. She can barely stand the sight of you. She isn't going to leave you a thing."

Jack was tempted to say that it seemed to him that Pepper Winchester couldn't stand the sight of anyone, maybe especially her daughter. "Frankly, I think she'll try to take it all with her before she leaves any of us a dime. But even if I'm wrong, I'm no threat to you."

Virginia looked skeptical. "*Please.* After that sympathy play you made at dinner? I see what you're doing, but it won't work. You're wasting your time."

"Is that why you pulled me in here? To tell me that?"

Virginia was tall like her mother, but without the grace. "Has my mother mentioned who else is coming to this gruesome reunion?"

"Your mother hasn't shared anything with me."

"Well, I'm worried." Her gaze bored into his. "I heard Enid and Alfred whispering between themselves. They seem to think Pepper might not be of sound mind. I'm betting they're thinking that they can somehow have her put away and take all her money."

Jack wasn't surprised to hear this. "God knows they've put up with her long enough. They probably deserve it." Enid acted as if she was the lady of the house, not Pepper. It surprised him that his obstinate grandmother put up with it.

"What Enid and Alfred Hoagland deserve is to be fired before they steal her blind," Virginia snapped.

"What if they've somehow coerced her into making a new will and leaving everything to them?"

"I can't see Pepper doing that under any circumstances. Haven't you seen the way she looks at Enid? She detests the woman. And no one is going to have Pepper committed. It would require a mental evaluation, and I'd put my money on Pepper passing with flying colors."

"You'd put *your* money on it?" Virginia said. "As if you had any money. I know that's not your car parked out there." She gave him a satisfied look. "I have connections. I had the plates run. That Cadillac belongs to the Galaxy Corporation. I assume you're employed by them. Or did you steal the car?"

"I borrowed the Caddie with every intention of taking it back," Jack said, bristling. He hadn't expected this of his aunt.

"And your *wife?* Did you borrow her, as well?" Virginia asked with a laugh, then waved it off. "I was only joking. She's right up your alley. I've seen the way she looks around the lodge, as if she's putting a price tag on all the furnishings."

Jack bit back an angry retort. It was one thing to come after him, but it was another to go after his wife. Even his pretend wife.

The irony didn't escape him. He was defending a woman he'd picked up on the highway. A stranger he didn't know beans about. But then, neither did his aunt.

"Josey likes antiques and comes from money," he said, feeling that might be true. "I can assure you, she isn't interested in Grandmother's."

"You don't look anything like Angus," Virginia said, changing tactics.

Jack laughed, determined not to let his aunt get to him. "I'm not going to argue this with you. My grandmother knows the truth, that's all that matters."

"Your *grandmother* is the reason you're a bastard. She didn't think your mother was good enough for Angus."

He tried to rein in his temper, but Virginia had pushed him too far. "Pepper never approved of any of the women her sons fell in love with. Or her daughter, for that matter. She controlled you all with money and a cushy life on this ranch. All except Trace. Is that why you hated him so much—because he couldn't be bought?"

The color had washed from Virginia's face. She stood trembling all over, her lips moving, but nothing coming out.

"But the truth is I wasn't the only bastard to come out of this house—was I, Aunt Virginia?"

JOSEY WALKED UP the narrow dirt road to a small hill before she stopped to look back at the sprawling lodge and the tall cottonwoods and the sparse pines that made the place look like an oasis in the desert.

The lodge was far enough off the main road that she felt relatively safe. From what she'd seen earlier, the main road got little use, not that the lodge could be seen by anyone just happening to drive past.

No one knew she was here. That was the beauty of it. So why couldn't she relax? Because her mother wouldn't be safe until she sent the money and got her moved.

Jack had said they would stay for the week, but Josey knew she couldn't make it that long. If there was just some way to send the money without having to leave here—or let anyone know where she was, she thought, as she walked back down the road in the diminishing daylight. It would be dark soon, and she had no desire to be caught out here alone.

But she wouldn't involve Jack any more than she had. She couldn't.

As she entered, she didn't hear a sound from down the hall. The door to the parlor was closed. She assumed Jack was still in there talking to his aunt, though she couldn't imagine what they might have to talk about. Unless Virginia was trying to talk him into doing away with Pepper and splitting the take.

They'd better cut Enid and Alfred in, Josey thought with a wry smile. The two gave her the creeps. If anyone was plotting to knock off Pepper it was one or both of them.

As she opened the door to the bedroom, Josey realized that Jack could have finished his talk with his aunt and be waiting here for her.

She was relieved to see the bedroom unoccupied. She closed the door behind her and stood looking at the large canopied bed. Playing married was one thing. But where was Jack planning to sleep?

The door opened behind her as if on cue. She turned to look at him, and he grinned as if he knew exactly what she'd been thinking.

"I'm sorry, where did you say you would be sleeping?" she asked.

"I was thinking we could negotiate something."

She smiled back at him. "Think again."

"I suppose sharing the bed is out of the question?"

"You suppose right."

"Don't you trust me?"

"Not as far as I can throw you."

"Now, honey," he said, reaching for her, "we can't let Enid catch us sleeping separately on our honeymoon."

Josey stepped away from him. "We can if we have a fight." She picked up a cheap vase from a nearby table, tossing it from hand to hand. "A lover's quarrel. You know newlyweds."

He was shaking his head, but still smiling. "No one will hear it if you break that."

"But Enid will see the broken glass in the morning when she comes with the coffee and catches you sleeping in that chair over there."

Jack launched himself at her and the vase, but he wasn't fast enough. The vase hit the floor and shattered like a gunshot. Jack's momentum drove them both back. They crashed into the bed and onto it, with Jack ending up on top.

"Now this is more like it," he said, grinning down at her.

Josey could feel the hard beat of his heart against her chest as she looked into those amazing blue eyes of his. The man really was adorable.

"I want to kiss you," he said quietly. He touched her cheek, his fingers warm.

She felt a small tremor. He could be so gentle that it made her ache.

"What will it cost me?"

"You want to pay for a kiss?" she asked, raising a brow, trying to hide her disappointment that he hadn't just kissed her.

"Is there any other way you'd let me kiss you?"

She hated that he made her sound cheap and mercenary. She'd only agreed to take his money for this week because it would have made him suspicious if she'd turned it down. Did he really think she was doing this for the money?

"I really—" The rest of her words caught in her throat as she realized he was untying her scarf. She grabbed for the ends to stop him—just not quickly enough.

"What the hell?" He pushed off her to a sitting position on the edge of the bed next to her, his expression one of shock and horror as he stared at her. "Josey... what—"

"It's nothing." She quickly sat up as she tried to retie the scarf to cover up the rope burn on her neck.

"Like hell," he said, reaching out to stop her as he took in the extent of her injury. "How did this happen?"

She didn't answer as she tried to take the ends of the scarf from him and retie them. "Please."

He held the scarf for a moment longer, his expression softening as he lifted his gaze to hers. "Who did this to you?" There was an edge to his voice, a fury.

"It has nothing to do with you." She pulled away, getting to her feet and turning her back to him as she clumsily tied the scarf with trembling fingers.

"This is why you were on the highway," he said, rising from the bed to come up behind her. "This is what you're running from."

She didn't deny it.

"I don't understand why—"

"No, you don't, so just forget it," she snapped. She finished tying the scarf and swung around to face him. "I took care of it."

He stared at her. "The only way to take care of it is to kill the person who did this to you."

Josey didn't dare speak into the dense silence that fell between them.

Jack seemed to be waiting for her to explain. When she didn't, he let out a curse.

She watched him grab one of the pillows and a quilt that had been folded up on the end of the bed. He brushed past her and dropped both the pillow and quilt onto the chair before leaving the room.

It was much later that she heard him return to the dark room and curl up in the chair across from her. She could hear him breathing softly and feel his gaze on her. She closed her eyes tight and told herself she didn't give a damn what Jack Winchester thought of her. It wasn't the first night she'd gone to sleep lying to herself.

She woke up just after two in the morning to find Jack gone.

Chapter Six

It was late by the time McCall reached her office in Whitehorse. She had brought evidence from the crime scene that needed to be sent to the lab in Missoula first thing in the morning.

Deputies had discovered a bullet on the outside of the car pulled from the river and in the headrest on the driver's side. Both were .38 slugs. Someone in camp had been armed. Deputies would continue their search in the morning for the weapon—and any more victims.

But McCall wasn't ruling out that at least one person had gotten away—possibly armed—from the crime scene.

"Any chance you'll be coming down to my place later?" Luke had asked as he rubbed the tension from her shoulders before she'd left the crime scene.

McCall had leaned into his strong hands, wanting nothing more than to spend the night with Luke in his small trailer curled against him. He was staying in the trailer out on his property until he completed their house. He planned to have it done before their Christmas wedding so they could move in together.

She couldn't believe how lucky she was that Luke had come back into her life.

"I'm sorry," she'd told him. "I'd better stay at my place near town tonight. This case—"

"I know." He'd turned her to smile at her, then kissed her.

He did know. He knew how much this job meant to her even though she'd fought taking the acting sheriff position. He'd encouraged her to run for sheriff when the time came.

"You sound like my grandmother," she'd said.

"Yeah? Well, we both know you aren't finished with your father's death, don't we?"

It was the first time he'd mentioned what he'd overheard the night he'd saved her life at her cabin. She hadn't had to answer, since there was no point. He was right. She wasn't finished, and she had a bad feeling her grandmother wasn't, either.

McCall pushed aside thoughts of her fiancé as she went to work.

George had assisted with taking their Jane Doe's prints. McCall entered them now into the system and waited. The chance of getting a match was slim at best. The Jane Doe would have had to been arrested, served in the military or had a job where her prints were required for security reasons.

That was why McCall was amazed when she got a match.

Her prints had come up from a prostitution charge. She'd served eight months and had only recently been released. Her name was Celeste Leigh of Palm City, California. No known address or place of employment. She was twenty-two and believed to be living on the streets.

McCall put in a call to Detective Diaz in Palm City

and wasn't surprised to find him still at work. Apparently he was getting a lot of pressure on the Ray Allan Evans Sr. murder because Evans had been the husband of Ella Vanderliner.

"I've got an ID on our Jane Doe," she said and proceeded to tell him about Celeste Leigh.

"Prostitution? I'm not surprised. From what we've discovered investigating his father's homicide, RJ was involved in a string of shady ventures that lost money, and his daddy had to bail him out. He was also known to frequent the lower end of town."

"Celeste was wearing a diamond engagement ring with a big rock on it. We found the receipt for it in the glove box of the car. It set RJ back a large chunk of change. Which might explain why her ring finger appeared to have been broken. I think RJ changed his mind about any upcoming nuptials."

Diaz swore. "The bastard broke her finger trying to take back the wedding ring? I guess I shouldn't be surprised given that he later hung her from a tree."

"Apparently, he'd been abusing her for some time."

"That fits with what we know about him. He'd been accused by other prostitutes of abuse, but they always dropped the charges. So what about the other noose?"

"We found Josephine Vanderliner's purse downriver from where RJ and Celeste were believed to have been camped. We'll continue dragging the river in the morning. Given the three sets of tracks, the two nooses and her purse, we're fairly certain Vanderliner was there with them."

"Keep me updated. I'll see if I can find some next of kin that need to be notified of Celeste Leigh's death."

McCall hung up and studied the photograph of Ray

Allan Evans Jr. again. He was blond, blue-eyed, movie-star handsome, but there was something about him that unnerved her, and would have even if she hadn't known anything about him.

It was in the eyes, she thought, as she pushed away the photograph and looked instead at the copy she'd made of Josephine Vanderliner's photo.

Vanderliner was pretty in a startling way. In the photo, she had her long, ginger-colored hair pulled back and wound in a loose braid. Her eyes were aquamarine, and she was smiling into the camera as if she didn't have a care in the world.

That had apparently changed, McCall thought, as she sighed and made another copy of the photographs to take to the *Milk River Courier* office come morning.

If there was even a chance that either RJ Evans or Josephine Vanderliner were still in the area, then residents needed to know and be on the lookout for them.

If they were in Whitehorse, the town was small enough that any stranger stood out like a sore thumb—especially this time of year. During summer a few tourists would past through on what was known as the Hi-Line, Highway 2 across the top part of Montana. But it was a little early for tourist season.

As McCall locked up and headed for her cabin beside Milk River, she glanced at the vehicles parked diagonally at the curb in front of the bars. None from out of state. Only one from out of town.

She left the mostly sleeping little Western town and headed home, praying neither suspect was anywhere near Whitehorse, Montana.

WHERE WAS JACK? Josey felt a chill as she glanced around the empty room. The door to the bathroom was open, the room empty.

She sat up, listening. The house seemed unusually quiet. Eerily so. She had a sudden urge to get out of there while she had a chance. What was wrong with her?

From the open window next to the bed, she heard one of the horses whinny, then another. She threw her legs over the side of the bed and hurried to the window.

A wedge of moon and a zillion tiny stars lit the black night. She could make out the horses moving around the corral as if something had set them off. She waited for her eyes to adjust to the darkness, surprised that the floodlight near the barn was out.

It had been casting a golden glow over the ranch yard earlier when she'd gone to bed. Her pulse quickened.

A breeze rustled the leaves of the cottonwoods, casting eerie shadows in the direction of the lodge.

Among the shadows, something moved.

Jack.

He crept along the dark edge of the buildings like a man who didn't want to be seen. He had something in his hand that occasionally caught the moonlight. A crowbar?

Josey watched him reach the end of the far wing, the one she'd noticed was older than the rest and had boards over the windows and doors. He disappeared around the corner.

Where was he sneaking off to at this time of the night and why? Apparently, she wasn't the only one with secrets.

JOSEY WOKE THE NEXT MORNING to the sound of running water. A few minutes later Jack came out of the bathroom wearing only his jeans and boots. His muscled chest was suntanned and glistening. He smelled of soap, his face was clean shaven, his blond hair was wet and dark against the nape of his neck.

She'd felt a wave of desire wash over her.

"Morning," he said, seeing she was awake. He seemed to avoid her gaze.

"Good morning." Well, if he wasn't going to say anything, then she was. "Jack—"

"I'll let you get ready and come down with you for breakfast," he said quickly. "Can you be ready in half an hour?"

She nodded, sensing the change in him. She'd hoped things would go back to the way they were yesterday, when he'd been playful and affectionate. It had been a game, this pretend marriage. But apparently yesterday had changed that after he'd seen the rope burn on her neck. Or did it have something to do with his late-night exploration?

She'd heard him come in just before daylight. He hadn't turned on a light. She'd listened to him stumbling around in the dark and caught a whiff of alcohol. Had he been drinking?

Now he didn't give her a second glance as he pulled on a Western shirt and left.

She lay in bed, hating this change in him. She knew he must be regretting picking her up on the highway, let alone proposing marriage, even a fake one. She touched the rope burn on her neck. What he must think of her.

If he only knew.

Well, what did he expect? she thought angrily, as she swung her legs over the side of the bed and headed for the bathroom. He didn't know a thing about her. He hadn't wanted to know a thing about her. All he wanted was a pretend wife to fool his grandmother. And she'd done her job just fine.

She took a quick bath and was ready when he returned.

He again gave her only a glance, his gaze pausing for a moment on the new scarf she had tied around her neck. She couldn't wait for her neck to heal enough that she could dispense with the scarves.

As they descended the stairs, Josey missed his warm hand on her back. She missed his touch almost as much as she missed the way he had looked at her.

Jack's grandmother glanced up as they entered the dining room, her gaze narrowing. The old gal didn't miss much. She must see that there was trouble in honeymoon paradise.

Josey felt uncomfortable, as if she was under scrutiny throughout breakfast. Even Virginia seemed to pick up on the fact that something was different between Josey and Jack.

"The two of you should take a horseback ride," Pepper Winchester said as they finished breakfast. "Show her the ranch, Jack. I know how you love to ride."

Josey started to say that wasn't necessary, that she didn't know how to ride, that the last thing the two of them needed was to be alone together, but Jack interrupted her before she could.

"I think that's a great idea," he said, getting to his feet. "I'll go saddle up two horses and meet you in the barn."

JACK WAS ALMOST SURPRISED when he turned to find Josey framed in the barn doorway. He wondered how long she'd been standing there watching him. A while, from her expression.

He hated the way he'd been treating her since seeing what some bastard had done to her. He couldn't help his anger. He wanted to kill the son of a bitch.

A part of him also wanted to grab Josey and shake some sense into her. How could she have let something like this happen? Clearly, she'd gotten hooked up with the wrong guy. Why had he thought her too smart to fall for a man like that? He was disappointed in her.

But it only amplified the fact that he didn't know this woman. Apparently not at all.

"You've never ridden a horse before, have you?" he said now. "I saw your expression at breakfast."

"That had more to do with you than horses," she said, as she stepped into the barn. "I woke up last night and you were gone."

He finished cinching down the saddle and turned to her. "I went downstairs for a drink."

Her eyes narrowed. "Before or after you sneaked outside with a crowbar?" she asked. She started to turn away when he grabbed her arm and swung her back around to face him.

"What are you doing here with me?" he demanded.

She looked into his eyes, and he lost himself for a moment in that sea of green. "I didn't have anything better to do."

He let go of her arm, shaking his head. "So we're both lying to each other. Be honest with me and I'll be honest with you," he challenged. "What are you running from? Or should I say *who* are you running from?"

She took a step back. "Whatever you're doing here, it's none of my business."

He laughed. "Just like whoever is after you is none of my business?"

"It's better if you don't know."

He gave her an impatient look. "I'd like to know what has you so scared."

"No, you don't." With that she turned as if to leave, but collided with Alfred Hoagland, who was standing just outside.

"I came to see if you needed help saddling the horses," the old man said, his two large hands on each of her shoulders to steady her. "Change your mind about going for a ride?"

"No," she said, pulling free of him and stepping back into the barn.

"I've got it covered, Alfred," Jack said.

The old man stood in the doorway for a moment. "Fine with me," he said before turning away.

Jack stepped past Josey to make sure Alfred wasn't still standing outside listening.

"Do you think he heard what we were saying?" she whispered behind him.

"Don't worry about it." He turned his back to her.

"Look, if you've changed your mind about this marriage—"

"I haven't," he quickly interrupted. "I'm sorry about the way I've been acting. Coming back here…" He waved a hand through the air. "It's hard to explain. I have a lot of conflicting emotions going on right now. But I'm glad you're here with me. Come for a ride with me. It's a beautiful day, and Enid packed us a lunch so we can be gone until suppertime. You have to admit, that has its appeal."

IT DID. Just like Jack did when he smiled the way he was smiling at her now. Earlier, she'd stood quietly studying him from the barn doorway as he saddled the horses. He'd been unaware she was there and she hadn't said anything, enjoying watching him.

He'd spoken softly to each horse, touching and stroking the horses in such a gentle way that she'd found herself enthralled by this side of the man.

Now she eyed her horse, wondering what she'd gotten herself into. Her horse, like Jack's, was huge. She told herself she could handle this. After everything she'd been through, this should be easy.

But when she looked at Jack she didn't feel strong or tough. She felt scared and hurt. It was crazy that what he thought of her could hurt so much, and it scared her that she cared. She barely knew this man she was pretending to be wed to, and his sneaking away from their room last night proved it.

Worse, she couldn't help thinking about what his reaction would be if he knew the truth. She cringed at the thought.

"Ready?" Jack swung up into his saddle with a fluid, graceful motion that made her jealous. Everything seemed to come easy for him, making her wonder about the story he'd told at dinner last night.

Apparently, he'd had a hard life, and yet it didn't show on him. Unless his bruises were deeper than her own.

She concentrated on attempting to copy Jack's movements. She grabbed hold of the saddle horn and tried to pull herself up enough to get a foot in the stirrup.

She heard Jack chuckle and climb down from his horse.

"Here, let me help you." He didn't sound upset with

her anymore. She wished that didn't make her as happy as it did. "Put your foot in my hands."

She looked into his face, overcome by the gentleness she saw there, and felt tears well in her eyes. She hurriedly put her booted foot into his clasped hands and, balancing herself with one hand on his shoulder, was lifted up and into the saddle.

The horse shuddered, and she grabbed the saddle horn with both hands, feeling way too high above the ground.

"Thank you," she said, furtively wiping at her tears.

"You don't have to do this."

He misread the reason for her tears. She nodded, not looking at him. What was wrong with her? She hadn't shed a tear throughout her recent ordeal, and here she was fighting tears? She was letting Jack Winchester get to her. Big mistake.

"I want to do this." She could feel his gaze on her and was relieved when he walked around and climbed back on his horse.

As her horse followed Jack's out of the barn, she looked at the vast country and took a deep breath. Her father always told her she could do anything she set her mind to. But her father had been gone for years now, and her mother no longer knew her.

They rode through tall green grass across rolling prairie, the air smelling sweet with clover. In the distance, Josey could see the dark outline of a mountain range. Jack told her they were the Little Rockies.

They'd ridden from rocky dry land covered with nothing but cactus and sagebrush into this lush, pine-studded, beautiful country. It surprised her how quickly the landscape changed. Even the colors. They ran in shades of silken green to deep purple by the time they reached the horizon.

They stopped on a high ridge deep in the Missouri Breaks. She felt as if she was on top of the world, the land running wide-open to the horizons as clouds bobbed in a sea of blue overhead. "It's amazing up here," she said, taking an awed breath.

"It's still lonely country," he said. "There isn't anything for miles."

"Your grandmother doesn't run cattle or grow any crops?"

"She used to, back when the family all lived on the ranch, but I'm sure she sold off the herd after we all left," Jack said. "All she had was Enid and Alfred, and you can tell by the shape the place is in that they haven't been able to keep up with maintaining the house and barns. I'm surprised she kept the horses, but I suspect Alfred must ride. I wouldn't imagine my grandmother's been on a horse in years."

"You used to ride as a boy?" she guessed.

He nodded. "My mother and I rode down here. It was our favorite spot."

She heard a wistfulness in his voice that she hadn't heard since they'd been here, a love for this country and a sorrow for the mother he'd loved.

"You miss this," she said.

He chuckled.

She could almost feel the battle going on inside him. He'd come here to even a score with his grandmother in some way. But a part of him wanted this, not the money, but the land, and not just to own it, but to ranch it.

"What would you do if your grandmother asked you to stay?"

"She won't."

"How can you be so sure of that?"

"Because I know her."

"Maybe she's changed."

He chuckled again. "Right. Anyway, it's too late."

Was it ever too late? She thought of RJ. Maybe some people were too bitter, too sick, too hateful to ever change. Maybe Jack's grandmother was one of them.

She listened to the breeze blow through the boughs of the ponderosa pines and wished she and Jack never had to go back to civilization.

"I'd run cattle on it the way this ranch was when I was a kid," Jack said suddenly. "I'd get wheat growing up on those high benches and alfalfa and hay. I'd make it a working ranch again instead of…" His voice trailed off and he laughed, as if at his own foolishness. "Just talking," he said. "I came up here to say goodbye."

They ate the lunch Enid had packed them with a view of the lake where the Missouri River widened into Fort Peck Reservoir. The water looked like a sparkling blue jewel hidden in this untamed, uninhabited country.

"I'm sorry about the way I reacted last night," Jack said after they'd finished a sandwich and soda on a large flat rock.

She nodded, a lump in her throat. This was the last thing she wanted to talk about.

"I was just so angry at the person who did that to you…" His voice trailed off. "And I took that anger out on you."

She understood more than he knew.

"Josey, I want to help."

She shook her head. "You don't know any more about me than I do you. I think it is best if we leave it that way."

"That's not true. You've met my family. You know where I was born. Hell, you practically know my whole life history."

"Just up to the age of six. I don't even know where you live now."

"Wyoming. Ten Sleep, Wyoming. How about you?"

She shook her head.

"Look, I know you're in trouble and it's because of a dangerous man." He raised his hand to keep her from interrupting him. Not that she was going to. So far he'd been dead-on. "All I'm saying is that maybe I can help."

Josey smiled, her eyes burning with tears again. She was touched and hated that she was. "Don't be so nice to me, okay?"

"I can't help myself." His gaze locked with hers.

She felt the heat in those eyes, the blue like a hot flame. Their thighs brushed as he moved, the touch sending a flurry of emotions racing through her.

Jack drew her into his arms before she could protest. His mouth dropped to hers as his strong arms encircled her.

His kiss was filled with passion and heat and, strangely enough, a gentleness like he'd shown with the horses, as if he knew to go easy with her because she would spook easily.

She did more than let him kiss her. She kissed him back, matching his passion and his heat, if not his gentleness, until she came to her senses and drew back.

He was looking at her, his eyes filled with a soft tenderness.

It was as if a dam burst. All the tears she'd repressed for so long broke free. He pulled her back into his arms, holding her as she sobbed, his large hand rubbing her back as he whispered soothing words she could neither hear nor understand.

MCCALL STOOD OUTSIDE the cold, sterile autopsy room waiting for George to come out and give her the results. The crime lab had flown in personnel to do the autopsy. George was assisting.

She'd had only a few hours' sleep before she'd called down to the Missouri River this morning to check with Luke. They were dragging the river and had been since daylight. So far, nothing.

George didn't look so hot as he came out of the autopsy room. "I figured you'd be waiting." He made her sound ghoulish. "The report should be typed up within an hour."

She shook her head. She didn't want to wait that long. "Just give me the highlights."

He sighed, looking exhausted and a little green around the gills. She figured he regretted taking this job and wondered how long he'd last.

"Could we at least sit down for minute?" he asked, and headed for the conference room.

She grabbed them both a cup of coffee from the machine and joined him.

"As you know, she had numerous signs of abuse," he said, as she handed him a cup of coffee and sat down. "Scars, cuts and bruises, cigarette burns. She had either been with a long-time abuser or…"

"She got off on it," McCall guessed.

He grimaced.

"So maybe the hanging was a sexual thing."

George looked even more uncomfortable. "With two women? There were two places where ropes had been tied to the limb."

McCall thought about it for a few moments as she sipped her coffee. "Maybe we were wrong about there being another victim. Maybe he'd hung her up there before and the limb had held the first time. This time, it didn't."

"I guess. But how do you explain the car in the river?"

She shook her head. "I guess it would depend on whether or not they were alone at that camp. We've just assumed Vanderliner was with the other two because she was seen with her stepbrother leaving the scene of the murder and we found her purse."

McCall rubbed her temples. "Also there were at least three different sets of footprints found at the scene, two women's-size types of sneakers and tracks that matched the loafer we found stuck under the brake pedal of the car."

"You're thinking the victim on the slab could have had more than one pair of sneakers," George offered.

"Or the other prints could be those of the missing Josephine Vanderliner. It would explain the other noose, and we have three different hair samples from the car, which was only a couple of days old. We know Vanderliner was in the car at some point because of the eyewitness but we don't know for how long. He could have dumped her and kept her purse."

"So we don't know if Vanderliner made it as far as Montana."

McCall nodded thoughtfully. "I just have a bad feeling she's here. Either in that river or on the loose. I stopped by the newspaper office early this morning. They're running photographs of both RJ Evans and Josephine Vanderliner. If either of them got out of that river, then someone has to have seen them. They were going to need a ride since the only tracks we found were for the car in the river."

"Great," George said. "One of them abuses women for the fun of it and the other is wanted for murder." He shook his head. "I hope you put something in the paper to warn residents in case they come across them."

"Armed and dangerous and possibly traveling together."

Chapter Seven

RJ felt like hell. His shoulder had quit bleeding. Fortunately the bullet had only furrowed through his flesh and missed the bone, but it hurt like a son of a bitch. He knew he had to get some antibiotics. If it wasn't already infected.

But right now he was more concerned about the blow to his head. The double vision was driving him crazy. That and the killer headache. Bitches.

Celeste had almost drowned him. Josey had shot him. He'd been damned lucky to get out of that car. He wondered where Celeste was. The last he'd seen her she had been sucked out of the car by the current.

He'd gotten his foot caught under the brake pedal. When he'd finally freed himself, he'd come up downriver in time to see Josey getting away. He'd been bleeding like a stuck pig and was half-blind from the blow on his head, but even crazed as he was, he knew he had to catch her or everything he'd worked for would turn to a pile of crap.

How had things gone so wrong? Maybe Celeste was right. Maybe it had been when he'd lost his temper and strung her up from that tree limb. He hadn't meant to kill her, just shut her the hell up.

No, where things had really gone haywire was when he decided to string up Josey next to her. Should have known that limb couldn't hold both of them. Shouldn't have left the pistol lying on that log by the fire pit, either.

But who knew either of those women could move that fast? He hadn't been that surprised when Josey had shot him. He'd expected something like that from her, but he'd never seen it coming with Celeste. She'd been like a wild animal when she'd attacked him.

He'd tied the ropes to the bumper of the car and strung up both women. When the damned limb broke, he'd thrown the car in Reverse, thinking he could run them down. But then Josey had shot at him and Celeste had come flying in the driver-side window at him, the rope still around her neck and dragging in the dirt. She'd knocked the breath out of him.

And with her pummeling him he hadn't realized he was still in Reverse, the car still going backward toward the river. The next thing he knew the car was in the river and he was underwater and Celeste, that stupid whore, was still fighting him.

Shuddering now at the memory of how close he'd come to drowning, he stumbled and almost fell. He'd climbed out of the river and gone after Josey. He knew she'd make a run for it. No surprise, she'd taken the backpack with the money and his gun in it.

He'd climbed the hill back to the single-track dirt road. That was when he'd spotted her. She had shoes, so she had made better time than him. He'd lost both of his in the river, and he was shot and hurt, and with nothing but socks on his bare feet the ground felt rough.

He'd seen her on the highway halfway up the

mountainside. Too far away to shoot her even if he'd had the pistol. Maybe with a rifle…

But then a pale yellow Cadillac convertible had roared across the bridge and up the other side, stopping three-quarters of the way up the mountain when the driver saw Josey standing beside the road.

RJ had picked up a rock and thrown it as hard as he could. It hit on the mountain below him and rolled down, starting a small avalanche. But of course it hadn't stopped Josey from disappearing in the Cadillac.

He didn't know how far he walked last night. He just knew he had to put some distance between him and the river. He'd finally laid down under a big pine tree and slept until daylight. The soles of his feet were bleeding through his socks.

He'd awakened this morning and realized he could see the highway from where he was on the side of the mountain and the cop cars. All that commotion. They must have found Celeste.

That was when he knew he was in trouble. He had to find Josey before the cops did. But he couldn't track her down in the shape he was in. He needed shoes, clothes, a vehicle, medicine and some drugs. He'd lost his stash in the car when it went into the water. He felt jittery and irritable. Soon his skin would be crawling as if there were bugs just under the surface.

He knew he couldn't get a ride. Not as bad as he looked. Not with cops and searchers crawling the area.

That's when he'd seen what appeared to be a roof in the distance and remembered when he and his father had come to Montana for an elk hunt. There used to be a bar at what was called Mobridge. As he remembered, there was also a house. Was it possible someone still lived there?

JACK LEANED BACK, the rock warm, the view incredible, and studied Josey.

She stood on the edge of the ravine, staring out at the wild terrain.

They hadn't spoken since the kiss or her tears. He'd held her until she'd quit crying, then she'd stepped out of his arms, seeming embarrassed, and walked to the edge of the ridge.

He'd waited, giving her time and space. He knew better than to try to push her and yet he wanted desperately to know who had done those things to her and what had her running so scared. What the hell kind of trouble had she gotten herself into and how could he make it right?

Jack chuckled to himself, realizing he'd been wanting to make things right since he was a boy and he'd seen the pain his mother had suffered.

With Josey, it was more complicated. She didn't want to involve him. Didn't she realize he was already involved? He'd become involved the moment he'd picked her up on the highway. He'd only gotten in deeper by kissing her. He wanted to help her. And if that meant getting this bastard who'd done this to her...

She'd said she'd taken care of it. He didn't like the sound of that. Had she killed the man? Was that why she was so afraid? Why hadn't she gone to the police then? Between the rope burn around her neck and the bruises he'd only glimpsed, she would have had a good case for self-defense.

The breeze ruffled her short, dark curls. He watched her raise her hand to push it out of her eyes. She was so beautiful. So strong and yet so fragile.

He knew he shouldn't have kissed her. But he hadn't been able to help himself. And he couldn't even promise that he wouldn't do it again.

She turned to look back at him. "I'm sorry about that."

"I'm not. I'm used to women crying after I kiss them." Just as he'd hoped, she smiled. "I suppose we'd better head back. We have a long ride ahead of us. Can't have Aunt Virginia passing out from hunger if we're late for supper. She is such a delicate thing."

Josey chuckled. "She's a lot like your grandmother that way."

"Isn't she though." He handed Josey her reins and helped her into her saddle.

"I'm from California, an only child, my father is dead, my mother—" Her voice broke. "She was in a car accident and never fully recovered."

"I'm sorry."

"I probably shouldn't have even told you that," she said, looking toward the horizon. "The less you know about me, the better off you'll be once I'm gone."

WITH JACK AND JOSEY OFF on a horseback ride and Virginia napping, Pepper Winchester took advantage of being alone with Enid.

She'd managed to keep her housekeeper from drugging her for some time now by getting rid of the food or drink Enid gave her privately, but she had to put a stop to it. Pepper knew her only hesitation was that she didn't want to have to fire Enid and her husband.

Not because she felt any kind of loyalty to them. She'd been more than generous with the two over the years. They must have a nice little nest egg put away.

No, it was because she didn't like change. The last thing she wanted was strangers on the ranch. Enid and Alfred had been fixtures on the place since Pepper herself had come to the ranch as a new bride. Was it any wonder they felt they belonged here even more than she did?

But she couldn't let Enid run roughshod over her anymore. Nor could she trust the woman. Pepper was sure the two wondered what she was up to. They knew her well enough to know that getting her family back to the ranch hadn't been an act of sentiment.

She found Enid in the kitchen stirring something boiling on the stove. It was impossible to tell what she was cooking. The woman really was a horrible cook. When Call was alive and the kids were all on the ranch, they'd had a real cook and Enid had been the housekeeper.

Once everyone was gone, there had been no reason to keep on anyone else, although Pepper couldn't remember firing the rest of the staff.

She suspected Enid had done it, since Pepper had been so distraught that her housekeeper and caretaker had taken advantage of it.

"Please turn that off," she said now to Enid.

Enid turned slowly to stare at her as if she couldn't believe what she was seeing. Had it been that long since she'd been in this kitchen?

Enid turned off the burner, then crossed her arms over her chest, leaning back against the counter next to the stove. "Well?"

Pepper bristled at Enid's insolent manner. She'd let

this happen and had only herself to blame. In her grief, she'd given up control of her home and her life to this woman and her husband. She now saw what a mistake that had been.

"I'm going to have to let you and your husband go." Her words seemed to hang in the humid kitchen air, surprising them both.

She waited for Enid to put up an argument. When she didn't, Pepper added, "I'm sorry."

To her surprise, Enid began to laugh. "Alfred and I aren't going anywhere."

Pepper couldn't believe her ears. "I beg your pardon?"

"You best give it some thought," Enid said, and started to turn back to whatever she was cooking.

Pepper felt her temper rise. "I've made up my mind."

Enid sighed and turned back to her, eyes narrowing into menacing slits. "Do you know how long I've been on this ranch?"

"That doesn't have anything to—"

"I've been here since before Call brought you here. I've heard every argument, seen it all, *know* you better than you know yourself." She lowered her voice. "*I* know where all the bodies are buried."

"Are you threatening to blackmail me?" Pepper demanded, barely able to contain her rage.

"If I wanted to blackmail you I could have done it a long time ago." Enid smiled. "Even now I wonder what that new acting sheriff would think if I told her just half of what I know about her grandmother."

Pepper's stomach twisted into a knot at the mention of McCall. Her heart was pounding so hard in her ears she had to steady herself, her hand going to the kitchen counter for support.

"I'd hate to see you have to spend the rest of your golden years behind bars." Enid sounded so self-satisfied that Pepper had to restrain herself from picking up one of the kitchen knives and ending this right here.

She might have done just that, except then she couldn't finish what she'd started. But once she knew the truth about Trace's murder…

"So, to answer your question," Enid was saying, "of course I'm not blackmailing you. I'm just saying you might want to reconsider." Enid turned and picked up the spoon she'd laid down earlier. "Of course, if you saw fit to put a little something in your will for Alfred and me, that would be greatly appreciated. We *have* been loyal servants on the Winchester Ranch almost our whole lives. Call, bless his soul, always said he didn't know what he would have done without us."

Pepper's gaze bored into the woman's back like a bullet at the mention of Call's name. She felt powerless and hated the feeling, even knowing that it wouldn't be for long. The day would come when she would turn the tables on Enid and it would be soon if she had anything to do with it.

"Why don't you sit down and have some of this soup I made?" Enid said. "You can tell me what you're up to getting your family back here to the ranch." She glanced over her shoulder at Pepper. "I told you, I know you better than you know yourself."

If that were true, Pepper thought, then Enid would be terrified of her and what she had planned for her.

"You're mistaken about my motives," Pepper managed to say, and started to leave the room. "I just wanted to see my family."

She was almost to the door when Enid's words stopped her.

"Some people think you've already lost your mind, locking yourself up all these years in this old place," Enid was saying. "Wouldn't take much for someone to think you're not in your right mind. Now why don't you sit down and have a little soup. I made it special just for you. It will calm you right down."

Pepper turned back to watch Enid ladle out a cup of the soup and stir something into it before setting the cup on the kitchen table.

"You'll want to eat it while it's still hot."

She stared at the cup of watery-looking soup, Enid's threat still ringing in her ears as she stepped back into the room, sat down at the table and picked up her spoon.

"A little of my soup, that's all you need," Enid said, as she went back to work at the stove.

Pepper took a bite. She gagged a little, the bile rising in her throat. She took another bite and felt the warmth of the soup and the drugs take hold. She put down her spoon.

Enid took the rest of the cup of soup and dumped it down the drain. "You should lie down for a while. You look a little peaked. I'm sure you'll feel better after a nap."

DINNER WAS A SOLEMN AFFAIR. Josey noticed that Jack's grandmother was especially quiet. Virginia drank her wine without incident, and Jack seemed lost in his own thoughts.

She was grateful he hadn't wanted to talk about what had happened on their ride. Josey was embarrassed. She never cried like that, especially in front of a stranger. And she needed to remember that was exactly what Jack was—a stranger.

As soon as dinner was over, she excused herself, saying she needed a little air, and went outside for a walk.

The air felt close. She was taken with the wild openness of this place. She could literally see for miles.

Josey thought about her mother and felt that old pain and frustration. For months she'd been trying to help her. Now she'd made things worse.

But once she got money wired to the new health-care facility and knew for sure that her mother had been moved...

She hadn't realized how far she'd gone until she turned around to head back. The sky had darkened. Thunderheads hunkered on the horizon to the west, and the wind had picked up, sending dust swirling around her. She raised her hand to shield her eyes, squinting in the direction of the Winchester Ranch lodge.

Lights were on downstairs. Fortunately, as Josey was leaving the house, Pepper had grabbed Jack, insisting he come with her. Otherwise, Josey was sure Jack would have wanted to tag along. She knew he worried about her and, like her, he must worry that the trouble after her might somehow find her here.

As she neared the house, the first drops of rain began to fall. The Cadillac sat out front where they'd left it yesterday, the top down. She noticed the keys were in the ignition, opened the driver-side door and slid behind the wheel. She whirred the top up, snapping it into place, then put up the windows and sat for a moment in the warm quiet, listening to the rain patter on the canvas roof.

She looked toward the house and thought of Jack. Through the parlor window, she could see shadows moving around inside. Jack and his grandmother?

Feeling almost guilty, she reached over and opened the glove box and dug around inside until she found the car registration.

The car was registered to Galaxy Corporation. The address was a post office box in Ten Sleep, Wyoming.

What was the Galaxy Corporation? And did this car even belong to Jack Winchester?

Josey hurriedly put the registration back in the glove box along with the Montana map, then changed her mind and opened the map.

Just as she had suspected. The town of Whitehorse had been circled. She struggled to read what had been written off to the east of it. Winchester Ranch.

A sliver of worry burrowed under Josey's skin as she stuffed everything back into the glove box and closed it.

She sat in the car, listening to the patter of the rain, staring at the old Western ranch lodge and wondering who she was pretending to be married to.

JACK HADN'T WANTED to let Josey out of his sight, but he'd been cornered by his grandmother after dinner and had no choice.

A fire burned in the small rock fireplace. It crackled softly as Pepper Winchester motioned for him to sit opposite her in the matching leather chairs.

"I'm sorry I ambushed you the other day," she said. "I shouldn't have done that."

Pepper Winchester apologizing?

"I had hoped you might have remembered something from the day of Trace's birthday party."

What was it she wanted him to remember? he wondered. Or was it something she wanted to make sure he didn't remember?

Suddenly, the room felt cold as a chill ran the length of his spine.

"I foolishly thought that if I just asked you right out, you would tell me the truth," she was saying.

Jack smiled to himself. Now this was more like his grandmother. He said nothing, waiting for the barrage he knew would follow. What he wasn't ready for was the tears as his grandmother began to cry.

She quickly stopped herself, getting up awkwardly and leaning heavily on her cane as she moved to the fireplace, her back to him.

"Why don't you tell me what this is really about?" he suggested, determined not to be swayed by her tears.

"You're right, of course." She didn't turn around as she brushed at the tears, her back ramrod straight. "I have reason to believe that one of you saw something from the window up there. I thought if you had that you'd tell me. After all these years I'd assumed there would be no reason for any of you to keep the secret any longer. I foolishly assumed that one of you would want the truth to come out."

Her candor surprised him as much as her apology and her tears had. He didn't know what to say.

"I know it's possible that I'm wrong," she said, making it sound as if she didn't believe it. "Maybe none of you saw Trace being murdered." She turned to face him. "You see now why it is so important that I find out the truth. I don't believe the killer acted alone. I'm basing that assumption on where Trace was killed—within sight of the ranch. The killer got him to that spot, I believe, for a good reason. Because someone else was watching from the ranch that day. I believe that person didn't know that you children were in that third-floor room with a pair of binoculars."

Jack was stunned. "You're saying you think someone from the family was involved in Trace's murder?"

"Yes, I do."

So that was what this was about. He couldn't believe what he was hearing, and yet even as a small child he was aware of the jealousy among the siblings.

"I intend to find out who that person is if it takes my last dying breath."

Jack stared at her. "That's why you invited us all back."

She nodded. "I would be a foolish old woman to think that I could make up for the past at this late date." She shook her head. "I won't rest until I find out the truth. Will you help me?" Her voice broke and he felt something break in him, as well.

He reached inside himself for all the hatred he'd carried for this woman the past twenty-seven years, but that fire that had consumed him for so long had burned down to only a handful of red-hot embers.

His words surprised him, since he didn't feel he owed this woman anything given the hell she'd put his parents through. "We were in the room that morning."

His grandmother slumped down onto the hearth.

"We'd heard stories about the room and wanted to see it."

"Whose idea was it to go up there?" she asked in a voice fraught with emotion.

"I don't recall. All the adults were busy with Trace's birthday preparations for that afternoon."

Pepper's eyes shone brightly in the firelight as if remembering.

"I'm sorry, but I didn't see anything." He'd been busy reading what had been scratched into the walls.

Her disappointment was palpable. "Did one of your cousins have a pair of small binoculars?"

He felt a start as he remembered the binoculars.

"Which cousin?" she asked, witnessing his reaction.

"I...I really don't recall." He'd been distracted. By the writing on the walls. And the girl. Jack had wondered where she'd come from and why he hadn't seen her before. He gathered she shouldn't be there, that she'd sneaked in, ridden over from the only close ranch nearby, the McCormick Ranch. He'd forgotten until now, but there'd been another girl with her, a younger girl who they all ignored.

"I remember Cordell and Cyrus fighting over the binoculars." Showing off for the older girl. "I honestly can't remember which one of them ended up with the binoculars."

Jack wondered what his grandmother would say if he told her about the girls? He wasn't sure what held him back. Certainly not loyalty to his cousins or their friends. He wasn't even sure why he'd told his grandmother what he had. Just for a moment there, he'd felt sorry for her, he supposed.

She nodded slowly, as if sensing he was holding back something. "I would think that if anyone saw their uncle being murdered, that boy would have had a reaction. He might not have told me, but I would think he'd have told his cohorts."

"You have to remember, I was just the nanny's kid," Jack said, digging up some of that old pain to remind himself why he was here. "My so-called cousins weren't all that fond of me. So if they had secrets, they kept them to themselves."

She rose, but with effort. He started to help her, but she waved his hand away. "If you should think of anything that might help me…"

Did she really think he was here to help her?

He was glad when his grandmother called it a night and he could go look for Josey. He was relieved to find her alone, sitting in the tire swing under one of the massive cottonwood trees. A rain squall had blown through, but it was dry under the trees. He loved the smell after a rain almost as much as he loved the scent of Josey's damp hair.

"You all right?" Jack asked, as he gave her a push. The rope tied to the limb overhead creaked loudly.

Josey jumped off and turned as if he'd scared her.

He remembered the rope burn on her neck and mentally kicked himself for being so stupid. "I'm sorry, I—"

"No, it's just that I get motion sickness on swings."

Right. "Dinner was fun," he said sarcastically, to change the subject.

"Wasn't it." She stepped from under the canopy of cottonwood limbs and turned her face upward. "Have you ever seen so many stars?"

"You don't see many where you live?"

She didn't look at him. "No. I live in the city."

He found the Big Dipper, one of the few constellations he knew. He wanted to know more about Josey, but he knew better than to ask. Whoever had hurt her made her afraid to trust. He could understand that.

"How did your talk go with your grandmother?" Josey asked, afraid he was about to question her.

"She talked a lot about Trace, my uncle who was murdered."

"What was that she asked yesterday about some room that is off-limits?" Josey asked.

He turned to look back at the house and pointed. The room was barely visible from this angle, as it was on the far wing set back against the hillside—the wing that had been boarded up. It was an odd wing, she noticed. If had been built back into the side of a hill and appeared to be much older than the original structure. As an afterthought, a room had been added near the back.

"That's the room?" she asked.

"That's it."

"What's in it?"

"Nothing. A window." He shook his head. "Nothing else. It's soundproof."

"Soundproof?" She realized he'd been in the room, just as his grandmother had suspected. "Why is whether or not you were in the room such a big deal to your grandmother?"

Jack looked like he wished she hadn't asked. "Between you and me? She thinks one of us might have seen my uncle Trace murdered." He nodded at her surprised reaction. "There were a pair of binoculars in the room. I never touched them, but the others were looking through them. She thinks one of them witnessed the murder. The alleged murderer confessed, but was killed. My grand-mother believes there was an accomplice, someone from the family, and that's why Trace was murdered within sight of the ranch."

"Well, if one of you kids had seen something, wouldn't you have told?"

"Maybe the kid did, and maybe whoever he told was the accomplice."

"That's horrible."

"It's also why she is getting us all back here, to inter-rogate us individually to get at the truth."

Josey jumped as she realized Enid was standing in the shadows off to the side.

"I guess you didn't hear me call to you," Enid said, stepping toward them. "I wanted to see if there was anything I could get you before I turned in."

"No," Josey and Jack said in unison.

"Well, fine then," the housekeeper said. She turned on her heel and headed for the house.

"That woman is the worst eavesdropper I've ever come across," Josey whispered. "I don't trust her."

"Me, either."

"The way she treats your grandmother, it makes me wonder."

Jack nodded solemnly. "It's almost as if she and her husband have something on Pepper, isn't it?"

Josey realized she was getting chilly. She started to head for the house when Jack touched her arm, stop-ping her.

"Thank you for being here. I mean that. No matter what, I'm not sorry."

"I hope you never are," she said, knowing he would be soon enough as they walked back to the house and their bedroom. Jack curled up in his chair. Josey thought she'd never be able to sleep, but, still tired from the long horseback ride that day, she dropped right off.

JACK WOKE TO A SCREAM. He bolted upright in the chair, momentarily confused. The scream was coming from the bed.

He shot to his feet and stumbled in the dark over to the bed. "Josey." He shook her gently, feeling the perspiration on her bare arm. "Josey," he said, shaking her more forcefully.

The scream caught in her throat. She jerked away, coming up fighting. She swung at him, both arms flailing wildly.

"Josey!" he cried, grabbing her arms and pinning her down. "It's me, Jack. You were having a bad dream." He released one of her wrists to snap on the light beside the bed.

She squirmed under him, then seemed to focus on him. He felt the fight go out of her, but her face was still etched in fear and she was trembling under him, her body soaked in sweat.

He let go of her other wrist and eased off of her, sitting up on the edge of the bed next to her. He could hear her gasping for breath.

"That must have been some dream," he said quietly, thinking of the rope burn on her neck. Whatever had happened to her was enough to give anyone nightmares.

"I'm okay now."

He wasn't sure if she was trying to convince him or herself. "If you want to talk about it…" He reached over to push a lock of dank hair back from her face.

"I can't even remember what it was about." She shifted her gaze away.

"That's good," he said, going along with the lie. He stood. "If you want I can leave the light on."

She shook her head. "I'm sorry I woke you."

"No problem." He doubted he'd be able to go back to sleep, but he returned to his chair, glad Enid had put them at the end of the wing away from everyone, so no one else heard the screams.

Josey turned out the light. He heard her lie back down. The darkness settled in. He listened to her breathe and thought about how a man would go about killing a bastard like the one who'd given Josey such horrible nightmares.

He also thought about how a man might go about keeping Josey in his life.

IT WAS WHILE HE WAS EATING in the kitchen at the house at Mobridge that RJ spotted the phone hanging on the wall.

He'd had to break into the house and had been surprised to find that it appeared someone still lived here.

That was good and bad. The good part was that they weren't home and he'd been able to find some clean clothes, a warm coat, boots that were only a little too big and some drugs to tide him over.

He'd also been able to find food. Not much in the refrigerator so he suspected they'd gone into town to shop. He made himself some soup, ate the canned meat straight from the can along with the canned peaches he'd found, leaving the empty containers on the table. It wasn't like they wouldn't figure out someone had been here.

It appeared a man and woman lived in the house, both older from the clothing he'd found. He'd gone through the woman's jewelry box. Nothing worth stealing. But he'd managed to scare up almost a hundred dollars from a cookie jar in the kitchen and the man's sock drawer.

He got up, searched around for a phone book and finally found one in a drawer. It had doodles all over the front along with an assortment of numbers.

He pulled a chair over so he could sit and opened the phone book to Whitehorse, the town up the road in the direction the yellow Cadillac convertible had been heading when the driver picked up Josey. There were only a few pages, so it didn't take long to find the numbers he needed. He started with gas stations. With towns so few and far between up here, the driver of the Cadillac would have filled up before going any farther up the road.

Three gas stations. He called each, coming up with a story about trying to find his brother-in-law. The clerks were all friendly, that small-town trust that he had a growing appreciation for with each call.

No luck there. He began to call the motels on the chance that the Caddie driver had dropped Josey at one.

He got lucky on his fifth call.

"I remember seeing a yellow Cadillac," a clerk at one of the motels told him.

RJ tried not to sound too excited. "There at the motel?"

"No, over in front of the clothing store."

RJ frowned. "You saw the guy driving it? Was there a woman with him?"

"No. Just a man when I saw him and the car."

He was disappointed. Maybe the guy had already gotten rid of Josey. It just seemed odd the guy would be shopping for clothing, unless…

That damned Josey. She probably cried on the guy's shoulder and suckered him in. RJ could understand being smitten with her. She was one good-looking woman. He'd wanted her himself.

Should have taken her, too, when he had the chance. He'd planned to, but Celeste had thrown a fit when he suggested the three of them get together. Once he'd given Celeste that engagement ring she was no fun anymore.

So let's say Josey got the driver of the Cadillac to buy her clothes. Then what else would she get him to do for her?

He tried the last motel, convinced he'd find Josey curled up watching television and thinking she'd gotten away.

"I saw the car," the male clerk said. "Sweet. One of those vintage restored jobs."

RJ couldn't have cared less about the work done on the Caddie. "So she's staying there at the motel?"

"The woman with him? No." The guy sounded confused. "I saw the *car* when I was getting gas at Packy's."

That was one of the numbers he'd already called. "Did you happen to notice if there was a woman with him? A woman with long, curly, reddish-blond hair, good-looking?"

The clerk had chuckled. "Good-looking, but she had short, curly, dark hair. And she wasn't with him then. I saw her in the car later."

"Wait a minute. So he didn't have her with him at the gas station, but you saw him with this woman later?"

"That's right. I passed the Cadillac. The cowboy was driving and the woman was in the passenger seat. I didn't get a really good look at her. She was kind of slumped down in the seat. But I saw she had short, curly, dark hair."

What? Slumped down in the seat? The answer came in a rush. Josey had changed her appearance. He wasn't sure how or when, but that had to be the explanation.

"Did you see which way they went when he drove out of town?"

"South."

"South?" Why would the driver go back the way he'd come? "On Highway 191 toward the river?"

"No, they took the Sun Prairie road. I was thinking I wouldn't take a car like that down that road."

RJ could only be thankful the cowboy hadn't been driving some nondescript sedan or this clerk would have never noticed him. "What's down that road besides Sun Prairie?"

The clerk laughed. "Well, there are some ranches, Fort Peck Reservoir, but they didn't look dressed for fishing. Mostly there's just a whole lot of open country."

RJ rubbed his temples. His head felt like it might explode. "So there is no way of knowing where he was going."

"Well, there wouldn't have been if he hadn't asked

me for directions when we were both getting gas in our rigs."

This clerk was on RJ's last nerve, plucking it like an out-of-tune guitar string. If this discussion had been in person, that jackass would be breathing his last breath shortly. *"Directions?"*

"To the Winchester Ranch. Didn't I mention that?"

Chapter Eight

Josey woke a little after one in the morning to find Jack's chair empty.

She sat up, listening. A breeze stirred the limbs of the large cottonwood tree outside the window. Shadows played on the bedroom floor, the curtains billowing in and out like breath.

Where was Jack? She slipped out of bed and went to the window. For a moment, she didn't see him. But just as he had the night before, he moved stealthily along the edge of darkness, staying to the deep shadows. He was headed like before toward the closed wing of the lodge.

She frowned and realized it was time she found out what her "husband" was up to. She feared that, whatever it was, if his grandmother found out it would get them kicked off the ranch. She wasn't about to admit that she was worried about Jack.

Grabbing the robe Jack had bought her, she shrugged into it, failing to talk herself out of what she was about to do.

At her door, she listened. No sound. Opening it, she crept out, carrying her cowboy boots. At the top of the stairs, she stopped. A dim light shone downstairs. It seemed to be coming from the kitchen.

Josey listened but hearing no sound tiptoed down the stairs to the front door. Easing it open, she stepped out, closing it behind her.

She hesitated on the front step to pull on her boots. Then she followed the same path Jack had taken, keeping to the shadows until she reached the far wing of the lodge.

It was an odd wing, she noticed. It had been built back into the side of a hill and appeared to be much older than the original structure. The doors and windows had been boarded up, but someone—Jack?—had removed the boards from the doorway.

The breeze picked up, the door blowing open a little wider as she stepped into the darkness of the boarded-up wing. The air was much colder in here and smelled musky, as if the wing had been closed up for some time.

Josey waited for her eyes to adjust to the darkness. She didn't move, hardly breathed as she listened. The only light bled in from the doorway. She'd left the door open, thinking it might be the only way she could find her way back.

At first she heard nothing but the sound of the breeze in the trees outside. Then her ears picked up a fainter sound coming from inside, a scratching noise that could have been mice. Or something larger.

She hesitated. Was it that important she find out what Jack was up to?

The answer was yes, she realized. She moved toward the noise, feeling her way along the dark hallway until she saw the shaft of light coming from under one of the doors.

Mice didn't carry flashlights, she told herself. She moved cautiously forward, stopping in front of the door. She listened to the scratching sound for a moment before she tried the cold knob.

It turned in her hand.

She took a breath. Was she sure she really wanted to know Jack's secrets? She eased the door open a few inches.

In the glow of his flashlight resting on one of the shelves, Josey saw Jack standing in front of a rock wall. Jack had a crowbar in his hand and was scraping mortar from between the stones.

The room appeared to be a root cellar with rows of shelves. There were dozens of old jars covered with dust, their contents blackened with age.

Jack worked feverishly, as if desperate to see what was on the other side of that wall.

Josey only had a moment to wonder about what she was seeing when a door slammed down the hall.

JACK FROZE, all his instincts on alert. Heavy footfalls echoed down the hall. The hall light flashed on. He swore under his breath and grabbed the flashlight, snapping it off as he turned to look toward the door.

The door was open. A figure was framed there. His heart caught in his throat. He knew that particular figure anywhere. Josey, dressed in only a robe and cowboy boots.

He started to take a step toward her, but she motioned him back as the heavy footfalls grew louder. Jack sank back into the dark shadows of the room, but there was no escape. He was caught. And so was Josey.

"What the hell are you doing in here?" boomed Alfred Hoagland's easily recognizable, raspy old voice. Through the doorway, Jack saw Alfred grab Josey by the arm.

Without a thought, he stepped toward the door, going to her rescue.

A giggle, high and sweet like a child's stopped him cold. *What the hell?* It took Jack a moment to realize it had come out of Josey.

"Are you daft?" Alfred demanded, letting go of her and stumbling back.

Josey seemed to come awake with surprise. She stumbled back into the wall, closing the door partway as she caught herself. "What…where am I?" She sounded both surprised and scared.

"Something wrong with you?" Alfred demanded, sounding a little afraid himself.

Josey let out a sob. "I can't have been sleepwalking again." She began to cry, covering her face with her hands. Jack had seen her cry and wasn't fooled.

Alfred cleared his voice, visibly uncomfortable. "You should get back to bed."

"I don't know where—"

Alfred let out a curse. "I'll take you." Jack could hear him grumbling to himself all the way down the hall as he led Josey out.

Jack waited until he heard the door close before he turned on his flashlight again. He couldn't chance that Alfred might get suspicious and come back. Taking some of the boards from the cellar shelving, he covered the spot where he'd been working. With luck, Alfred wouldn't notice if he did come back.

Jack knew he had Josey to thank for covering for him tonight, but he was furious with her. She'd taken a hell of a chance. She had no idea how much danger she'd put herself in.

As angry as he was at her for following him and butting into his business, he was also grateful and more than a little awed. Who was this amazing woman? It made him wonder what he saved her from on the highway. Had she felt she owed him? Well, they were even. He'd make sure she wasn't that foolhardy again.

But even as he thought it, he realized his aunt was apparently right about one thing. He and Josey were definitely a pair.

JOSEY HAD BEEN IN BED when Jack returned to the room. She pretended to be asleep, listening to him slip in and undress in the pitch blackness of the room.

Finally, he settled into the large chair.

She lay awake, listening to his breathing, knowing he, too, was still awake and just feet from her. She thought about rolling over and offering to share the bed with him. For the first time since they'd gotten "married," she felt they really were in this together.

But she remained mute, not daring to say the words because she knew right at that moment she was feeling scared and alone and would have given anything just to be held in his strong arms.

She knew, too, what would happen if she invited him into her bed.

"Josey?"

She froze, then said quietly, "Yes?"

"Don't ever follow me again."

She lay perfectly still, hearing the anger in his words and feeling her own fury race through her veins like liquid flames. She'd saved the bastard's bacon. "No need to thank me," she said sarcastically.

"We both have our secrets. Stay out of mine and I'll stay out of yours."

In the darkness, she touched the rope burn on her neck and felt the sting of tears. Sleep finally came as a godsend.

RJ DIPPED HIS FINGERS into the salve and touched it to his shoulder, grimacing with pain. He glared into the cheap mirror as if Josey was on the other side, relishing at the thought of the pain he would heap on her.

"I'm coming for you, bitch, and when I find you I'm going to hurt you in ways you never dreamed."

He opened one of the containers of prescription pills he'd found in the medicine cabinet. All of the pills were at least a year old, but if he took enough of them, he might be able to numb the pain, if not kill any infection.

Downing the pills, he took a drink and listened.

He felt better. His vision had cleared some and if he'd had a concussion, it seemed to be getting better. He'd turned on the radio, but hadn't heard any news, so he figured no news was good news.

Josey was smart. If he was right, she'd conned the driver of the Cadillac and was now on the Winchester Ranch miles from town. Hard to find, was what the clerk had said when RJ had made him give him the same directions he'd given the Cadillac driver.

Yeah, not that hard to find. He just hoped she

stayed put. He figured she would. She'd feel safe. Her mistake.

He wanted to go after her right now. No holds barred. But even in his dazed state, he knew that would be stupid.

First, he had to take care of himself. Get his strength back, patch up his wound. Hell, he wasn't going anywhere without a vehicle.

Josey always seemed to land on her feet. He hadn't been worried about her going to the cops—not with a murder rap hanging over her. She knew what would happen to her mother if she ended up behind bars. The thought made him frown. She had the money in the backpack. Would she try to get her mother moved out of the rest home his father had stuck her in?

Hell, yes. He stormed out of the bathroom, picked up the kitchen phone and called the nursing home.

"Just wanted to check on Ella Vanderliner. I mean Ella Evans," he said, when the night nurse answered.

"I'm sure she's asleep. May I ask who's calling?"

"Good. So she's still there?"

"I'm sorry, I didn't catch your name."

He hung up. Maybe he'd been wrong about Josey. Maybe her first thought had been to save her own skin without any thought to her mother.

He glanced in the bedroom at the soft-looking bed and thought about curling up for a while, but knew he couldn't chance it.

He'd gotten almost everything he'd needed here and he didn't want to push his luck. Now he just needed wheels. Unfortunately, all he'd found around this place was some old, broken-down, rusted farm equipment. No vehicle he could steal.

That meant he'd have to hit the road and hope someone stopped to give him a ride. But first he'd find a place to get some sleep in the pine trees again. His head would be clearer in the morning.

He wandered back into the bathroom, pocketed all the pills and a large bottle of aspirin. Pulling on the stolen coat, he took one last look around the kitchen, found some stale cookies and left Mobridge behind.

THE NEXT MORNING Josey woke to find Jack standing on the small balcony outside their room. He looked as if he had the weight of the world on his shoulders. For so long, she'd been so involved in her own problems that she'd been blind to anyone else's. That was what had gotten her into this trouble. Had she been paying attention—

She slid out of bed, wrapping her robe around her, and stepped out on the balcony next to him. Without giving it any thought, she put her arm around Jack as she joined him.

He glanced over at her, his smile shy, apologetic. "I'm sorry I snapped at you last night when I should have thanked you. But I was upset. You shouldn't have followed me."

She looked over at him, her eyes narrowing. "You mean the way you shouldn't have untied my scarf?"

He had the good sense to look chastised. "I wanted to help you."

"And why do you think I followed you last night?"

His gaze locked with hers. "You shouldn't be worrying about me. You have enough—"

"You can tell me what you're after," she said, lowering her voice. "I'll help you. You helped me by bringing me here." He started to argue the point. "Don't even bother to tell me you didn't know I was in some kind of trouble."

He smiled at her and touched her face. "Still," he said, shaking his head, "it's probably better that we don't know everything about each other."

His words cut like a knife, even though she agreed with him. They both had dark secrets, and yet living here pretending to be lovers was another kind of hell.

She pushed off the balcony railing and into the cool darkness of the bedroom, only to stop short at the sight of Enid standing in the middle of the room holding a stack of clean towels.

"I didn't think anyone was here," she said. Her expression left no doubt in Josey's mind that she'd heard everything.

JACK MENTALLY KICKED HIMSELF at the hurt expression on Josey's face as she'd left him on the balcony.

A moment later, he heard Enid's voice and swore. That damned sneaky woman. She'd probably heard everything. His fault. He should have been more careful.

Enid would take what she'd heard to his grandmother, sure as the devil.

But with a start, he realized he didn't care. Let her run to Pepper. Maybe it would be better if Pepper sent him packing. Hadn't he always known he might leave here empty-handed?

The bedroom door closed behind Enid, and he saw Josey standing in the middle of the room looking worried over what the woman had overheard. A wave of desire washed over him so strong, he thought it might drown him.

"She heard everything," Josey said, as he stepped into the bedroom, closing the French doors behind him.

He nodded, realizing he would have only one regret if he had to leave here—and it had nothing to do with what was or wasn't behind that rock wall in the closed wing.

"We should get down to breakfast," he said, his voice thick with emotion.

She didn't move as he stepped deeper into the room. "I think I'll skip breakfast," she said.

He started to talk her out of it, hating the thought of eating alone with just his grandmother and his aunt. But he saw the stubborn determination in the set of her jaw and decided to let it go.

They'd reached an impasse.

"I think I'll go for a horseback ride. Would you like—"

"No, thank you. I'll just stay in my room and read. I have a headache." Her words made it clear who'd given it to her.

"Should I have Enid send you up something to eat?"

Josey gave him a look of warning.

"I'll tell her not to disturb you, then." He stood for a moment, wanting to say all the things he felt, but unable to find the words. It was one thing to pretend they were husband and wife. It was another to get too close, and yet something like metal to magnet drew him to her. He wanted this woman. And not just for a week.

He had to fight every muscle within him not to reach for her.

As he descended the stairs, he found his grandmother waiting for him and groaned inwardly. Could this morning get any worse?

"Jack, may I speak with you?" Pepper led the way down to the parlor before he could answer.

The moment he stepped into the room, closing the door behind him as his grandmother instructed, she asked, "Why did you come here?"

Enid hadn't wasted any time. "Because you invited me and I wanted to see the ranch again."

His honest answer seemed to surprise his grandmother, who raised a brow. "I know you blame me for your unhappy childhood."

"My childhood wasn't unhappy."

"I kept your father from marrying your mother."

"Only until I was six. My father was an alcoholic and my mother spent her life trying to save him. Worse things happen to kids." He thought of his grandmother's children, that awful room on the third floor and what he'd seen scratched into the walls.

"I'm no fool," she snapped. "I know you want something from me, but I don't think it's my money."

As Josey said, the woman was sharp. "I have my own money, so it seems I came here to enjoy the ranch." He got to his feet. "Speaking of that, I'm going for a horseback ride."

"Alone?"

"Josey is resting. Please tell Enid she doesn't want to be disturbed."

Another raised brow. "Enid seemed to think that the two of you are going your separate ways when your week here is up."

"Enid should mind her own business." He saw that his grandmother had no intention of letting him leave it at that and sighed. "Josey and I, well, we think we might have acted in haste. Probably a little time apart would be good after we leave here," he said honestly.

Pepper's eyes narrowed, but when she spoke she said, "Enjoy your horseback ride. Don't go too far alone."

"Yes, I wouldn't want what happened to my grandfather to happen to me," he said, and saw his grandmother's expression darken.

PEPPER TOLD HERSELF she didn't care one way or the other about Jack and Josey's marriage, and yet she found herself climbing the stairs to the far wing. She'd noticed there was trouble between the two of them, but things seemed to have been a little better after their horseback ride yesterday.

Now, though, something seemed to have happened to drive them apart again. It seemed odd to her that Jack would go off on a horseback ride by himself. It was the first time he'd left Josey alone.

"Jack said you were resting, but I wanted to check on you," she said when Josey answered her knock.

The young woman looked uncomfortable.

"He's gone for a horseback ride. I thought you and I might…" She looked past Josey into the bedroom. *Her* bedroom when Call was alive.

"Would you like to come in?" Josey asked with obvious reluctance.

Pepper stepped into the room, fighting off the memories that assailed her. She and Call had shared this room from the first night she'd come to the ranch. Had she ever been happy?

Yes, at first she'd been deliriously happy. Naive, foolish, blind with love, but happy. It had lasted at least a week. Maybe even a month before she'd realized what a controlling bastard she'd married.

And yet she'd stayed, believing that he would change. She silently scoffed at the thought now. There'd been a time when she really believed that love could conquer all. Why else had she not only stayed with him but also had five children with him?

"Would you like to sit down?" Josey offered.

Pepper smiled at the young woman. She was kind and thoughtful, clearly from a good family.

"Thank you, I think that would be nice." She took one of the chairs, noticing as Josey removed a folded blanket and pillow from the other chair.

Josey must have seen her expression and smiled ruefully. "I'm sure you've heard that Jack and I have been having our problems."

"Enid is a terrible old busybody," Pepper said, anxiously anticipating the day she would be able to get rid of the woman for good. Impulsively, she reached over and took Josey's hand. "I know you and Jack aren't legally married."

Josey opened her mouth as if to explain, but Pepper waved her off. "Jack thinks I'm an old fool. Of course I had my lawyer investigate. I like to know who is sleeping under my roof."

"I feel I should apologize for letting you believe—"

"Oh, don't look so aghast. I like you. I was truly sorry to find out the two of you *weren't* married. You're good for Jack, and from what I've seen, he's good for you, as well."

JOSEY DIDN'T KNOW what to say. She had to admit that Pepper Winchester had caught her completely off guard.

"Are you shocked that I'm not upset? Or that I actually care for my grandson?"

Again the woman had caught her flat-footed. Before Josey could speak, Pepper laughed, easing the tension in the room.

"I am capable of love and caring. I like Jack. I'm sorry I hurt him and his mother. But there is nothing I can do about that. You live to be this old, you, too, will have regrets. I unfortunately have more than my share."

"You are definitely a surprise," Josey finally said, relaxing a little.

Pepper smiled at that. "I just remember what it's like to be in love."

Josey started to protest that she wasn't in love with Jack, but stopped herself. Even if she and Jack weren't legally married, they were still supposed to be in love. And she did care about Jack. Too much.

"Jack seems to think that the reason you're asking your family back to the ranch is because you're not satisfied with the results of your son's murder investigation," Josey said, needing to change the subject.

"That's true."

"I thought someone confessed."

"Yes. Unfortunately, that person is dead, and I have reason to believe that there was a second person involved. I have no proof."

"You think Jack knows something?"

Pepper smiled secretively. "I guess time will tell. If there is any chance that the person responsible for

Trace's death hasn't been brought to justice…" She shook her head. "It's something I need settled before I die."

"I can't believe it would be someone in your family."

"I've made a lot of mistakes in my life, but my greatest ones were with my children. Their father was a harsh disciplinarian. Too harsh. I didn't protect the older ones. But when Trace was born…" She cleared her throat.

"Would you like some water?" Josey asked. Pepper nodded, and she stood and went into the bathroom, returning with a glass of cold water.

"I should have stopped Call sooner," Pepper said, after taking a sip. "I should have done so many things differently. By then my older children had no respect for me, and in my guilt I avoided them. That rift grew wider as Trace became my life, the only part I cared about."

Josey wondered why Jack's grandmother was confessing all this to her. Just minutes before she'd opened the door to Pepper, she'd promised herself that she wasn't going to get any more involved with this family. In fact, she'd been thinking that the best thing she could do was to make an excuse to leave sooner.

"If one of my older children had anything to do with Trace's death, then I am to blame for it." Pepper nodded, tears in her eyes. "But I still want justice and I will still get it."

Josey felt a chill at the woman's words as Pepper set down the glass on the end table and rose, picking up her cane.

"Thank you for listening to an old woman ramble,"

she said, seeming embarrassed. "I hope you don't think ill of me."

"No," Josey said. As she rose to escort Pepper out, she thought of her own father. He would have killed for her. He also would have demanded justice had anything happened to her. But he was gone, and there was no one to protect her or see that justice was done.

"Please don't give up on Jack," Pepper said. "He needs you. I don't think he realizes how much. He prides himself on his independence and taking on the world alone—but then you are a lot like that yourself, aren't you?"

Josey was startled that Pepper had realized that about her. "Sometimes we have to take on things alone because there isn't anyone else," she said, echoing her earlier thoughts.

"But you aren't alone anymore. You have Jack."

"Yes," she said, feeling guilty at how wrong Pepper was about that.

Chapter Nine

McCall had known that once the news hit the radio and newspaper the calls would start coming in. Most of them were from residents who'd seen someone suspicious hanging around the alley, heard a noise out back or thought someone had been in their house.

Her deputies were running themselves ragged checking on suspicious characters, only to find the suspect was a relative of a neighbor or nothing at all.

When she took the call from the dispatcher she was expecting just another bad lead.

"It's Frank Hanover down at Mobridge," a man said. "We just got home from Billings and found our house has been broken into."

"What's missing?" McCall asked, thinking Mobridge was near the Missouri River, near the crime scene.

"Clothes, some of my shirts and pants, a coat, as far as I can tell. Cleaned all the drugs out of the medicine cabinet, ate some food and left a mess."

She sat up straighter, remembering the house at Mobridge. It was back off the road, no other houses around.

"Took a pair of my boots," Frank was saying.

"What size do you wear?" she asked.

"Eleven." He seemed to hesitate. "Is that important?"

It was to her. Ray Allan Evans Jr. wore a size 10½ loafer. He could make do with a pair of size 11 cowboy boots real easy. "What else was taken?"

"About a hundred dollars in cash, the wife and I estimate. That's all that we've found missing so far."

"Did he take one of your vehicles?"

"Weren't none to take," Frank said.

So RJ was still on foot. "I'm sending a deputy. Please try not to touch anything that the intruder left. You said he made a mess in the kitchen? Please leave it."

"He used our phone, looks like since he left the phone book out and a chair pulled up to it. Probably ran up our long distance bill," Frank grumbled.

"What's your number out there?" McCall asked, and wrote it down. As soon as she hung up, she called the phone company and asked for the phone log on recently dialed numbers.

"I'm sorry, but we're going to need a warrant to do that or permission from the customer. We'll need those in writing. You're welcome to fax them to us. That would speed things up."

McCall cursed under her breath. "I'll get back to you." She then called Frank Hanover back, then called a deputy who was still in the area and sent him over to pick up the written permission slip from the Hanovers.

She wanted to know if Frank Hanover was right and RJ had called someone. She needed to know where he was headed. She'd called in extra officers to help search the area near Mobridge, even though she suspected he was long gone.

He would be looking to steal a vehicle. It was just

a matter of time before he found one. She just prayed
that no one would be driving it.

RJ DIDN'T KNOW how long he'd been walking up the
dirt road when he heard the sound of an engine.

At first he thought he was hallucinating. It had been
so long, and he'd been straining so hard to hear one.
Praying for one, if he could call it praying. More like
wishing on a curse.

He turned and saw what appeared to be a dark-
colored pickup headed in his direction. RJ swallowed,
his throat dry as he stuck out his thumb.

He'd cleaned up at the house, but he knew he still
looked pretty rough. He feared no one would stop for
him, so he was surprised when the driver slowed, then
braked to a stop.

Sun glinted off the windshield, and it was a moment
before he saw the lone driver, an old man dressed in a
straw hat, flannel shirt and blue overalls.

He felt a wave of relief. One old farmer behind the
wheel.

RJ would have shouted with glee if it wouldn't have
made him look insane.

Both windows were already down on the old pickup.
"Trouble?"

RJ stepped up to the open passenger-side window as
dust settled around him. "Car broke down a good ways
back by the river."

"You been walking this far in the wrong direction?"
the farmer said with a laugh. "If you'd gone the other
way, you have reached Highway 191 and gotten a ride
a lot quicker than this."

As if RJ didn't know that. He'd opted for the less

traveled dirt road for a very good reason. The highway was too visible. He couldn't take the chance since he knew the California police would have put out an APB on him and Josey by now.

"Well, hop in. I can take you as far as Winifred, that's where I'm headed."

RJ couldn't have cared less where Winifred was as he opened the pickup's door and climbed in. He wouldn't be going that far anyway.

The pickup smelled of hay and possibly manure. It didn't matter. RJ couldn't believe how good it felt not to be walking. The boots he'd borrowed had rubbed blisters on both feet. He leaned back as the old farmer got the rig rolling and watched the land slip by, a sea of undulating green.

The farmer made several attempts to make conversation before turning on the radio. He picked up a station in Whitehorse, Montana, that, according to the farmer, played a polka of the day at noon.

The news came on. Ray tensed as he heard first Josephine Vanderliner's name and description, then his own, followed by a warning that both were considered armed and dangerous. He wished he was armed as the farmer reached under his seat and pulled out a tire iron.

JOSEY WATCHED THE SUN drop toward the dark outline of the Little Rockies in the distance. The spring day was hot and golden and held the promise of summer.

The prairie glowed under the heat. It was so beautiful and yet so alien. She wondered what this kind of isolation did to a person and thought of Pepper Winchester and the Hoaglands.

For the life of her she couldn't imagine what this

ranch must have been like when all the Winchesters had lived and worked here. Children running up and down the long hallways. The kitchen would have been bustling with activity, the whole ranch alive with sounds.

Josey wished she could have seen it. She sighed and looked to the road, anxious for Virginia to return from town. Earlier, she'd caught Virginia as she was leaving. The idea had come to her in a flash.

"Would you do me a huge favor?" Josey had asked her and seen the woman's irritation. "I just need to get some money wired to my mother's rest home."

Virginia's interest had picked up instantly. "Oh, honey, your mother's in a rest home? Why, she can't be very old. What's wrong with her?"

"Just give me a moment to get the money and the address." She'd run back up the stairs, telling herself this was the only way. No one knew Virginia. And it wasn't like involving Jack. Virginia couldn't get in trouble over this since she really was an innocent bystander.

Josey had dug through the stacks of hundreds, choosing bills free of blood. She'd already set up her mother's transfer, planning to move her mother from the horrible rest home where her stepfather had stuck her—to one where he couldn't find her.

Virginia's eyebrow had shot up when she saw the wad of money.

"I wasn't sure I could get a check cashed anywhere up here, and everything with Jack happened so fast..."

His aunt had pursed her lips in disapproval. "Marry in haste and... Well, you know." She seemed a little upset that Josey hadn't satisfied her curiosity about her mother.

"Here's the address. They're expecting the money. I can't thank you enough for doing this."

Virginia had left then, promising to bring her a receipt and let her know that the money had arrived.

Neither Virginia nor Jack had returned and it was getting late. Josey got more restless by the moment. Tired of watching for both of them, she turned away from the window and went into the bathroom to bathe before supper, wondering if Jack would be back by then.

Her bruises were healing. So was the rope burn on her neck. Soon she wouldn't have to wear the scarves. But she would have to disappear. As long as she was free, her mother should be safe.

She closed her eyes as she slid down into the warm water filled with bubbles. Once her mother was safe and she was sure nothing could change, then she would deal with the fact that she was wanted for murder and she had no way to prove her innocence.

She opened her eyes and climbed out of the tub, wishing she could go to the police and just get it over with. As she toweled herself and pulled on the bathrobe, she told herself that maybe if the police knew what had happened—

No, RJ was right. She would fry, and what would happen to her mother?

She thought about the rest of the bloody money in the armoire and felt nauseous as she opened the bathroom door and stepped out. Either way, she would never see her mother again, she thought, as she looked through her clothes for something to wear to supper.

"Are you all right?"

She jumped as Jack touched her shoulder. She hadn't heard him return.

He looked so concerned, she was filled with guilt for dragging him into this, even if it had been his idea. She'd only been thinking of herself. She hadn't considered the spot she was putting him in.

"You scared me."

"I'm sorry." He sounded as if he meant it. The last of the day's light shone on his face through the open French doors, accentuating the strong lines of his face. "Sorry about a lot of things."

"Sorry you brought me here?" She felt a little piece of her heart break off and fall.

"No," he said. "No, you're wrong about that. If I've been distant it's just because…" He raised his hand, signaling to her to wait a moment, then walked over and locked the bedroom door. "Enid won't be coming back in without us knowing it," he said, as he dragged a straight-back chair from the small desk in the corner and wedged it under the doorknob.

"Jack?" Josey said. He turned to her, and she saw the look in his eyes. She'd noticed that he seemed different after his ride. More relaxed. More like the Jack she'd met on the highway.

"You want the truth?" he asked.

She swallowed as he moved toward her.

"I think it's time I was honest with you. I've been pushing you away because if I don't…"

JOSEY'S GREEN EYES widened in alarm—and something that seemed to simmer on the back burner as he moved toward her, his gaze locked with hers.

It had always been so easy to lose himself in that sea of green. He stopped just inches from her, saw her eyes fire as he reached for her robe sash and slowly untied it.

"Do you have any idea what you're doing?" she asked, her voice breaking.

He chuckled. "It's been a while, but I think I remember how it goes."

She placed her hand over his to stop him, her eyes searching his. "Jack—"

He knew all the reasons they shouldn't take this pretend marriage any further than they had. Hell, he'd listed them at length on his long horseback ride today.

"I want you. That, Josey, is the truth." He looked into her eyes, then he gently pushed her hand away and untied the robe sash. It fell open to expose bare flesh.

He slipped his hands around her slim, bare waist and felt desire spread through him, a fire rushing through his veins.

His gaze still locked with hers, he inched his hands up to cup her full breasts in each palm. She let out a sound and arched against him. He felt her nipples harden against his palms.

Slowly, his hands moved upward. He eased the robe off her slim shoulders. It dropped to the floor, and for a moment he was taken aback at how beautiful she was.

"I want to make love to you," he whispered.

Josey let out a soft moan and he felt something give inside him. He'd never wanted anything the way he wanted this woman.

His palms skimmed over her small waist to her hips. Cupping her perfect derriere in both hands, he dragged her to him, no longer able to stand another moment without kissing her again.

Her lips parted as his mouth dropped to hers. He

heard her moan again and felt her working at the snaps of his Western shirt, and then his chest was pressed against her warm, full breasts, her nipples hard as stones, and he was carrying her to the canopied bed.

JOSEY WRAPPED THE ROBE around her and stepped to the window, the white sheer curtains billowing in on the evening breeze. She breathed in the unfamiliar scents as if only just now aware of them. Everything felt new and fresh, the day brighter. She hugged herself, smiling as she closed her eyes and turned her face up to the warmth of the sunset, reveling in the memory of making love with Jack.

Jack still lay on the bed behind her. She could feel his gaze on her. It heated her skin more than even the evening warmth. She would never forget the feel of his hands, his mouth, his body. His gentleness. His passion. He'd consumed her, filled her, fulfilled her.

"Come back to bed," he said softly. "We don't have much time. If we don't make an appearance at supper, I'm afraid there will be hell to pay."

She smiled to herself and was about to turn back when a flash of light caught her eye. The sun glinted off the bumper of a vehicle coming down the road toward them.

Josey froze, her pulse thundering in her ears.

"What is it?" Jack asked, sensing the sudden change in her. He pulled on his jeans and joined her on the balcony.

Her heart began to pound louder as she saw that there was something on top of the SUV roaring up the road. A light bar. And on the side of the vehicle a Sheriff's Department logo.

"It must be my cousin McCall Winchester," he said, as a woman with long, dark hair climbed out of the patrol car. Even from this distance Josey could tell she was wearing a sheriff's uniform.

"What do you think she wants?" Josey asked, fighting to keep the terror out of her voice. She'd thought she was safe here. That Jack was safe. She should never have involved him.

"My grandmother must have invited her for dinner," he said, as he drew Josey inside the bedroom and shut the French doors. "What's wrong?"

"Jack, I'm really not up to meeting her." She felt the heat of his gaze. He'd known she was in trouble. Now he knew it was with the law. "I should have told you—"

He touched a finger to her lips. "I'll take care of it." Jack's gaze locked with hers. "You're trembling. You should get back in bed."

"Jack—"

"It's going to be all right." He pulled her to him and kissed her. "You can meet my cousin some other time. Don't worry, I'll make apologies for you. I shouldn't have taken you on such a long horseback ride yesterday. I'd hate to think you're coming down with something."

She closed her eyes and wished they could just stay in this room forever. Become recluses just as his grandmother had done for twenty-seven years. No one had known for sure whether she was alive or dead. Nor had they cared.

She opened her eyes and grabbed for him as he started for the door. "I can't let you get in any deeper."

He took her in his arms, planted a kiss in her hair, then pulled back and smiled. "I'll be back as quick as I can. Lock the door behind me."

JACK LEFT JOSEY and went downstairs. He had known Josey was in trouble, but he'd just assumed it involved a man—not the law. As he descended the stairs, he had flashes of their lovemaking. He knew it had probably been a mistake, but even given what he now knew about his "wife," he couldn't regret it.

Enid opened the front door and Jack slowed on the stairs. He'd heard about McCall when the news had come about Trace Winchester's murder and the role Trace's daughter, a sheriff's deputy, had played in helping solve the crime—including almost getting herself killed.

So he'd been curious about his cousin the cop. He'd heard she'd been promoted to acting sheriff—their grandmother's doing, he would bet. Pepper Winchester might have been a recluse for the past twenty-seven years but she was still a force to be reckoned with, especially considering all the land she owned and the Winchester fortune. Which was surprising, given all the stories he'd heard about where that fortune had come from and at what cost.

He thought of the stories his mother had told him, and now he wondered how many of them were true. He had to remind himself that his mother had believed everything Angus Winchester had told her, and look where that had gotten her.

Still, he'd believed at least one of those stories was true. That's why he'd come here. Strange how long ago that seemed and, maybe more startling, how it had become less important.

McCall looked up as he came down the stairs. He couldn't hide his shock. She looked exactly like his grandmother had at that age.

She smiled at his surprise. "You must be Jack." She held out her hand. He stopped to shake it.

He found it amusing how wrong his grandmother had been. He recalled overhearing, when he was six, Pepper saying her son Trace had eloped with a local tramp who was lying through her teeth about the baby she was carrying being her son's. Clearly, Ruby Bates hadn't been lying. McCall was a Winchester.

"Oh, I see you two have met," Pepper said, appearing from down the hall. "Where is your wife?" she asked Jack.

"She isn't feeling well. I think she might have picked up a bug. I shouldn't have taken her on such a long horseback ride, as hot out as it was yesterday."

His grandmother looked suspicious. "McCall was looking forward to meeting her."

He turned his attention to the acting sheriff. "I'm sure you'll get to meet her when she's feeling better. It isn't like we're going anywhere for a while."

RJ TURNED OFF the first side road he came to. Now that he had a ride, all he could think about was sleeping in a real bed tonight.

His shoulder hurt like hell, and he worried that it was infected. Wouldn't that be a kicker if he died from a stupid flesh wound?

He felt himself coming down from the rush of killing the farmer. He'd been glad when the old fart had pulled out the tire iron. Taking it away from him had almost been too easy. He'd smacked him a couple times with it, then reached over and opened the old man's door, shoving him out before sliding over behind the wheel to stop the pickup.

Once he'd gotten rid of the body, his head ached again but he knew he had to start thinking more clearly.

The pickup was old and dark colored, like a zillion others in this part of Montana. But he did stop and smear some mud on the license plate. He could camp out somewhere, hide the pickup, but he was counting on the farmer's body not being found for a while.

Eventually someone would call the sheriff's department to notify them that the old guy was missing. But in the meantime, RJ decided to press his luck.

He would drive to Billings, the largest city in Montana, where he could get what he needed—and not be noticed. It was out of his way by a few hours, but he couldn't chance going into Whitehorse. Too small. People noticed outsiders in that kind of town.

He shoved the farmer's hat down on his head and drove toward Highway 191. Tonight he would break into a pharmacy and steal the drugs and medical supplies he needed. He would sleep in a motel room bed, charging the room to the credit card he'd found in the old guy's wallet, and he'd have a nice meal.

Eventually, the cops would track the expenditures. But he would make sure they never connected it to him. Or at least make sure they couldn't prove it. Later tonight he would ditch the pickup and get himself a new ride, one no one in Whitehorse would recognize. Then he'd see about getting himself a gun.

Chapter Ten

Move! Josey grabbed her clothes and quickly got dressed, her mind racing. She found her backpack and opened the armoire, dumping the old clothing out and reaching for the money. Just touching it made her sick to her stomach.

But she couldn't leave it here, and she knew the day would come when she would need it to hire herself a good lawyer. In the bathroom, she retrieved the gun and dropped it on top of the money in the backpack.

Her gaze fell over the room, stopping on the canopy bed and the rumpled sheets. Her heart broke at the memory of the two of them making love there earlier. She'd given herself to Jack completely, surrendering in a way she'd never thought possible. He'd been so gentle, so loving. She thought of the passion that had arced between them. Had she been a romantic, she would have said they were made for each other.

But she was a realist, and because of that she knew making love with him had been a mistake. She was a woman wanted by the law. How could she have been so foolish to fall for Jack?

The realization struck her like a train. She'd let herself fall in love with this cowboy from Wyoming. Now there would always be this empty place inside her heart that only Jack Winchester could fill.

She took one last glance around the room. All she knew was that she had to get out of here, get away, far away. Once she knew her mother was safe…

Josey jumped at the sound of an engine turning over. Rushing to the window, she saw the sheriff's department car pulling away. Her hammering heart began to slow, then took off again as she heard the tap at the door.

"Josey, it's me."

She rushed to the door and into Jack's arms. All her plans to escape, to run far away, to keep her distance from this man went out the window the moment she saw the smile on his face.

"My cousin just stopped by because my grandmother had been nagging her to," Jack said. "She's on some big case and couldn't stay but a minute. She was disappointed, though, that she didn't get to meet my wife."

Relief made her weak as Jack locked the door, swept her up in arms and carried her back to the bed.

"All I could think about was getting back to you," he whispered against her hair. His mouth found hers.

She tried to speak, but he smothered her words with kisses. As he began to make love to her, all reason left her. There was no other place she wanted to be but in Jack's arms.

PEPPER WATCHED HER GRANDDAUGHTER drive away. The pride she felt surprised her, as did the guilt. She wished she'd known McCall sooner. She'd lost twenty-seven years of McCall's life. Her own fault.

She brushed angrily at the sudden tears that blurred her eyes, surprised by them and these feelings. She hadn't believed for a moment that the baby Ruby Bates had been carrying was her son Trace's. Because she hadn't wanted to.

But the two had produced McCall, and there was little doubt she was a Winchester. She hadn't even needed to see the DNA test. The young woman looked just like Pepper had at that age.

Trace had been her baby, her undeniable favorite, and she'd been sick with worry because she knew she was losing him. He'd married Ruby Bates because she'd been pregnant. Or maybe because he really had loved her. Pepper had never really known. Trace was dead, and maybe even Ruby didn't know the truth.

Not that it mattered. They had produced McCall, and she made up for everything.

It still amazed her that McCall seemed to have forgiven her for her past sins, unlike her children and even her other grandchildren. McCall knew that she'd tried everything to get Trace to dump Ruby and come back to the ranch.

So maybe Trace had loved McCall's mother. Loved McCall even though she hadn't been born before he was murdered. After all, according to McCall, it had been her father's idea to name her after her grandfather Call.

She wiped her tears as the dust from McCall's patrol car settled over the wild landscape, hating these sentimental emotions and wondering if she should have just left well enough alone and died in her sleep without ever getting her family back to the ranch.

"Mother?"

She turned to see Virginia standing in the doorway.

She'd been so lost in thought, she hadn't heard her enter.

"I'm bored to tears. I'm going into town again. Can I get you anything?"

"No, but you should ask Enid if she needs any groceries, since you're going," Pepper said.

Virginia made a face. "She already gave me a long list. I hope to be back by supper. Enid wanted to know if you knew if Jack and his wife would be joining us. Apparently, they missed both breakfast and dinner."

A good sign, Pepper thought. "Tell Enid to plan on it. If they decide to skip another meal, that will be fine also."

Virginia didn't look happy about being asked to relay the message to Enid, but acquiesced. "Too bad Enid is such a horrible cook. I can't understand how you have survived eating her food all these years."

Her daughter had no idea.

AS MCCALL DROVE BACK to Whitehorse, she thought about her relationship with her grandmother. She'd never even laid eyes on the woman until last month. But since that time her life had changed—and Pepper Winchester had had her hand in that.

She wasn't sure why she'd forgiven her grandmother for denying her existence for more than twenty-seven years. Maybe she saw herself in Pepper Winchester—and not just the fact that they resembled each other. Or maybe what had brought them together was the shared loss of a father and son. McCall had never gotten to know her father. Trace had been killed before she was born. Her grandmother's loss had been even greater because Trace had been her favorite, and losing him had made her lock herself away for the past twenty-seven years.

A call pulled McCall out of her reverie. "I've got Sharon Turnquist on the line. She says her husband is missing." Sharon farmed and ranched with her husband John south of the Breaks.

"Put her through."

"John left to go into Winifred and never got there," Sharon said, sounding worried and scared. "Neighbors are out looking for him, driving the road south, thinking he must have gone off somewhere along the way."

The Turnquist Ranch was a good fifteen miles from Mobridge on a narrow dirt road that wound through the rough badlands country. What were the chances this wasn't connected to Ray Allan Evans Jr.?

"I've got a deputy down that way," she said. "I'll have him help in the search. You let me know when you find him."

She hung up and called to make sure that the deputy she'd sent down to Mobridge had returned with a signed agreement from the Hanovers. Both had been faxed to the phone company, she was informed.

McCall hung up feeling antsy. She just hoped to hell that RJ hadn't stumbled across John Turnquist. She knew the elderly farmer and his wife. You couldn't ask for two nicer people.

Unfortunately, John was the kind of man who would stop and offer a ride to anyone walking along the road. This was rural Montana, where people still helped one another. Even strangers.

JACK AND JOSEY finally came up for air and realized they were both starving. They laughed and played in the huge clawfoot tub before getting dressed in time to go downstairs for supper.

There was an unspoken truce between them, Jack thought. It was as if they knew they didn't have much time together—although right now, feeling the way he did, he couldn't imagine a day without Josey in it.

He was surprised when Virginia was the one late for supper. She came into the lodge complaining about the road into Whitehorse, the dust, the distance, the rough road. She plopped down at the table, announcing she was starved as she distractedly thumbed through the newspaper she'd bought in town.

"Do you have to do that at the table during supper?" Pepper asked with no real heat behind it.

Jack had noticed that his grandmother didn't seem to be herself. She appeared even more distracted than even Virginia.

"I picked up the Whitehorse newspaper since everyone in town was talking about the front-page article," Virginia said, as if she hadn't heard her mother. "A car was found in the Missouri River south of town after a fisherman hooked into the body of a woman. You can't believe the rumors that are flying around town. What has everyone so worked up is a rumor that the woman was found with a noose around her neck. Someone had hung her!"

Josey's fork rattled to her plate.

Jack's gaze shot to Josey. All the color had drained from her face.

"Virginia!" her mother snapped. "We're *eating*."

"Why didn't McCall tell us about this?" Virginia demanded of her mother. "This must be the big case she is working on. Everyone is supposed to be on the lookout for possibly two individuals who might have been hitch-hiking from somewhere near the Fred Robinson Bridge on the Missouri River crossing."

Jack heard all the air rush from Josey's lips. Her fingers gripped the table as if she were on a ship tossed at sea.

"They believe the driver of the vehicle got away after the car went into the water and that both suspects are believed to be armed and dangerous!" Virginia said, scanning through the story. "Apparently, they are both wanted for questioning in a murder case in California. The photos of them aren't very good in grainy black-and-white."

Josey stumbled to her feet. "I'm sorry, I—" She rushed out.

Pepper threw down her napkin, silverware clattering, and shoved back her chair. "Don't you ever know when to shut up, Virginia? Go after her, Jack. That woman could be the best thing that ever happened to you. Don't be like your father."

Jack was already on his feet before his grandmother had even spoken. He'd been so shocked by the news Virginia had brought home, it had taken him a few moments to move. He snatched the newspaper from Virginia's fingers.

"Oh, God, you don't think she's pregnant already, do you?" he heard his aunt say as he rushed from the room.

THE CALL CAME IN late that evening from the deputy McCall had sent out to the Turnquist Ranch.

"One of the other ranchers spotted a body down in a gully," the deputy told her. "It's John Turnquist. I put in a call to the coroner. He's on his way out. Thought I'd better let you know. There's no sign of the pickup he was driving. His wallet's missing, as well. His wife said he didn't have much money in it, but did have several credit cards."

RJ. "Tell her not to cancel the credit cards just yet," McCall said. "We might be able to track him that way. We'll need numbers on the cards so we can work with the companies, and we're going to need a description of that pickup."

"There's something else," the deputy said. "Can't be sure until George gets here, but it looked like John was beaten with something before he was dumped out and rolled down into the gully."

She swore under her breath. "Well, at least now we know what Ray Allan Evans Jr. is driving. Let's find this bastard before he finds his next victim."

JOSEY RAN TO THEIR ROOM at the end of the empty wing, her heart pounding in her ears.

Celeste's body had been found. But the heart-stopping news: RJ was alive. He'd gotten away. She knew what that meant. He would be coming after her. Probably already was.

She stopped pacing to stand in the middle of the bedroom, her mind racing. She had to get out of here. She had to—

At the sound of the door opening behind her, she spun around.

"Talk to me," Jack said quietly, as he closed the door and locked it.

She shook her head and took a step back. "I need to get out of here."

"Josey, you have to tell me what all this has to do with you." His words were heavy with emotion as he put down the newspaper. "After what's happened between us, you owe me that."

She tried to swallow. Her stomach roiled. "I've already involved you. I can't—"

"Josey." He took a step to her, his big hands cupping her shoulders. "I can't help you if you don't tell me—"

"It's all too..." She waved a hand through the air, unable to even form words to describe what had happened to her. "You don't want any of this. Let me leave. Pretend you never picked me up on that highway."

"I can't do that." He sounded filled with anguish.

She stared at him in disbelief. "Aren't you just a little worried that I'm a murderer?"

His blue eyes lit with something akin to love as he took hold of the ends of the scarf around her neck and slowly began to untie it.

"Don't." The word came out a whisper.

"This is why I don't believe you're a killer," he said softly. "Someone did this to you. Just as someone did it to that woman they found."

She fought back the horrible memories. "You don't understand. You could be arrested for harboring a fugitive. Jack, everyone is looking for me, the police in California, the sheriff here in Montana, and..." Tears filled her eyes.

"And the person who hurt you. That's what has you so terrified." Jack thumbed at her tears, then kissed her. "But you're going to tell me because you know you can trust me."

She smiled at that. "The last man who told me to trust him almost killed me."

"I'm not that man."

No, Josey thought. Jack Winchester, whatever his secrets, was like no man she'd ever met. And right now, she suspected he might be the only person alive who'd believe her story.

AFTER BREAKING INTO a small older pharmacy and getting everything he needed, RJ had gone back to his motel and seen to his shoulder before going to sleep. He'd picked a Billings motel where he could park the pickup so the clerk couldn't see it. The clerk had been half-asleep when he'd checked in and hadn't paid any attention to him, anyway. He'd worn the hood up on the sweatshirt he'd taken from the Mobridge house just in case, though. No way could the man be able to make a positive ID of him.

He'd set his alarm for just after midnight and had come up with a way to get rid of all the evidence and the truck. Since hotwiring these damned new cars was next to impossible even if he knew how, he decided to take a more direct approach.

He drove around until he found a rundown bar on the south side of Billings. Then he crossed the river, and found an old abandoned farm house. Driving into the yard with his lights off, he parked the truck behind one of the out buildings.

He'd seen enough *CSI* to know exactly how arsonists set fires. With the pack of cigarettes he'd bought at a convenience mart and the extra gas in the back of the truck, he'd soaked the front seat and set the makeshift fuse.

He'd been about a half mile away, walking down the road, when the pickup blew. RJ smiled to himself as he walked the rest of the way to the bar. The back parking lot was cloaked in darkness. Ideal for what he had in mind.

The jukebox blared inside the bar, one of those serious drinkers' bars where patrons went to get falling-down drunk. There was a pile of junk behind the bar and a stand of pines.

Given the late hour, it wasn't long before a man came stumbling out of the bar, clearly three sheets to the wind. RJ stayed hidden in the dark behind one of the cars and waited until the man started to put his key into the door lock before he called to him.

"Harry?" RJ called, pretending to be drunk as he approached the man, the tire iron behind his back.

The man turned.

"Oh, sorry, I thought you were Harry Johnson." RJ was close now, close enough to smell the man's boozy breath.

"Nope, maybe he's still in the bar." The man turned back to his car, fumbling with the keys.

RJ hit him in the kidneys, then brought the tire iron down on the man's skull. He went down like a ton of bricks.

Unfortunately, the drunk was heavier than he looked, especially considering he was now dead weight. RJ dragged him behind the pile of junk and laid a scrap of sheet metal over him like a blanket.

He figured it would be a while before anyone found the guy and probably even longer before someone started searching for his vehicle.

Picking up the keys from the ground where the

man had dropped them, RJ opened the car door and climbed into the large older model American-made car. He swore. The man was a smoker, and the inside of the car reeked.

Well, beggars couldn't be choosers, as his father used to say. Just the thought of Ray Sr. made him grit his teeth. He wasn't the least bit sorry that old son of a bitch was dead.

RJ started the engine, turned on the radio, pulled away from the bar and headed for Whitehorse. Like the driver of the yellow Cadillac, he had the directions to the Winchester Ranch.

"It's out there and gone," the clerk had told him. "About as remote as it can get."

Josey didn't know it, but she'd chosen the perfect place to end this.

MCCALL WASN'T SURPRISED to hear from Detective Diaz in Palm City, California. She figured he was calling for an update, and while she had little in hard evidence, when she finished telling him what they had so far, he came to the same conclusions she had.

"That sounds like him," the detective said. "RJ skated on more than a few run-ins with the law, from breaking and entering, theft and assault to allegations from prostitutes who claimed he'd abused them. None of them ever made trial. I'm sure his father paid the people off."

McCall heard something in his voice. "And Josephine Vanderliner?"

"She went through a wild time when she was younger, nothing big. Speeding, drinking, a couple of marijuana possession charges, but she's been out of trouble since her mother's accident."

"What about Ray Sr.?"

"Nothing on the books, but he was living pretty high on the hog and running out of money fast when he married Ella Vanderliner."

"What about her car accident?"

Diaz chuckled. "Like minds. There was some question since it was a single car rollover. She had been drinking. The daughter was convinced it was foul play, saying her mother never had more than a glass of wine."

McCall could almost hear him shrug. "You said the mother is in a nursing home? Have you checked it to see if Josephine has called or stopped by?"

Diaz cleared his voice. "Actually, that's why I called. The mother was apparently moved, but the home swears they have no idea where."

"Someone had to sign her out."

"Apparently her daughter had made arrangements before…" His voice trailed off.

"Then she must have known she was going to come into some money," McCall said.

"It does give her more motive for killing Ray Sr.," Diaz agreed. "The battle she was waging in court was for control of her mother, which means control of her mother's money."

"Ray Sr. wouldn't have wanted that to happen."

"Nope," Diaz agreed. "But then neither would his son, RJ."

Chapter Eleven

On the way to the Winchester Ranch, Ray popped some of the pills he'd stolen and realized he felt better than he had in days. He could hardly feel his shoulder and he was thinking clearly, maybe more clearly than he ever had.

He'd realized how crucial it was to his plan that he found Josey. He wanted the money in that backpack, but more important he needed to make sure she never surfaced.

Once she was dead, he would inherit his father's money—which was the Vanderliner money. His father had been broke when he married Ella Vanderliner. It had been a godsend when she'd gotten into that car wreck and he'd gained control over all her money—including Josephine's, as luck would have it.

RJ laughed, wondering if his old man had planned it that way. Maybe the acorn hadn't fallen that far from the tree after all. But if that was the case, Ray Sr. had been holding out on him all these years.

Worse, he'd had to put up with this father's lectures every time he'd gotten in trouble when it was possible his old man was just like him. Hell, wouldn't it be something if he'd gotten his predilection for rough sex from

Ray Sr.? That would explain why his mother had taken off years ago and why his old man had paid to keep her in the style she'd become accustomed to, until she drowned in her fancy swimming pool.

RJ realized with a chill that his father might have been behind that accident, as well. But if true, then he really hadn't known his father at all.

He wheeled his train of thought back to his own problem: Josey Vanderliner. His fear now was that a judge would put Ella's care in Josey's hands. Unless Josey was arrested for murder, of course.

But RJ wasn't willing to put his life in the hands of a jury. He hated to think who would be more believable on the stand. That sweet-looking Josephine Vanderliner with the mother who was practically a vegetable. Or himself.

No, Josey had to disappear off the face of the earth. This was one body that could not be found.

Then he would surface and blame all of it on Josey. With her fingerprints on the weapon that had murdered his father, he didn't think he'd have that much trouble selling his story to the police. At least not in California.

It would be harder to explain the rest of what had happened. He thought he could sell the cops on a story that Josey had taken him and Celeste hostage. He had the bullet wound to prove that Josey had shot him. The rest he could say he didn't know anything about. He could say Josey had knocked him out and he came to underwater in the car. Let them try to prove he had anything to do with Celeste's death or that of the rancher.

Once he was cleared of any wrongdoing, he would be in charge of Josey's mother's care—and her money.

He'd put the old lady in the cheapest rest home he could find, one that cost even less than the one his old man had stuck her in. She wouldn't know the difference anyway.

"TALK TO ME, JOSEY," Jack said. He took her hand and led her over to the bed. As he sat down on the edge, he pulled her down next to him.

"I should never have involved you in this."

"It's too late for that," he said quietly. "You knew this woman they found, didn't you?"

Josey closed her eyes for a moment. "Her name was Celeste. I didn't know her last name. I'd never laid eyes on her before a few days ago."

Jack could feel Josey trembling and see the terror in her eyes, the same terror he'd seen the day he'd picked her up on the highway. He tried hard to hide his own fear as he asked, "Did you have anything to do with what happened to her?"

"No," she said with a shudder. "But I was there. I saw RJ unraveling. I saw it coming and I knew what he was capable of. I'd seen him…" Her voice broke.

"Why don't you start at the beginning."

She stared into his eyes for a long moment, then nodded slowly. He waited while she collected herself.

"You aren't going to believe me. I hardly believe it myself."

He squeezed her hand. "Don't worry. I'll know if you're lying."

She smiled at that. "You think you know me that well?"

"Yeah," he said simply. "I do."

Josey took a breath and let it out slowly. "I guess

it starts with my family. My father was Joseph Vanderliner."

Jack's eyebrows shot up. "*The* Joseph Vanderliner of Vanderliner Oil?"

She nodded. "That's the reaction I've been getting all of my life."

"I knew you came from money, just not that much money," he said. "I read that your father died a few years ago, and your mother…"

"She took my father's death hard. She was never a strong woman. I hadn't realized how weak she was until she married my stepfather, Ray Allan Evans Sr."

"You didn't like him."

"At first I thought he was all right. Until my mother had a car accident. The police said she'd been drinking, but she didn't like alcohol. She never had more than a glass of wine and usually not even that."

"This accident. Was your mother…"

"She survived, but she suffered massive head trauma. She will never recover." Her voice broke again. "Ray Sr. put her in a nursing home and took over her finances, which included my own. My father had died suddenly and hadn't updated his will, so my inheritance was still tied up with my mother's. I had a job at Vanderliner Oil, but when Ray Sr. took over he had me fired. I sued him, because I desperately needed to get my hands on my inheritance so I could take my mother out of that horrible rest home he'd stuck her in and get her proper care."

Josey rubbed a hand over her forehead. "My father's will was just ambiguous enough that my stepfather had control over not only all of my mother's and my money, but Vanderliner Oil, too. And he was spending the money as if there was no tomorrow."

She let go of his hand and stood up, pacing in front of the bed. "I should have been suspicious when my stepfather called and said he wanted to settle out of court, no lawyers. He had arranged, he said, to give me part of my inheritance as a show of faith. All I could think was that if I could get my hands on enough money I could help my mother. I should have known it was a trap."

MCCALL HUNG UP from her call to Detective Diaz and heard the fax machine buzz. She walked down the hall and checked. Sure enough, it was the phone logs she'd been waiting for from Frank Hanover's house.

Her gaze went to the most recent calls, her heart starting to pound. There were five calls made during the time Frank said he and his wife had been in Billings.

All but one of the calls had been to Whitehorse, Montana numbers. McCall took the list back to her office, picked up the phone and dialed the out-of-state number first. A rest home? Hadn't Detective Diaz told her that Josephine's mother was in a rest home?

After she'd established that Ella had been in that rest home, she hung up, wondering why RJ had called there.

McCall dialed the first Whitehorse number.

"Packy's," a woman answered.

Why would RJ call a convenience mart?

McCall hung up and checked the other numbers. A call to the other two convenience marts in town. The rest were to motels in town.

She stared at the list. RJ was looking for someone.

She called the next number and recognized the woman's voice who answered at the hotel. "Nancy, it's McCall Winchester. Did you get a call from someone inquiring about a woman?"

Nancy Snider laughed. "Is this a crank call?" she joked.

"I have two missing persons, both considered armed and dangerous, and it seems one of them is searching for the other one. Help me out here. According to my phone log, the call would have come into the motel at eight-forty last night."

"Sorry. Now that you mention it, I did get a call last night."

"Man or woman calling?"

"Man. He asked if his girlfriend was staying here."

"Did he describe her?"

"Long, red-blond hair, curly, carrying nothing more than a backpack. Said they were supposed to meet up, but she got mad at him. Said he was worried about her."

"What did you tell him?"

"Said I hadn't seen her. Then he asked about some guy driving a yellow Cadillac convertible. Said she might be with him."

"A yellow Cadillac convertible?"

"Said it was one of those old ones with the big fins," Nancy said. "Told him I hadn't seen it, either."

But McCall had.

JOSEY CONTINUED TO PACE the bedroom, too nervous and upset to sit still. "When I got to the house, my stepfather was waiting. I could tell at once that he'd been drinking." She hesitated.

"He made a pass at you."

She laughed nervously. "How did you—"

"I know people."

"I slapped him. He became angry. I picked up a bronze statue he had on his desk in his library. He backed off and went to the wall safe, opened it and showed me the stacks of money—*my* money."

"How much money are we talking?"

"A little over a million in the safe," she said, and saw Jack's eyes widen.

"And the rest of your inheritance?"

She'd known he would realize she had more than that coming. "He had a letter releasing the rest of my inheritance to me. It was…sizable." She swallowed. "Ray said, 'Come get it, then get out.' I was wary. I said, 'Do you have something I can put it in?' He'd laughed and called out, 'RJ, get the lady something to put her money in.'"

"RJ," Jack repeated.

"Ray Allan Evans Jr." She swallowed again, her throat dry. "He appeared and I realized he'd been waiting in the next room."

Jack swore under his breath. "The two of them had set you up."

"RJ brought in an old backpack. It's the one I had when you picked me up on the highway. He tossed me the empty backpack and I moved to the safe just wanting to get the money and get out of there."

Jack listened, holding his breath.

"As I started loading the money into the backpack, I heard Ray Sr. order his son to get him a drink."

She took a breath and let it out slowly, remembering how everything had happened so fast after that. "I saw RJ. He had gone to the bar but he'd come back with only a bar rag. His father had taken a step toward me, saying something I didn't hear or just don't remember because of what happened next."

She was breathing hard now, the memory making her nauseous. "I had put the bronze statue back on Ray's desk. RJ walked past the desk, picked up the statue using the bar rag and struck his father in the back of the head. He hit him twice. I felt the spray of blood—" She was crying, remembering the way Ray Sr. had fallen at her feet.

Jack nodded as if he'd seen it coming. So why hadn't she? She'd known they were up to something, but she'd never dreamed…

"I must have been in shock. The rest is a blur. RJ was saying that his father never planned to let me leave with the money—or the legal document freeing up my inheritance. He shoved me aside. I was just standing there, staring down at Ray Sr. I could tell he wasn't breathing. The bronze statue was lying next to him covered with his blood. There was so much blood. RJ was frantically loading the money into the backpack. I saw it was splattered with Ray's blood."

"Let me guess. He wouldn't let you call the cops," Jack said.

"No. He said the only prints on the bronze statue were mine and that he would swear I'd killed his father for the money. Everyone knew about the legal battle I had been waging against my stepfather."

Jack swore. "They set you up and then he double-crossed his father."

Josey nodded. "I refused to go anywhere with him, but he pulled a gun and dragged me out of the house by gunpoint. When we got outside, he shoved me into the back of a car I had never seen before. That's when I saw that there was a woman in the car who'd been waiting for him."

"Celeste."

Josey nodded slowly. "She drove us to a secluded place while RJ held a gun on me. I thought they were going to kill me right there. I'd seen RJ kill his own father in cold blood. I knew he would shoot me without a moment's hesitation."

"Surely this Celeste woman—"

"She was excited, as if this was some great adventure. She didn't seem to notice the blood on RJ's clothing or that he had a gun. But he didn't kill me there. While he duct-taped my mouth, my wrists and ankles and shoved me into the trunk, she showed me the diamond ring RJ had bought her. He'd told her they were going to get married and then go on a long honeymoon."

"My God." Jack rose from the bed and took her in his arms.

"Oh, that was only the beginning," Josey said, as she leaned into his broad chest. "And now RJ is out there somewhere looking for me."

Chapter Twelve

RJ thought about taking a page out of Josey's playbook and drastically changing his appearance. But his last haircut and highlighting job had cost him a bundle and he wasn't about to ruin that with some disgusting dye job.

He decided he would just have to wear the farmer's straw hat to cover up most of his blond hair. His bigger concern was gasoline.

There was no way he could chance stopping at a station once he left Billings. There were only two towns between there and Whitehorse—Roundup and Grass Range, both small—and he'd heard on the radio that people were looking for him.

So he bought a gas can, put it in the trunk of the car he'd borrowed from behind the bar and filled it in Billings. Fortunately, the car had a large gas tank. The last thing he wanted to do was run out of gas before he found the Winchester Ranch.

His plan was to get to the ranch early enough that he could watch the comings and goings. He had no way of knowing how many people were on the place or how to find Josey. Once he had her, she would tell him where the backpack was with the money in it. At least the money better be in it, he thought.

There was always the chance that she wasn't even on the ranch anymore, but if the yellow Cadillac was there, then he would at least be able to find out where Josey had gone.

The drive was a lot longer than the clerk who'd given him the directions had led him to believe. This place was from hell and gone on miles of narrow dirt road. He was getting annoyed, the drugs he'd taken starting to wear off, when the right rear tire blew.

JACK COULD SEE how hard this was for Josey, but he had to know everything. It was the only way he was going to be able to help her. And no matter what she told him, he knew he would help her any way he could.

He'd never planned to let himself become emotionally involved with this woman, especially knowing from the get-go that she was in some kind of trouble.

But she'd brought out every protective instinct in him, and somewhere along the way he'd found himself falling for her.

"I realized he'd framed me for his father's murder, and the only reason he didn't dump me beside the road was because he needed to make it look as if I'd taken off with the money. I knew something else."

"He couldn't let you live," Jack said.

She nodded. "With his father dead and my mother unable to take care of herself, RJ would be in charge of everything my father had built. I knew he would destroy Vanderliner Oil, spend until he lost it. But I was more worried about what would happen to my mother.

"RJ was all drugged up, flying high, thinking he'd

just pulled off the perfect crime. I had no idea how far he'd driven before he stopped. I thought he was going to kill me then, but he just let me out long enough to go to the bathroom, give me some water and a little something to eat. Apparently, he didn't want me dying in his car and smelling it up."

"He didn't give you any idea where you were headed?"

Josey shook her head. "I asked him to let me ride in the backseat and promised I wouldn't cause any trouble. I wanted to know where we were. I also didn't stand a chance of getting away bound up in the trunk. With my wrists taped behind me, what could I do anyway?"

"So he agreed."

"I think he did it because he was already over Celeste," Josey said. "She was complaining about everything, especially about having to guard me whenever we stopped for gas or he had to run in and get food. At one point, she told him she wasn't going any farther unless he dumped me."

Jack shook his head in disbelief. "She was as cold-blooded as he was."

"The money was part of the appeal. At one point, they thought I was sleeping, and I heard him explain to her that he had to make sure no one found my body and that was why they were going to a place he and his father had hunted in Montana."

"You had to be terrified."

"I watched for an opportunity to get away, but as drugged up as RJ was, he never let down his guard. He seemed ultraintuitive to even the slightest movement by me. By the time we reached Montana I realized he was going to get rid of not only me, but also Celeste. Unfortunately, she hadn't figured that out yet."

McCALL GOT THE CALL about a possible suspect sighting in Billings and hoped the recent incidents down there were RJ's doing only because it would mean he was nowhere near Whitehorse or the Winchester Ranch.

"We had a drugstore break-in," the cop on duty told her. "He sprayed something over the video camera, but missed a small spot. It was definitely a white male. Could be this Ray Allan Evans Jr. you're looking for."

"We believe he was injured at the scene and might be in need of medical supplies."

"Drugs and medical supplies were stolen. That same night a man was killed behind a bar and a pickup truck was set on fire near there. We also had a break-in at a house not far from the bar. A handgun was taken."

That sounded like her man. McCall made a note to see if Sharon Turnquist could get her the serial number on her husband's pickup. "What about the murdered man's car?"

"Missing." He rattled off the make and model and license plate number.

McCall was betting that RJ was now driving it.

After she hung up with the Billings police, she phoned the rest of the numbers that RJ had called. A few of the people who'd talked to him either hadn't come in yet for their shifts or had the day off. She asked for their numbers and tracked them down.

"Sure, I remember talking to him," the young male clerk at one of the motels told her. "He was trying to find his girlfriend. They'd gotten into a fight and she took off with some other guy. The guy did have a great car though. It was one of those Cadillacs with—"

"What kind of information did you give him?" McCall interrupted.

"Pretty much the same as the other guy—directions to the Winchester Ranch."

"The other guy?"

"The cowboy driving the Cadillac convertible. He was getting gas at Packy's the same time I was."

"Was he traveling alone?"

The clerk laughed. "The second guy asked me the same thing. I told him about the woman I saw with the cowboy. Didn't match the description he gave me of her, but he sounded like she was the one he was looking for."

Didn't match the description? "What did the woman look like?"

"Pretty with short, curly, dark hair."

The same way her grandmother had described Jack's wife, Josey.

Josey. Josephine. The moment McCall hung up, she dialed her grandmother's number at the ranch. The phone rang and rang. Her grandmother didn't have voice mail, but she had an old answering machine. When it didn't pick up, McCall realized there could be only one reason why.

The phone line was out.

In the middle of winter it wouldn't have been unusual for the phone line to be down. But this time of year?

It seemed odd. RJ could have reached the ranch by now, but would he cut the phone cord in broad daylight? It was more likely he would watch the place and hit it tonight.

Without cell phone service anywhere near the ranch, there was no way to reach her grandmother to warn her.

McCall feared it was too late to warn any of them as she jumped in her patrol car and, lights and siren blaring, headed for the Winchester Ranch.

RJ SHOULDN'T HAVE BEEN SURPRISED to find no spare tire in the trunk. He pulled out the tire iron and beat the trunk lid until it looked like the craters on the moon. He felt a little bit better after that.

Back in the car, he downed a half-dozen pills, then drove until there was no rubber left on the tire and the rim buried itself in a rut. The car wasn't going any farther, he thought with a curse, then realized it was blocking the road to the ranch. With an embankment on one side and a ravine on the other, no one would be coming down this road tonight.

He studied the directions he'd been given under the dome light. If he was right, he could cut off some of the distance by going across country. He drank the last of the twelve-pack he'd bought in Billings. It was hot and tasted like crap, but he didn't want to get dehydrated and it helped the buzz he had going.

There was just enough gas left in the can in the trunk to soak the front seat pretty good. He lit the car and, taking the map, dropped off the side of the road and headed what he believed was southwest. The night was cloudy, but earlier he'd seen the moon coming up in the east.

He heard the *whoosh* as the car caught fire, and he was glad there wasn't much gas in the tank. Even if the car did explode, though, he doubted the sound would carry clear to the ranch. He'd hate for them to have even an inkling of what was coming.

As he topped a rise, he realized he couldn't be that far from the ranch. Pleased that maybe things were turning out as they were supposed to for once, he counted the minutes before he'd see his stepsister again.

IT HAD GOTTEN DARK out. All Josey wanted to do was finish the story so Jack would understand why she had to get out of there. It was getting later, and the breeze coming in through the French doors was almost cold. She feared another storm was brewing on the horizon, and she worried about the road out of the ranch if there was a thunderstorm. She'd heard Enid say that when it rained here, parts of the road became impassable.

"When Celeste heard that we were going to camp, it was the last straw," she said. "We'd been eating fast food for thirty hours, sleeping in the car, and Celeste was ready for the good life RJ had been promising her. Also, he'd been popping a lot of pills so he could keep driving straight through, and he was acting oddly. When we reached the camp, RJ cut me free of the duct tape and tied me to a tree with part of the rope he'd brought along. I thought I might stand a chance since the rope was much less restricting than the tape.

"That night he and Celeste got into a huge argument. RJ demanded she give back the engagement ring. Celeste went ballistic and started hitting him. He grabbed her and tried to take the ring off her finger. The next thing, she was screaming that he'd broken her finger, howling with pain. He hit her and she went down."

Josey stepped to the open French doors to look out into the darkness for a moment, hugging herself against the cold, against the thought of RJ and what he was capable of. "He'd been playing with the extra rope he'd brought. But it wasn't until then that I saw he'd fashioned two lengths with nooses at the ends. RJ was saying something about Montana being the last of the old West. He tied one end of the rope to the bumper of the car, threw the other end over a limb near the water and looped the noose over Celeste's neck and pulled it tight. He abused her all the time. It seemed to be their thing, but this was different. Then he came for me saying it was time to hang the bitches."

She looked back at Jack and saw the pain and fury in his face before hurrying on. "I fought him, but he was too strong for me."

"That's how you got all the bruises."

Josey nodded. "I must have passed out because when I woke up, RJ was in the car, the motor running and I was being dragged by my throat. Celeste had come to and she was screaming for him to stop. He kept going in the car until we were both hauled off our feet and were hanging from the tree limb. I remember gasping for breath. Then I heard this huge crack as the limb broke, and the next thing I knew I was falling. The moment my feet hit the ground, I tore the noose from my neck.

"I had seen where RJ had laid down the gun when he was hitting me. I ran for it. I grabbed the pistol and spun around. Celeste still had the noose around her neck, but she'd found RJ's knife he'd used to cut the rope earlier. RJ saw her and hit the gas in the car. She sliced through the ropes before they went taut again."

Josey closed the French doors and stepped back into the room, still hugging herself against the memory— and the cold fear. "RJ threw the car into Reverse and headed right for her. I had the gun in my hand. I fired, but missed him, hitting the car instead. I fired again. I heard him cry out. I'll never forget the murderous look in his eye. Then he must have realized he was still in Reverse and headed for the river.

"It happened so fast. Celeste threw herself through the driver's-side open window. They were struggling as the car crashed into the river. Celeste had RJ in a headlock. RJ was wounded and trying to fight her off. Neither seemed to notice or care that the car was sinking. I grabbed the backpack and ran, still holding the gun.

"When I finally did stop on a rise to look back, I didn't see either of them. By then I'd realized that if I had any hope of getting my mother out of that awful place Ray Sr. had put her in, I couldn't turn myself in. At least not before I wired the money to the facility I'd set up for her the night I met Ray Sr. to pick up the money. Now all I have to do is make sure my mother is safe, then go to the police and—"

"RJ is still out there," Jack broke in. "It's going to be your word against his, and as you said, your fingerprints are on the murder weapon. If you turn yourself in, you'll go to prison—and what will happen to your mother?"

"I hid her. He won't be able to find her." But even as she said the words, she knew her mother wouldn't be safe.

"And what happens when this money you have runs out?"

Josey raked a hand through her hair. "Don't you think these are the things I've been trying to figure out?"

"I know," he said, taking her in his arms. "That's why

we need to figure them out together. I can finish what I came to do tonight and we can get out of here."

She pulled back to look into his face. "Jack—"

"We're in this together now. I just need you to trust me and stay in this room," he said. "We'll leave first thing in the morning. I know of a place we can go until we can make sure your mother was moved and is safe. Then—"

"You're planning on going after RJ," she said. The thought of Jack being in danger terrified her more than RJ coming after her alone. "No. I can't let you do that."

He cupped her shoulders in his hands. "We can talk about this later. I need to go. There is something I have to do. It's from a promise I made a long time ago. I feel I have to do this. Stay here. I'll try not to be long. Keep the door locked." He touched her cheek, a tenderness warming his blue eyes. "I'm not going to let anything happen to you. Get packed and wait for me. I'll hurry."

IT WAS DARK when McCall came around the corner in her patrol SUV, and her headlights flashed on the burned vehicle in the middle of the road. She pulled up, grabbed her flashlight and got out, half hoping to find RJ's body in the car.

Instead, she found footprints and tracked them a short distance in her flashlight beam. They were headed southeast toward the Winchester Ranch.

RJ had a good walk ahead of him. As she climbed back into her SUV, she could only hope he stumbled across a rattlesnake or broke his leg in a prairie dog hole. Backing up, she turned around and returned to the main road. Unlike RJ, she knew another way to get to the ranch that would be faster than walking. She considered calling for backup, but changed her mind. From the single set of footprints, RJ was alone. McCall figured he was after Josey Vanderliner, also known as Mrs. Jack Winchester.

The only thing McCall didn't know was how her cousin Jack fit into this.

RJ LET OUT a low whistle under his breath when the saw the Winchester Ranch. It looked like a damned hotel. Who were *these* people?

With a sinking feeling, he realized he was screwed if all those rooms were full of people. He'd never be able to find Josey—let alone get her out of there. Even with the gun he'd stolen in Billings, he couldn't take on everyone in the place.

He reminded himself he had no choice. Getting rid of Josey had become more than just something he needed to do to seal the deal on his father's death. It had become personal, he thought, as he rubbed his shoulder. If it wasn't for the pills he kept popping, he would be in horrible pain. As it was, his shoulder was a constant reminder of why he had to find Josey and finish this.

He moved down the hillside in the dark to the back of the massive log structure. Finding the main phone line coming in was child's play, since the pole was right behind the house. There was even a yard light nearby, so he wouldn't have to use the small penlight he'd brought.

But when he reached the spot where the phone line entered the house, he found that someone had already beat him to it. What the hell? The cord had definitely been cut. A sense of dread raced through his veins like ice water. Who would have done this?

Suddenly he wasn't so sure about finishing this here. Maybe he should just cut his losses, steal one of the cars, take some back road across the Canadian border. But he knew he wasn't going anywhere without money.

Still, this felt all wrong.

He moved around to the front of the place, staying in the shadows, the fine hairs on his neck standing on end. He came to a window with a light behind it and crouched down to listen.

He could hear a radio playing and someone banging around in the pots and pans and mumbling under her breath. He took a peek through the crack between the curtains. A small, elderly woman appeared to be cleaning up the kitchen in angry bursts.

RJ waited to see if anyone else showed up. When no one did, he moved along the edge of the house, staying to the dark shadow of the building.

He heard more voices, saw another lighted window, and eased forward. The window was open a crack, and he could hear two women talking.

"Give me a reason to stay here, Mother."

"Virginia, you have to do whatever it is you need to do."

"Can't you just say you want me to stay? Is that so hard for you? Or say you want me to leave. If it doesn't make any difference to you, that's the same as telling me to leave."

The older-sounding woman sighed deeply. "Why does everything with you have to be so dramatic? You've done nothing but complain since you got here. Why would you want to stay?"

RJ heard the younger one sniffle as if crying.

"Maybe I'd like to see my brothers and my nephews," she said, sounding hurt. "When are they arriving?"

"I don't know, Virginia. As you pointed out, they may not come to see me at all. I haven't heard from them. Or the rest of my grandchildren."

"I can't believe they won't."

"Perhaps they are less worried about their inheritance than you are," the older one said.

"You know, Mother, you deserve to die alone on this ranch with just Enid and Alfred here with you, both of them just waiting for you to breathe your last breath. I wouldn't be surprised if they helped that along one day."

He heard the scrape of a chair, then heavy footfalls and the slamming of a door. He listened but heard nothing more. Apparently, this place wasn't full. So far he'd only seen an old lady. But the daughter had mentioned two others, apparently caretakers.

As he started to move, he heard another sound, this one coming from outside the house. He pressed himself against the side of the house and stared out into the darkness.

Someone moved in the distance. Someone who seemed to be sneaking along the outside of the building—just as he had been doing.

The person who'd cut the phone line?

He waited until he saw the figure disappear inside a door at the far end of a separate wing of this monstrous place.

RJ waited for a moment, then followed.

IT DIDN'T TAKE Josey long to pack after Jack left, since she'd already started it earlier. She checked, though, to make sure she hadn't forgotten anything. Then she checked the gun she'd stuffed in the top of the backpack. She had only four bullets left. She hoped she wouldn't have to use them, but knew she would if they ran across RJ. As drugged up as he probably was, she wasn't sure it would be enough to stop him. The thought of killing him made her shudder. But she wouldn't let him hurt Jack, no matter what.

As she crossed in front of the French doors, she glanced out into the darkness, wondering where RJ was. Jack had said he wouldn't be able to find them on this ranch so far from everything. But Jack didn't know RJ.

Josey felt anxious, wishing Jack would hurry. They needed to get out of here, for their sakes and his grandmother's and Virginia's. She remembered Enid and Alfred. They seemed like they could take care of themselves.

She put the gun back into the top of the backpack and pulled the drawstring closed. Silently, she prayed that her mother had been moved to the new health-care facility and that RJ couldn't get his hands on her. That would be Josey's one weak spot, and RJ would capitalize on it if he thought of it.

With everything done, she turned out the lights and stepped to the window. She knew where Jack had gone. What she still didn't know was what was so important behind that rock wall. He'd said it was something he'd promised to do a long time ago. She knew Jack was the kind of man who stood by a promise no matter what.

What scared her was just that. He was risking his life and hers. So what was behind that rock wall? Hidden treasure? The famous Winchester fortune Jack had told her about?

No, she thought. Knowing Jack it was something much more important.

Standing on the balcony in the darkness and cold, Josey wondered when the exact moment was that she'd fallen in love with Jack Winchester. Had it been that first kiss in the Cadillac? Or when he held her while she cried on that high ridge during their horseback ride? Or was it when he'd taken her in his arms and carried her over to the bed? Sometime over the past few days she'd begun to realize she was no longer pretending. She felt like his wife.

With a start, Josey realized that she'd just seen something move along the edge of the far building—the same one Jack was in right now. It couldn't be Jack. He'd left a long time ago. Unless something—or someone—had held him up.

She stared hard into the blackness at the edge of the building, fear gnawing at her insides. If not Jack, then—

Alfred. The old man was sneaking along the edge of the building. He must have seen Jack go into the closed wing earlier. Or suspected that's where he was headed. What would Alfred do when he caught Jack opening that old rock wall? Why would he care?

She thought about the other night when Alfred had caught her in that wing. Had he gone back to make sure no one had tampered with the wall? Then that would mean he knew something had been hidden behind it.

Her heart began to pound.

What was he up to?

As he stepped to the edge of the far wing, the moon

slipped from behind the clouds. Her skin went clammy, fear closing her throat, as she saw what Alfred gripped in his hands. An ax.

Chapter Thirteen

Jack had made some progress on the rock wall the past two nights. He worked harder and faster tonight, anxious to get back to Josey. He didn't believe there was any way that her homicidal stepbrother could find her, and he'd made sure he had the Cadillac keys on him so she didn't do anything crazy like leave on her own.

He wished he could just let this go, but he'd promised his mother and himself years ago that he would see that Pepper Winchester got what she deserved. Today was that day. Then he could put this place and all that behind him.

But even as he thought it, Jack realized that something had changed in him. For years he'd been waiting for an opportunity to get back on this ranch and see what was behind this wall. It had always been there, that need to finish things in Montana. It hadn't mattered how well his life or his career had been going in Wyoming. There had always been this mission hanging over his head.

Now, though, his thoughts kept returning to Josey, and he realized just how much he'd changed since he'd met her. It was all he could do to keep chipping at the mortar. Did he really need to know what was behind this wall anymore?

The mortar in the wall was old, more than forty years. He chipped out another stone and set it aside. As he shone his flashlight into the space behind the wall, he could make out what looked like a large bundle wrapped in cloth.

His pulse kicked up a beat. Hurriedly, he removed another rock. There was definitely something in there. Something wrapped in what appeared to be an old canvas tarp.

For so long he hadn't been sure if his mother's story was even true. After all, she'd heard it from Angus Winchester, her lover, the man who'd lied to her for years.

Jack worked another rock out, and then another. Just a few more and he would be able to see what had been hidden for all these years behind this rock wall.

AFTER SEEING ALFRED with the ax headed for the wing where she knew Jack was working, Josey grabbed the gun out of the backpack and tore out of the room at a run. She heard someone call to her as she threw open the front door, but she didn't look back as she sprinted toward the closed wing.

The air chilled her to her bones. That and the fear that had her heart in her throat. There was no sign of Alfred as she ran the length of the building. She skidded to a stop as something moved out of the darkness just before she reached the door into the closed wing.

A low rumbling sound filled the air, and she froze as she saw the old dog. It blocked the way, the hair standing up on the back of its neck, a low growl coming out of its throat.

It took a step toward her. She raised the gun, but knew she wouldn't be able to shot it. "Nice dog," she whispered, and took a step away from it and the side of the building. The dog remained where it was. She took another step, then another, frowning. The old dog acted almost as if it was protecting something.

A bone? She squinted into the blackness at the edge of the building. Her blood suddenly ran cold. At first she thought it was a fawn deer or some other animal that the dog had killed and was only protecting its food.

But then she caught the glint of metal and saw that something was protruding out of the center of the dead animal. An ax.

"Oh, my God," she breathed as the moon broke free of the clouds, and she saw Alfred lying on his back, the ax buried in his chest.

Her mind whirled. Who would…? Jack! Where was Jack?

She turned and ran the last few steps to the door into the closed wing.

JACK REMOVED THE LAST ROCK in his way. Kneeling down, he picked up one end of the tarp. The canvas, rotten after all these years, disintegrated in his fingers.

The first thing he saw was what was left of a boot. He suddenly felt weak as he stared at what lay beyond the boot—a mummified body. Call Winchester.

Jack sat back on his haunches, surprised at the range of emotions that rushed through him like a wildfire. He'd dreamed of the day he would fulfill his promise to his mother. He'd expected revenge to taste sweet. Finally Pepper Winchester would get what she deserved.

But there was no sweetness, only a deep sorrow in him as he looked at what he knew were his grandfather's remains. He'd spent his adult life working hard to succeed in business, waiting for the opportunity to break down this wall and show the world who Pepper Winchester really was. It was going to make it all that much sweeter that she was still alive and would know who uncovered her deadly secret.

Jack waited for the relief, the elation, the smug satisfaction. He finally had proof that his grandmother had killed her husband and hidden his body behind this rock wall, just as his mother had heard.

He'd gotten what he'd come for. He didn't give a damn about any inheritance. Now all he had to do was call his cousin the sheriff and let her take it from here. He could wash his hands of this place that had haunted him all these years.

But what he hadn't expected was to feel a connection to this ranch or this family. He hadn't expected to meet Josey or fall in love. Or feel anything for his grandmother, let alone a dead grandfather he'd never known.

Jack heard a sound behind him. Josey, he thought. Of course she wouldn't be able to stay in the room. She would be worried about him. She would— He turned and saw the figure framed in the doorway.

PEPPER WINCHESTER had been coming out of the parlor when she'd seen Josey racing down the stairs as if the devil himself were after her.

"Call the sheriff," Josey had cried. "I have to get to Jack."

She'd tried to stop the girl to make sense of what was happening, but Josey had rushed out without answering.

The fear in the young woman's face had sent an arrow of panic through Pepper's own heart.

"What is wrong with that girl?" Virginia demanded, coming out from her room at the back wing.

"Stay here. Call the sheriff. Tell McCall there's some kind of trouble."

Her daughter's eyes widened in alarm. "You're not going out there."

But Pepper was already following Josey. She couldn't move as quickly, and once outside it took her a few minutes for her old eyes to adjust to the dark. She caught a glimpse of Josey running toward the closed wing of the lodge.

That building was actually the first homestead. Call had workers add on to it, the lodge expanding, as his grandiose plans developed, into what it was today. But Pepper remembered his stories about his parents living in what people would call an old shotgun house. Long and narrow, the hall ran straight through every room to the back door. Only this one didn't have a back door. The house ended in an old root cellar tucked into the hillside.

She saw Josey stop, heard the old dog growling even from here. As she worked her way in that direction, Pepper realized it had been years since she'd ventured out of the house. She wasn't used to walking on uneven ground, even with her cane. She felt exposed out here and suddenly afraid as she saw Josey give the dog a wide berth before slipping past the dog and disappearing into the door of the wing Pepper had Alfred close off years ago.

She quickened her pace, gasping for breath, as she

realized that what she had feared for more than forty years was about to come true.

RJ WAS MOVING down the hallway toward a scratching sound and a sliver of light under one of the doors, when he heard someone come into the house behind him. He quickly stepped into one of the darkened rooms, pressing his back against the wall.

He'd heard the dog growling, heard someone trying to soothe it. He'd expected whoever it was to run back to the house screaming after seeing the old man's body with the ax buried in it.

Rubbing his wounded shoulder, RJ swore under his breath at the pain. He hadn't seen the old man until it was too late. He'd sensed someone behind him in time to avoid the brunt of the ax. But the wooden handle had hit his shoulder.

The ax had stuck in the side of the log house. As the old fool had tried to wrestle it free, RJ had hit him, knocking him backward. Then, close to blacking out from the pain of the blow on his already injured shoulder, RJ had furiously jerked the ax from the wall and swung it as hard as he could. It stuck with a suctioning sound.

RJ had looked around, but he hadn't seen anyone else. *One down,* he'd thought. Then he'd heard an odd noise coming from within the building. He'd looked for a way into this wing and found an old door where someone had removed the boards that had been tacked over it.

Someone was in there working at this hour? There was a chipping sound, then a scraping sound, as if something large was being moved across the floor.

He'd opened the door, listened, then stepped through,

and was partway down the hall when he'd heard some-one come in behind him.

Now he held his breath, wondering what was going on and why everyone was headed for this particular part of the strangely built house. The only light was a faint glow coming from under a door farther down the hallway. Where he stood there was total darkness. But he could feel a draft and realized that the window across from him, although partially boarded up, had a hole in the glass between the boards the size of a small rock.

Tentative footsteps moved in his direction. RJ pulled the gun he'd stolen from his jacket pocket, half wishing he'd brought the ax with him. He didn't dare fire the weapon for fear of who it might attract. He'd have to use it as a blunt force instrument. He'd had some experience with that.

As he listened to the footsteps growing closer and closer, he heard something outside the building that made his heart beat faster and his stomach drop. Through the broken window came the whine of a car engine in the distance.

It was headed toward the house, which meant there was another road into the ranch.

McCALL HAD TURNED OFF her lights and siren as soon as she'd gotten out of town; she hadn't needed them because of the lack of traffic. Now she stopped in a low spot and killed her headlights and engine. She reached for her shotgun. She was already wearing the Kevlar vest under her jacket and had her Glock in her holster. Both the shotgun and the pistol were loaded and ready to go.

Easing open the door, she slid out and started down

the road. Over the first rise, she saw the lodge sprawled against the mountainside. She could hear the wind in the cottonwoods as she neared the creek. The antique weather vane on the barn turned slowly.

She pulled up short as her eyes picked up movement in front of the house. Someone was walking toward the far wing. She heard the tap of a cane on the gravel. Her grandmother? Where was she going?

McCall began to run, hoping to hell her grandmother wasn't armed and would mistake her for a trespasser. But she wasn't about to call out and warn RJ that she was coming. She'd have to take her chances with her grandmother.

VIRGINIA PEERED OUT THE WINDOW, seeing nothing. Where had her mother gone? The old fool. Well, she wasn't going out there after Josey, who'd probably just had a spat with her husband. Newlyweds!

She looked around, wondering where Enid and Alfred were. They lived in the wing opposite the kitchen and laundry rooms. Virginia realized she hadn't heard a peep out of either of them.

And it certainly wasn't like Enid to miss anything. Why hadn't she come out when Josey had come tearing through the house and both Virginia and her mother had raised their voices to call after her?

Virginia thought the whole thing ridiculous, but she stepped to the phone and began to dial 911 before she realized the line was dead.

She slowly put down the receiver. Her cell was useless out here; in fact, her grandmother didn't even own one and with good reason. Cell phone coverage was sketchy in this part of the county.

The huge old place seemed too quiet. She shivered and hugged herself, wishing her mother would come back and assure her there was a good reason the phone line was down.

Should she stay in here and wait, or should she go out and see what was going on herself? Maybe her mother needed her.

The thought actually made Virginia laugh out loud.

The wind buffeted the old glass at the window, making her jump. She'd been so busy listening to the house that she'd failed to realize how hard the wind was blowing. It thrashed the cottonwoods outside, sending leaves swirling across the yard.

She tried to convince herself that the wind had knocked down the phone line, just as it used to when she lived here. But she knew something was terribly wrong. She could feel it.

She eased open the front door and peered around the corner, hoping to see her mother. A gust of wind nearly wrested the door from her hands. She stared into the darkness. Was that Pepper headed for the old wing of the house?

She let out a small cry as ice-cold fingers bit into her upper arm. The door slipped from her fingers and swung open, banging against the wall as she swung around.

"What are you doing?" Enid demanded.

The elderly housekeeper looked odd. Or maybe it was the way the wind blew her hair back from her face in this dim light.

"You scared me half to death," Virginia snapped. "You have to quit sneaking up on people like that. You're going to give my mother a heart attack."

"It would take more than that to kill your mother."

Enid glanced down the hallway in the direction of Pepper's room. "Where *is* your mother?"

"She's gone outside after Josey."

Enid pushed past her, fighting the wind to see.

Virginia heard her mother scream like a wounded animal, the sound getting caught up in the howl of the wind, as Enid began to run awkwardly in the direction Pepper had gone.

Virginia slammed the door, then hurried down to her room and locked herself inside.

RJ KNEW HE COULDN'T BE SEEN where he was standing in dense shadow, and yet he'd almost blown it—he'd been so surprised to see Josey walk past the room where he was hiding in plain sight.

He wanted to laugh. Could his luck get any better than this? He felt he was on a roll. Nothing could go wrong.

The hardest part was waiting until he heard her footsteps stop. Still, he waited as he heard a door creak open. He started to take a step when he heard Josey speak—and a man answer.

Perfect. RJ took a cautious step out, then another. The door to the room down the hall was open now, a dim light spilling out. He could hear their voices, but couldn't make out what they were saying. Something in the tone, though, told him this was the driver of the Cadillac parked out front, the cowboy who'd saved Josey. Or thought he had, RJ thought with a smile.

He eased down the hallway, stopping as soon as he could hear what they were saying.

PEPPER TEETERED on her cane as McCall reached her.

"What is going on?" Pepper demanded, her voice warbling with emotion.

McCall steadied her for a moment, following her grandmother's gaze to the body lying in the shadow of the house and the old dog sitting next to it.

"It's Alfred," her grandmother said. "He has an ax in his chest."

McCall could see that. "What are you doing out here?"

"Josey rushed out of the house saying to call you because Jack was in trouble. I came out to find out what was wrong."

Josey, McCall thought, looking around the ranch yard. "I want you to go back to the house." At the sound of a sole crunching on the gravel, McCall swung around to see Enid. She had stopped short of where her husband lay dead next to the door. She had her hand over her mouth.

"Enid," McCall said, going over and taking hold of her arm. "I want you to take Pepper back into the house. Do you hear me?"

The ancient housekeeper nodded slowly.

"Now! Both of you, and stay there." McCall moved along the building, glancing back to see that neither old woman had moved. Damn it. She didn't have time to herd them back to the house. She reached the end of the building and saw where the boards had been removed.

The door into the old section of the house was open. Cautiously, she moved toward it.

FOR A MOMENT, Josey stood, her heart in her throat, afraid to breathe.

"Jack?" she whispered, as she stared into the dark room. The gun was in her hands, one finger on the trigger. She knew RJ might have already gotten to Jack. That if anyone was in the room it could be RJ, standing in the dark and laughing at her.

A light flashed on, the beam pointed at the floor.

Her finger brushed the trigger and jerked away. "Jack!" she cried. She lowered the gun and rushed to him. Her relief at seeing him unharmed made her throat swell with emotion. She could barely get the words out. "Alfred. He's dead. RJ—" The rest was choked off as she saw the hole in the wall and what lay just inside it. "Oh, my God. Who—?"

"My grandfather," he said, taking the gun from her and laying the flashlight on one of the shelves so the beam wasn't pointed at them. "My mother had heard stories from people who used to work on the ranch about Alfred rocking up a wall in the old wing the day Call Winchester disappeared."

The mention of Alfred brought back the horrible scene just outside. The words spilled out of her as she felt the urgency return. "I saw Alfred earlier carrying an ax and headed this way, so I came to warn you, but..." She shuddered as she met Jack's eyes. "He's dead. The ax is in...his chest. RJ's here."

Jack gripped her arm with one hand. He had the gun he'd taken from her in the other. "Come on, let's get out of here."

They both seemed to hear the creak of a floorboard behind them at the same time. Turning toward the doorway, Jack stepped in front of her as they were suddenly blinded by a bright light.

JACK BLINKED, covering his eyes as he shielded Josey from the man standing in the doorway holding the gun on them.

"Drop the gun," the man ordered, and lowered the flashlight so it wasn't blinding Jack.

Jack knew he could get off at least one shot before RJ fired. He couldn't take the chance that Josey might be hit.

He had risked her life for revenge. He would never forgive himself. But he knew even if they'd left earlier, one day RJ would have caught up to them. This encounter had been inevitable.

Jack just would have liked to be more prepared.

He felt Josey behind him, heard the small sound she made and knew this was indeed her stepbrother, RJ Evans, the man who'd framed her, hurt her and planned to kill her.

In the diffused light from the flashlight in his hand, Jack saw that RJ was tall and blond, with eerie blue eyes. He looked strong and solid and armed. Jack had to believe that RJ wouldn't want to kill them here in this room, that he would get an opportunity to save Josey. It couldn't end like this. He would do anything to save Josey.

"I said drop the gun. Now!"

Jack dropped the gun to the floor at his feet.

RJ smiled. "Hey, Josey. Shocked to see me? I thought you might be surprised that you hadn't killed me." He sounded angry, his words slurring a little as if he might be drunk or on drugs. "Could you have hidden someplace more hard to get to?" His gaze shifted to Jack. "And you must be the guy with the Cadillac convertible. Nice ride. I think I'll take it when I leave here."

Behind him, Jack felt something hard and cold suddenly pushed against his back. The crowbar. Josey slipped it into the waistband of his jeans.

"Now kick the gun over here," RJ ordered.

JOSEY KNEW how this would end. She knew what RJ was capable of, his cruelty unmatched. He would make them both pay, Jack for helping her and putting RJ to all this trouble, and Josey—

She couldn't think about that or the fear would paralyze her. This had to end here. The last time she'd shot at RJ it had been to stop him from killing both her and Celeste. She'd sworn then that she would never fire another gun, especially at another person.

RJ stepped forward before Jack could kick the gun over to him in a swift movement that caught both her and Jack by surprise. He caught Jack in the side of the head with the butt of his weapon.

Jack started to go down and Josey saw her chance. She dropped to the floor, snatched up the gun Jack had dropped and fired blindly at RJ. The gunshots exploded in the small room, deafening her, as she saw RJ stumble backward toward the doorway. His flashlight clattered to the floor and went out, pitching the room in blackness.

The air had filled with five shots. Josey knew she'd had only four in the gun she was holding. That meant RJ had gotten a round off. Her heart leaped into her throat at the thought that Jack might have been hit. If the blow to the head from the butt of the gun hadn't killed him, then the shot could have.

"Jack?" For a moment, the silence was deafening. Then a chill skittered over her skin as she heard RJ chuckle. He knew there had only been six shots in the pistol. He knew she was no longer armed.

She could hear him feeling around in the dark for something. His gun? Had he lost it? Then her heart began to pound wildly as she heard him crawling toward her. "Jack?" No answer.

She was filled with agony and terror that Jack was dead. Her plan had backfired. Somehow Jack had gotten in the line of fire.

She scuttled backward from her sitting position on the floor until she hit the rock wall. Her fingers felt rocks and dried mortar. She felt around frantically for a rock small enough that she could use as a weapon, but found nothing.

Remembering the hole Jack had made in the wall, she felt around for it, thinking that if she could get through it—

As she tried to scramble to her feet, disoriented by the blackness, RJ's hand closed like a vise around her ankle. She screamed, grabbing a handful of dried mortar from the floor and throwing it where she thought his face should be.

He let out a scream of his own, clawing at her now with both hands as she tried to fight him off. But RJ had always been too strong for her.

McCALL HAD JUST STEPPED through the doorway and had started down the hall when she heard the five shots. She snapped on her flashlight. With her weapon drawn, she hurried down the hall.

She couldn't tell where the shots had come from. The sound had echoed through the wing. So she was forced to stop at each door, before moving forward again.

Behind her she heard a door open and spun around to see her grandmother standing in it, wide-eyed. Damn the stubborn woman. Hiding behind her was Enid.

McCall couldn't take the time to argue with them. She waved for them to stay back, knowing the effort was useless, as she moved forward down the hallway.

She hadn't gone far when the hallway light switched on. She swore. Her grandmother or Enid had just alerted whoever had fired those shots that they were no longer alone.

IN THE SUDDEN LIGHT, Josey saw that at least some of the four shots she'd fired had hit their mark. RJ had left a wide smear of blood on the floor as he'd crawled after her. He had pulled himself up into a sitting position and managed to get hold of her wrist, twisting it until she was sure he was going to break it, then pulled her facedown in front of him.

But when the lights had come on, her gaze had gone instantly to where she'd heard Jack fall. He lay just feet away. His eyes were closed and she could see that his shirt was soaked with blood. She stared at his chest, praying to see the rise and fall of his breath.

Please, God, let him be alive.

RJ let go of her wrist to grab a handful of her hair. He jerked her head up and slapped her almost senseless. "I'm talking to you, bitch. Look at me when I talk to you. I want you to be gazing into my eyes when I rip your heart out."

He'd already ripped her heart out if he'd killed Jack. She had fought RJ until he'd gotten her down on the floor. His face was scratched where she'd made contact, his eyes red and running tears, his cheeks gritty with mortar. He kept blinking and swearing as he tried to clear them.

But it was the way the front of his shirt blossomed with blood that gave her hope. "You're in no shape to rip my heart out," she said, meeting his gaze. She would fight this bastard to the death. "You're going to bleed to death on this dirty floor."

He laughed, a gurgling sound coming from his throat, that even gave him pause. A new cruelty came into his eyes. He wasn't going to die alone, the look said. He let go of her long enough to pull the knife from the sheath strapped to his leg.

Out of the corner of her eye, Josey caught movement. She wanted to cry in relief. She wanted to look in Jack's direction to make sure she hadn't just imagined it. But she did neither. She kept her gaze locked with RJ's, afraid of what he would do if he knew that Jack was alive.

Josey didn't move, didn't breathe, as RJ put the knife to her throat.

JACK CAME TO SLOWLY. The blow to his head had knocked him senseless. He lay perfectly still, listening to RJ threatening Josey. It was all he could do not to leap up and attack the man.

But first he had to be sure that RJ wasn't still holding a gun on her.

He moved his head as quietly as he could until he could see RJ sitting, leaning against the stack of rocks Jack had removed from the wall. He was turned slightly, so he wasn't facing Jack, but he didn't have his back to him, either.

Jack saw that RJ's shirt was soaked with blood. There

was a wide trail of blood on the floor where it appeared RJ had crawled over to Josey. He now had hold of Josey's hair and was holding her in front of him at an odd angle.

The last thing Jack remembered was the sound of gunfire. At first he'd thought RJ had unloaded his weapon on Josey. But now he could see Josey's gun lying within her reach. He could only assume it was empty or RJ would have taken it from her. She didn't appear to be wounded, but Jack couldn't know that for sure until he got a better look at her.

Shifting just a little, he felt the crowbar at his back and eased it out behind him. He knew he would get only one chance if RJ was still armed. He would have to make it count.

"You know, RJ, you might have pulled it off," Josey was saying. Jack realized she was stalling, giving him time. "The way you set me up when you killed your father, that was brilliant."

"Thanks." RJ sounded touched that she thought so. "I hated that mean old son of a bitch. I don't know why I didn't kill him sooner."

Jack heard something in RJ's voice and the way he was trying to catch his breath. He was bleeding badly and Jack suspected Josey had nicked a lung.

"Where you went wrong was taking Celeste along with you."

"Tell me," RJ agreed, struggling with each breath.

Josey had to have heard it, as well. She would be thinking that if she kept him talking…

Slowly, methodically, trying not to make a sound, Jack worked his way to a crouch. RJ's threats covered most any noise Jack had made.

"She was only after your money," Josey said. "I think you're better off without her."

"Uh-huh," RJ agreed. "You aren't going to suggest that I hook up with you, are you?" His laugh sounded as if he was underwater. "A woman who shot me not once, but twice?"

It wasn't until Jack was ready, the crowbar in his hand, that he saw a glint of metal and realized what RJ was holding to Josey's neck.

MCCALL HEARD VOICES and followed the low rumble down the hallway, then stopped just outside the room. She heard a man's voice, threatening to kill someone. Not her cousin Jack's voice. RJ's? She could only assume so.

Then she heard a woman's voice, scared, but in control. Josey Vanderliner? Where was Jack? Hadn't her grandmother said something about Josey going after Jack?

Leading with the weapon, McCall swept it across the room, taking in the scene and making a decision in that split second.

She'd heard everything said within the room and knew that RJ had some kind of weapon in his possession and planned to kill Josey. He sounded bad, but she knew that some men, especially those that took certain drugs, didn't die easily.

When she saw the knife RJ was holding to Josey's throat and her cousin Jack armed with a crowbar and ready to risk his life for this woman he called his wife, McCall didn't hesitate. She pulled the trigger.

Chapter Fourteen

It was chaos after that. Jack lunged forward even as RJ fell away from Josey, the shot to his head killing him instantly. Jack lunged, knocking the knife away from Josey's throat with the crowbar in the same instant McCall fired.

McCall heard her grandmother and Enid behind her. Heard the gasps. Jack was cradling Josey in his arms. Past them, McCall saw the hole in the rock wall and what appeared to be a mummified body lying in what was left of an old canvas tarp.

"It's Call Winchester," Enid cried. "Just like Alfred said."

McCall rounded up everyone and got them all back to the house, but not before she'd seen the expression on her grandmother's face as she looked at the mummified body behind the wall.

"I'm going to need statements from all of you," McCall announced after going to her patrol car and calling for backup, an ambulance and a coroner. "Starting with you. I assume you are Josey Vanderliner?"

Josey nodded.

"The rest of you just sit here quietly."

She took Josey down the hall to the first room McCall

had ever seen in this house just a month ago. It had taken a while, but her grandmother had accepted her as a Winchester.

Now, though, McCall was wondering if that was such a good thing, as she turned on the small tape recorder she'd retrieved from the patrol SUV.

"Tell me what happened here tonight," she said to Josey, and listened to the horrific story the young woman told, beginning with the murder of Ray Allan Evans Sr. in Palm City, California, and finishing with RJ holding a knife to her throat.

"I heard him confess to the murder of his father," McCall said, when Josey finished.

"Jack didn't know anything."

McCall smiled, thinking that her cousin was a Winchester. He knew something was up with this woman he'd picked up on the road. He'd helped her disguise her looks and given her a place to hide out. But she kept those thoughts to herself, secretly admiring Jack. There would be no charges of harboring a criminal since Josey Vanderliner had been a victim herself.

After that, McCall talked to Jack. "You knew there was a body behind that rock wall?"

"I thought it might just be a rumor."

She nodded. "Do you believe Enid that her husband, Alfred, killed Call Winchester?"

Jack grinned. Even though he was blond and blue-eyed, McCall saw the Winchester shining through. "I would have no idea."

She laughed, shaking her head. "The old gal got to you, too."

"I don't know what you're talking about," Jack said.

Enid repeated the same story she'd told on the way

to the house, swearing that Alfred had killed Call and that the only reason she'd kept silent all these years was that Alfred had threatened to kill her, as well.

McCall didn't believe a word of it.

Her grandmother looked pale by the time she came into the room. She sat down heavily, still holding her cane, appearing a little dazed.

"You must have wondered what happened to your husband," McCall said to her grandmother.

Pepper looked up, her eyes misting over. "I loved your grandfather. But it was a relief not to ever have to see him again because I *did* love him, and being around him hurt so badly, loving and hating him at the same time."

McCall was surprised at her grandmother's honesty. "What did you think happened to him?"

"You know this country. I thought eventually we'd find his body. I also thought he might have just taken off, put this life behind him. Your grandfather, well, he'd had other lives before I met him. I never knew where he got his money or how. But I did know that he liked the idea of reinventing himself. But to see him behind that wall…" Her voice broke. "Will the coroner be able to tell how he died?"

The question made the hair stand up on the back of her neck. "Probably not," McCall said slowly.

"I know what you're thinking, but I couldn't do that to him. I couldn't wall him up like that. Call was afraid of small spaces." She shuddered and wiped her eyes.

As McCall shut off the tape recorder, she didn't know if she believed her grandmother or not, but she wanted to.

JACK SANK DOWN into the bubbles, the water as warm and soothing as the feel of Josey's body tucked in front of him in the big clawfoot tub.

He pressed his face against hers, breathing in her scent, thanking God that she was all right.

They hadn't said much since McCall had allowed them to come upstairs and clean up. Their clothing would be taken as evidence, but since the acting sheriff had witnessed what had happened and had heard RJ confess to his father's murder, they had both been cleared.

"I thought I'd lost you," Jack said.

Josey cupped his face in her hands, her gaze taking him in as if memorizing every feature. "You aren't the only one. I was so worried that if the blow to the head didn't kill you then the one shot RJ got off did." There were tears in her eyes.

"You realize I'm not going to let you go."

She smiled almost ruefully. "Jack, we're virtually strangers."

"After what we've been through?" he scoffed, as he pulled her to him. "And we could have years to get to know each other better if you would say you'll really be my wife. I know this isn't much of a proposal—"

She touched her fingers to his lips. "This is the second best proposal I've ever had. The first was a few days ago on the highway."

He kissed her fingers, then removed them from his lips. "Well? Willing to take a chance with me?"

"One question. What is the Galaxy Corporation?" She looked chagrined. "I checked the registration in your car after you kept sneaking off in the middle of the night."

"It's a business I started that puts kids together with ranches. Oftentimes the kids are from the inner city or have been in trouble. I twist the arms of rich landowners, people who own large amounts of land but spend only a week or two actually at the ranch, to let the kids come work the place. Most ranch managers are fine with it as long as the kids are supervised. You can't believe what hard work and fresh air does for these kids."

She heard the love in his words for both ranching and kids. She should have known the Galaxy Corporation was something like that. "Did I mention how much I love you?"

"No." But his grin said he liked it. "I should tell you, though, I don't make any money doing this. Fortunately, it turns out that my mother's family had money. That helped get the corporation going so that now it is self-supporting."

Josey laughed. "I have a ton of money, more than I will ever spend. What?" she said, when she saw his expression.

"I don't like the idea of marrying someone who—"

"Can expand your kids-on-ranches program?" she asked.

He smiled at her. "Still—"

"The answer is yes. If you still want to marry me."

He looked into her beautiful green eyes and felt his heart soar like a hawk. "I don't want to spend another day away from you."

"You won't have to. My mother is safe. McCall checked for me. I will want to move her closer to wherever I'm going to be, that's all I need. Well, maybe not *all* I need." Desire sparked in her gaze. "I need you, Jack Winchester."

They made love in the tub, slowly, lovingly, a celebration of life. It wasn't until they were drying off that Jack broached the subject.

"My grandmother has asked me if I'd like to come back to the ranch at some point. I told her I would have to talk to you. I think everything that has happened has changed her. Well, at least a little. I know you probably have nothing but bad memories here and there is more than a good chance that my grandmother had something to do with my grandfather being put behind that stone wall, you know."

"Jack, you love this place and I love you."

"But after everything that's happened, not to mention the secrets that these walls have seen…"

She stepped to him, wondering at how fate and maybe a whole lot of luck had brought Jack Winchester into her life. She wanted to pinch herself. "I will be happy wherever you are."

He grinned as he reached for her, drawing her back into his arms. "I was thinking we should elope and go on a long honeymoon, then if you still mean it, maybe we'll come back here for McCall's wedding at Christmas and see how things go."

Josey kissed him, remembering that day on the highway when he'd come roaring up the hill in his old Cadillac convertible and had stopped for her. She remembered his handsome face beneath the brim of his Western hat. But what she remembered most was that boyish grin of his.

"Pepper said she would give me a section of land so we could build a house of our own," Jack said between kisses, as he carried her over to the bed. "We'll need lots of room for all those kids we're going to have together. I'm thinking a half dozen."

Josey laughed as he lowered her to the bed. She pulled him down. "It is definitely something we can negotiate," she said.

"I love you, Josey," Jack said, grinning. "Taking you for a wife was the smartest thing I ever did."

* * * * *

CLASSIFIED COWBOY

BY
MALLORY KANE

DID YOU PURCHASE THIS BOOK WITHOUT A COVER?
If you did, you should be aware it is **stolen property** as it was reported
unsold and destroyed by a retailer. Neither the author nor the publisher
has received any payment for this book.

All the characters in this book have no existence outside the imagination of
the author, and have no relation whatsoever to anyone bearing the same name
or names. They are not even distantly inspired by any individual known or
unknown to the author, and all the incidents are pure invention.

All Rights Reserved including the right of reproduction in whole or in part in
any form. This edition is published by arrangement with Harlequin Enterprises
II B.V./S.à.r.l. The text of this publication or any part thereof may not be
reproduced or transmitted in any form or by any means, electronic or mechanical,
including photocopying, recording, storage in an information retrieval system,
or otherwise, without the written permission of the publisher.

This book is sold subject to the condition that it shall not, by way of trade or
otherwise, be lent, resold, hired out or otherwise circulated without the prior
consent of the publisher in any form of binding or cover other than that in
which it is published and without a similar condition including this condition
being imposed on the subsequent purchaser.

® and ™ are trademarks owned and used by the trademark owner and/or its
licensee. Trademarks marked with ® are registered with the United Kingdom
Patent Office and/or the Office for Harmonisation in the Internal Market and
in other countries.

First published in Great Britain 2011
by Mills & Boon, an imprint of Harlequin (UK) Limited,
Eton House, 18-24 Paradise Road, Richmond, Surrey TW9 1SR

© Ricky R. Mallory 2010

ISBN: 978 0 263 88530 9

46-0611

Harlequin (UK) policy is to use papers that are natural, renewable and
recyclable products and made from wood grown in sustainable forests. The
logging and manufacturing processes conform to the legal environmental
regulations of the country of origin.

Printed and bound in Spain
by Blackprint CPI, Barcelona

Mallory Kane credits her love of books to her mother, a librarian, who taught her that books are a precious resource and should be treated with loving respect. Her father and grandfather were steeped in the Southern tradition of oral history and could hold an audience spellbound for hours with their storytelling skills. Mallory aspires to be as good a storyteller as her father.

Mallory lives in Mississippi with her computer-genius husband, their two fascinating cats and, at current count, seven computers. She loves to hear from readers. You can write her at mallory@mallorykane.com or via Harlequin Books.

For my Daddy, who loves reading my books.

Chapter One

"Hey! What the hell are you doing?" Texas Ranger Lieutenant Wyatt Colter slammed the door of his Jeep Liberty and crossed the limestone road in three long, crunching strides.

It had taken him longer than he'd intended to get here. Jonah Becker's spread was huge—as big as Comanche Creek, Texas, was small. Becker had twelve thousand acres. The entire city limits of Comanche Creek would fit in the southeast corner of the spread.

Right now, though, Wyatt was much more concerned with the northwest corner, where human bones had been unearthed by the road crew, which Becker had fought so hard to keep off his land.

This small piece of real estate was Wyatt's crime scene, and the owners of the two mud-spattered SUVs had breached it. Where in hell was the deputy assigned to guard the scene?

Just as he drew in breath to yell again, the growl of a generator cut through the damp night air. A large spotlight snapped on with an almost audible whoosh. He headed toward it.

"Ben, hit your light!" a kid yelled. His long-billed

baseball cap sat askew on his head, and his pants looked as if they were going to fall off any second.

A second light came on. Now that there were two lights, Wyatt could see more people. He had to get this under control now, or his crime scene would be totally contaminated.

"Hey!" Wyatt grabbed the kid's arm.

"Ow, dude. Watch the shirt."

"Where's the deputy sheriff?"

"I don't know." The kid shrugged and peered up at Wyatt from under his cap. "What's the nine-one-one?"

"The nine-one-one is you're stomping on my crime scene. Who the hell authorized you to be here?"

"My boss the hell did, dude."

Wyatt tightened his fist in the boy's shirt. "I'm not *dude*. I'm Lieutenant Wyatt Colter, Texas Ranger. Now, who authorized you to be here?"

The kid's eyes bugged out. "I, uh, I'm an anthropology major. This is part of my Forensics 4383 course. If we're lucky, we'll see signs of murder on the bones."

Wyatt's anger skyrocketed. He twisted his fist in the kid's shirt, showing him he didn't appreciate his comment.

"Those are human beings," he growled. "Show some respect."

"Y-yes, sir."

Forensics course. He should have guessed. The students were from Texas State. They were here with Dr. George *Something,* the head of the Forensics Department. He'd been called in by Wyatt's captain. And without asking, he'd brought a bunch of ghoulish kids with him.

No way was Wyatt going to allow students to stomp all over this scene. He had a very good reason for

wanting to make sure nothing—and that meant *nothing*—
went wrong.

This time.

As the head of the Texas Rangers Special Investigations Unit, Wyatt hadn't been surprised when he was
assigned to investigate a suspicious shallow grave containing badly decomposed remains. What had surprised
him was that his assignment was in this town.

The last time Wyatt had seen Comanche Creek, it
had been through a haze of pain and the stench of
failure as he was loaded into an ambulance two years
ago.

The idea that he was here now, to possibly identify
the body of the woman he'd failed to protect back then,
ignited a burning in his chest. He absently rubbed the
scar under his right collarbone.

"Where's your boss?" he snapped.

"Over there."

Wyatt looked in the general direction of the kid's
nod. There was a group of people standing inside the
tape, right in the middle of his crime scene. He caught
flashes of light as one of them took pictures.

"Which one?"

"In the hoodie."

Wyatt raised his arm an inch, nearly lifting the kid off
his feet. All three had on hooded sweatshirts. "Try
again."

"Ow, dude! I mean, sir. The black hoodie. Taking
pictures."

Wyatt let go of the kid and turned on his heel.

So the forensic anthropologist was going to be his
first problem. He was the only member of the task force
that Wyatt knew nothing about. He'd been appointed by
the captain.

Wyatt had chosen the rest of the team. He'd picked Reed Hardin, the sheriff of Comanche Creek, and Jonah Becker's daughter Jessie, because of their familiarity with the area. He had hopes that Ranger Sergeant Cabe Navarro's presence would ease the tension between the Caucasian and Native American factions in town.

He'd never worked with Ranger Crime Scene Analyst Olivia Hutton, but she had an excellent reputation, even if she was from back East.

It was the captain's idea to use an anthropologist from Texas State University. "They have one of the premier forensics programs in the United States," he'd told Wyatt.

"And besides, the governor's looking for positive press for the new forensics building and body farm Texas State just built."

Great. Politics. That was what Wyatt had thought at the time. And now his fears were realized. The professor was trying to take over his crime scene.

"Well, Dr. Mayfield," Wyatt muttered. "You might be the head of your little world, but you're in my world now."

As he strode over to confront the professor, he took in the circus the guy had brought with him. Two spotlight holders, plus four other students milling around. Add to that three rubberneckers drooling over his crime scene, and it equaled nine people. And that was eight— nearly nine, too many.

He stopped when the scuffed toes of his favorite boots were less than five inches from the professor's gloved hand and toeing the edge of a shallow, lumpy mud hole.

"Hey, Professor."

The guy had hung his camera around his neck and was now holding a high-intensity pocket flashlight. He shone it on Wyatt's tooled leather boots for a second, then aimed it at a white ruler with large numbers on it, propped next to what looked to Wyatt like a ridge of dirt.

"Okay," Wyatt muttered to himself, pulling his own flashlight out and thumbing it on. *En garde*. He crossed the other man's beam with his own. "Hey. Excuse me, *Professor?*" he said loud enough that heads turned from the farthest spotlight pole.

Wyatt heard drops of rain spattering on the brim of his Stetson as the guy thumbed off the flashlight and pushed his hoodie back. Wyatt spotted a black ponytail. *Oh, hell.* This was no gray-haired scholar with a tweed jacket and Mister Magoo glasses. He was a long-haired hippie type.

Just what he needed, along with everything else. He hoped the guy didn't have a *cause* that could interfere with this investigation.

The professor rose from his haunches and lifted his head.

"Hey to you." The voice was low and throaty.

Low, throaty and undeniably feminine. Wyatt blinked. It matched the pale, oval, feminine face, framed by a midnight-black crown of hair pulled haphazardly back into a ponytail.

He'd heard that voice, seen that face, wished he could touch that hair, before.

"Oh, hell," he whispered.

"Yes, you already said that."

Had he? Out loud? He clamped his jaw.

She turned to look at the kid with the spotlight. "Let's get that canopy back up. It's starting to rain."

Then she gestured to the two standing beside her. "Help them. No. Leave my kit here."

Then she tugged off her gloves and wiped a slender palm from her forehead back to the crown of her head. The gesture smoothed away the strands of hair that had been stuck to her damp skin, along with several starry droplets of rain.

Wyatt wasn't happy that he remembered how hard she had to work to tame that hair.

"I have to say, though, I'm really fond of *hey*. You're just as eloquent and charming as I remember," she said.

He felt irritation ballooning in his chest. He could show her eloquent and charming.

No. Screw it. She didn't deserve to see his charming side. Ever.

"The name listed on the task force was George Mayfield, from some university. *Not* Nina Jacobson," he informed her.

Her lips, which were annoyingly red, turned up. "Texas State. And that's right. It was supposed to be George Mayfield. Think of this as a last-minute change."

"I'm thinking of it as a long, thick string being pulled. Where's Spears?"

"Who?"

"The deputy who's supposed to be guarding my crime scene."

"Oh. Of course. Kirby." She smiled. "He's very helpful. I told him he could leave."

"And he *did?*"

She nodded.

He was about two seconds away from exploding. He lowered his head, and water poured off the brim of his Stetson, onto her pants.

"Oh!" she cried, brushing at them. "You did that on purpose."

"I wish," he said firmly, working hard not to smile. "I want these people out of here."

"No."

"What? Did you just say no?"

"That's right. *No.* I need them here. It's already started to sprinkle rain. If we're not careful, we're going to lose evidence."

That reminded him of what she had said about the canopy. "You took down the canopy? Have you totally contaminated the scene?"

"The canopy was collapsing. It was about to dump gallons of water right into the middle of the site."

He glowered at her. "Well, I'm not having a bunch of college brats stomping all over my crime scene. This is not a field trip. It's serious business. More serious than you may know."

Nina's pretty face stiffened, as did her sweatshirt-clad shoulders and back. "I am perfectly aware of how serious this find is. You, of all people, should understand just *how* aware I am."

Now his eyes were burning as badly as his chest. He squeezed them shut for a second and took a deep breath, trying to rein in his temper. "Get them out of here," he said slowly and evenly.

Nina's eyes met his and widened. To her credit, she lifted her chin. But she also swallowed nervously, and her hand twitched. She showed great control in not lifting it to clutch at her throat.

But then, she'd always showed admirable control, unlike her best friend, Marcie. It had baffled him how the two of them—so completely different—had ever become so close.

He held her gaze, not an easy task with those intimidating dark eyes, until she faltered and looked away.

He'd gotten to her, and he was glad. Last time they'd seen each other, she'd had the final word.

It's your fault. My best friend could be dead, and it's all your fault. You were supposed to protect her.

She stepped past him with feminine dignity and walked over to the kid whose pants were still drooping.

He heard him say, "Yes, ma'am." Then he heard her say, "Okay, guys. Let's put this equipment away. We're done for the night. We'll get started again in the morning."

Wyatt turned and found Nina staring at him. "They're done, period, Professor."

This time her chin went up and stayed up. "We'll see about that tomorrow, Lieutenant. And I'm not a professor. I'm a fellow."

Wyatt felt a mean urge and acted on it before his better judgment could stop him. He shook his head. "No, Professor, you're definitely *not* a fellow. I can attest to that."

"Go to hell," she snapped.

"Charming," he muttered.

She turned away, so quickly that her ponytail almost slapped her in the face, and followed the students to the SUVs.

Wyatt took off his hat and slung the water off the brim, ran a hand through his hair, then seated the Stetson back on his head. The rain had settled into a miserable drizzle, the drops falling just fast enough to seep through clothes and just slow enough to piss him off.

He went back to the Jeep and got a roll of crime-scene tape. Obviously one thickness of yellow tape around the perimeter wasn't warning enough. Not that twenty thicknesses would actually keep anyone from getting to the newly discovered grave, but the tape, plus the deputy, who was supposed to be here by midnight and guard the scene until morning, would be a deterrent.

At least for law-abiding folks.

By the time he was finished retaping the perimeter, three times over, most of the equipment was gone from the site and the two SUVs had loaded up and left.

He looked at his watch. Eleven o'clock. An hour until Sheriff Hardin's second deputy arrived. He debated calling Hardin and reaming him and his deputy for leaving the crime scene unguarded. But he could just as easily do that tomorrow morning.

He crossed his arms and surveyed the scene. At least the rain had stopped for the moment. He took off his hat again and slapped it against his thigh, knocking more water off the brim, then seated it back on his head.

Propping a boot on top of a fallen tree trunk, he stared down at the shallow, jagged hole in the ground, his mood deteriorating.

The rain had released more odors into the air. The fresh smell of newly turned earth was still there, seasoned with the sharp scent of evergreen and the fresh odor of rain-washed air. Still, he couldn't shake the sensation that he could smell death. Even if he knew bones didn't smell.

A frisson of revulsion slid through him, followed immediately by remorse. He propped an elbow on his knee and glared at the hole, as if he could bully it into giving up its secrets.

Are you down there, Marcie?

So now he was talking to dead people? He reined in

his runaway imagination sharply. If the remains unearthed here were those of his missing witness, Marcie
James, at least her family and friends would have
closure.

And he would know for sure that his negligence had
gotten her killed. As always, he marveled at his un-
realistic hope that somehow Marcie had survived the
attack that had nearly killed him. Still, he recognized
it for what it was—a last-ditch effort by his brain to
protect him from the truth.

She was dead and it was his fault.

He heard the voices arguing with his, like they
always did. His captain, assuring him that the Rangers'
internal investigation had exonerated him of any negligence. The surgeon who'd worked for seven hours to
repair the damage to his lung from the attacker's bullet,
declaring that he ought to be a dead man.

But louder than all of them was the one low, sexy
voice that agreed with him. The voice of Nina Jacobson.

*My best friend is gone. She could be dead, and it's
all your fault. You were supposed to protect her.*

He rubbed his chin and tried to banish her words
from his brain. He needed to put the self-recrimination
and regret behind him. Whether or not Marcie James's
death was his fault wasn't the issue now.

Identifying whoever was buried in this shallow hole
was. For a few moments, he got caught up in examining
the scene. This was the first time he'd seen it. The kids
had erected the canopy, so the area underneath was dark.

But Wyatt could imagine what had happened. The
road crew that was breaking ground for the controver-
sial new state route that cut across this corner of Jonah
Becker's land had brought in its bulldozer. It had dug
into this rise and unearthed the bones.

The discovery of the bodies—combined with the fact that the ME couldn't make a definitive identification of the age, sex or time of death of any of the victims—had reopened a lot of old wounds in Comanche Creek.

Marcie James's kidnapping and disappearance two years before had been the latest of several such incidents in the small community in recent years.

About three years prior to Marcie's disappearance, an antiques broker who had been accused of stealing Native American artifacts from Jonah Becker's land had disappeared, along with several important pieces. Everyone thought Mason Lattimer had skipped town with enough stolen treasure to set him up for life. But none of the pieces had ever surfaced.

Then, less than a year after Lattimer's disappearance, a Native American activist leader named Ray Phillips had vanished into thin air after a confrontation with Comanche Creek's city council and an argument with Jonah Becker.

One odd character vanishing was a curiosity. A second disappearance was noteworthy. But a third in five years?

That the third person was an innocent young woman scheduled to testify in a land-deal fraud case connected to a prominent local landowner cemented the connection between each of the bodies and that landowner—Jonah Becker.

It had taken less than twenty-four hours to rekindle the fires of suspicion, attacks and counterattacks in the small community of Comanche Creek. The warring factions that had settled into an uneasy truce—the Comanche community, the wealthy Caucasian element and activist groups on both sides—were suddenly back at each other's throats.

Wyatt straightened and took a deep breath as he surveyed his surroundings. The moisture in the air rendered it heavy and unsatisfying. He unwrapped a peppermint and popped it into his mouth. The sharp cooling sensation slid down his throat, and its tingle refreshed the air he sucked into his lungs.

Jonah Becker and his son Trace had both protested the state's acquisition of this corner of their property for a newly funded road, although the state of Texas had paid them. From what Wyatt could see of the area, the fact that they wanted to keep it despite the generous compensation was suspicious on its face.

To him, the land was barren and depressing. Anemic gray limestone outcroppings loomed overhead. The worn path that served as a road was covered with more limestone, crushed by cow and horse hooves into fine gravel, which sounded like glass crunching underfoot. Scrub mesquite and weeds were just beginning to put on new growth for spring.

Wyatt knew that in daylight he'd see the new blooms of native wildflowers, but a splash of blue and yellow here and there couldn't begin to compete with all that gray.

He pushed air out between his teeth, thinking longingly of his renovated loft near downtown Austin. The houseplants his sister had brought him for his balcony were much more to his liking than this scrub brush.

Just as he started to crouch down to take a look at the area Nina Jacobson had been photographing, he heard something. He froze, listening. Was it rain dripping off the trees? Or a night creature scurrying by?

Then the crunch of limestone from behind and to the left of him reached his ears.

In one swift motion he drew his Sig Sauer and whirled.

Chapter Two

"Whoa, cowboy," a low amused voice said.

Wyatt carefully relaxed his trigger finger.

Nina Jacobson. Son of a…

He blew out breath in a long hiss and holstered his gun. "I told you to get out of here."

"No. You told me to—and I quote—'get them out of here.'" She lifted her chin and stared at him defiantly. "I did that. For now."

He set his jaw. "Great. So we've established that you can follow directions. Good to know. Follow this one. *You* get out of here. Now."

She shrugged. "No can do. No transportation."

His gaze snapped to the empty road where the SUVs had been parked. Then back to her. First her face, then her left shoulder, which was weighed down by a heavy metal case, and on down to her right hand, where it rested on the telescoping handle of a small black weekend bag.

Oh, hell. He raised his gaze to meet hers.

Her eyes widened, and like before, he was grimly pleased that he could so easily intimidate her. He knew the effect of his glare. He'd seen it in the faces of suspects, subordinates and, occasionally, friends.

"Then you better start walking," he muttered, turning and propping his boot up on the fallen tree trunk again.

"Not a chance, cowboy. I'm staying with my site. I need to get some more pictures." Her hand moved from the bag's handle to the camera around her neck.

"It's not your site. It's my crime scene."

She didn't answer. Wyatt felt a cautious triumph. Maybe he'd won. Of course, he knew he was going to have to take her back to town, so she scored props for that. But there was no way she was going to turn his crime scene into a field trip for a bunch of students.

No way. He set his jaw and got ready to tell her to get into his Jeep.

"The ME said *he* thought there were two bodies." She spoke softly, but her tone got his attention.

Reluctantly, he slid his gaze her way. "*He* thought? Does that mean you don't?"

She stepped over the crime-scene tape and dropped to her haunches at the edge of the hole. He started to stop her, but she'd piqued his curiosity, so he followed her and crouched beside her, sitting back on his heels.

She slid her narrow, powerful flashlight beam over the clods of dirt and debris left by the road crew. After a couple of seconds he picked up on the pattern she was tracing.

Across, up, down and back. Then she moved the beam back to where she'd started and traced the pattern again.

"What? What are you showing me?" he asked.

"Look closer."

"If I look any closer, I'll fall in."

She laughed, a sexy chuckle that impacted him like a bullet straight to his groin. Surprised at his reaction, he shifted uncomfortably and swallowed hard to keep from groaning aloud.

"See this?" She shone the beam on her starting point and slid the light back and forth, over what looked like a ridge in the dirt. "That's a human thigh bone."

Adrenaline shot through him again. "That?" He pulled his own flashlight out of his pocket. "How can you tell?"

"I'm a forensic anthropologist. Bones are my business."

"What else can you tell about it? Is it male? Female? Child? Adult?"

She shook her head as she fished a brush out of her pocket. She telescoped the handle of the brush and leaned over to run the bristles across the surface of the bone. The dirt covering the bone was a mixture of dust and mud, so brushing at it didn't accomplish much.

"It's not a child. But making all those determinations is never quite as easy as the TV shows make it seem. Now look at this." She swept the beam of light across and up, then back across.

"Another thigh bone?"

"Go to the head of the class, cowboy." The beam moved again.

"And a third," he said, tamping down on his excitement—and his dread. One of those bones could be Marcie's. "Three thigh bones? Everybody has two, so was the ME right? There are two bodies in here?"

"Not so fast. These closest two may be similar in size, but the three femurs are all different," she said, with the same lilt in her voice that he was trying to keep out of his.

"Three? You're saying they're from three different people?" He looked at her, dread mixing with excitement under his breastbone. *Three sets of bones.* Three people gone missing in the past five years. Was it going to be that easy? "That's three different thigh bones, laid out like that?"

She met his gaze, her dark eyes snapping. "Yeah. Exactly. Look at that placement. They're crisscrossed in a star pattern. I suppose it could be chance that they ended up like that." He shook his head, but she wasn't looking at him. She had turned back to the bones and was brushing at them again. She gasped.

"What is it?"

"I think this largest bone has a piece of pelvis attached. That could definitely tell us if it's a male or female." She leaned a fraction of an inch farther forward and brushed at the far end of the bone. "Damn it," she muttered.

"What now?"

"The ground's too wet. I'm going to have to wait to unearth the bones."

"I guess you can't just pick them up."

She laughed shortly. "No. There might be something attached to them—clothes, another bone, a piece of jewelry. No. I have to be very careful to avoid destroying evidence."

"But you're absolutely sure the three bones are different."

She sat back on her haunches and tilted her head to meet his gaze. "Absolutely."

"Are you thinking…" He couldn't finish the sentence. He needed to know if one of those bones belonged to Marcie James.

Dear Lord, he hoped not.

Nina's face closed down immediately, and he saw a shudder ripple along her small frame. She needed to know, too. He understood that. But she had a very different reason.

She shook her head. "I can't say yet." Her voice had taken on a hard edge—the outward manifestation of an obvious inner struggle between her love for her friend and her professional detachment.

She hissed in frustration as she collapsed the brush handle, wiped the bristles against her jeans-clad thigh and then put the brush in her forensics kit.

"I need to build a platform so I can get to the bones without disturbing the site any more than it already has been." She informed him. "I can't rule out the possibility that this is a Native American burial site."

"Burial site? Are the bones that old?"

She shook her head. "I don't think so. I'll need to clean them and test them to be sure. But the layout of the land around here is consistent with the places the Comanche chose for their sacred burial grounds. I didn't see the site before excavation started, but the level of rise and the general shape suggest the possibility."

Wyatt grunted. He'd thought the same thing as soon as he'd gotten his first glimpse of the scene. The thought had gone out of his head once he'd seen the kids milling around.

"As soon as I can study the bones, I can give you the sex and race. However, to estimate the time of death requires more testing and equipment. Fresh bones will glow when exposed to ultraviolet light. The fluorescence fades from the outside in over time. Still, my opinion right now is that these bones are recent. As soon as I get them cleaned up, I can look at them under my portable UV lamp. Then I'll take samples for DNA analysis."

Wyatt's chest felt tight. There were only a few reasons that DNA would do her any good. "For a positive ID," he said quietly.

Nina nodded solemnly. "For a positive ID."

Both of them knew whose DNA they were thinking of.

He stared down at the three ridges. "So, Professor, I guess you need your students and their spotlights to help you get the platform built and extract the bones."

"That's right, cowboy." Her eyes glittered with triumph as she stood and pulled a cell phone out of her pocket.

He stood, too. "Tomorrow."

"Tonight. You just agreed that I need them." She flipped the phone open.

"Tomorrow." He folded his hand over hers, closing the phone. A funny sensation tingled through his fingers. For a second he thought the phone had vibrated.

She looked at their hands, then up at him. "Give me one good reason why not tonight. I told you I need some more pictures, and I do not want anybody disturbing the bones."

"Because I'll be overseeing every stick, every bone, every clod of dirt that's removed, and I need some sleep."

"Speaking of clods," she muttered, pulling her hand away from his. "It's dangerous to delay. This rain could turn into a deluge and bury the bones again. Any disturbance of the site increases the chances for contamination."

A pair of headlights appeared, coming around the curve beyond a thick stand of evergreens.

Wyatt checked his watch. "That's Deputy Tolbert. I didn't realize it was midnight already. That settles it. He's here to guard the site tonight. He'll make sure it's not disturbed. You and I are heading into town."

"I'll stay with the deputy."

"No, you won't."

"But the weather—"

"No more rain in the forecast."

"I need to—"

"I said no." He didn't raise his voice, but there went her eyes again, going as wide as saucers.

He gave a small shrug. "You'll get more done in the daylight."

He could practically see the steam rising from her ears, but she pressed her lips together and nodded once, briefly. He knew she'd been informed that as the senior Texas Ranger on the task force, he was in charge, even of the civilian members.

"Fine," she snapped. "Can I at least call my team and let them know what I've found and what I'm going to need in the morning?"

"Be my guest," he said, putting his hand to the small of her back, his gentle but firm pressure urging her away from the crime scene.

They stepped over the yellow tape as Deputy Tolbert's white pickup rolled to a stop and he jumped out.

"Deputy." Wyatt held out his hand.

Tolbert ignored Wyatt's hand and eyed Nina appreciatively.

Wyatt watched him with mild distaste. He'd sized up Shane Tolbert the first time he'd met him, over two years ago. The designer jeans and expensive boots, plus what Wyatt's sister called *product* in his hair, had pegged him as a player back then, and from what Wyatt could see, nothing had changed.

"Nina Jacobson. Gorgeous as ever. I didn't know you were going to be here." Tolbert touched the brim of his hat, then glanced sidelong at Wyatt. "Lieutenant Colter." His voice slid mockingly over Wyatt's rank.

Wyatt stopped his fists from clenching. Tolbert grated on his nerves, but Reed Hardin had hired him, and the sheriff seemed to be a good judge of character.

Tolbert and Marcie James had dated, although they'd broken up by the time Marcie was tapped to testify. It didn't stretch Wyatt's imagination to figure out that Tolbert was one of the people who blamed Wyatt for Marcie James's death.

"So, Nina," Tolbert continued, "what did you find? Doc Hallowell thought there might be two bodies in there."

Wyatt shifted so that he was a half step between Nina and Tolbert. "She'll be back in the morning with her team to start examining the evidence." He felt rather than heard Nina take a breath, so he spoke quickly. "We're heading to town. I'll be back here by nine in the morning, if not before. You know the drill. Don't let anyone close except Dr. Jacobson and her team. Call me if anything happens."

Tolbert's eyes narrowed. "I do know the drill, *Lieutenant*. Happy to oblige."

Wyatt directed Nina toward his Jeep. He'd talk to Sheriff Hardin first thing in the morning about the burr under Tolbert's saddle. If Shane Tolbert was going to be a problem, Wyatt needed to know.

"I DON'T LIKE leaving the burial site unguarded all night," Nina said.

Texas Ranger Lieutenant Wyatt Colter took a sharp right onto the main road into Comanche Creek. "The *crime scene* is guarded. Or did you miss your buddy Deputy Tolbert? He was the one in the black cowboy hat."

"I don't trust him."

Wyatt's head turned slightly, and she felt his piercing eyes studying her. It took a lot of willpower to meet his gaze. Finally he turned his attention back to the road. "Any particular reason?"

"Other than how mean he was to Marcie when they were dating?"

"They dated for how long? A year?"

"Something like that. Maybe eighteen months. Long enough for Marcie to figure out what kind of man he was."

"And what kind of man is that?"

"A loser. A coward. An abuser."

"He hurt her?" A dangerous edge cut through Wyatt's voice.

Nina bit her lip. She shouldn't have gone that far. She really didn't have any proof of abuse. Marcie had never admitted any specific mistreatment. "She just said he could be mean."

"Mean how?" He slowed the Jeep as they passed the high school and turned onto Main Street.

She should have known better. Wyatt Colter wasn't the kind of man to dismiss anything he heard or saw without sticking it under his personal microscope. Right now he was focusing that scope on Shane Tolbert, and she understood why.

Tolbert was guarding *his* crime scene. Wyatt considered it his duty to know everything there was to know about the deputy.

Nina wasn't sure how or why she had suddenly become an expert on Wyatt Colter. But she was definitely not comfortable with her newfound insight.

Time to change the subject. "I'm supposed to have a room at the Bluebonnet Inn."

In the watery glow from the streetlights, Nina saw Wyatt's jaw flex. She almost smiled. He was upset because she'd deflected his question.

"With your students?" he asked.

"No. They're staying on campus at West Texas Community College. The college made arrangements for us to have one of their chemistry labs as a temporary forensics lab, so we don't have to drive for an hour each way to the Ranger lab each time we need something. That's why I was so late getting out to the site. I was setting up the equipment."

"Is a community college lab going to be good enough? I can arrange for a driver—"

"It's really nice. Brand-new. All the chemicals a girl could ask for, as well as sterile hoods and some very nice testing equipment. Obviously there will be specific sophisticated tests that can be done only at a forensics lab, but for the most part, it's got all the comforts of home." She smiled.

For a few seconds, Wyatt didn't speak. "So you're the only one who rated a hotel room?"

"Perks of the job," she murmured as he pulled into a parking place in front of the Bluebonnet Inn, a two-story Victorian with double wraparound porches and sparkling clean windows. It was one of the original buildings in town. "Wow. Betty Alice has really fixed up this place."

He didn't comment, just turned off the engine and reached for the door.

"You don't have to—" *Oh.* For a second she'd thought he was getting out to walk her to the door. But that wasn't it. His jaw action earlier hadn't been because she'd changed the subject. "Don't tell me you're staying here, too? Well, isn't that…convenient." She sighed. She'd finagled herself onto this project, knowing she'd have to put up with Wyatt Colter. Relishing the opportunity.

He'd been so arrogant two years ago, pushing Marcie to testify against Jonah Becker and assuring her that she didn't have to worry. That as long as she was under the protection of the Texas Rangers, she'd be safe.

Marcie had trusted him. Everyone had. And no wonder. Not only did the very large, reassuring shadow of the Texas Rangers envelop the entire state of Texas and everyone in it, but Wyatt Colter himself exuded competence, assurance, *safety*.

It was the first thing Nina had noticed about him when she'd met him back then.

From his honed jaw and the cleft in his chin to his confident, deceptively casual stance, from his intense blue eyes to the long, smooth muscles that rippled with reined-in power beneath his clothes, he was the perfect personification of the Texas Rangers. And as long as he was guarding Marcie, nothing could possibly happen to her. He'd promised her.

Well, something had happened.

And it was Wyatt Colter's fault. Her best friend was gone—likely dead—because he'd never once doubted his ability to keep her safe.

When Nina had called in a favor to get on this task force, she hadn't thought any further than her determination to be a thorn in Lieutenant Colter's side and to find justice for Marcie. She hadn't bargained on spending this much time this close to him.

Still, at least this way she could keep an eye on him.

While Nina's thoughts whirled, Wyatt got out of the Jeep and headed for the front porch. As he climbed up the steps, it started raining again. He removed his hat and slapped it against his thigh, then glanced back at her before disappearing inside.

She could read his thoughts as easily as if they were printed in a cartoon bubble above his head.

Open your own door. No double standard for Wyatt Colter. If she wanted in on the task force in place of George Mayfield, then she should expect to be treated like him or any other member of the team.

Little did he know, that was fine with her. Gestures like opening doors, holding seats, paying for dinner all came with strings attached. And Nina didn't like strings.

She was here in an official capacity. She *expected* to be treated like any other member of the task force. While it was true that there was a chance that the site could turn out to be archeologically significant, Nina wanted nothing more than to find out what had happened to Marcie.

Well, that and to keep an eye on Colter. Not that she thought he was less than honest and aboveboard. She just didn't want to take any chances. This find could remove the haunting grief that had enveloped her for the past two years.

Marcie and she had been paired as roommates at Texas State, and despite their very different personalities, they'd become fast friends. Marcie had been there for Nina when Nina's father died and when her brother was killed in combat in Iraq. She'd been Nina's family. There was no way Nina was going to pass up this chance to find out what had happened to her friend.

The town was split. Half of the people thought Marcie had been killed. Her kidnapping had never resulted in a ransom notice. She and her mysterious kidnapper had just disappeared.

The other half figured she had got cold feet and arranged the kidnapping herself to get out of testifying against Jonah Becker, one of the most powerful men in the state of Texas. But if Marcie were alive, why hadn't she contacted anyone in all this time?

Of course, Nina wanted Marcie to be alive and well,

but there was one huge obstacle to that theory. If Marcie had arranged her own kidnapping, that meant she was responsible for shooting Texas Ranger Wyatt Colter.

And Marcie wouldn't have done that. Nina couldn't see her shooting anyone. Not even to save her own skin.

Through the glass front door of the Bluebonnet Inn, Nina saw Wyatt glance back toward her. With a wry smile, Nina opened the passenger door and climbed out, leaving her forensics kit on the floorboard at her feet. She hefted her weekend bag by its handles.

Wyatt was disappearing up the dark polished stairs by the time she got to the front desk.

"Hey there," the round-faced woman said on a yawn. She'd obviously been asleep until Wyatt had slammed the front door. "I'm Betty Alice Sadler. Welcome to the Bluebonnet Inn. Can I help you?"

"Nina Jacobson. I have a reservation. I apologize for getting here so late."

"That's all right," the woman said, tapping the keyboard with her index finger. "I'm always happy to have a guest. Let me just look here."

Nina sighed. "Oh, I forgot. The reservation is in the name of George Mayfield, Texas State University Anthropology Department."

"Ah. Of course." Betty Alice eyed her curiously. "This is about those bodies on Jonah Becker's place." In Betty Alice's Texas drawl, the word *bodies* sounded sinister. "Will Mr. Mayfield be joining you?"

"No." Nina didn't see any need to explain.

However, Betty Alice obviously thought she deserved an explanation. She waited for a few seconds, hoping to get one, but Nina just stood there calmly.

"Well," Betty Alice drawled finally and hit a few more keys. "I'll need your ID."

Nina handed over her driver's license and glanced at her watch. Betty Alice yawned again and sped up the check-in process. Apparently she was ready to get back to sleep.

She handed Nina a room key—a real key, to room 204 on the second floor. "If I'd known you would be here instead of—" Betty Alice glanced at the computer screen "—Mr. Mayfield, I could have given you the pink room. I keep it for my female guests."

Nina winced inwardly as she pictured how the *pink room* would be decorated. She didn't need a pink room. She just needed a room. She was exhausted, and eight o'clock was going to come very early.

"That's very nice of you, but I'm sure room two-oh-four will be fine. Do you have Wi-Fi?"

Betty Alice beamed at her. "We surely do. My niece hooked it up—or whatever you do with Wi-Fi. *And* it's complimentary."

Nina thanked her and headed up the stairs.

"Say, Nina Jacobson."

She turned around to find the woman pointing a finger at her. "I thought I recognized you. You were Marcie's friend. I remember you were staying here when she disappeared and that Texas Ranger got shot."

"Yes, that's true," Nina said, forcing a smile.

"Oh, my goodness." Betty Alice's hand flew to her mouth. "I remember him, too. Lieutenant Colter was the one who got shot."

Nina nodded, doing her best to suppress a yawn.

"Oh, honey, run along. Here I am, just talking away, and you're asleep on your feet." Betty Alice shooed her toward the stairs and turned around to head back to her own room behind the desk.

When Nina got to the second floor, Wyatt was holding a full ice bucket in one hand and pushing his key into the lock of room 202 with the other.

He turned his head and his offhand glance morphed into annoyance as his eyes lit on the key in her hand.

"That's right," she said, brandishing the key with a gaiety she didn't feel. "Howdy, neighbor."

He scowled. "Good night," he said and went into his room and closed the door.

"Good night, cowboy," she muttered.

After an ineffectual attempt to get mud off her black hoodie and jeans, and a defeated glance at her favorite work boots, which were beyond any help she could give them tonight, Nina took a hot shower.

By the time she had slipped on a bright red camisole and panties and was ready for bed, her mind was racing with her impressions of the burial site.

She settled into bed with both pillows behind her back and the pad and pen she always kept in her purse. She rested her pad on her bent knee and wrote the date, the location and her name. Beneath that she jotted a note to herself.

Ref: report of State Highway Dept regarding unearthing of remains. Attach copy.

Then she let her thoughts float freely. She'd type up an official report later on her laptop, but right now what mattered was getting her first impressions down before she lost them.

Incredible find. Texas Ranger Lieutenant Wyatt Colter has claimed it as his crime scene, but it's likely to be of archeological significance.

Appearance consistent with indigenous burial grounds.

Important to note that condition of the find suggests a possible hoax. Three unique thigh bones, laid out in a star pattern. Accidental? Or placed by someone? All three femurs appear to be of recent origin. The largest is certainly male. But I need to measure and examine all three to estimate gender.

Nina stopped and closed her eyes. Bones were her business, but that didn't mean she was immune to the idea of handling remains that could turn out to be those of her best friend.

A wave of nausea slithered through her, and her eyes pricked with tears. What if one of the bones was Marcie's?

Marcie. Sweet and kind, but impulsive, and maybe even a little bit self-destructive. Definitely not the best judge of character.

"Oh, Marcie, what did you get yourself into?"

Chapter Three

Nina shook off the renewed grief over losing her friend. She couldn't afford to get emotional. She needed to concentrate on the bones.

She reached for her camera and viewed the flash photos she'd taken.

She tried to view the three thigh bones in close-up, but the exposures were too dark. She'd have to send them to Pete, the graphics expert at the university, to have them corrected and enhanced.

She glanced at her laptop. She ought to send the photos tonight so Pete could get to work on them as soon as he got in tomorrow. The sooner she got the enhanced photos back, the sooner she could make more specific determinations of age, sex and time of death.

Still, in the morning she'd be able to look at the bones themselves. She glanced at her watch and yawned. Tonight it was more important to get her first impressions down on paper.

She continued writing.

Bones too covered with dirt and mud to tell much more. Already dark when we arrived at the site at 8:30 p.m.

History. (See fax from Ranger captain.) Two days ago road workers were breaking ground for a state route on land owned by Jonah Becker when they unearthed bones, which the foreman suspected were human.

The foreman stopped the ground breaking and called Sheriff Reed Hardin, who called the county medical examiner. The ME found the bodies "too decomposed and mixed up to identify" (i.e., skeletonized) and requested help from forensics experts.

Because of the state of decomposition and the fact that three people have disappeared from the area in the past five years, Sheriff Hardin called in the Texas Rangers, who were responsible—

Nina paused, then crossed out that last word.

—who were involved in one of the disappearances. The Rangers put together a Special Investigations Task Force.

Nina paused, clicking the cap of the ballpoint pen she held. If the site was a Native American burial ground…

Her pulse jumped slightly. She couldn't deny her excitement. New burial sites were rare. A junior professor getting a chance to be the principal on such a find was even rarer.

In fact, she wasn't sure why Professor Mayfield had acquiesced so easily when she'd asked him to let her take his place on this task force. Maybe he already knew the site wasn't old.

That thought gave her mixed feelings. She'd love to have a significant find with her name on it. On the other hand, she couldn't forget the real reason she'd requested to be on this task force. That could be Marcie lying out there. If it was, then she deserved a proper burial, as well as closure.

Nina clicked the pen angrily. Who was she kidding? If her best friend had been murdered, she deserved *vengeance*.

Nina twisted her thick black hair in her left fist and lifted it off her neck. Glancing down at the pad, she saw that she'd written *vengeance* and then underlined it three times.

She crossed through it and took a deep breath. *Okay, Dr. Jacobson. Get it together. You're a professional.*

Plan: Tomorrow students will construct a plywood platform from which we can extract the bones with as little disturbance of the site as possible. Until I can determine whether the site or any part of it is of archeological significance (a historic burial site), I am compelled to treat the entire site thusly.

First order of business: take samples of the three femurs for physical examination, dating and DNA extraction.

Nina chewed on the cap of the pen and read back over what she'd written, but she found it hard to concentrate. At least she'd gotten her first impressions down. She could add to it tomorrow.

She set the pad and pen on the bedside table, set her cell phone alarm for 7:00 a.m., and then turned off the lamp and sank down into the warm bed. But light from a streetlamp reflected off her camera lens. She turned her back to it.

It would take only five minutes to transfer the photos and send them.

"Tomorrow," she whispered to herself.

Tonight, the camera taunted her.

Sighing, she threw back the covers and turned on the lamp. She retrieved her laptop and booted it up, then grabbed the camera and transferred the photos into an e-mail and sent it off to Pete.

By the time she was done, her arms and legs were thoroughly chilled. She turned off the lamp and dove under the covers.

Despite how tired she felt, it took her a long time to fall asleep. To her surprise, it wasn't thoughts of the burial site or the identities of the remains buried there that kept her awake.

The image that seemed burned into the insides of her eyelids was of Wyatt Colter lying in a matching double bed not forty feet from hers, his broad bare shoulders and torso dark against the white sheets. Was he also having trouble sleeping?

Even if he was, she doubted it was because he was picturing her lying in bed this close to him. More likely, if he were fantasizing about her, it was a dream of watching her mud-covered backside recede as he ran her out of town.

She sniffed and squeezed her eyes shut. She had no idea why she couldn't stop thinking of Wyatt Colter. Probably she was just too tired to concentrate on anything rational, and too excited about the case to calm her mind for sleep.

She concentrated on her breathing, counting each breath until she dozed off. But as soon as sleep

claimed her, an image of Wyatt rose in her vision—
in boxers. In briefs.

In nothing.

"Stop it, Nina!" she growled as she turned over and
pounded the pillow again.

Finally her breathing relaxed, and her brain began
to banish the sensual but disturbing images.

A SHRILL RING pierced Nina's eardrums.

She moaned and squeezed her eyes shut. It wasn't her
phone. That wasn't the theme from *Raiders of the Lost
Ark*.

Which one of her neighbors had gotten a new, hide-
ously loud tone? She pushed her nose a little deeper
under the covers.

"Colter."

The low, commanding voice reverberated through
her. Her eyes sprang open.

Colter. Bones. Marcie. Her thoughts raced. Had
something happened at the site?

She sat up and kicked off the covers, squinting at the
clock on the bedside table.

Four o'clock in the morning. She'd been asleep for
over three hours. It didn't feel like it.

"Son of a… No. You stay there." Wyatt's voice,
even through the connecting door, was deep, harsh,
commanding.

She held her breath listening, her heart fluttering
beneath her breastbone. She pressed her hand against
her chest.

Fear? No. She wasn't afraid of Wyatt Colter. Maybe
a little intimidated by his larger-than-life presence. But
her reaction was definitely not fear. Now, if she were a

criminal, she'd be afraid. Or a subordinate who'd screwed up.

"Have you called Hardin?"

Something *had* happened.

She shot up out of bed, grabbed her jeans and pulled them on, balancing on tiptoe as she zipped and fastened them. She didn't even bother combing her hair, merely twisted it into a ponytail as she thrust her feet into her muddy work boots.

"Call him. I'll be right there!" Wyatt's voice brooked no argument.

Just as she pulled the Velcro straps on her boots tight, Wyatt's door slammed. The picture hanging over her headboard and the glass lamp on the bedside table rattled.

She shoved her arms into her hoodie and threw open the door to her room. Wyatt's broad shoulders were just disappearing down the stairs.

"Hey, cowboy. Wait for me!" she called.

His head cocked, but he didn't slow down.

She started out, then realized she didn't have her camera. It took only a fraction of a second to decide. If she went back, he'd be gone.

She vaulted down the stairs two at a time, landing at the bottom with a huff and a scattering of dried mud.

"What the hell are you doing?" Wyatt growled. "Go back to bed."

Betty Alice poked her head out from the door behind the desk in time to hear Wyatt's words. Her eyes sparkled, and she snorted delicately.

Nina's face heated, and she sent Betty Alice a quelling glance. To someone who didn't know what was going on, she supposed Wyatt's words had sounded suggestive.

"Go on." Wyatt sounded like he was shooing a disobedient dog.

"Not a chance, cowboy. Where are we going? Did something happen at the site?"

"*We* aren't going anywhere."

"You can't keep me away from my bones," she declared pugnaciously.

"*Your* bones?"

Now Betty Alice's pupils were dark circles surrounded by white.

"It might be your crime scene, Lieutenant, but I'm the forensic anthropologist. They're my bones." Nina lifted her chin. "That was Deputy Tolbert, wasn't it? Something happened at the site."

Wyatt blew air out in a hiss between his teeth and tossed a peppermint into his mouth.

"Got another one of those? I didn't get a chance to brush my teeth."

He glowered at her, but she kept her expression carefully neutral. Finally he dug into his pants pocket and pulled out a cellophane-wrapped disk and tossed it toward her. She swiped it out of the air with no effort.

"Thanks," she said. "I'll pay you back." She was pretty sure she heard another growl as he spun on his boot heel and headed out the front door.

WYATT DIDN'T SAY a word on the drive out to the crime scene. He was in no mood to deal with Nina Jacobson. Against his better judgment—almost against his will— he cut his eyes sideways. They zeroed in on that red lacy thing that peeked out from under her half-zipped hoodie.

The red lacy thing and the creamy smooth flesh that it barely covered. He growled under his breath as his body reacted to what his eyes saw.

Snapping his gaze back to the dirt road, he clenched his jaw and lifted his chin. *Forget what Nina Jacobson is or isn't wearing,* he warned himself.

He had enough on his plate right now. If there was one thing he knew, it was how to separate his personal and professional life.

Yeah. Separate them so well that one of them no longer existed. His awareness turned to the slight weight of the star on his chest. That star, with its unique engraving and aged patina, represented who he was.

Wyatt Colter, Texas Ranger.

And as he knew very well, there was no place in a Ranger's life for personal complications.

"Would you at least tell me what Shane said?"

Nina's voice broke into his thoughts. It was breathy and low—sultry. Like a hot summer Texas storm. Like her.

He didn't bother to answer her.

Shane Tolbert had sounded groggy, embarrassed and angry all at the same time. But that was nothing compared to how he was going to sound—and feel—once Wyatt had ripped him a new one, right before he did the same for Sheriff Reed Hardin.

Wyatt's first act upon hearing about the discovery of the bodies less than forty-eight hours ago had been to demand two guards on the crime scene twenty-four hours a day. Sheriff Hardin had countered that one guard per eight-hour shift was plenty. "Nobody's bothered the scene," the sheriff had said. "There were a few folks who drove up there on the first day, right after the road crew discovered the bones. Most notably Daniel Taabe and a couple of his cronies, who wanted to know if what the road crew had unearthed was a historical burial site. But after that…nothing. My deputies can handle things just fine."

Wyatt had requested the extra men from his captain, but the captain had sided with the sheriff.

Now, as he'd known he would be, Wyatt had been proven right. If there had been two men guarding the site, this wouldn't have happened.

He roared up to within a few feet of the crime-scene tape and slammed on the brakes.

To his amusement, Nina uttered a little squeak when the anti-locking brake system stopped the Jeep in its tracks.

He jumped out, leaving the engine running. He stalked over to Sheriff Hardin's pickup, where Deputy Tolbert was sitting on the tailgate, with Doc Hallowell and the sheriff hovering over him.

"Need to go to the hospital?" Sheriff Hardin was asking as Wyatt walked up.

Doc Hallowell shook his head. He reached inside the black leather bag sitting beside Tolbert.

"Sheriff," Wyatt said.

"Lieutenant." Hardin didn't look at him. He pointed a pocket flashlight at Tolbert's head. "That's a nasty cut."

"I'm going to stitch it right here," Doc Hallowell said, searching in his bag, "as soon as I can dig out my suture kit."

A doctor making a house call or a crime-scene call. Wyatt shook his head. Small towns. They were a mystery to him.

"What happened?" Nina asked from behind him.

Wyatt wished he could pick this damn crime scene up and transport it to a secure location. He desperately needed some time alone here. Just him and the crime scene, and maybe Olivia Hutton, the top-notch crime scene analyst. He could use her expertise, but while she was available to him as part of the task force, she hadn't been called in yet, since this was classified as a cold case. He made a mental note to call her and ask her opinion.

Tolbert looked up at Nina sheepishly. "Got myself conked over the head. I heard something and went to investigate. I'm thinking there were at least two of them. One to distract me and the other to bash my skull in." He winced as Doc Hallowell poured alcohol on the gash on the back of his head. "Ow! I guess I'm lucky I've got a thick skull."

From the corner of his eye, Wyatt saw the thinly disguised look of disgust on Nina's face. She *really* didn't like Tolbert.

"Doc," Wyatt said. "can I look at that cut before you start working on it?" He pulled out his own high-powered flashlight and shone it on the deputy's skull.

The gash looked fresh, of course. And it was edged by an inflamed strip of scalp, which disappeared into Tolbert's hair. As far as he could tell, it had been made with a honed-edged instrument, like the edge of a plate or a board, or maybe even a hatchet, if it wasn't too finely sharpened.

The doctor had trimmed the hair around the gash, and now he was stitching it, quickly and neatly. Wyatt watched with casual interest as he tied the stitches. He counted seven.

"Any idea what they hit you with?" Wyatt asked.

Tolbert shook his head. "No clue. Something with an edge. Maybe the back side of an ax. You see how much it bled."

Wyatt gestured to Nina. "Professor, can you get a couple of photos of the wound?"

"Hey," Tolbert said, ducking his head. "It's humiliating enough without a record of it."

Nina snapped a couple of shots.

"I need it for a match with a possible weapon," Wyatt explained.

"Stay still, Shane," the doctor said. "I'm almost done."

"They just hit you once?" Wyatt asked.

"Ow, Doc!" Tolbert exclaimed, blinking as Nina's camera flashed. "Are you done yet?"

Hardin took a step backward. "Lieutenant Colter? Looks like Doc's getting Shane fixed up. Why don't we check out the crime scene?"

Wyatt looked at Tolbert, then at Hardin. He had a lot more questions for the deputy, but the sheriff obviously wanted him at the crime scene—or away from Tolbert.

"You mean nobody has checked out the damage yet?" Wyatt replied.

When Wyatt turned to head over to the burial site, he saw that Nina was there. As he watched, she crouched down to sit on her haunches—the exact position she'd been in earlier.

Only this time he knew who she was. How could he have thought she was a middle-aged, sedentary professor of anthropology? Granted, it had been raining and she'd been cloaked by that oversize black hooded sweatshirt. But looking at her now in the same position, he couldn't believe he'd mistaken the feminine curve of her back and behind for a male's.

She pushed the hood of her sweatshirt off her head and shone the beam of her high-powered flashlight along the ground.

By the time they walked up beside her, she had sat back on her heels, her face reflecting disgust and anger.

"One of my bones is missing," she said.

Chapter Four

"Which one?" Wyatt burst out. "Which bone is missing?"

Nina shook her head. "Whoever did this made a mess. Tromped all over the site. But I think it's the largest one. The one that had a piece of pelvis attached to it." She looked up at him, her dark eyes snapping.

Wyatt shone his flashlight over the ground. "Can you get casts of these prints?" he asked the sheriff.

Hardin crouched down and studied the ground. "It's pretty wet, and he was slipping in the mud. But yeah."

"You're sure?" Wyatt asked.

Hardin nodded. "Deputy Spears can handle it."

"Make sure he finds the sharpest print," said Wyatt.

Hardin frowned. "Look, Lieutenant, if you want to call in your own crime scene investigator—"

"No!" Nina exclaimed.

Wyatt's gaze snapped to her.

"Sheriff, if your deputy can cast the prints over there, I'd appreciate it." She pointed. "I *really* don't want anyone else trampling the site."

Wyatt shook his head. "Professor—"

Nina stood. "First of all, I'm a certified crime scene investigator, so *I* can do it if you insist. But I have no doubt that Sheriff Hardin and his men know what they're doing. Let them cast the prints over there while I extract the other two bones. I'll process this area for trace evidence while I'm at it."

It probably couldn't hurt for her to handle the crime scene. And the boot prints at the edge of the shallow hole were clearer, anyhow. He nodded at Hardin.

Beside him, Nina sighed in obvious relief.

The sheriff rose, dusting his hands against each other, then propping them on his hips.

"Can we get them done now?" Wyatt asked.

This was why he didn't like small towns. Everything moved at a snail's pace. This was a crime scene— a major crime scene. It might tell them of the disappearances that had haunted Comanche Creek for the past several years. It might hold evidence of what had happened to Marcie James.

And yet the people who could provide the answers— the doctor, the sheriff, the deputies—seemed to operate with a "we'll get around to it" mentality.

Hardin sent Wyatt a hard glance. "Can we get a thing or two straight, Lieutenant?"

"Happy to. As long as it cuts down on the delays." Wyatt nodded.

"This isn't Austin. We might be kind of slow here compared to your Texas Ranger pace, but we can do the job," Hardin replied. "I've already called Deputy Spears and told him to get back out here. Once he's here, he'll get the footprints cast. Do you think that'll be time enough for you?"

Wyatt clenched his jaw. "That's fine. Spears. He's the one who abandoned the crime scene, isn't he?"

"He didn't abandon it." Hardin countered. "Dr. Jacobson, a member of *your* task force, assured him that she would be responsible for the scene until Tolbert came on at midnight."

"Nobody on *my* task force but me has that authority, Sheriff. Is that clear?" Wyatt grumbled.

Reed Hardin's mouth flattened, but he nodded.

Wyatt felt a twinge of regret for his tone. "Thanks," he muttered. "When can I talk to Deputy Tolbert?"

"Any time, Lieutenant. I would like Doc to release him first."

Wyatt nodded. "What's the story with him, anyhow? I know he and Marcie James were dating at one time. Apparently she told Nina he could be abusive."

"I said *mean,*" Nina interjected as she bent down again to study the indentation where the missing bone had lain.

Hardin nodded. "Right. Abusive might be too strong a word. Shane's got a temper, but he's a good deputy. He's competent. Might even call him a go-getter." Hardin's mouth quirked up in a smile. "I wouldn't be surprised if he has his sights on being sheriff one day."

"You trust him that much?" asked Wyatt.

"Whether or not he could become sheriff has nothing to do with how much I do or don't trust him. It's a matter of competence," replied Hardin. "In fact, that's one of the things I admire about him. He's gone to school on his own time to take classes on crime scene investigation. He's pretty knowledgeable."

"Yeah?" Wyatt's mental radar buzzed. So Tolbert was *pretty knowledgeable* about CSI. "Where'd he get his degree in hostility?"

Hardin shrugged. "That he comes by naturally. His dad, Ben Tolbert, has always been a drinker and a woman chaser. Knocked Shane around some until he got big enough to fight back."

"And once he got big enough?"

"I doubt you're asking that question without knowing the answer."

Wyatt nodded. "He has a suspension on his record. Excessive force."

"It was a domestic dispute. Single mother's boyfriend came home drunk and decided to whale on her eight-year-old for leaving his bike in the driveway. He broke the boy's arm. Shane broke the guy's nose."

Wyatt looked at Hardin with new respect. Suspending the deputy was the right thing to do, but it couldn't have been easy to put a black mark on his record for avenging a child. Especially given Tolbert's own childhood.

"Ever hear anything about trouble between him and Marcie James?"

Hardin shook his head. "You know how people can talk sometimes. I remember once she hurt her arm. Claimed she'd pulled a muscle playing tennis."

"Did you check it out?"

"Doc said it could have been twisted in a fall."

"Could have."

Hardin nodded. "I kept an eye on her, but I never saw anything else. Shane seemed to care about her. I don't remember why they broke up."

"What do you think about the missing bone? Who in Comanche Creek would attack your deputy and steal one of the bones?" Wyatt looked toward the burial site, toward Nina. As he watched, she stood and shed the hooded sweatshirt, leaving her in nothing but the little red thing. He swallowed.

"I don't have a clue," Hardin said. "I know there were people who were upset about Marcie testifying in the land fraud case, but it's hard to imagine that any of them could have killed her."

"The professor says the bones are recent."

Nina tugged the red camisole down over her low-slung jeans as far as it would stretch, which wasn't far, then picked up a fallen branch. After testing it with her weight, she stuck one end into the ground and braced herself as she reached across the shallow mud hole. She stretched precariously, straining toward something Wyatt couldn't see.

"What are you getting at?" Hardin asked.

"Could Shane have faked the attack so he could destroy evidence?"

Hardin sent him a questioning look.

"Maybe he knows whose bones are buried in there." Wyatt spoke without taking his eyes off Nina. The scrap of shimmery red material rode up her back, leaving a good eight inches or so of bare midriff between its hem and her jeans.

"You're suggesting Shane killed Marcie James? No way. He was torn up about Marcie's disappearance."

Wyatt swallowed, trying to concentrate on Hardin's words. "I want to question him as soon as possible," he said gruffly.

Nina reached a fraction of an inch farther, and Wyatt got a view of the underside of her breasts. He winced. In about three seconds, she was going to fall face-first into the muddy crime scene—not to mention expose her breasts—if somebody didn't rescue her.

At that very instant, she almost lost her grip on the branch.

"No problem," Hardin answered. "You can talk to him later this morning at my office. Say ten o'clock?"

"Make it nine. I'll be there," Wyatt tossed over his shoulder as he stalked quickly over to the shallow hole. He bent and scooped Nina up with one arm, grunting quietly. She was more solid than she looked. And her breasts were soft and firm against his forearm.

"Ack!" she squawked as he plopped her down a couple of feet away, on solid ground. "What? You!"

She got her feet under her and stood. When she swiped at a lock of hair that had fallen over her brow, she left a trail of mud. "I almost had it."

"What you *almost* had was a face full of mud. You could have ruined my crime scene. As an *anthropologist*, I'd think you'd know that falling into the middle of a find would contaminate it."

"I wasn't falling."

"The hell you weren't. What were you after?"

"I'll show you." She lifted her chin and walked imperiously over to the edge of the shallow hole.

Wyatt tried not to smile as he followed her. She had no idea that she looked like a tomboy, with mud streaking her face and wisps of hair flying everywhere.

"Damn it," she muttered and turned back toward him.

No. He corrected himself. With the curve of her breasts and the delicate bones and muscles of her shoulders and collarbone showing, not to mention the outline of her nipples under the red camisole, a tomboy was the last thing she looked like.

"What is it?"

"I don't see it now." She patted her pockets. "I need my flashlight. It's in my hoodie."

Wyatt clenched his teeth in frustration as he bent down and retrieved her hooded sweatshirt.

"Here. You need to put it on, anyhow." He couldn't stop his eyes from flickering downward, to the top of her breasts.

"What? Why?" She looked down, made a small distressed sound, thrust her arms into the massive sleeves and wrapped the sweatshirt around her.

With an effort, he turned his attention away from her to study the general area where she'd been reaching.

She pulled out her flashlight and turned it on.

"What were you trying to reach?" he asked again, hearing the frustration in his voice.

She aimed the beam. "Something bright."

"Bright?"

"Like metal. I think it might be a piece of jewelry."

"Or a gum wrapper."

She shrugged, still searching with her flashlight. "Oh. There!" She held the light beam steady.

"That clod of dirt?" Wyatt squinted at the unsightly clump of mud and something fuzzy and tangled. "It looks like it came out of a sewer pipe."

"Can you get it? I want it intact."

"Let me have that stick." He put his weight on the branch, bending it slightly to test it. Then he leaned on it.

"Use this." She handed him a small tool.

"What's this?"

"A trowel."

He sent a glare sideways toward her. "Keep the flashlight on the clump of dirt."

Bracing himself, he reached. Her prize was farther away than it looked. She'd have definitely ended up facedown in the mud.

By stretching his shoulder nearly out of joint and straining his biceps, he managed to slide the blade of the trowel underneath the clump. Holding his breath, he lifted it. Then he eased backward until he was balanced on his own two feet on dry ground.

"Hold on," Nina said.

Wyatt froze. "What?" he snapped, his arm muscles quivering with effort.

"Just stand still for a minute." She held her flashlight in her left hand and a pair of tweezers in her right. She probed the clump cautiously.

Finally, she found what she'd been looking for, judging by the hiss of breath he heard. She fished a small plastic bag out of her pocket, slid her find into it, sealed it and marked it. Then she retrieved a larger bag and held it out for Wyatt to drop the clump into.

"What was that you put in the small bag?"

"That was what I saw. I think it's a necklace. Let me seal and mark this, and we'll look at it." He heard the nervous excitement in her voice. She quickly sealed the bag containing the clump of dirt and wrote something on it. Then she held up the small bag. "Hold the flashlight for me?"

Her fingers trembled as she held the bag under the beam. She turned it this way and that, and used her fingernail to maneuver the object inside.

Wyatt watched, trying to make sense of what he saw. A narrow chain of some kind. Shiny, like fine gold.

"Oh, dear heavens," Nina breathed. "It is…" Her voice broke.

"Is what?"

Nina looked up at him. There was enough light for him to see a suspicious brightness in her eyes. "It's Marcie's necklace."

Her words slammed into his chest like a physical blow. *Marcie's necklace*. He hadn't realized that he'd held out hope that Marcie could still be alive. That somehow, against all odds, and despite his failure to keep her safe, she'd managed to survive.

"Marcie's? How can you be sure?" He held his

breath, dreading her answer. She'd been Marcie's best friend. If anyone could positively ID Marcie's possessions, she could.

But she didn't answer him. Her attention was on the contents of the bag, and her hand was trembling.

"Nina?"

"Look at it." Nina held the bag so the flashlight beam sparkled off a cluster of tiny diamonds embedded in the clump of dirt.

Wyatt squinted. "Wait. Is that *hair?*"

She nodded and took a shaky breath. "Human. Long. Blond. And see the diamonds? They form an M. I know this is Marcie's necklace because…" Her voice broke. "Because I gave it to her." She took a shaky breath and straightened.

Wyatt met her eyes and found them stone cold and filled with hostility.

"That means," she said harshly, "that one of those thigh bones is Marcie's."

Chapter Five

"Let me have the necklace and the hair. I'll give it to Sheriff Hardin and then get you back to town. You're obviously freezing." Wyatt's voice was gruff, disapproving.

"No," Nina said through chattering teeth. She clamped her jaw and consciously relaxed her hunched shoulders. "You're not getting rid of me that easily. I'm keeping the evidence. You called me in to do the collecting and analyzing, and I'm going to do it." She kept her arms folded, so he couldn't see her shivering.

Her hoodie was only slightly better than nothing. It was damp from where she'd dropped it on the ground, and she could feel a glob of cold, slimy mud sliding down between her shoulder blades. In spite of her determination, she shuddered.

Wyatt's jaw tensed. "Technically, my captain called in your *boss*, not you."

Nina lifted her chin and glared at him. His gaze narrowed, as if he was tired of dealing with her.

She studied his rugged features. He wasn't handsome. Not by Hollywood standards. His jaw just missed being too prominent. The cleft in his chin bordered on too deep. His wide, straight mouth barely kept his nose from looking too long. And his eyes were a clear, dark blue that she'd never seen in eyes before.

And those eyes were on her.

"I tell you what," he said. "The Ranger lab has DNA on file for Marcie. Divide that sample with me, and I'll have the lab test it against Marcie's."

Nina's fist tightened around the evidence bag. His suggestion was entirely reasonable, so why was her instinctive reaction not to let one single hair out of her sight? As soon as the question popped into her head, she knew the answer. It wasn't that she didn't trust the Rangers, or even Wyatt Colter. It was that she held in her hand the answer to the question that had haunted her for two years. Was Marcie dead or alive?

Wyatt raised a brow.

Nina nodded. "We'll need a witness to oversee the transfer of evidence." She glanced over at Tolbert's pickup. "The doctor."

Wyatt fetched Doc Hallowell, and within minutes the division and transfer of evidence were taken care of. Wyatt made a short phone call, then came back over to watch Nina lock her evidence bag in her forensics kit, along with the record of transfer.

"The courier will be here within an hour," he said.

"Thank you." She folded her arms, feeling the chill of the early morning seeping under her skin. "You know, Marcie was my friend. All I came here for was to find out what happened to her. I can't abandon her until I know."

Wyatt's eyes darkened, like storm clouds obscuring the sky. "Your involvement borders on conflict of interest."

She held his gaze. "If that's true, then you being head of the task force is definitely a conflict."

"Come on," he snapped. "Let's get you into the Jeep."

"No." She shook her head. "I never should have left the site. I'm staying here until my students can build the platform and erect a fence."

Wyatt's blue gaze narrowed. "Like hell you are," he growled. "You'll be frozen solid long before daybreak. The sheriff's got it covered."

"The sheriff may have the *crime scene* covered, but the burial site is my responsibility."

"Nope. It's my responsibility. You are a member of this task force—at least for now. I'm the head of it. Do you understand what that means?" He looked down at her from under the shadow cast by the brim of his Stetson.

She pressed her lips together and stared back at him, losing a little bit of credibility when she couldn't keep her chin from trembling with cold.

"It means I can have you replaced."

"On what grounds? I'm perfectly capable of handling this job."

"You're of no use to me if you can't follow orders."

"Orders?" She bristled.

A corner of his mouth twitched. "Orders. Now get in."

She stood her ground. "I'm the forensic anthropologist—"

He took a step forward. "Get in the vehicle."

She backed up. "I have a perfect right to stay here if I want to."

"Get. In."

Nina realized everybody had stopped talking and was staring in their direction. She didn't dare take her eyes off Wyatt, though. No telling what he'd do.

"What are you going to do?" she snapped. "Make me?"

"If I have to."

"How?"

He lifted a hand to the brim of his hat and pushed it back about an inch, enough to chase the shadows away from his eyes. "I could shoot you, I guess. But that would be messy."

She kept her chin up. "I've already lost one thigh bone. I don't want to lose another."

Suddenly he was in her face. "You risk losing a lot more than a thigh bone if you stay out here all night. Now, do I have to pick you up and put you in the vehicle myself? Or are you going to go on your own?"

She darted a quick, involuntary glance around. Everyone was watching them. She felt the sting of heat as a flush rose to her cheeks.

"I'm a Ph.D. You can't just *pick me up* and *put me* anywhere. Everyone's watching."

Wyatt inclined his head, and his eyes sparked dangerously. Obviously he didn't care.

Anger sent blood rushing to her ears and scalp. "Fine," she snapped. "If you trust the sheriff to keep your *crime scene* safe until daybreak, I suppose I do, too." She tossed her head. "No reason for everyone to stick around until then."

She felt Wyatt's eyes on her back as she trudged over to his Jeep and climbed into the passenger seat. He'd left the engine running, and the warmth hit her chilled skin like the first blast of a hot shower. She shivered uncontrollably for a few seconds.

The temperature gauge on the dashboard computer read forty-nine degrees. Not exactly freezing. But her sweatshirt was damp, not to mention the knees and seat of her jeans. And that slimy mud was beginning to dry on her back. The temperature didn't have to be freezing to cause hypothermia.

She looked out the window and saw that every eye was on her. And they were all smiling. Even Tolbert. Her face flushed with heat.

Then, as she watched, Wyatt aimed his intimidating glare at them, and one by one, they turned their attention back to what they were doing.

She felt an absurd gratitude toward him, and that made her mad. He didn't deserve her gratitude, for two reasons. First, it was his fault the men had been staring in the first place. He'd been out of line threatening her, even if he was in charge. Second, her oldest, dearest friend was missing and presumed dead because of him. She wasn't sure what he could have done to stop the armed kidnappers who'd grabbed Marcie, but he was a Texas Ranger. He'd sworn to protect her.

As for herself, she intended to have him at her side when she analyzed those thigh bones, but not because she trusted him to protect her. In fact, her reasoning was just the opposite.

She wanted him there because if one of the bones was Marcie's, she was going to need somebody to blame.

WYATT GLANCED back at the Jeep as he headed over to talk to Sheriff Hardin. There was a glare on the rain-spattered windshield, but he could make out Nina's black hair. He didn't have to see her face to know her accusing eyes were following him.

He supposed it was fitting that he was saddled with her reproachful presence as he worked to get to the bottom of Marcie's disappearance. After all, he'd lived for two years with her voice in his head.

It's your fault.

"What did your bone collector find?" Hardin asked, cutting into his thoughts.

"A clump of hair and a necklace that may have belonged to Marcie James."

"Where are they? Get them to me and—"

Wyatt shook his head. "Nope. Nina's tagged them. She's got the chain of custody."

"Are you sure she ought to be doing that? She was Marcie's best friend."

Wyatt's hackles rose, but he knew the sheriff had a valid point. It was the same point he'd just raised to Nina. "I trust her for that very reason. She's determined to find out what happened to her friend."

Hardin sent Wyatt a telling look. "Word is she's already decided who's responsible."

Wyatt shrugged as if that fact didn't concern him. "Maybe. Can't say I disagree with her. Besides, whether we like it or not, these are cold cases. And with the state of the remains, it's more up her alley than CSI's."

"What did you need the doc for?"

"We need to positively ID the hair as Marcie's. So the professor divided the evidence into two bags, with the doctor witnessing the transfer of some of the evidence from her to me. I've got a courier coming to take it to the Ranger Forensics Lab. We have Marcie's DNA on file. If the clump of hair is a match, we should know within twenty-four hours."

The end of his sentence was almost drowned out by the sound of a four-wheeler roaring up. Wyatt looked across the road and saw Trace Becker, Jonah Becker's son, climbing off the vehicle and heading their way. He remembered Trace mostly because of his hair-trigger temper and the two-by-four chip he carried on his shoulder.

There was a reason Wyatt had recommended Becker's daughter Jessie instead of Trace to work with them on the task force.

Trace stomped toward them, his chin stuck out pugnaciously. "What the hell's going on, Reed?"

Hardin held up a hand. "Now, Trace, calm down."

"Calm down?" Trace stormed. "This is the second time I've been disturbed tonight. Around ten I saw so much light out here that I thought we had a fire. Now there's another commotion on *my* land, and nobody bothered to contact me to let me know what was going on."

His land? Wyatt opened his mouth, but Hardin beat him to the punch. "Did you come down here earlier, Trace?"

Trace took a split-second too long to answer. "Earlier? What do you mean?"

"When was the last time you were here?" Wyatt broke in, narrowing his eyes as he studied Trace's cowboy boots. There was mud clinging to the sides.

Trace scowled at Wyatt for a couple of seconds, as if trying to place him, then turned back to Hardin. "I ran out here this afternoon to check on the burial site. Spoke with Deputy Spears for a bit, then headed back to the house to finish up some paperwork."

"And later, when you saw the lights?" Hardin asked.

"I stepped outside to see what was going on and realized they were spotlights, not a fire," Trace replied.

"Yeah? And then?" Wyatt broke in.

Trace cocked his head. "And then I went back inside."

"You weren't curious? Worried about what was going on up here?"

"I told you I had paperwork." Trace growled. "Are you calling me a liar?"

"I'm asking if anyone can vouch for you."

"Vouch for *me?* What the hell? You've got a lot of gall, standing here on *my* property, telling me I need someone to *vouch* for me." Trace turned to Harding. "Who the hell is this guy, anyhow?"

Wyatt took a step forward. "Lieutenant Wyatt Colter, Texas Ranger. I'm in charge of the task force looking into the remains that were found on *your father's* land."

Trace turned on him, only to be stopped by Hardin's hand on his arm.

"We're just trying to find out what happened," Hardin said. "Now, if your dad or Jessie can confirm that you didn't leave the house—?"

"They can't," Trace broke in. "Jessie's out of town, and Dad…" Instantaneously, his whole demeanor changed. "He's not doing so well. And all this isn't helping." He swung his arm in a sweeping gesture. "Reed, I asked what's going on."

Wyatt studied Trace. He was barely holding it together. His fists were clenched at his sides, and despite the chill in the air, he was sweating. Was he really worried about his father, and indignant about the intrusion on the Becker spread? Or was he afraid of what the Ranger task force would uncover?

Hardin sent Wyatt a telling look, then stepped over and patted Trace on the back.

"Somebody hit Shane over the head. He called us as soon as he woke up. When Doc finishes sewing his head up and we check out what his attacker was after, things will calm down out here. You know we've got to do our jobs." As he talked, he maneuvered Trace toward his four-wheeler. "Why don't you get back down to the house and make sure your dad's okay? We've still got a lot of work to do here, but don't worry. I'll keep you in the loop."

Wyatt bristled at Hardin's kid-glove handling of Jonah Becker's belligerent son. He was half-inclined to grab him and run him in for making threats against law enforcement. But while this was his jurisdiction, Comanche Creek wasn't his town and these weren't his neighbors. He was an outsider, so he needed to maintain a cordial relationship with Sheriff Reed Hardin.

He arched his neck and consciously relaxed his shoulders. The sheriff's words had calmed Trace down, so Wyatt kept his mouth shut. He'd talk to Hardin later about getting Deputy Spears to check Trace's and Tolbert's boots against the tracks around the site.

The ground was damp from the rain. Unlike the limestone road, the mud ought to show every footprint and the tracks of every vehicle that had come near.

As Trace's four-wheeler faded in the distance, the sound of a big engine filled his ears. He turned and saw a pickup roaring up.

"That's Kirby Spears," Hardin said from behind him.

"The deputy who let Nina talk him into leaving the crime scene unguarded."

"Tell you what," Reed said on a sigh. "You discuss who can authorize what with your bone doctor, and I'll do the same with my deputy."

"I haven't met him yet."

"Let's take care of that right now." Hardin led Wyatt over to the deputy's truck and introduced them. Then he turned to Wyatt. "You're coming to my office around nine tomorrow morning, right? Woody—Mayor Sadler—just called me about what's going on. He'll meet us there."

Wyatt got the sheriff's message. They'd accomplished all they could for the moment, and since it was already after four o'clock in the morning, everyone was going to be sleep deprived and grouchy, anyway.

"See you at nine," Wyatt said. Turning on his heel, he headed for his vehicle. He still had to deal with Nina until he could get her back to the Bluebonnet Inn.

He climbed into the driver's seat, put the Jeep into gear and headed back to town. The heated air was laced with the earthy smell of mud and rain, but underneath those expected odors was a totally unexpected one.

The subtle scent of roses. He gave in to the urge to take a deep breath, even while he lectured himself.

Nina Jacobson was a distraction, not an attraction. His body disagreed, as the sudden tightening in his groin emphasized.

He clenched his teeth and pressed his lips together, concentrating on the dark country road. He owed it to Marcie to find the person responsible for her death. He couldn't afford to let anything or anyone distract him.

No way.

"What?" Nina asked.

"What?" His response was automatic.

"You said something."

Had he? He pulled up in front of the Bluebonnet Inn. "Eight o'clock is going to be here before you know it," he muttered, opening the driver's-side door.

He glanced over at her. In the pale glow of his overhead light, with those big dark brown eyes and her ponytail coming loose, she looked like a bedraggled puppy.

He had to bite his cheek to keep from smiling. There was a reason people couldn't resist puppies. He deliberately tore his gaze away from hers.

Nina got out, wrapping her hoodie around her. She grabbed her forensics kit and stalked to the front door of the inn.

Wyatt was there before her. He opened the door and

held it, ignoring her suspicious glance. "You've got the evidence, right?" he asked.

"Do I look like this is the first time I've done this?" As soon as the words were out of her mouth, she regretted them, because Wyatt's blue eyes sparkled with mischief, and the corner of his mouth twitched. "Well, it's not," she said quickly. "I've assisted Professor Mayfield on several cases. Even if you're not impressed by my credentials, you should be impressed by his."

"I'm thinking that's why the captain requested *him* for the task force."

She was not going to let him bait her. Not going to get drawn into an argument. "If you're so concerned about my abilities—"

No. Don't go there. "Call Dr. Mayfield," she finished lamely as she pushed past him to climb the stairs.

At the top, she fished in her jeans for the room key. Finally, her fingers closed around it, and she unlocked her room door. She felt a tug on her drooping ponytail. Her head whipped around.

Wyatt held out his hand, streaked with mud. "Looks like you're going to need another shower," he commented. "Try not to make too much noise." He yawned and checked his watch. "I'm planning on getting three hours of sleep before I have to get up."

Nina made a face at him, but it was wasted energy. He'd already disappeared into his room and closed the door.

She let herself in and turned on the overhead light.

And gasped.

Someone had been in her room.

Chapter Six

Nina's fingers flew to her mouth as she stared at the bedside table. Her camera wasn't where she'd left it. She glanced around the room, trying to remember if she'd moved it.

Her gaze lit on her weekend bag. Had she stuck the camera inside with her laptop? The bag didn't look like it had been disturbed.

She shook her head. No. Her last thought before rushing out the door to catch up with Wyatt had been that she'd forgotten her camera. She remembered glancing back at it sitting on her bedside table.

Stay calm, she told herself. This was a small-town B and B. Betty Alice certainly knew that Nina and Wyatt were gone. Maybe she always got up by 5:00 a.m. Maybe she'd come in to bring fresh towels, and decided that the camera shouldn't be sitting out in plain view.

Or maybe she'd just been curious about the pictures. Even Betty Alice, with all her homespun giddiness, probably knew how to view stored pictures on a digital camera.

She stepped farther into the room and glanced apprehensively toward the bathroom. What if whoever had come into her room was still here? Not wanting to look like a wimp in front of Wyatt, she stepped over to the bathroom door and flung it open.

Empty.

She let out the breath she hadn't realized she'd been holding. Nothing looked out of place in the bathroom. The towel she'd used was draped over the shower curtain rod, and the floor was still puddled with water where she'd stood to dry off. So Betty Alice hadn't come in to replace the dirty towels.

Turning around, she spotted her camera sitting on the lower shelf of the bedside table.

Again, her thoughts turned to that split second when she'd paused to decide whether to grab her camera. She shook her head. She hadn't moved it.

Someone else had.

She started toward it, then stopped, taking a deep breath. Her camera could have been moved innocently, but did she dare make that assumption? What if whoever had stolen the thigh bone from the burial site had deleted her photos or taken her SD card to remove any proof that there were three unique thigh bones there in the first place?

Her logical brain immediately offered up reasons why that didn't make sense. Surely the medical examiner had taken photos. And that begged the question, had the ME's evidence been tampered with?

She glanced toward the door that connected her room with Wyatt's. For a couple of seconds she considered not telling him. But if her pictures were missing, it could impact the case, and she could hear him now if she left it until tomorrow. So she rapped on the door.

At first she didn't hear anything. Then the screech

of old pipes assaulted her ears, and below that sound, Wyatt's deep voice, although she couldn't make out what he said.

She rapped again, and the knob twisted right under her hand.

He stood there with his hand on the knob. No shirt on, and damp, tousled hair dripping water onto his forehead and shoulders.

He had a towel in his hand, and he wiped its edge across his face and then looked up at her from under wet lashes. When he met her gaze, he frowned. "What's wrong?"

"It's probably nothing…" she began.

"What?" he barked, looking past her and into her room.

"Somebody moved my camera."

His eyes met hers as if deciding whether she was credible, then he pushed past her. When he did, she felt damp heat wafting from him and smelled clean water, fresh soap and peppermint. The combined scents made her knees weak.

Since when did water, soap and peppermint smell like a hero? And why would she even think of that word in connection with Wyatt Colter, of all people?

He slung the towel back around his neck, the gesture sending graceful undulations along the muscles of his bare back and shoulders. "Where is it?" he said.

He still had on his khaki dress pants, but the belt was gone and the pants hung enticingly low, just covering the curve of his buttocks.

"Professor?"

"What?" She blinked. "The camera? Oh, it's on the bottom shelf of the bedside table." She went around him, trying her best not to touch him, and pointed.

"There. The problem is, that's not where I left it. When I left, it was sitting on top of the table."

"Are you sure?"

She bristled. "Yes," she said icily. "I wouldn't have bothered you if I'd had any doubt. Was anything moved in your room?"

He shook his head, sending droplets of water raining down on his tanned shoulders. One drop hit the back of her hand. She rubbed it into her skin.

"Have you touched it? Checked it to see if they did anything to it?"

She shook her head, staring at the damp hair at the nape of his neck. A drop of water rolled lazily down the back of his neck. Her mouth went dry.

He turned to look at her.

"No," she said quickly. "No. I left it where I found it."

He crossed the room to the table.

"Should you glove?"

He lifted the camera by its strap. "You go ahead. Check to see if your card's still in there. This is the camera you were using earlier, right?"

"Yes." She still held her forensics kit in her hand. She opened it and pulled out a pair of exam gloves and quickly donned them.

Wyatt lifted the camera up to the light. "I can't see the card slot."

Nina took the camera in her gloved hand. "It's on the bottom. The card goes inside here." She pointed, flipped open the tiny hinged door. "It's still there." She pressed the preview button. "My photos are still here."

"That's good. What about the rest of your things?"

"I don't think anything else has been touched. My laptop is in my bag."

"You checked?" And there was that note of censure in his voice again.

"No. But the bag hasn't been moved."

He looked at it. "How can you be sure?"

"Because I'm sure. Before I went to sleep, I put the laptop in my bag and zipped it closed. It's exactly where I left it, next to the bathroom door."

"And are those—" he nodded "—exactly where you left them?"

Those were a pair of white silk panties.

Nina bent her head over the camera until her suddenly hot cheeks cooled off a little. "That's right," she said. "Exactly. What do you want to do with the camera? Fingerprint it?"

Wyatt took his time shifting his gaze from her panties on the floor to the camera in her hand. He shrugged. "We could, but I'm betting either it's been wiped clean or whoever handled it has no prints on file."

"Still, someone was in here. They obviously looked at the photos. What if it was the same person who knocked out Shane?"

He shook his head. "How did they get in? Your windows are locked from the inside, and the door was locked, right?"

She looked at the windows. They were locked. She hadn't noticed him studying the room. He was good.

"And nothing's out of place in my room," he noted.

"Are you sure?" She asked. It was a silly question. If he'd observed all that about her room in the few seconds he'd been in here, it was a cinch that he'd already given his own the once-over.

He didn't even bother to nod.

"Whoever knocked out Shane probably knows Betty Alice," she said.

"Unless she's right in the middle of all this—the disappearances, the theft of the thigh bone—she'd never let someone roam through here in the middle of the night."

"You think Betty Alice looked at the photos?"

"It makes sense. She or some other busybody that works or lives here. Betty Alice is the mayor's sister. This is a very close-knit community—make that two very close-knit communities—on one side, the Caucasian element, and on the other, the Native Americans. There was a lot of hostility between them when I was here before…" He stopped, and she saw his jaw tense. "And it doesn't seem to have changed much," he added gruffly.

"Then we should probably get out of here before she or someone else steals evidence or—"

"Whoa." He held up a hand. "Not so fast."

"You don't think we need to move?"

"To where? The dorm at the community college, with your students?" He shook his head. "I'd rather not. For one thing, it would cause a stir. Everyone would want to know why we moved. My suggestion is to keep all the evidence locked up. Back up photographs, notes and any other important information or transfer to a secure location." He gave her a tiny smile. "I doubt we have to consider Betty Alice dangerous. But I'd rather be here, so I can keep an eye on her. Who knows? The fact that she's the mayor's sister may come in handy for us."

Nina nodded. Everything he said made sense, but the fact remained, someone had been in her room and had touched her things.

"Are you okay?" Wyatt asked.

Nina frowned. "Okay? Sure I'm okay. What do you mean?"

"Why don't we change rooms? The chain on my door isn't broken. You'll feel safer."

"The chain?" She turned to look at the door to the hall. She hadn't noticed that her chain was in two pieces.

"Later this morning I'll let Betty Alice know that it needs replacing."

"I don't need to move. I'm fine." She gave a short little laugh.

Wyatt picked up her weekend bag, carefully avoiding the panties, and set it on her bed. "Still, I'd feel better. Pack up and we'll switch. Then if anything happens, you can just yell." He went back into his room.

Nina quickly packed up her things and took them through the connecting door into Wyatt's room. He was waiting for her.

"Okay. Not much time left until daybreak," he said. "Make the most of it."

"I've still got to take a shower," she said on a sigh.

The look he gave her was fleeting but intense. "There's a clean towel in there."

Then he stepped through the door. "See ya later," he muttered.

Once the door was closed, Nina set her weekend bag on the floor and opened it, moving her laptop to get to her clothes.

She sighed as she stepped into the bathroom. If she didn't literally have mud drying on her back, she'd skip the shower and fall straight into bed.

Oh, no. The bathroom was still warm and steamy. The clean, fresh, minty scent of him permeated the air. A shiver that had nothing to do with the temperature skittered through her. Her knees went wobbly again.

For a few seconds, she stared at the damp towel he'd

folded and left on the back of the toilet. It took will-power not to pick it up and hold it to her nose. It would be warm and clean and minty, like him.

With stoic deliberation, she left the towel where it was. She turned on the shower and took out her rose-scented shampoo and body wash. Taking the cap off the shampoo, she breathed deeply of its sweet, familiar scent.

A slight breath of mint didn't have a chance against a bottle full of roses, she hoped as she peeled off her muddy sweatshirt and jeans.

WYATT STARED AT the rumpled bedclothes and thought about Nina in that little red camisole and red panties scooting around between those sheets, trying to get comfortable.

He was pretty sure just from looking at her that she wasn't the kind of woman who'd wear underwear that didn't match. Or maybe he just hoped she wasn't, because some day he'd like to see her in red bikini panties and nothing else—or maybe black ones. Of course, snowy white would work, too.

He swallowed and debated placing his head under the water faucet again—this time with cold water running.

He pushed his fingers through his damp hair, then rubbed the back of his neck and sighed. If he was planning to get any sleep tonight—today—he needed to get to it. A glance toward the connecting door told him it was closed. He'd noticed when he'd first entered the room that, although there was a keyhole in the door, there was no key. He'd checked to see if his room key fit it. It didn't.

As he'd climbed the stairs last evening, he'd overheard Nina declining Betty Alice's offer of what she'd called the pink room. With a grimace, Wyatt formed a mental picture of that room. He smiled at her quick refusal. Nope. He couldn't picture her in pink. Not with that midnight black hair and those sultry lips.

She just wasn't a pink kind of woman.

Purple maybe. Black definitely. And he'd like to see her creamy skin in that color that seemed to disappear... Didn't they call it nude?

But the red was his favorite. Bloodred. Like rich, velvety roses.

Any more of this kind of thinking and he was going to have to douse more than his head in cold water.

It took him only a couple of seconds to straighten out the bedclothes. Then he stalked over to the opposite side of the double bed and pulled the covers back and lay down.

But to his dismay, the other side of the bed wasn't far enough. His nostrils were still filled with the scent of roses, and when he turned over, he somehow ended up with a long black hair tickling his cheek.

He punched his pillow and turned over again. Even so, every time he managed to drift off to sleep, some part of Nina's body rose up in his mental vision.

Her breasts, their gentle swell hidden and yet highlighted by the shimmery red camisole she'd had on. Her bottom, barely covered by the low-slung jeans.

He knew nothing about her. He'd only met her three times. Once at dinner with Marcie and him, during which Marcie seemed to be trying to fix the two of them up. Then on that awful day when Marcie was kidnapped.

And last night.

He took a deep breath. Running around in a slinky,

revealing little camisole didn't fit his perception of her. However, being so excited about a forensic find that she forgot what she was wearing—*and* didn't notice what she was exposing—did.

Growling, he groped along the bedside table until he found the little pile of peppermints he'd set there with the rest of his pocket litter. Grabbing one, he peeled off the wrapper and popped the mint into his mouth, relishing the cool, sweet bite on his tongue, and the way the sharp mint taste and smell banished the last dregs of roses from his nostrils.

He turned over on his back, threw an arm over his eyes and directed his thoughts toward the next step in his investigation. He was scheduled to meet with the sheriff and his two deputies at nine o'clock. And with Mayor Sadler. He'd mentioned wanting to talk to Trace Becker, but they hadn't arranged anything.

Wyatt considered calling Hardin to make sure Trace would be there, but it was just after six in the morning, and he was pretty sure the sheriff was asleep—or at least trying to catch a nap.

Two hours. Wyatt took a deep breath. He had two hours to nap. He changed position again and tried to wipe his brain clean of thoughts and images. He even managed to stop thinking about Nina's body. The only image he wasn't successful in banishing was the look on her face when he'd opened the connecting door.

She'd looked terrified.

The trouble was, she'd seemed only slightly less frightened when he'd closed it after they'd switched rooms.

He couldn't blame her for not feeling safe with him. After all, they were here now because he had failed to keep Marcie James safe two years ago.

This time, no matter what he had to do, no matter what the cost, he would not fail.

He'd find Marcie—or her killer. And while he was at it, he'd make sure nothing happened to Nina.

Chapter Seven

Just before nine o'clock, Wyatt walked up to the two-story white limestone building with a triple arched front. Looking at it, he had the same reaction he'd had two years ago. It was hard to believe it was really the sheriff's office.

To Wyatt, it looked more like a facade for an old-style Western movie. He paused with his hand on the glass doorknob and checked the sign again.

"It's the right place," an enticingly deep feminine voice said behind him.

Wyatt turned and met a pair of dark, snapping eyes in a heart-shaped face framed by straight black hair. Her lips were bright red and matched the red shirt she had on. The rest of her outfit, a leather fringed vest, suede gauchos and tooled leather boots, might have looked costumey on another woman, but she carried it off like a star.

"I know, but it still feels like I'm walking into the middle of an old Western movie."

"I'm Ellie Penateka," she said, holding out a perfectly manicured hand.

Wyatt didn't know the name, but he was pretty sure he'd seen her before, back when he was here guarding Marcie James. She'd be hard to miss anywhere. He grasped her hand briefly, then pushed the door open and stepped back to let her enter first. "Nice to meet you," he muttered.

"We'll see," she whispered. She sent him a wink as she walked past.

Wyatt followed her down a wide hallway and through a door located midway. A young woman with dark red hair looked up and smiled at Ellie, then stood and gave him the once-over.

"You must be Lieutenant Colter," she said. "Sheriff Hardin is waiting for you. Through there."

Wyatt let Ellie lead as they walked through a small office with two desks—probably the deputies' office.

When Ellie opened the door marked Sheriff, Wyatt stopped in dismay. The room was crammed full of people. He frowned as he zeroed in on Sheriff Hardin, sitting behind his desk.

Hardin shrugged. He looked as irritated as Wyatt felt.

Wyatt paused for a couple of seconds to take an inventory.

On the opposite end of the room from Hardin's desk, Shane Tolbert sported a bandage on the side of his head and was soaking up sympathy from a man and a woman Wyatt didn't recognize.

He did know the large man with the weathered, rugged face and salt-and-pepper hair, whose hip was propped on the edge of Hardin's desk. It was Woody Sadler, the mayor of Comanche Creek and, from what he recalled, a very good friend of Hardin.

Standing next to Sadler was Jerry Collier, head of the county land office and Marcie's former boss. He was a weasely guy with a pinched face and a "don't ask me" attitude.

To Wyatt's left stood a medium-height, well-built man with ruddy skin and black hair anchored in a single braid down his back. He was dressed in a starched and ironed denim shirt and faded jeans. On his wrist, just above his watch, was a beaded rawhide bracelet. It wasn't a huge leap to the conclusion that he was Daniel Taabe, the leader of the Native American faction in Comanche Creek. He met Wyatt's gaze, and his brows drew down in a scowl.

He wasn't the only one. Everyone had stopped talking and had turned to glare at him. There were eight people in the room, and each one of them was packing their share of hostility. It hit Wyatt in palpable waves, like a hot, dry summer wind.

Hardin stood and stepped around his desk to shake hands with him.

"I thought we were meeting with Tolbert and Mayor Sadler," Wyatt said evenly.

"Apparently word got around. A lot of people want to know what's going on out there," Hardin replied.

Ellie crossed the room to stand next to Taabe. She said something to him, and he nodded.

"You know everybody?" Hardin asked Wyatt.

Wyatt nodded. "Most of them. Who are the two standing over there with Tolbert?"

Tolbert grinned and elbowed the man next to him in the ribs.

"That's Billy Whitley. He's the county clerk. And next to him is his wife, Charla," Hardin said.

Wyatt nodded. "Right. I remember the names from the transcripts. The DA questioned them about Becker's shady land deal."

"Marcie claimed that Billy was paid to alter some documents. But any proof that Marcie had…"

Hardin's words slammed into Wyatt's chest like the bullet he'd taken two years ago. Any proof of bribery connected with the land deal that Jonah Becker had tried to broker had died with Marcie.

"Where's Trace Becker?" Wyatt asked.

"I didn't tell him about the meeting," Hardin confessed.

"What about the boot prints? Did your deputy cast them?"

Hardin nodded. "Yep. Kirby will bring them in when Shane relieves him. He did tell me he thinks the boots are a size twelve. Same size Kirby wears himself."

"Any distinguishing marks?"

"Don't know yet."

"What size does Tolbert wear?"

"Twelve." Hardin looked at his watch and stood. "Folks, this is Lieutenant Wyatt Colter of the Texas Rangers. He's heading the task force that's investigating the bones found on Jonah Becker's land."

Wyatt felt the slight weight of the silver badge pinned to his chest as he met each person's gaze in turn. He took his time, staring into each pair of eyes a split second longer than politeness dictated. It was designed to make people uncomfortable—especially people with something to hide.

And usually, that was everybody. What they were hiding might or might not affect the case he was working on, but it was almost a cliché. *Everybody* had something to hide.

The only one of the eight who wasn't flustered was Daniel Taabe. He gazed back at Wyatt calmly.

Wyatt sent him a barely perceptible nod and turned back to Hardin.

Hardin opened his mouth, but before he could speak, everyone started shouting questions and complaints.

"Hold it!" Hardin yelled. "Just hang on a minute. Except for Shane and the mayor, every single one of you showed up without an invitation."

"Reed." Mayor Sadler stood. He didn't raise his voice, but everybody else in the room grew quiet. The mayor held out a big, work-roughened hand to Wyatt. "Lieutenant, welcome back to Comanche Creek."

Wyatt didn't miss the touch of irony in Mayor Sadler's tone. He doubted that anyone could have missed it. It was a cinch that, even if he didn't know them, they all knew him and what his connection was to the town.

He took they mayor's hand and shook it. "Thank you, Mayor Sadler—"

"Lieutenant," Mayor Sadler interrupted him. "Gathered here this morning are some of Comanche Creek's most prominent citizens. We're all concerned about the, uh…remains that were unearthed over on Jonah's land. What can you tell us about what's going on up there?"

Wyatt felt all their eyes on him. This wasn't his preferred way of working, but he'd make do. He'd never seen the advantage in meeting with a roomful of people, all asking questions at once. He much preferred to work one-on-one. He found it easier to draw out someone when it was just the two of them. He was intimidating, and he knew it.

Although he was a good judge of character and a good reader of body language, he knew very little about the people gathered here.

Wyatt took a deep breath. "I'm sure you realize, Mayor, that it's going to take more than a cursory examination of the crime scene and the remains to give us the information we need. We have a forensic anthropologist going over the entire area. As soon as she has definitive information that can be shared with the public, we'll let you know. In the meantime—"

"I've got a question," Jerry Collier said. "Just how many bodies are in that hole?"

Wyatt took his time answering. He met every pair of eyes in the room again, this time observing each person's reaction to Collier's question.

As before, Daniel Taabe's dark eyes held his gaze calmly. Ellie Penateka's dark eyes snapped with amusement and, unless Wyatt was badly mistaken, a touch of flirtation.

Charla's head was lowered like a bull's. Her lips were flattened disapprovingly, and her dark eyes gleamed with open hostility. Her husband, Billy Whitley, seemed to have a perpetual smile on his face— a distinctly unpleasant smile. To Wyatt, he looked like a hyena that had just finished a meal.

Tolbert gingerly touched the bandage on his head and averted his gaze. Wyatt was convinced that the deputy hadn't told him or anyone else everything that had happened out at the crime scene the night before.

Wyatt slid his gaze past Hardin to Woody Sadler. The mayor's deeply lined face looked worried and impatient. Next to him, Jerry Collier's beady eyes shone with excitement, as if he were about to learn a dark secret.

Well, Wyatt wasn't spilling any secrets today. He was here to gather information, not to impart it. So he wasn't about to get into how many bodies had been discovered or any other specifics.

"Mr. Collier, we don't know how many bodies yet," he finally said. "That's a question Dr. Jacobson will have to answer. And she won't be answering it until we've made a thorough investigation of the entire area."

"How long will that take?" Charla asked.

Wyatt shrugged. "No telling. I can tell you this, though. The fewer interruptions we have, the faster we can get to the bottom of this."

"What's that supposed to mean?" Charla snapped.

"It means just what it sounds like," Wyatt returned. "Last night, as I'm sure you all know by now, Deputy Tolbert was attacked, and the crime scene was compromised."

"We talk plain out here, Lieutenant," Billy Whitley said. "What the hell do you mean, *compromised?*"

"I mean, somebody stole one of the bones." Wyatt couldn't watch everybody at once, but he concentrated on soaking up the reaction to his words. His statement was no surprise to anyone in the room. Word had spread fast. "This is going to make Dr. Jacobson's job harder. Not to mention that whoever took that bone contaminated the crime scene. I have a feeling that was the attacker's intent."

Tolbert spoke up. "I gotta say, I feel really bad about letting down my guard."

A few murmurs of protest arose.

Tolbert waved his hands. "No, no. I should have been more alert. When I heard the road crew had dug up those bones, I figured it was another Indian mound. There's been a few uncovered around here." Tolbert turned his gaze to Wyatt. "It's hard to wrap your brain around the idea that some dried-up bones you're looking at could belong to somebody you knew." He paused. "Somebody you dated."

Charla laid her hand on Tolbert's arm in a comforting gesture.

"Now I have a question," Wyatt said. Since he was here, he might as well find out what he could. "Why would anyone pick that isolated corner of Jonah Becker's land to bury a body?"

The tension in the room went up several notches. Wyatt waited. Eventually someone would be compelled to break the silence.

It turned out to be Jerry Collier.

"That's a good question," he said eagerly. Wyatt noted the glare Charla aimed at Collier, who wasn't paying any attention to her. "That limestone road's old, from back when Jonah's grandpappy and everybody else got around on horseback. It's four miles from town, and it's far enough away from everything so that it's dark and quiet. For years kids used to go out there to park. Time was, everybody knew about Dead Man's Road."

Collier's words hung in the air. For a few seconds it seemed like nobody even breathed.

Dead Man's Road.

Then Mayor Sadler cleared his throat. "Jerry, it musta been you out there parking, although I can't for the life of me figure out who'd have gone out there with you."

Everyone laughed.

The mayor went on. "Kids today don't even bother trying to find a deserted place to park. Hell, they do everything right out in the open."

"Why do they call it Dead Man's Road?" Wyatt asked.

Collier answered. "Long time ago, an old Injun stayed in that cabin up the hill. Old man Becker let him alone. He died twenty years ago. My grandma says he must have been over a hundred years old. Most of the kids quit going over there when he died. I think they thought the cabin was haunted."

"Okay, folks," the sheriff said. "Jerry, if you're through spreading gossip, maybe we can get this over with. I hope you all feel better about what we're doing to figure out what happened out there. Now, Lieutenant Colter and I have things we need to discuss—official business relating to the crime. If you'll excuse us—"

"Sheriff," Wyatt broke in. "Since everybody's already here, maybe I could conduct a few interviews." He paused, observing each person's reaction to his words.

"What the hell?"

"Hey, I don't have time—"

"Is he accusing—"

"Hold it!" Mayor Sadler's voice quieted the small crowd immediately. He pushed the brim of his white Stetson up off his forehead. When he did, the rattle-snake tail attached to the band rattled. "Now, folks, we've got a heck of a problem here. You know it and I know it. Marcie James's disappearance was a tragedy. It's the lieutenant's job to figure out what happened out there on Jonah's land. Now, I'm going to guarantee to him that each and every person in this town will cooperate." He looked at each person. "I'm counting on you all to not make me out a liar."

There were low grumblings, but nobody protested.

"Who has time to talk to the lieutenant right now?" asked the mayor.

The room suddenly went quiet as a tomb.

Chapter Eight

The mayor straightened and cocked his head. "Now listen here. I said, I'm counting on you all. Shane, I know you can take time to answer the lieutenant's questions right now. And Jerry. Who else? Billy? Charla?"

Billy Whitley spoke up. "No can do, Woody. I told you Charla and I are headed into Austin today."

"No problem," Mayor Sadler said. "Just make sure you get with the lieutenant." He turned to Wyatt. "Well, Lieutenant. As you see, a lot of folks have places to go and things to do. S'pose you could schedule your interviews for later?"

Wyatt opened his mouth to answer, but the mayor wasn't finished.

"Tell you what. You can use my conference room next door, in the courthouse. The building's a dead ringer for this one. I'll even have my assistant set up the times for you. Just let her know when you're available and who you want to talk to." He slid a card out of his breast pocket and handed it to Wyatt. "Here's my office number. My assistant's name is Helen."

Wyatt nodded, feeling a little like a chastised schoolboy. Mayor Sadler had made all the arrangements for his questioning of the townspeople, and at the same time he'd manipulated him into doing it when and where *he*, not Wyatt, wanted it done.

Mayor Sadler was a sly one. Wyatt wasn't keen on questioning people under the watchful eyes and ears of the mayor and his staff, but in light of Mayor Sadler's perfectly reasonable compromise, any insistence on his part would only evoke more hostility.

Wyatt cleared his throat. "Sure. I'll just need to—"

The mayor settled his hat back down on his head and headed for the door. The small crowd took that as a signal and began to disperse. Charla and Billy took off, and Jerry Collier sidled over to Tolbert and whispered something to him.

"Lieutenant."

Wyatt turned. It was Daniel Taabe. Wyatt held out his hand. Taabe's handshake was firm, and he looked Wyatt straight in the eye.

"I understand Dr. Jacobson is treating the site as a possible sacred burial ground."

"That's right. I can't answer any questions about that, though. That's her area."

Taabe nodded. "Of course. I want assurance from you that any evidence you find will be discussed with me. As I'm sure you can appreciate, my interest is in protecting sacred Comanche rites and rituals, and preserving historically significant finds."

"The only thing I can assure you is that I plan to find out the truth about what happened out there. If I can, I'll see that you get the information as soon as I can release it."

"I'd like to be involved on the front end."

Wyatt nodded. "So would everybody else here. I can't give you special privileges, Mr. Taabe."

Taabe's black eyes narrowed slightly. "What if I

provide three men to help guard the site? One for each shift."

Wyatt eyed him. Just how trustworthy was he? Same question went for the men he was offering. The extra help would ease Wyatt's mind a lot. And if there was a Native American guard on each shift, along with local law enforcement, then maybe the result would be like the fox, the goose and the grain, and there would be no more midnight attacks.

He gave Taabe a slight nod. "I'll check with the sheriff. See what he says."

Taabe's head dipped slightly. "Good enough."

Beside him, Ellie frowned. "Daniel, he practically—"

Taabe moved one hand, an almost imperceptible gesture. Quieted, Ellie pressed her lips together tightly, but she didn't say anything else.

Taabe continued. "Lieutenant, one more thing. If it's all right with you, I'd like to talk with you somewhere other than in Mayor Sadler's office." Taabe's mouth turned up in a wry smile.

Wyatt nodded. "Fine with me. Where would you like to meet?"

"I'm headed to my office now. Would you be interested in talking there once you're finished here?"

Wyatt agreed and made a note of the directions to Taabe's office. They exchanged phone numbers; then Taabe and Ellie left.

As Wyatt stepped over to Hardin's desk, he noticed Collier had walked over to stand with Shane Tolbert. They were sharing a laugh.

"Well?" Hardin asked, dropping into his desk chair.

Wyatt shook his head. "Curious bunch of people," he commented quietly as he took in the area around Hardin's desk.

He remembered Hardin as superorganized. His desk reflected that, as did the calendar hanging on the wall. It was marked in block letters, with appointments and neatly printed notes.

"You ain't seen nothing yet," Hardin commented wryly as he rubbed his eyes.

"Yeah. I'm sure." Wyatt turned his attention to Collier and Tolbert. "If you had to say who stole that bone last night, who would you finger?"

Hardin leaned back in his chair and clasped his hands behind his head. "That's a tough one. I like to stay neutral and let the facts speak for themselves."

"I do, too, but there's sure not much to go on." Wyatt lowered his voice. "How likely is it that Tolbert saw something and isn't telling us?"

Hardin took a deep breath. "Can't say. It'd depend on who or what he saw."

Wyatt pushed his fingers through his hair. So Hardin didn't trust Tolbert. Not completely. "What about Collier? Whitley? The mayor?"

"This is a small town. People here have known each other for years—some for all their lives. There's a lot of loyalty and a lot of resentment among the folks that live here."

"Okay, what about this? Why would Daniel Taabe offer men to help guard the crime scene?"

"He did that?"

"He said he wanted to be in the loop—to know what we find as soon as we find it."

Hardin shrugged. "He's real interested in preserving Comanche history. Maybe he wants to watch over the site in case it is a sacred burial ground."

Wyatt caught Tolbert's eye and nodded, indicating he was ready to talk to him. "Or?"

"Or he knows what we're going to find out there."

"That's what I figure," Wyatt said. "In fact, my guess is that every single person who came here this morning knows more than they're saying."

NINA DUCKED as the massive rock rolled over her head. Then she slid through the quickly narrowing space between the metal door and the stone floor, her hand outstretched, her fingers only millimeters away from the treasure.

Phone. Ringing.

She woke up with the theme from *Raiders of the Lost Ark* echoing in her head. For a moment, she didn't remember where she was. Nothing looked right. Her bedroom faced the morning sun, and the windows in her apartment had white drapes, not blue shutters.

Bluebonnet Inn. Wyatt Colter. Bones.

She sat up, the sleepy haze gone from her brain, and picked up the phone.

"Hello?" she said, clearing her throat.

"Dr. Jacobson?" It was Todd, her student assistant who'd organized the spotlights the night before. She pulled her phone away from her ear and squinted at the display.

Nine o'clock. Hadn't she set her telephone's alarm for seven?

"Todd? Are you at the site?"

"Yep. Sorry to bother you and all, but it's like nine o'clock."

Nina pulled the band out of her hair and shook her head, stifling a yawn. "I know. Sorry. I must have forgotten to turn on my alarm. Send someone to pick me up. How much work have you gotten done?"

"Well, that deputy dude's giving us a hard time. He's pretty grouchy."

"Shane Tolbert?"

"Nah, this is the guy who was here when we got here last night. Spears or something. We've got the ramp built to the edge of the yellow tape, but he won't let us past there. We can't get started on the platform until we can get inside the tape."

Nina blew out a breath in frustration and threw back the bedclothes. "You tell him— No, wait." She stopped. "I'll call Sheriff Hardin and Lieutenant Colter." Her gaze lit on her forensics kit. *The samples*. "Who's still back at the school?"

"Nobody. Everybody's here. I was hoping we'd have the platform built by now."

"Good. But I need someone to help me process some evidence." She didn't even have to think about who she wanted. Julie Adams was her best lab student by far. "Send Julie to come and get me right now. The Bluebonnet Inn. Tell her it's programmed into the navigation system on both SUVs. I'll be ready. And hang in there, Todd. Prefab everything you can while you're waiting. The sheriff or the lieutenant will call Deputy Spears in a few minutes."

"Will do."

"Todd, have you talked to Pete today?" She knew she'd successfully e-mailed the images of the three thigh bones to Pete at Texas State, but it would make her feel better to hear that he'd received them and forwarded them to the Ranger Forensics Lab.

"Nope."

"Okay. I'll check with him. Tell Julie to hurry. I'll be waiting downstairs." Nina hung up and washed her face, brushed her teeth and ran a comb through her hair, before anchoring it with a hair band. Jeans and a T-shirt and white athletic socks came next.

Then she picked up her cell phone again and checked the alarm. It was set to Silent. She growled under her breath. She never forgot things like that. But she'd had more excitement in the past twelve hours or so than she'd ever had in her life—ever.

She threw her cell phone and her camera into her purse, grabbed her forensics kit and her boots and headed downstairs in her stocking feet.

By the time she got to the bottom of the stairs, the smell of coffee and something heavenly and fresh baked filled her senses. She gazed longingly toward the dining room, but she didn't have time for coffee, much less breakfast.

She headed for the front door.

"Morning, Nina."

She turned toward the cheery voice. It was Betty Alice, with a steaming mug in her hand.

"Here. I poured you a cup of coffee. There's sugar and cream on the sideboard in the dining room."

Nina took a deep whiff. "I really don't have time—"

"Of course you do. Now you go on in there and sit down." Betty Alice guided her to a dining-room chair. "And give me those."

Betty Alice took Nina's boots, leaving her hand free to accept the mug of coffee, which it did seemingly without her permission.

Dear heavens, it smelled good.

"These boots are a disgrace. I'm going out to knock all this dried mud off of them."

"Mrs. Sadler, I really don't—"

"Call me Betty Alice, dear. And eat a piece of

cinnamon loaf." She wagged her finger at Nina. "You're way too skinny."

With that she was gone. The screen door slammed behind her.

Nina saw a coffee carafe, cream and sugar, the cinnamon loaf, and a bowl of fruit sitting on the sideboard.

Maybe she could afford a few minutes for a mug of coffee. She set her forensics kit on a chair and fixed her coffee. She usually took it black, but the thick cream and the bowl full of raw sugar were too much of a temptation to ignore.

She took a long swallow. That first swallow of coffee was always her favorite moment of the day, but this was different—and way better. She couldn't remember why she seldom take the time to really savor her coffee. It was a grave error, one that she was going to correct immediately.

Then she dug into the food.

By the time Betty Alice came in, Nina had eaten half a bowl of fruit and a slice of cinnamon loaf, and was about to finish her coffee.

"There you go, hon. Your boots are just inside the door, and it looks like you need another cup of coffee. Let me—"

"No," Nina said firmly. "I really don't have time. My student should be here any second."

Betty Alice's eyes lit up, and she took a quick breath, but Nina deflected it.

"Can you give me Sheriff Hardin's phone number? I need to check with him on something."

"Of course."

As Betty Alice rattled off the number, Nina programmed it into her phone, then dialed it.

"Hardin," he said briskly.

"Sheriff Hardin, this is Nina Jacobson. I just talked to one of my students. For some reason your deputy won't allow them to construct the platform we talked about yesterday. He's stopped them at the perimeter of the site—of the crime scene."

"Did Lieutenant Colter authorize a platform?"

"Of course he did. It's the only way we can gather evidence without destroying the site. You were there."

"I didn't hear anything about a platform. I'll call Deputy Spears, but, Dr. Jacobson, when you need something from one of my employees, please have Lieutenant Colter ask for it."

Nina's ears burned at the sheriff's tone, but she knew better than to argue. It would only waste breath, because she was sure she knew the reason Hardin insisted on having Wyatt contact him.

It was Wyatt's rule.

"Yes, sir," she snapped. "I'll do that. Thank you." She hung up and made a quick call back to Todd to let him know the sheriff was calling Deputy Spears.

When she hung up, Betty Alice stepped in front of her. "Before you go, I want to apologize. Lieutenant Colter asked me about fixing the broken chain on your door. You really should move into the pink room. It's so much prettier, and all the locks are new."

"No." Nina wasn't about to be separated from Wyatt. She liked being close enough to him to know when he got a phone call in the middle of the night. "No. The room I'm in is fine."

"Nonsense. I don't want you to be nervous."

"I'm not nervous. But I did want to ask you who came into my room in the early morning hours, while we were at the grave site."

"Why…no one." But Betty Alice's gaze wavered. "Why would you think that?"

She knows something.

"Someone was in my room while we were at the crime scene. Whoever it was looked at the photos in my camera. Who was here between four o'clock and six o'clock?"

Betty Alice laughed nervously. "Oh my. You sound like the policemen on *Law & Order*."

Nina gazed at her steadily.

"My only other guest is a man who's visiting his son at the community college."

"Whoever went into my room had a key."

Betty Alice's cheeks turned red. "You know, now that I think about it, my niece came over to do some work on the wireless Internet service, but she wouldn't—"

"At four o'clock this morning."

"I don't know. Oh, dear." Tears started in her eyes.

"What is it?"

"I am so sorry. She's only seventeen. I'm afraid she has a crush on Reed—Sheriff Hardin. Maybe, maybe she wanted to see if you had taken any photos of him."

Nina eyed her suspiciously. Was she telling the truth? Or trying to cover up for someone? Nina decided not to push her. She might need Betty Alice's cooperation. "No damage was done, but let her know that if anything else of mine or Lieutenant Colter's is touched again, she could be charged with interfering with an investigation. Or, if you prefer, I could talk to her."

Betty Alice's eyes widened in shock. "No, please. I promise you she won't go into either of your rooms again."

"Good. Thank you."

The innkeeper patted her cheeks with her palms.

"Goodness. Let's see. I was going to tell you something. Oh, I remember. While you're gone today, I'll get that chain fixed. And I'm sure the key to the connecting door between your room and the lieutenant's is around here somewhere. Probably in one of my kitchen drawers." She stopped, letting the words hang in the air.

To her surprise, Nina felt her own cheeks heat up. No matter what she said, Betty Alice was going to take it the wrong way. But she didn't want that door locked. For some reason, she felt a lock would put more than a physical barrier between herself and Wyatt. He'd think she'd asked for it.

And truthfully, Nina liked the idea of being a mere wooden door away from Wyatt. Just so she could know what he was up to, of course.

"No." Nina shook her head and smiled. "I wouldn't want you to go to any trouble."

Betty Alice's eyebrows rose. "I understand completely," she murmured as she turned to refill Nina's mug.

Nina opened her mouth to protest the woman's assumption that there was something between her and Wyatt. But she'd started it, by insisting on staying next door to him. If she tried to explain the real reason she didn't want to move, what would she say? That she was torn between blaming him for her friend's disappearance and feeling as if his mere presence was enough to keep her safe from all harm?

She couldn't even explain that to herself.

Chapter Nine

Males. Nina couldn't make sense of them.

She glared at the two femurs laid out on the examining table in her makeshift lab.

She measured the head of the smaller thigh bone with the vernier caliper. The diameter, while less than that of the other bone, was still well within the testing parameters for males and quite a bit larger than the range established for females.

Of course, the ranges were averages. Still, it would take a *very* tall woman to have a thigh bone as large as the minimum assigned to males, and Marcie was only five-four.

Pulling down the lighted magnifying lamp, she studied the two bones. Judging by the fusion of the heads, it was obvious that both individuals had been well into their twenties. It would take more than a lone thigh bone to estimate the age any more closely.

Now if she had their skulls, she'd know the sex, age and possibly the race of each one. A more in-depth examination and the use of tables developed over years of study would even give her the time and possibly the cause of death.

Nina turned to the counter where her laptop was and

quickly recorded her initial estimates of the sex and heights of the two victims.

Then she laid a yardstick next to each bone and photographed it. Referring to the latest version of long-bone indicators of height in humans, she estimated the height of the smaller man at five feet eight inches.

The second bone was longer. Nina's calculations put him at five feet eleven inches.

As she typed that information into the computer, Nina's heart and gut twisted. The evidence proved that neither of these bones was Marcie's. And she was ninety-nine percent sure that the missing femur was the longest of the three—much too long to be her friend's.

She blew breath out in a long sigh. So who were the men whose bones she was studying? And where was Marcie?

She'd have to send scrapings to the lab to test nitrogen levels and fluorescence before she could pinpoint the men's ages.

She turned back to her laptop and searched through e-mails, looking for the message she'd received from the forensic technician at the Ranger lab.

There it was. She printed it and its attachments. They were summaries of the medical records of Mason Lattimer, the antiques broker who'd disappeared from Comanche Creek five years before, and Ray Phillips, the Native American activist who'd gone missing a couple of years later.

She glanced over the first sheet, gleaning the pertinent facts. According to his medical records summary, at his last doctor's visit, Mason Lattimer was forty-four years old and in excellent health, except for some osteoarthritis in his knees and hips, for which he took anti-inflammatory tablets.

The arthritis might help with identification, but almost everyone over forty had some evidence of degenerative bone disease.

She looked at the second sheet. The only medical record for Ray Phillips pertained to a ten-year-old visit to the health department for a tetanus shot. At the time he'd been nineteen. The nurse who'd administered the shot had noted no illnesses or injuries.

Nina sighed. Not much to go on.

"Why isn't this door locked?"

The commanding voice cut through the air like a saber. Nina jumped and whirled.

Wyatt stood in the doorway.

"And why aren't you answering your phone?"

"I'm busy," she said shortly, turning back to the table. "How did you find me?"

He laughed shortly. "You weren't at the crime scene, and you weren't at the inn. It wasn't much of a stretch to figure out the next most likely place. These doors should be locked."

"It's a community college. It has security. And, anyway, there's someone around all the time."

"There's nobody here right now."

She didn't answer him. Her mind was still focused on the two cleaned thigh bones on the table.

"You've been here only one day, and your room has already been broken into. Sheriff Hardin doesn't have the manpower to keep a guard with you at all times. It's after seven. How were you planning to get back to the inn tonight?"

Nina knew he'd said something, but she wasn't sure what. She bent a little lower over the magnifying lamp. There was a nick near the head of the femur tagged number one. Straightening, she glanced at the white board where she'd written the significant facts about each of them.

"What's wrong?" he asked.

It was irritating how easily he read her. Generally, the reaction she got from people was that it was impossible to know what she was thinking.

Dr. Mayfield had said once that she could unearth proof of the lost continent of Atlantis and the bones of Adam and Eve in the same day, and no one would know it by looking at her.

"What makes you think something's wrong?" The question might have been an automatic response, but truthfully, she really wanted to know how he could read her so easily. It was almost as disturbing as her sense that she knew all about him.

Before she realized he'd moved, he was at her side. "Those the thigh bones? Are they the only bones you were able to find?"

She blew out a frustrated breath, then crossed her arms and leaned against the table edge. "As it happens, once I was able to convince Sheriff Hardin that you really had given the okay to build a platform, Todd finally got it finished—late this afternoon. He and Julie, my two best graduate students, are sifting through the dirt and mud, looking for more remains."

"Good. What have they found?"

She glared at him. "Do you think you could retract that ridiculous order you gave to Sheriff Hardin that no one but you can authorize *anything* having to do with the site?"

Wyatt started to shake his head.

"It would cut down on *delays*."

He glared at her, and she knew she had him. "I'll tell

Hardin you can make decisions dealing with extracting the remains."

"Thank you." She relaxed a little. It was a huge victory for him to trust her with a little of his responsibility. "By the way, speaking of the sheriff, I want him to talk to Betty Alice's niece…scare her a little."

"You figure it was her niece who snooped around in your room?"

She shrugged. "That's what Betty Alice said. I'm more inclined to believe it was Betty Alice herself. It will be interesting to see what she does when Sheriff Hardin contacts her niece."

Wyatt's mouth turned up. "I'll tell Hardin to warn Betty Alice about tampering with evidence."

"Good. Thanks."

"Professor? The bones?" he prodded.

"Oh, right. We have two males here. I'll start with the bone tagged as number one. Judging by its length, he was five feet eight inches tall. It's hard to determine weight with so little to go on, but I'd estimate that he was average weight for his height. He was over twenty-five…could have been as old as fifty. I'm basing that on some early indications of osteoarthritis. Here, where the head of the bone is nicked, I can see some reduction in bone density."

"What about when he died?" Wyatt was frowning at the white board.

"I can't determine that with the resources I have here. That kind of testing requires a fully functioning forensics lab." She handed him the two sheets of paper. "I'll need to take bone scrapings to send to your Ranger lab so they can perform those tests. Meanwhile, take a look at these. Mason Lattimer and Ray Phillips's medical records."

"The two who disappeared from Comanche Creek in the past five years."

"Right. The size of the second femur," she continued, "indicates a male, five feet eleven inches. Again, hard to say about his weight. He was younger, maybe thirty."

He looked at the sheets of paper in his hand and then at the white board. "Then those two thigh bones could be Lattimer and Phillips."

"It's possible, but I can't be sure. Not without more to go on."

"But you're sure both bones belonged to males?"

She didn't even bristle at his question. She understood that it came from concern and frustration. Because she felt exactly the same way.

He'd expected an in-depth analysis. That was her area of expertise. So she knew he was surprised by her uncertainty of the weight of the two men.

"The diameter of the head of the femur in males is larger than that of females. A female thigh bone with a head in the size range of a male's would be an anomaly. At best, it would probably indicate a height of more than six feet."

Wyatt grimaced slightly. "And Marcie was under five-six."

"That's right." Nina pressed her lips together.

Neither she nor Wyatt was going to get closure. Not today. Maybe not ever.

"So that means…"

"Marcie's not there."

"Maybe she's underneath the other bones?"

Nina shook her head. "Not unless the entire site got turned upside down, or these two were put there after she was. I don't think that happened."

Wyatt stared at her, and she could see his brain working to sort the information into a rational, understandable format. To force it to make sense. She waited, knowing he was going to fail. She knew because she'd already been through it herself.

"Are you saying Marcie might be alive?"

"No, I'm not." Her voice held a jagged edge. She stood. "Come over here." She led the way to a small laminar flow hood. "This is what I did this morning," she said as she opened a pair of surgical gloves and slipped them on. "Here's the clump of hair. I extracted the necklace from right about here. Now, take a look at the hair's roots. That's blood."

Wyatt was standing so close to her that she could smell the peppermint on his breath and feel his tension.

"Blood?"

She nodded. "I managed to get enough to type it. It's the same type as Marcie. She was O-negative, and so is this."

"The blood is Marcie's blood type. It's Marcie's hair." Wyatt's words were a statement rather than a question.

"There are a lot of people with O-negative blood. We have to wait for the DNA match from the Ranger lab, but…" Nina's breath caught, and her eyes filled with tears. She carefully returned the clump of dirt-encrusted hair to the evidence bag and sealed it.

Wyatt swallowed hard. The curve of Nina's back and her bowed head gave him the answer he'd expected. They might not have found Marcie's bones yet, but that was her blood, her hair, her necklace that they'd pulled from that sad shallow grave.

The faint hope that had burned inside him flickered wanly, like a flame in the wind. Very little doubt remained. The evidence that Marcie was dead was piling up.

"What else have you got to do tonight?" he asked.

"What else?" Nina looked up at him. The glitter of moisture in her eyes took him aback. Although he supposed it shouldn't have. Marcie had been her best friend. Of course she'd held out hope, no matter how faint, that her friend was still alive.

"Have you eaten?"

She stared at him blankly.

"I'll take that as a no. Come on. I'm buying." He wasn't sure why he felt like he had to cheer her up when his own world was falling apart. It was one thing for a witness to disappear. Protected witnesses were not always happy about being protected. A surprising number of them ditched their protector or resigned from the program.

But this—this new information, which the professor had gleaned from just a few hours of study—meant that Marcie hadn't just disappeared. The evidence pointed to murder. Her hair, her blood, her necklace had been recovered from a shallow grave. It was only a matter of time before they found her bones.

As soon as the tests confirmed her identity, the entire case would be reopened. And this time he could lose his badge.

WYATT PAID THE CARHOP and took the bag. "Thanks," he said, waving away the change.

Nina grabbed the bag. "It has been way too long since I had one of Bud's grilled cheeseburgers."

Wyatt glanced up at the neon sign. Bud's Burgers and Shakes, Since 1953. "You take a perfectly good cheeseburger and *fry* it? Bread, pickles and all?"

"Don't knock it," Nina said as she bit into her sandwich, which did smell really good. "Think of it as a grilled-cheese sandwich with beef. Mmm."

Her appreciative murmur reverberated inside him

like a roomful of violins. He gritted his teeth as he dug into the bag for his own ordinary burger and fries.

They sat in his Jeep and ate, while the carhops glided back and forth on their roller skates, taking orders and delivering food.

Wyatt acted mildly interested in their activity while he polished off his food and settled back to watch Nina eat. By the time she finished, he'd decided if he could give her one-fifth the enjoyment she was getting from that burger, he'd be over the moon—and so would she.

He'd also decided that if he didn't stop thinking like that, he'd end up embarrassing himself.

"So you grew up here, too? Like Marcie?" he asked when she finally crumpled up the wrapper and licked her greasy fingers before cleaning them with a paper napkin.

She shook her head. "No. I've never lived in a small town. Not sure I'd ever want to."

"Not even for grilled cheeseburgers?"

She smiled and licked a dollop of mayonnaise off her lower lip, something he'd have liked to do for her. He groaned inwardly and looked away.

"I guess you live in San Marcos because of the university?"

"No. I live in Austin," she replied.

Wyatt sent her a thoughtful glance. "What part?"

"Lady Bird Lake area. Travis Heights."

"No kidding? I live a few blocks away from the lake. So did you grow up there?"

"No. In San Antonio. I met Marcie when we were paired as roommates at Texas State." She laughed. "Marcie wanted to major in anthropology. It took her only one visit to the body farm to decide it wasn't for her."

"Yet you two stayed friends."

Nina looked at him as if trying to decide if she'd rather share her memories of Marcie with him or cut him off at the knees for daring to talk about her best friend.

"My dad and my brother died within seven months of each other. It was an awful time. But Marcie was the one person I could count on, no matter what. She was always there for me…"

Wyatt silently finished Nina's sentence. *Until your negligence got her killed.* He balled up his burger wrapper and his napkins and stuffed them down into the bag.

"Ready?" he asked and pulled out of the parking spot without waiting for an answer. He headed back toward the Bluebonnet Inn, on the other end of Main Street.

"Did you talk to Shane and Trace Becker?" she asked as he parked the Jeep in the limestone parking lot.

"Becker never showed. But, yeah. I talked to Shane. After Hardin let all the bigwigs in town meet with us in the sheriff's office."

"Bigwigs? Like the mayor? I'm sure he was there."

Wyatt nodded. "He was. And Jerry Collier, Marcie's boss. She'd told me that the fraudulent land deal was Jonah Becker's idea. But Collier was the one she was afraid of."

Nina nodded. "I know. I think she was afraid of what he'd do if she testified."

"Right," Wyatt agreed. "That's why she was in our custody. Without her testimony, there was no proof that Collier or anyone else had done anything illegal." Wyatt swallowed the bitter taste of failure. "Some guy named Whitley was there, with his wife. You know them?"

"I don't think so. I met only a few people who were in and out of her office fairly regularly." She paused. "So you questioned Shane?"

Wyatt nodded. "He couldn't tell me anything more

about who attacked him last night. He said he was about to get into his truck to warm up for a few minutes, but when he walked around to the driver's-side door, someone hit him from behind."

"That's consistent with the state of the ground by the driver's-side door and the mud on his knees and hands. He didn't see anything? Not even the attacker's shoes?"

"He said he was too dazed. He about fell all over himself apologizing to everybody in Hardin's office for not stopping the guy."

"Hmm. Did you ask him anything else?"

"I got his shoe size. Twelve. Same as the castings from the crime scene. Which makes sense. And I questioned him about Marcie. Asked him if he thought her body might be buried out there. He looked surprised and upset, as if he'd never thought of that. According to him, he loved her. Said he was going to ask her to marry him. Said they'd talked about it."

"Oh, right. He's such a liar."

"They didn't talk about it?"

"*He* might have talked about marriage. But if Marcie did, it was only to tell him to dream on. She was through with Shane for good after that last…" She paused as though realigning what she was about to reveal.

"Last what?"

"Nothing," she said, crossing her arms. "What did Jerry Collier say?"

Wyatt saw that Nina wasn't going to say anything else about Tolbert and Marcie. He'd ask her later, when she was less defensive.

"Collier got real nervous. Kept fooling with a ballpoint pen till I thought I was going to have to take it away from him. I don't get why Marcie was afraid of him."

Nina shook her head. "Of course you don't. You're

a tall, strong, intimidating man. Marcie was five-four and weighed one-twenty at the most. Plus, Collier was her boss. He could have ruined her life with nothing more than a few well-placed words in her personnel file."

Chapter Ten

Nina's words gave Wyatt pause. He wasn't used to looking at the world through different eyes—certainly not a woman's.

"I never thought about it that way. You're right. It's hard for me to understand how anyone could be afraid of a little pip-squeak like Collier. Although I can guarantee you, Collier would never go up against Shane Tolbert in a physical confrontation. What's he? Maybe five-eight? Shane towers over him and outweighs him by at least thirty pounds."

A shudder rippled across Nina's shoulders.

He doubted it was entirely from the cold. Now that she'd made him aware of the difference in the way a man and a woman view other people, he could imagine what she was thinking.

She was probably picturing just how small and helpless Marcie had been next to Tolbert.

"You're cold," he observed. "Let's go inside. I'll make you a cup of coffee."

She didn't protest. Wyatt got out and went around to open the door for her, but she'd already climbed out of the truck and was heading inside.

He followed, watching her perfectly shaped backside

and wishing he didn't understand exactly why she was so determined to ignore any polite gesture from him. Wishing, for many more reasons than one, that he could go back in time and have a second chance to save Marcie.

Upstairs he took off his shoulder holster and washed his face and hands. Then he put on a pot of coffee and knocked on the connecting door. "Ready for coffee?" he called.

"Sure," he heard. "Just give me a minute."

He fixed himself a cup, black with lots of sugar, and sat down in the desk chair, leaving the slipper chair for her.

When she knocked lightly on the door and opened it, he gestured her in.

She'd changed into long, flowing pants and a matching top. She'd taken her hair down. Having it loose around her face had transformed her from a professor into a woman. The dark frame of her hair softened her features and made her skin look enticingly creamy and soft.

He forced his gaze away from her kissable face. Looking down, he saw that her feet were bare, with pink nail polish gracing her pretty, sexy toes. He groaned inwardly. When had he ever thought toes were sexy?

She headed straight for the coffeepot. "This is what I love about B and Bs," she said. "Real cream and a sugar bowl full of real sugar."

Wyatt watched her load up her mug with sugar. He had a strange urge to talk with her about sugar, about coffee, about how much he wanted to run his fingers through her black hair, but not only was that a waste of valuable time, which he could be using to get one step closer to what had happened to Marcie, it was also a surefire way to be shot down.

She hated him. She blamed him for her friend's death. They would never be friends. Talking about the grilled cheeseburger earlier was probably the closest they'd ever get to friendly conversation.

So there was no point in him waiting until she was less defensive to ask her about Marcie. There would never be a better time.

He decided to plunge right in. "You said Marcie was through with Shane for good after the last…something."

The teaspoon Nina was using to stir her coffee rattled against the side of the cup. "Last something?" she repeated, without looking at him.

He compressed his lips. She knew exactly what he was talking about. "What did you mean?"

She sat down on the slipper chair and flipped her hair back over her shoulder with one hand. "You think it was Shane who kidnapped Marcie? You think he killed her? I don't like him, and I certainly have no reason or desire to defend him, but I don't think he kidnapped her. For one thing, he didn't have time. He was there after the attack. Later I mean. After you were taken away in the ambulance."

"I know," he said gruffly. "I've read all the depositions, all the eyewitness accounts, all the interviews with everyone who could have possibly had any reason to stop Marcie from testifying. Nobody was anywhere, and nobody saw anything."

"What about you? What did you see?"

Wyatt rubbed his fingers across his forehead. How had the conversation ended up here? He started to change the subject back to what Tolbert had done to Marcie, but he made the mistake of meeting Nina's gaze. Her dark eyes were wide and pleading, and again he wished he could turn off the strange intuition that told him what she was thinking.

She wanted answers. Closure. Something to help her make sense of what had happened to her friend. The one person who had been there for her.

He blew his breath out between clenched teeth. He owed her that much. Not that he knew anything that would make her feel better. "You remember where we were staying, don't you?"

"Of course. That house just off Main Street, the one that was for sale by the bank. Marcie wanted me to stay there with her, but you wouldn't allow it, so I was staying at the inn."

He nodded. "That's right. I should have moved her back to Austin, into a safe house. Then I could have kept her whereabouts secret. Here in Comanche Creek, there might as well have been a big neon sign over the house. But the attorneys were sure it wouldn't take but a few days, and they wanted her available for depositions and questioning. I agreed, because I was sure there wouldn't be a problem. Hell, it was a local land fraud case. Everybody in town probably knew who was behind it, and Marcie was the only one who'd had the nerve to speak up. With her testifying, I figured others would come forward, and the whole thing would be settled within another day or two."

Nina started to shake her head. Was she going to tell him not to blame himself? He doubted it. Anyhow, it was two years too late for that.

He went on. "So that morning we were up early. The judge wanted to get the preliminary hearing started by nine o'clock. So it was around eight o'clock when I went out to check around and start the car." He leaned forward and put his elbows on his knees and stared at his hands.

After a moment he spoke again. "I heard a sound

from the house. I ducked behind the car just as a bullet hit the car door. Then three more shots. I could see a shadow standing at the front door, so I pulled my gun and ran toward him but…" He stopped. His chest was tight. He took a long, unsatisfying breath and stood, looking out through the blue shutters on the windows.

"That's when you were shot."

"I hit the ground, but when I tried to roll up and shoot again…" He shrugged. He hadn't been able to get back onto his feet. There had been a two-ton weight pressing on his chest. He'd raised his gun and fired, but it was like he'd lost control of his gun hand. All he'd been able to hear were his wild shots hitting the wooden siding.

Nina spoke from behind him. "I heard the shots all the way over at the inn. Then Betty Alice's phone started ringing off the hook." He heard the clunk of her cup as she set it on the desk. "I remember that by the time I got downstairs, everyone knew you'd been shot and the sheriff had rushed to Marcie's house, but she was gone, and there was blood on the kitchen floor."

Wyatt turned. Her eyes were bright with tears. Somehow that hurt his chest more than the memory of the bullet's impact.

"I'd give anything if I could have been there to process that scene myself," he confessed. "By the time I could do anything, the house had been cleaned up and sold. I wanted to examine that door. The person I saw had come from inside the house. I'm sure of it."

Nina made a small sound. "Inside? Surely you don't think it was Marcie?"

He shook his head. "She screamed. I heard her say 'Don't shoot.' No. It wasn't her. But whoever it was managed to get into the house somehow—with or without her permission. And of course, the blood was

O-negative. Just like Marcie's." He rubbed his forehead again. "I've been over the files a dozen times. But that's not the same as being there."

Nina looked down at her hands, then up at him again. "Wyatt, I—"

"If there's anything you know—anything at all—tell me. About Tolbert, about Marcie. About anyone else she mentioned talking to. I just need answers. Once I know all the facts, maybe I can finally figure out what happened."

Nina's dark eyes assessed him for a fraction of a second. "Marcie was so nervous about testifying. That's why she called me. To give her moral support. Plus, as soon as she was done giving her testimony, we were going on a cruise."

"Did she say why she was nervous? Who she was afraid of? I'm thinking it had to be somebody besides Collier."

"Jonah Becker?"

Wyatt gave a quick nod. "That'd be my guess. It's hard to believe Collier would have the guts to do anything on his own. Did Marcie ever mention Becker to you?"

"No."

"From what she told me, most of the information she had came from overheard telephone conversations. I'm not totally convinced that her testimony would have been enough to hurt Collier, much less Becker." Wyatt watched Nina and waited.

"She used to say that Jerry Collier was *creepy*. Apparently he was always trying to cut a deal with somebody."

"Did she ever talk specifics?"

Nina shook her head. "One of the worst things she

told me she'd seen was Collier and Daniel Taabe getting into a fight."

"Right. That fight was what precipitated the investigation. It was Taabe who brought the original charges of land fraud against Jerry Collier. I talked to him today. He believes that Marcie's sympathy for the Native American cause contributed to her disappearance."

"He could be right. Marcie thought the Comanches were getting the raw end of the deal."

"Taabe's not shy about showing his resentment for the town leaders. He offered me his help in the investigation."

"Are you going to accept it?"

Wyatt shook his head. "Can't afford to. I'm afraid allowing him access to the site could become a powder keg. One tiny spark and I'd have an explosion on my hands."

Nina nodded. "Did you talk to anyone else?"

"I tried to get an interview with Billy Whitley and his wife, Charla, but they weren't available. All I know about them is that they're big friends with Tolbert and they can't stand Taabe."

"I don't know them. I never heard Marcie mention their names."

"I'm going to try and talk with them tomorrow." He paused, studying her. "So if the fight between Collier and Taabe was the worst, what did she tell you that wasn't the worst?"

Nina licked her lips. "I told you, we didn't talk about the town that much. I do remember her talking about those two men whose medical records the Ranger lab sent me."

"You mean Lattimer and Phillips, the guys who disappeared? Marcie knew them?"

"I don't know. She worked at the land office for nine years, ever since she graduated."

"What did she say about them?"

Nina looked at him thoughtfully. "It was a long time ago. But it had something to do with Native American artifacts and burial grounds, and… Oh, that was it. One of them was buying up ancient artifacts. The other one, Phillips, was the leader of the Comanche community, and the two of them came to blows over some missing artifacts."

"When was this?"

She rubbed her temple. "It was one small conversation years ago. We were celebrating something. Maybe it was when I'd just gotten my PhD."

"I'll ask Hardin about it."

"I can tell you that when the land fraud came to light, Marcie mentioned them again. She said she was afraid she'd end up disappearing, like they did."

Wyatt nodded. Marcie had told him that, too. He should have asked her who she thought was responsible for Lattimer and Phillips disappearing. "What about her and Tolbert?" he asked. "Did she think he had anything to do with those two? You still haven't told me what happened that made Marcie decide she was through with him."

"When I called to tell her I'd booked us a cruise for the week after she was supposed to testify, she said Shane had been pestering her, wanting to see her. Wanting to talk to her about the case."

"When? While she was in my custody?" Wyatt thought back. Marcie had had her cell phone, but Wyatt didn't remember hearing her talk to Shane Tolbert.

Nina shook her head. "Just before. She agreed to meet him one last time, but then when she told him she didn't want to see him again, he threatened her."

Wyatt waited.

"He told her she was his. And if he ever saw her with another man, he'd…" Her throat moved as she swallowed.

"He'd what?"

Nina's eyes widened, and she swallowed nervously. "He'd kill both of them," she whispered.

He'd expected something like that, but the words hit his ears like a stunning blow. *Kill both of them.* Was Shane Tolbert capable of killing? Had the deputy shot him?

"Wyatt?"

He blinked. "What?" He realized she'd said something.

"I said, do you think Shane shot you?"

"The bullet they pulled out of my lung was never matched to a weapon. According to the file, the Rangers tested every gun in Comanche Creek."

"Your *lung?*"

Ah, hell, he thought. That had slipped out. It sounded like a bid for sympathy.

"I thought…" She'd turned pale. Her skin looked translucent against the backdrop of that dark hair.

He didn't wait to find out what she thought. He stood. "I don't trust Tolbert, but he *was* attacked. You saw that head wound. Seven stitches isn't child's play."

"No. It's very serious."

As was her voice.

"Wyatt? I didn't show you the pictures I took, did I?"

"Which ones?"

"Of Shane's head wound."

He shook his head, but she was already up and heading through the connecting door. Within seconds she was back with her camera. "Take a look at this."

He looked at her photos of the cut on Tolbert's head. There was a red stripe, emphasized by the camera's flash, next to the bleeding laceration.

"Do you see it?" Her voice was laced with excitement and impatience.

He didn't answer. He wanted to see what she saw.

"That red streak. It's a *hesitation* wound. Can't you see it?" she asked.

"I see it." He handed the camera back to her. "I noticed it that night, but do you really think Shane conked himself on the head?"

"Do you think he stayed politely still while someone else took a practice blow?"

He had to give her that point. "You know how hard that will be to prove. The redness has already faded."

She sighed. "I know. And the inflammation of the laceration will have spread to cover it."

He nodded, then gestured toward the coffeepot. "You want some more coffee?"

She shook her head. "I'll never get to sleep if I drink any more."

He took her cup, trying to ignore the way his fingers tingled where they brushed hers. Trying to ignore how she jerked her hand away from his accidental touch.

"You said you didn't get to question Whitley?" she asked.

He set the cups down, then propped a hip on the edge of the desk. "No. I want to, though. He and his wife acted like they were furious that I'd even dare to question them. I got maybe three minutes with Mayor Sadler, most of which he spent talking. Making sure I understood just how much he does for this town." He paused. "And Trace Becker never showed up. What do you know about him?"

"Not much. Marcie called Trace a spoiled brat. She did say she wouldn't be surprised if he was in on the illegal land deal with his father and Collier." She yawned. "Excuse me. I guess I'm more tired than I realized."

"What are you planning to do in the morning?" Wyatt asked. "Go to the site or back to the lab?"

"I trust my students to handle the extraction of the bones. I want to do those scrapings of the thigh bones and send them to the Ranger lab."

"So you've got somebody to pick you up?" He was interrupted by his cell phone. It was Hardin. He answered it.

"Lieutenant? It's Reed Hardin. I just got a call from Daniel Taabe."

"Something happen?"

Nina sat up straight, her sharp gaze holding his.

"You could say that," replied Hardin. "He says he found a hatchet in the back of his pickup. A hatchet with blood on it."

"Where are you?" asked Wyatt.

"Wait. That's not all. He said he also found a bone."

"He found a bone?" Wyatt asked.

"A *bone?*" Nina echoed. "Is it my thigh bone?"

"I'm headed out to Daniel's place now." Hardin gave him directions. "I'll be right there." Wyatt hung up his phone and reached for his shoulder holster.

Nina stood. "I'm going with you."

"No, you're not." Wyatt slipped the holster on and checked his weapon.

"Yes, I am. Somebody found my missing bone, didn't they?"

Wyatt cursed under his breath. He was going to have to be a lot more careful with her around.

She headed back to her room. "I'll be ready in five minutes."

"Three, or I'm leaving." It was an empty threat, and he knew it. He reached for his windbreaker. She was right. If it was the missing thigh bone, she needed to be there. He wasn't taking any chances of contaminating the evidence. The stakes were too high—for him, for the town and for Marcie.

Chapter Eleven

Daniel Taabe lived west of Comanche Creek, in a white clapboard house with a screened porch and a tin roof. They passed a trailer park, a few large new homes set back from the road and several houses that appeared to be the same age as Taabe's.

Sheriff Hardin was already there, along with Deputy Spears. They had a big spotlight on the backseat of Taabe's truck, and Spears was crouched down, examining the floorboards with a flashlight, while Hardin stood talking to Taabe.

Wyatt parked the Jeep and got out. Out of the corner of his eye, he saw Nina heading straight for the truck.

"Lieutenant," Hardin said as Wyatt approached. He was holding a small spiral notepad and a ballpoint pen.

"Sheriff. Mr. Taabe," said Wyatt.

Daniel Taabe was frowning. His black hair was unbraided and loose. It looked damp, as if he'd just washed it.

Hardin's face was dark with worry. Wyatt couldn't blame him. If the acknowledged leader of the Native American community here was arrested, things in Comanche Creek were liable to get real ugly, real fast.

"What happened?" asked Wyatt.

Hardin pushed his hat back off his forehead. "Daniel called me about seven thirty, told me he went to get something out of his truck and noticed a small hatchet and a bone in the backseat. Says he knows they weren't there when he got home from town around lunchtime."

Wyatt nodded and waited for Hardin to offer up more information. He was certain that the hatchet was the weapon used to knock out Shane Tolbert and the bone was the one missing from the crime scene. Therefore, this discovery fell under his jurisdiction, and he had every right to march over to the truck and claim the evidence. But as much as he wanted to do that, he owed the sheriff a little courtesy.

"Kirby's checking out the truck. I see your bone collector came along." Hardin paused. Wyatt didn't speak, so he continued. "I was just asking Daniel if he saw anybody around his truck earlier."

"I was about to tell the sheriff that kids come around here all the time," said Taabe. "I hire them to do odd jobs. It keeps them busy. There were three here this afternoon, cleaning out the stables."

Hardin clicked the ballpoint pen. "Who were they?"

"Tim Hussey, Andy Jones and Kirk Foote. You wouldn't know them." Taabe's voice held a note of indignation.

"Did you see any of them hanging around your truck?" asked Wyatt.

"No. As I told the sheriff, I did not see anything."

"I take it your truck wasn't locked," Wyatt continued.

"I have no reason to lock it."

"You didn't go out to the stables while the boys were working?" asked Wyatt.

Taabe shook his head. "Of course I did. I spent

nearly two hours out there with them. I like to show them the right way to treat the horses."

Wyatt nodded. "And when they left?"

"I was still in the stables," replied Taabe. "I had a couple of mares whose hooves needed trimming."

Wyatt persisted, frustrated with Taabe's polite yet uninformative answers. "So you don't know if one or more of the boys did something to your truck."

"Yes, I do. They didn't," Taabe asserted.

Wyatt's jaw ached. "Would you mind telling me how you know?"

Taabe's mouth softened into a smile. "I'd be happy to. The stables are there, east of my house. My truck was parked where it is now, right in front of my door." He paused and lifted his head, as if sensing something. Then he pointed to the north. "I always watch the boys leave. They went north."

Wyatt leveled a gaze at him and waited.

"The only time someone could have approached my truck without me knowing was when I was inside my house, taking a shower."

"And that was when?" Hardin asked.

"Shortly after the boys left. Around five."

"You always follow the same routine?" Wyatt interjected.

Taabe smiled again. "Generally."

Wyatt turned toward the cab, checking on Nina. Spears was still searching inside the truck. Wyatt could see flashes of light as the deputy took pictures. Nina was examining the ground beside the door.

"Do you have any further questions for me?" Taabe asked. "Because I'm expecting someone."

As Wyatt stalked over to Taabe's truck, a pair of headlights appeared in the distance. He watched as they grew closer, until a white pickup pulled up several feet from where they were standing.

Ellie Penateka jumped out, dressed in faded, torn jeans and a figure-hugging yellow top. She went straight to Taabe's side and asked him what was going on.

So she was the company Daniel Taabe was expecting.

Wyatt would have liked to hear their conversation, but he needed to know what Nina had found out about the bone.

"Professor," he said, dropping to his haunches beside her.

"Yes, cowboy?" she retorted without lifting her head. Her flashlight beam played along the hard, dusty ground.

"What are you looking for?"

"Checking for prints."

"The ground looks pretty hard—" Wyatt began just as she uttered a triumphant murmur.

"There." She aimed her flashlight at a point about eighteen inches in front of her.

Wyatt saw the faint edge of what appeared to be a boot print. A large one.

"Hold this." She handed him her flashlight and retrieved a tape measure from her pocket. After placing the tape alongside the print, she snapped several photos.

"Can you get a casting of that? We could compare it with the print from the crime scene."

"I don't think so. The ground's too dusty. But we can compare the boot size. This one appears to be a size twelve." She pocketed the tape measure and pushed herself to her feet and dusted her hands together.

Size twelve. The shoe size of Tolbert, Daniel Taabe,

Deputy Spears and who knew how many others in town. With the ground that dusty, there would be no way to see any details of the boot's sole.

"What about the bone?" he asked.

Her mouth flattened, and she gave a small shake of her head.

Wyatt's pulse sped up. She'd figured something out about the bone, and she wasn't happy about it.

As if to confirm his conclusion, her fist tightened around the lanyard attached to her camera.

"I'll show you," she said and stalked toward his vehicle.

NINA HEADED TOWARD WYATT'S Jeep Liberty. She'd done her best to hang on to her professional detachment, but what she'd found in the back of Daniel Taabe's truck had her heart still pounding and her palms clammy with shock and fear.

"Deputy Spears had already photographed and bagged them," she said, reaching for the back door.

She threw the door open and stepped back.

Wyatt glanced at her sidelong. "What's wrong, Professor?" he asked as he played the flashlight beam over the bags sitting on the backseat.

She scraped her teeth over her lower lip, not trusting herself to speak.

After a few seconds of scrutiny, Wyatt bent and studied the contents of the bags. "That hatchet could match Tolbert's head wound."

Nina didn't answer.

"What's that?" Wyatt asked, zeroing in on the second bag. "That's not the missing thigh bone." A camera flash sent a dark shadow along the sharp, tense line of Wyatt's jaw.

"No, it's not."

He turned the flashlight toward her. "Nina?"

She swallowed. "It's a pelvic bone. From a female."

"A female."

For a moment neither of them spoke, but to Nina, it was as if someone were screaming into a loudspeaker.

A female pelvic bone. Was it Marcie's? Wyatt cleared his throat. "Is it from the crime scene?"

"The mud is consistent."

"You don't sound sure."

"I can't afford to jump to any conclusions." But she already had. And they terrified her. "I need to get it back to the lab and test it."

Again, the silence between them was deafening.

Finally Wyatt nodded. "And I need to take Taabe in and question him."

"You're going to arrest him? You think he attacked Shane? Why would he call the sheriff to report finding the hatchet if he's the one who attacked him?"

"Maybe he's trying to throw suspicion off himself. It's a common mistake that guilty people make."

"I don't see him as violent. He seems to be more about peace than trouble." She looked over her shoulder. Taabe was talking calmly with Sheriff Hardin. "Who's the woman? She's beautiful."

Wyatt grunted noncommittally. "Ellie Penateka. Hardin tells me she's very active in the Native American community. Apparently she's leading a petition to reclaim Comanche land in this area. She's campaigning to get a casino built here."

"She's also campaigning to get Daniel Taabe," Nina muttered.

"What do you mean?" Wyatt asked.

"Just look at them. They're trying to act as if nothing's going on, but look at that body language."

"So you're an expert on the language of the body, as well as of the skeleton?"

His voice was close to her ear—too close. She got a whiff of sharp, sweet mint, and a sense that he knew how uncomfortable he was making her.

"It doesn't take an expert to know when two people are that attracted to each other," she said. "Look how she's standing. She's completely open to him. And he's the same way. I'd bet you a month's salary they're lovers. Or if not yet, they soon will be."

"Not a bet I'm willing to take," he muttered just as a camera flash blinded her.

"What the hell?" Wyatt said, stepping away from her. "Spears, what are you doing?"

"Sorry, sir. That was an accident," replied the deputy.

Nina blinked, trying to get rid of the after-burn inside her eyelids.

"Are you done with Taabe's truck?" Wyatt asked him.

Reed Hardin walked over. "We're just about to take it in, Lieutenant. We've got a small fenced parking lot behind the office. We'll keep it there."

"Good. I'll bring Taabe in," Wyatt announced.

"You think that's necessary? He's not going anywhere," Hardin said.

Wyatt nodded. "I want to question him before he has a chance to get his story together."

Hardin sent Wyatt an odd look. "Daniel Taabe has had his story together all his life."

Nina listened to the two of them while Deputy Spears handed her the bags of evidence that he'd collected.

"Dr. Jacobson?" Spears said. "Is that everything? Do you need me to explain my notes?"

"I don't think so, Kirby. Everything appears to be pretty self-explanatory. You've got the swabs labeled and the fingerprint sheets. And it looks like you did a good job with the hatchet and the bone."

Spears seemed to swell up. "Thank you, ma'am. I mean Dr. Jacobson."

"I'll call you if I have any questions," Nina told him.

"Okay. Good." The deputy stuck his hands in his pants pockets, then pulled them out again. "Well, I need to drive Daniel's truck back to town. I'll—I'll wait to hear from you. I mean, I hope I don't. Because I hope I did everything right, but—"

"Thank you, Deputy," said Nina. "I just need your camera, so I can send the images to the Ranger lab for processing."

"Uh…" Spears sent a look toward Hardin.

"It's all right," Nina reassured him. "I'm holding the chain of custody. I'll give you a written receipt."

Spears handed the camera over to her.

"Thank you," she said to Hardin. "I'll get you copies—"

"Let's go," Wyatt snapped.

Nina jumped. He'd walked up behind her. He didn't wait for her to acknowledge that she was ready to go. He just rounded the front of the Jeep and got in the driver's seat.

She opened the passenger door. "As soon as I put the evidence bags in my kit."

"Hurry up."

She deposited the bags the deputy had given her into the metal evidence kit, and closed and locked it. Then she checked the bone and the hatchet again, telling herself she was being careful, but knowing that she might be goading Wyatt a bit. He deserved it, ordering her around like that.

Finally she closed the back door and climbed in the passenger side. She'd barely gotten her door closed and her seat belt on before he pulled away in a spray of dirt and limestone gravel.

"What is wrong with you?" she cried. "The bone could fall off the seat, the way you're driving."

"You should have secured it better."

She understood at least part of why he was agitated. She felt the same way. Ever since she'd first laid eyes on the pelvic bone, her chest had been tight with tension, and tears had been pushing closer and closer to the surface.

The bone had belonged to a *female*. And as every anthropologist knew, the pelvic bone was *the* definitive feature distinguishing male from female.

She now had a bone that could be Marcie's.

It was taking all her strength not to give in to her emotional side, so she certainly wasn't going to be drawn into his little tantrum.

After a few seconds, he muttered something.

"What?" she asked.

"I said I hate small towns."

She bit her cheek, trying not to smile and appreciating the momentary diversion. "I don't care for them, either. You can never find a decent yoga class or a really good cappuccino."

He growled.

She bit her cheek again. "What happened?"

His hands were white-knuckled on the steering wheel, and the irritation and frustration radiated from him in waves. "Sheriff Hardin didn't think it was necessary to arrest Taabe." Disgust colored his words.

"I suspect he's right. Arresting Daniel could stir up a lot of trouble in town."

Another growl.

"I take it you don't agree."

His shoulders moved in a shrug. "I don't like delays."

"Ah, yes. I recall. Or people who disagree with you." She cringed, fully expecting him to squeeze the steering wheel hard enough to break it, but to her surprise, he consciously relaxed his hands, and his jaw even quit bulging quite so much. "What's your rush to arrest Daniel Taabe? Just what do you think he will do tonight if he's not in jail? Head for the border?"

He didn't answer.

"Want to know what I think he'll be doing tonight?"

Wyatt sent her a quick, quelling glance. "No."

"I think he and Ellie Penateka—"

"I said no."

"Okay, but I guarantee you Daniel Taabe will still be here tomorrow for you to question to your heart's content. Do you want to know why?"

"No."

"Because he and Ellie are in love."

Wyatt scowled at her. "And you know that."

"I told you earlier, it's obvious in their body language. Not to mention they can't take their eyes off each other."

He frowned, as if he wanted to ask her something, but he didn't. He drove in silence, while Nina turned her attention back to the digital photos Spears had taken.

"Kirby did a good job," she said finally.

"Kirby?"

"Deputy Spears. I mean, he must have taken three shots of each drop of blood, but at least he erred on the side of thoroughness."

"What about fingerprints? Did he find any?"

"There are some, but I'll need to send them to the lab to be matched. Of course, Daniel's will be all over, and depending on how long it took him to notice the bags in the backseat, he might have smeared or destroyed any new prints."

She kept thumbing through the photos. She squinted at a close-up of the pelvic bone. Was there something odd about the bone's surface? Or was it just a trick of the light?

She opened her mouth to tell Wyatt to take her to the lab so she could get started on testing it tonight, but at that moment the last shot Kirby had taken came up.

The one he'd accidentally snapped of her and Wyatt.

Oh, no, she gasped to herself. Then she went totally still, holding her breath. Had she said that out loud? Wyatt didn't react, so she must not have.

It was a wonder that she hadn't, because what she was staring at was a photo of the two of them, and they could be a dead ringer for Taabe and Ellie.

She and Wyatt were standing close together. Wyatt's head was bent toward hers. His expression was hot, even passionate, and his posture was open, powerful, protective.

She was leaning toward him, her neck slightly arched, as if opening herself to his kiss.

That wasn't what they'd been doing, but judging by the picture, it could have been.

What she'd told him about Taabe and Ellie echoed in her brain. *I'd bet you a month's salary they're lovers. Or if not yet, they soon will be.* She moaned silently.

"What?"

She jumped. "I didn't say anything."

"Yes, you did."

She turned off the camera. "Take me to the lab at the college."

"No. It's too late."

"I want to look at this bone. There's something odd about it."

"Tomorrow."

"Hey, cowboy, you're the one who said you didn't like delays."

He turned onto the road that led to the Bluebonnet Inn. "And you pointed out that I don't like people who disagree with me. So why do you keep doing it?"

"To irritate you?" she snapped.

"That would be my guess," he shot back.

She looked at her watch. "It's only... Oh."

"It's only what time?"

She bit her lip. "Almost midnight."

"Right. Still want to start a whole new set of tests?"

"Actually, yes. I don't have to tell you what it means that this pelvis is from a female."

"Are you positive that it came from the crime scene?"

She glared at his profile. "It's a bone, it's got mud smeared all over it and it showed up with a bloody hatchet that matches Shane's description of the weapon in his attack."

Wyatt stopped the Jeep in front of the inn and killed the engine. He turned and gazed at her steadily.

"Okay. I can't say for certain, not without the tests. Which is why I want to go to the lab." She tried to suppress a yawn but wasn't successful.

"See? You can't start all that testing tonight. You're exhausted. You'd probably screw up the tests. I need to take you upstairs and put you to bed."

He looked at her, his blue eyes twinkling, and a hot

thrill coursed through her at the idea of him lifting her in his arms and carrying her upstairs like Rhett Butler.

She swallowed, and the twinkle in his eyes faded, replaced by an intensity she hadn't seen before—not even when he was ready to throttle Sheriff Hardin for refusing to arrest Taabe.

He looked like…

She swallowed. He looked like he did in the photo. Hot, powerful, passionate.

Something caught and started to burn deep inside her. She lifted her chin just slightly. For an indefinable time they stared at each other.

Then Wyatt blinked and opened the driver's-side door.

"Tomorrow," he said gruffly.

Chapter Twelve

By the time Nina was ready for bed, she could barely hold her eyes open. She yawned and looked longingly at the turned-down covers. But her brain was still churning.

She had so much evidence and so few answers. And now a female pelvic bone had been added to the mix.

If it was Marcie's…

She couldn't go there. Just like Wyatt had reminded her, nothing was certain until she had the test results.

Test results. Her gaze snapped to her laptop. She needed to check her e-mail in case the forensics lab had sent her the results of the DNA comparison of the hair found at the crime scene.

Within a few seconds she was watching, her heart in her throat, as her new messages downloaded.

And there it was. Sender? The Ranger Forensics lab.

It was short. No wasted words. Attached please find…

Nina opened the attachment and scanned it quickly. Professional and to the point, and precisely what she'd expected.

She'd written several reports just like this, without once thinking about the real, grieving people on the receiving end of the information. Never again, though. She would never be able to stare at a set of remains again without remembering the grief that flooded her heart this minute.

Or the sense of loneliness.

A tear slid from her eye and rolled down her cheek. She wasn't a forensic anthropologist—not right now. She was a grieving friend. A quick swipe with her fingers got rid of the tear, but not the weight of sadness.

She turned and looked at the closed door that separated her from Wyatt, worrying her lower lip with her teeth. She needed to tell him; he needed to know.

It was as important to him as it was to her. Maybe more. After all, he was responsible.

Wasn't he? As much as Nina needed someone to blame, the longer she knew Wyatt, the harder it was to blame him.

She knocked on the door between their rooms. When he didn't answer right away, she was afraid he'd already gone to sleep. Should she wake him? She knocked again, lightly, then turned the knob, fully expecting the room to be dark.

But the soft glow of the bedside lamp lit the room—the empty room.

Too late, Nina recognized the warm scent of steam and bleached towels and soap.

She needed to get out of here—now.

Then the bathroom door opened, and there he was, right in front of her, dressed in nothing but briefs, with a towel hanging from one hand.

He was scowling, but as soon as his gaze met hers, his expression changed. "What's the matter, Professor? You okay?"

"I shouldn't have…" Nina stumbled over her words. "It can wait." She took a step backward.

"Hang on!" He grabbed the pair of sweatpants that were slung over the back of a chair and pulled them on. Then in one stride, he was at her side. "Now, what is it? Did you hear something? Has someone been in your room again?"

She shook her head. "I—I just checked my e-mail. The results are back on the hair."

"Yeah?"

Nina heard the fear and anticipation in his voice. He was as anxious to know the results as she had been.

And he'd be just as devastated.

She took a deep breath, filled with the odor of fresh clean skin and soap. She scraped her lower lip with her teeth and felt cool air on her cheek as another tear spilled over. "The DNA from the hair was a match with Marcie's. No question."

His gaze narrowed. After an instant of unnatural stillness, he brushed his fingers tenderly across her cheek. The slight touch sent a sweet, sad ache through her.

"We expected that," he murmured.

She squeezed her eyelids shut, trying to stop any more tears. Of course, it did no good. "I know," she whispered. "It's just hard."

"Yeah. It is." He pulled her close, cradling the back of her head in his palm.

She pressed her face into the hollow between his neck and shoulder, where his skin was warm and damp. Beneath its silky surface, his firm, vibrant muscles rippled, and his chest rose and fell with his strong, steady breathing. She slid her arms around his waist, just to absorb more of the comfort he offered her.

She missed Marcie.

"Something in me never let her go," she whispered. "I believed she was out there somewhere. That she was waiting for something—waiting until she felt safe enough to come back."

He pressed his cheek against her hair. "Are you okay?" he asked.

"Yes. I am." She laughed quietly. "I don't know why I'm acting like this."

"You've got a right."

She hugged him tighter, pressing her nose into his damp flesh, breathing deeply. His closeness and scent were comforting, she told herself. Her insides were warm and glowing from his gentle embrace and their shared sadness—not hot and liquid because she craved the taste of him on her tongue.

He pressed a kiss to the top of her head, a sweet, protective gesture at odds with the quick, staccato beat of his heart.

Her own pulse sped up, and her breasts, already taut and full where they pressed against his chest, suddenly grew ultrasensitive.

She pulled away.

His hand slid from the back of her head to her neck, and his thumb brushed across the line of her jaw gently, caressingly. "Do you want to leave?"

She shook her head, not knowing if she was answering him or wishing he would stop talking. The way she was feeling right now couldn't be described in words.

Words only complicated everything.

He nodded, as if he knew what she was thinking and agreed. She felt the movement of his head against her hair. Before he could speak, she pressed her fingers against his lips.

To her surprise, he opened his mouth and slid his tongue along her fingertips. She gasped.

He lowered his head, pushing her own fingers to her mouth, sending even more heat to her core. She slid her hand around to his nape, where his hair was damp and tousled, and pulled his head closer.

And accepted his kiss.

When their lips touched, he sighed—a ragged expulsion of breath. Hesitating, he hovered there, the full center of his lower lip barely grazing hers.

Without thinking about the consequences, she ran her tongue over the seam that linked their lips.

With a gasp, he let his mouth cover hers, and their tongues met. He tasted just like she knew he would. Hot and sweet and minty, with an undercurrent of something dark and delicious.

Then his hands were around her back and pulling her to him. The thin silk of her camisole seemed to melt as he imprinted his body on hers. Her nipples tightened until they ached. Her thigh muscles contracted reflexively, responding to the rising heat his touch was coaxing from her sexual center.

Wyatt tore his mouth away and studied her face, his eyes as hot and blue as a flame of pure oxygen. "Professor? I don't want to take advantage—"

Her fingers curled into fists. "You're not," she grated.

"You sure about this?"

She couldn't answer. She had no breath. All she could do was kiss him again, more deeply.

That was all the answer Wyatt needed. He picked her up and laid her down on the bed, then lowered himself beside her. It was all he could do not to rip away the delicate material of her panties and camisole.

But he restrained himself. Instead, he caressed her

bare skin, feeling her abs and thigh muscles contract when his teasing fingers touched them. He slid his fingers under the thin band of elastic and inched her panties lower and lower.

His immediate goal was to savor every second of this fantasy—this small moment out of time.

Neither one of them was exactly rational right now. Especially not Nina. She was grieving for her friend. Seeking comfort.

Later, when she was thinking clearly, he knew for a fact that she'd regret this momentary lapse of reason. But he wiped that thought from his head. If this was the only chance he ever got to act on the longings she'd generated in him from the first time he'd met her, he'd take it.

Every second of it.

The first time he'd laid eyes on her two years ago, he'd wanted to sink his fingers into her thick dark hair and watch it slide like black silk across his skin.

He'd wanted to skim his tongue across every inch of her creamy, petal-soft skin. If her face and the tops of her breasts were that creamy and smooth, what would the softer skin of her tummy feel like?

And the protected, sensitive skin of her inner thighs?

And the even softer, erotically charged skin of…

His hardness throbbed as her hands, busy pushing his sweatpants down, brushed it.

"Keep going," he breathed as he pushed the black satiny camisole up. Her belly and abs were as taut and shapely as they'd felt under his fingertips. He brushed his palms across the underside of her breasts. She moaned aloud and shoved his sweatpants farther down.

He kicked them off.

Then he sat up and brought her with him, holding

her so he could tongue her nipples. She arched, giving him easier access, and in one sleek movement, wrapped her legs around his waist.

She raised her arms so he could yank off her camisole.

Her breasts were beautiful, perfectly shaped—perfectly sized. Not small, yet not too big. He could spend eternity there, touching, tasting, savoring.

But Nina wanted more. Without saying a word, she let him know that she was ready. She tightened her legs. She threw back her head and moaned as he feasted on one creamy globe and then the other.

And finally, she fisted her hands in his hair and forced him to look up into her eyes.

"Now," she said, holding his gaze. "Now."

He laid her down and raised himself above her. "I don't want to do something you're not ready for—" he began, but she stopped his words with her fingers.

He thrust, and she took him in.

He gasped aloud as her heat enveloped him. She was so tight, so hot, so perfect. He sank hilt-deep, hearing the hitch in her breathing as he began to move.

She ran her fingers down his shoulders to caress his biceps, then back up, as she met him thrust for thrust, matching his rhythm. And the whole time she watched him. Her gaze never wavered.

Wyatt moved slowly, taunting them both with long strokes that brought him closer and closer to losing control.

Each time he moved, she moaned, low and breathy, and moved to match his rhythm.

After an indefinable time, he felt his muscles tense, felt the sweet, hot fire that signaled his coming release. He slowed down. "Let's take it easy," he hissed softly.

Nina shook her head. "No. Let's take it hard."

Matching words to deed, she ground against him, pushing him, demanding more, until he couldn't hold back for another second.

Then the fire ignited and spread. At the same time, he felt the change in her. The catch in her breathing, the tiny contractions, which told him she was as close as he was. So he pumped up the rhythm and made sure they came together.

NINA AWOKE TO SUNLIGHT streaming in through the window and the rhythmic sounds of Wyatt's long, smooth breaths. He was on his back, with the sheet angled across the edge of his hip.

She was curled up on her side, and for a while, she just lay there and watched him breathe. His brown hair was tousled, softening his features and making him look innocent and young.

His mouth was curved in a slight smile. The eyelashes, which were barely darker than his hair, lay against his cheek like fringes, hiding the intense blue of his eyes.

She traced the line of his jaw to the cleft in his chin with her gaze. Then down the elegant line of his neck to his chest.

There, below his right collarbone, was a scar. An ugly, jaggedly curved scar that disappeared under his arm.

Where he'd been shot. Where they'd cut the bullet out of his lung. Her throat contracted until she could hardly breathe.

She'd been shocked when he said he'd been shot in the lung. She'd thought the bullet had hit his shoulder, and nobody had ever told her any differently.

When they'd taken him away on a stretcher, with the

EMTs shouting commands and hustling everybody out of the way, she'd been resentful at so much hoopla over a shoulder wound. Tough guys on TV still chased villains after being shot in the shoulder.

Meanwhile, whoever had shot him had disappeared into thin air, with her best friend as his captive.

She'd yelled at Wyatt as they rolled the stretcher past her. She remembered her exact words.

My best friend is gone. She could be dead, and it's all your fault.

"I'm so sorry," she whispered silently as her gaze traced every inch, every millimeter of damaged skin. It shone pale against his tanned flesh, like the silver star he wore pinned to his shirt. And like the Ranger badge, the scar was a symbol of his courage.

He'd taken a bullet to his lung trying to save Marcie. He could have died.

Her breath caught in a near sob. How could she have been so wrong about him?

Each and every person who became a Texas Ranger took an oath to protect not only the state of Texas and their fellow Rangers but any innocent person.

These were men of legend. Heroes.

Heroes. She nodded to herself and sighed. How wonderful to be the recipient of such protection, such courage, such caring.

If she were looking for a hero, she could certainly do worse than Wyatt Colter. Against her better judgment, almost against her will, she reached out to touch the scar. Her fingers hovered over his skin, trembling with emotion.

They'd made love last night, more than once. If the fact that she was in his bed wasn't proof that it hadn't been a dream, the soreness between her thighs was.

Many people would say that what they'd done was

the ultimate intimacy. That nothing could bring two people closer together.

But right now, her desire to touch his scar, to feel the place where the deadly bullet had entered his flesh, felt much more intimate.

She slid her gaze from the tip of her finger to the curve of his scar, then up to his face—and met his sleepy gaze. "Oh!" she gasped.

He caught her hand in his. "Good morning," he muttered without taking his eyes off her. He stared at her as heat rose in his eyes. Then slowly he pressed her fingers to his chest.

To the rough, damaged skin of his scar.

Tears welled in her eyes. Embarrassment? Maybe. An awful ache at the pain he'd felt? Certainly.

"I'm sorry," she said.

The heat in his gaze flickered and changed to blue ice. He took his hand away. "Why? You didn't wake me."

"N-No," she stammered. "I meant—"

"It's getting late." He threw back the covers and got up, reaching for his clothes.

His brusque dismissal sent chills up her spine. She opened her mouth to say…what? She had no idea.

He headed for the bathroom, his clothes in his hand. A couple of seconds later, the pipes creaked. He'd turned on the shower.

She lay there staring at the closed bathroom door. Why had he deliberately pressed her hand against his chest—against his scar—and then acted as though he didn't know what she was apologizing for.

Then it hit her. He did know what she'd meant.

He hadn't misunderstood her apology; he'd rejected it.

Oh, she'd made a big mistake. She should have

known better. She'd never been cut out for casual relationships.

She knew—because she'd tried them before. But
her idea of a relationship included trust and safety. And
in her experience, casual was the antithesis of safety.

Quickly, she scanned the floor for her panties and
camisole, but she didn't see them. Feeling around in the
rumpled sheets, she finally came up with them.

By the time she had slipped them on and was ready
to dart through the connecting door and back to her own
room, Wyatt had appeared from the bathroom. He'd
showered and put on dress khakis, but he hadn't shaved.
His hair was still wet, and his chest and abs were damp.

She kicked the sheets away from her legs. "I've got
to shower, too," she mumbled just as a knock sounded
on the door. She froze, then pulled the sheets up again.

Wyatt reached for his holster, slung over the back of
the desk chair.

"Lieutenant?" Betty Alice's cheerful voice cut the air
like a paring knife. She knocked again.

Nina stared at Wyatt, who frowned and held a finger
up to his lips.

She shook her head and pointed toward the connecting door, silently asking for a couple of seconds to
escape into her own room, but he ignored her plea.

He opened the door, swinging it wide, toward the
bed. If Betty Alice didn't come all the way into the
room, she wouldn't see Nina.

Why it mattered to her what Betty Alice saw or
didn't see, Nina couldn't say. Maybe because of the
smirk on the woman's face when Nina had refused to
change rooms. Or when she'd declined the offer of a
lock on the connecting door.

Her face burned. She should have let Betty Alice install that lock.

"I found this on the desk this morning when I opened up," Betty Alice was telling Wyatt. "When I saw what the envelope said, I thought I'd better bring it right up to you."

"Did you see who brought it?" he asked.

"Why, no, I didn't. I got up about an hour ago to start my cinnamon loaf. It must have been before that, because I can hear the door from my kitchen, but not from my bedroom."

"Do you leave the front door unlocked?"

Betty Alice laughed. "No, but probably half the people in town know where the spare key is—under the doormat. This is a friendly town, for the most part. Anybody can get in if they really want to."

"Thanks."

Nina heard the dismissive tone in Wyatt's voice. Apparently Betty Alice didn't.

"Well? Aren't you going to see what it says?" she asked.

"I appreciate you bringing it up to me."

There was a pause of a few seconds. Then, "Well, I guess I'd better be getting downstairs. My cinnamon loaf needs to come out of the oven."

Wyatt closed the door. He didn't budge, and Nina held her breath until Betty Alice's footsteps faded down the hardwood stairs.

Finally, he looked at the note in his hand and then at Nina.

She got the message. She was dismissed, just as Betty Alice had been. He wanted to read his note in private. She ducked her head. "It won't take me long to shower and dress. If you don't mind running me out to the site, I'll catch a ride back to the lab with one of my students." She jumped up and sprang toward the connecting door.

"Wait."

She turned her head, feeling naked in her black camisole and bikini panties.

Wyatt had crossed to the writing desk and picked up an ornate letter opener. "It's addressed to you, too. Lieutenant Colter and Dr. Jacobson." He held it up to show her.

She got a glimpse of plain block letters before he slit the top of the envelope. He shook the folded sheet of paper out onto the desk and used a pen and the letter opener to ease it open.

Nina took a couple of wary steps toward him, still feeling viciously exposed in her underwear. As he opened up the note, she spotted another piece of paper inside.

His eyes scanned the sheet of paper, and he cursed. Then cursed again as he used the letter opener to flip over the enclosed rectangle. As she watched, his brows shot up and his face drained of color.

"What is it? Wyatt?"

"Damn it!" he growled. "Can you lift prints off paper?"

"Sure," she said. She was beginning to get scared. Wyatt looked as if he'd seen a ghost. "The lab at the community college has the necessary chemicals. What does the note say?"

"It says, 'I'll contact you about this in a few days.'"

"About what?"

Wyatt's gaze met hers. His eyes looked somehow hot and icy at the same time. His jaw muscles bulged.

"Wyatt?"

"This," he bit out. "Take a look."

She stepped over to the desk. There, looking dark

against the white of the note paper, was a photograph. Nina stared in disbelief. Her heart raced so fast, she felt like she couldn't take a breath. "Dear heavens," she whispered. It took a moment before she could say anything else. "Is that the date stamp?" She pointed to the right lower corner of the photograph.

"Yeah. It's dated the first of this month." Wyatt's voice was void of emotion.

Nina squinted. "This *year?*"

He didn't answer, but he didn't have to. She knew it was.

She intertwined her fingers together and pressed the knuckles against her mouth. A slightly hysterical chuckle escaped her lips. "So I'm not crazy?"

"If you are, then I am, too."

"You see what I see? A picture of…" Her voice died. She swallowed and tried again. "Of Marcie, date stamped a week ago."

She stood there, her mouth dry as a bone as Wyatt met her gaze. Then she said, "That means Marcie's alive."

Chapter Thirteen

Nina stared at the photograph of her best friend. "Who could have sent this? Marcie's kidnapper?"

Wyatt didn't speak. He looked as stunned as she felt.

"Do you think it's a fake? That date could have been added in a computer program."

He nodded.

Neither one of them spoke for a few seconds. Then Wyatt said, "Get your kit."

She was already at the door. She popped into her room, grabbed her forensics kit and her camera and hurried back without even stopping to put on a robe.

She took several shots of the note and photo, then pulled on gloves and bagged the note and the photo.

"Get dressed. I want to get this tested for fingerprints now," Wyatt told her.

She locked the evidence bag in her kit and headed back to her room. By the time she'd showered and dressed, Wyatt was gone. So she hurried downstairs.

He was standing near the foot of the stairs, with a cup of coffee in his hand, scrutinizing the front desk and lobby as if he could force them to yield up the secret of who had delivered the envelope.

He turned and held up his cup as she stepped off the last step.

She shook her head. "No. I'm ready to figure out what's going on here."

He nodded in agreement. "I just got a call from the sheriff. The footprint castings revealed a size twelve boot with an indentation on the right rear of the heel."

"Does he have a match?"

"He said Tolbert and Spears both wear a twelve, as do Trace Becker and Daniel Taabe."

"So either of the deputies could have left that print."

"Or Becker, snooping around. This brings into question Taabe's claim about the bone and hatchet left in his truck, too. That boot print you photographed could have been his own."

"What about our fingerprint? Should we try to lift it here at the college or take it to Austin?"

He set his cup on the desk and headed for the door. "Is there an advantage to driving for an hour to get to the Ranger lab?"

"For a possible fingerprint ID, probably none, unless you'd rather have someone other than me do the matching."

"I want it fast. If that picture is real…" He stopped, and Nina knew his brain was whirling with all the implications, just like hers was.

"Then Marcie's alive," she said, her voice quavering. "And either she or her kidnapper sent this picture to us."

Wyatt climbed in the Jeep and started the engine, while Nina stowed her forensics kit in the backseat and got in on the passenger side. She was thoughtful as Wyatt backed out of the parking space.

Marcie was *alive*. But that wasn't the most shocking thing.

For two years, Nina had prayed that her friend was still alive, but in all that time, she'd never considered the consequences.

If Marcie really was alive, then she'd faked her death, and worse…

"Wyatt, do you think it was Marcie who shot you?"

Wyatt grimaced to himself as he deliberately loosened his fingers from the steering wheel and put the vehicle in gear. Nina's mind was fitting the pieces together exactly the same way his was.

And both of them were venturing into dangerous territory.

"Professor, our job is to get the facts—not speculate."

Nina's breath whooshed out in a sigh. "You're right. I know. But I can't stop thinking about it, trying to figure it out. Because if Marcie's not dead, then…" He knew where she was headed. "Then we've got a third body. A female."

He heard in her voice how close she was to falling apart. Again, he knew how she felt. And again, he had to rein her in for her own sake. "You've got to stay calm. Stay rational. Hopefully we'll have an answer soon. If there's a fingerprint on the paper or the photo, you'll lift it. The Ranger database has the prints of just about everyone in Comanche Creek."

"But if the photo's a fake—"

"You're going to test the DNA from the pelvic bone. One way or another, the facts will give us the answer."

"The facts."

Her voice was steadier now. He'd managed to tap into her rational brain and stop her imagination from spiraling out of control.

Now if only he could stop his.

"How likely is it that you can get a print from the paper?" Maybe if he could get her to talk about facts and science, it would help him to stop rehashing all the ways he could have prevented Marcie from being kidnapped.

"Lifting prints from paper is dicey at best," she said.

He could tell by the tone of her voice that he'd successfully distracted her.

She went on. "The note was written on copy paper, which is relatively smooth compared to bond. And because of its acid content, it should hold the print well. But any ordinary TV buff should know to use gloves to handle a note. So I don't hold out much hope. The photo may be a different story. Glossy photo paper is an excellent medium for prints."

"Yeah," he commented. "I've ruined a few photos by touching them before the ink was completely dry."

She didn't respond to his effort at conversation. He glanced sidelong at her and saw that she was deep in thought.

He just hoped she was mulling over the best way to lift any fingerprints she found, rather than asking herself which scenario was worse—that her best friend had let her think she was dead, or that she'd been in the clutches of a kidnapper for two years.

AN HOUR LATER at the community college lab, Wyatt closed the door behind the courier. "Okay. The courier is on his way to the Ranger lab with the scrapings from the pelvic bone."

"Good," Nina said distractedly. She turned the head of the lighted magnifying lamp a fraction of an inch. *There. Finally. A decent print.* She straightened with a groan. "I think I've found one."

Wyatt stalked over and stood behind her chair as he peered through the large magnifying lens. "Where is it?" He bent to get a good look at her handiwork.

"On the back of the photo. I couldn't find one decent partial on the paper. And this is the only one on the photo."

"Good job." He put his hand on her shoulder, surprising her.

And thrilling her. And not just because of that moment, she remembered their wild night of lovemaking. Thrilling her in a way she'd never felt before.

Even after last night, she was surprised that he would cross the line between professional and personal with even that small gesture of a hand on her shoulder. He was so steeped in the responsibility of his position as a Texas Ranger.

She had to be careful, though. Even if he was a Ranger, he was still a man. She knew nothing about him.

Until last night all he'd been to her was the man who had let her friend die.

As far as she knew, for him their night together had been no more than a way to pass the time until this investigation was over and he could go back to his life and she to hers.

"Professor? Dazzle me with your knowledge."

"Right." She blinked and forced her brain back to the job at hand. "The photo was printed on a home photo printer, using standard four-inch-by-six-inch glossy photo paper. The glossy side can yield a print of lab quality. Like you said, getting a fingerprint on a photo can ruin it. But what people don't know is that even the back side of glossy paper is slick enough to take a great print."

"And that's where you found this one?"

"Here. Take a look." She slid her chair a little sideways so he could look through the magnifying lamp at the back of the photo. When he bent his head, his hair brushed her cheek.

She swallowed, doing her best to ignore the mint on his breath, the heat that radiated from his body and her instantaneous response to his closeness.

"Wow," he muttered. "It's almost a complete print."

Her heart swelled with pride. "Wow" was a supreme compliment, coming from him. "He probably left it while he was putting the paper in the printer. He was super careful about touching the front but didn't think about the back."

"Well, it's a beauty."

"I've still got to lift it." She pushed the magnifying lamp out of the way, thinking Wyatt would move away, but he didn't. Nor did he remove his hand. "I need room," she said reluctantly, quashing the urge to tilt her head and press her chin against his fingers. "This isn't going to be easy."

He straightened and gave her shoulder a squeeze before removing his hand.

She took a sheet of fingerprint film and peeled off the protective paper, and slowly and deliberately applied the sticky film to the back of the photo. Then lifted the fingerprint.

She held the clear film up to the light. "I got it," she whispered.

"Okay," Wyatt said, excitement evident in his voice. "Let's get it scanned in and compare it with the database."

Within a few minutes, Nina had uploaded the fingerprint to the Ranger database in Austin.

Wyatt made a quick call to the lab. "Liz said it will probably take a few hours to run through all the fingerprints," he told Nina a few minutes later. "I let her know the scrapings were coming in and told her to run them specifically against Marcie's DNA." He assessed her. "I'm betting you haven't eaten, and I know you didn't get much sleep last night."

She felt her face heat up. Of course he knew. He was there. He was the reason she hadn't slept. And neither had he. She grabbed the fingerprint sheet out of the scanner and placed it in a file folder. It was something to do until the heat in her cheeks dissipated.

"So you want to get some lunch?" he asked. "Then I'll take you back to the inn so you can take a nap. Liz promised to call me when the run finishes."

She looked at her watch. "I was hoping Todd would have some bones for me to look at by now."

As if on cue, the door to the lab opened and Todd backed in, carrying a large crate. "Guess what, Dr. Jacobson?" he panted as he set the crate gingerly on the lab table.

"You found more remains," said Nina.

Todd beamed. "Not just remains. Skulls. At least parts of skulls."

Nina's heart jumped. "Skulls? How many?"

Todd shook his head. "I'm not sure. They're mostly in fragments. But there are a few large pieces, and one really nice specimen. Mandible, maxilla, and zygo-matic…all intact, with teeth."

"What the hell does that mean?" Wyatt broke in.

Nina grinned at him. "Basically it means jaw, chin and cheekbones."

"That sounds good," Wyatt replied.

"It's great. The teeth could provide a definite ID." She turned back to Todd. "But you couldn't possibly have found nothing but skull fragments."

Todd beamed again. "There's a lot more coming, but I knew you'd want the skulls first."

"Get it all in here, and get Julie to come help us," said Nina. "We need to match bones to bones so we can figure out how many sets of remains we have here. We're going to need more tables."

She met Wyatt's eyes and knew he was on the same page as she was. Maybe with all the bone fragments Todd and Julie had unearthed, she could finally get a handle on just how many sets of remains had been dumped into that shallow grave.

And whether any of them belonged to Marcie.

Wyatt inclined his head. "So I'm guessing you'll be busy here for a while," he said.

She nodded, her mind already on the contents of the crate Todd was opening.

"Okay, then," said Wyatt. "The mayor's assistant has some appointments lined up for me this afternoon. Maybe I can finish interviewing everyone. I'll be back here by three-thirty or four. We can get something to eat. Okay?"

Nina watched as Todd lifted the partially intact skull out of the crate. It was still covered with dirt and mud, but Todd was right. It was a beautiful specimen.

"Set it over there, and let's get started cleaning it up." She pointed at an empty table, then looked around. "Wyatt? Did you say three-thirty?"

But he was gone.

BILLY WHITLEY CURSED AND let the front legs of his straight-backed chair drop against the hardwood floor of the mayor's conference room with a thud. "That is a damn lie," he barked. "Get my wife in here. She'll tell you."

Wyatt eyed the man narrowly. He didn't like him.

Not one bit. Of course, that shouldn't make a difference. Facts were facts. Evidence was evidence. Personalities shouldn't factor in.

"Marcie James stated in her sworn deposition that you accepted money to alter certain documents you had access to as the county clerk. Are you saying Marcie lied under oath?"

Billy slapped his breast pocket. He was either a smoker or an ex-smoker, and the gesture was a clear indicator to Wyatt that he was nervous about something. "Are you saying I'm lying now?"

Wyatt pushed a photocopy of Marcie's deposition across the table. "Just going by the facts. Here's her statement. It's highlighted right there."

"I can't believe it." Billy shook his head rapidly as he pushed the paper back toward Wyatt. "She was a sweet girl. I don't know why she'd tell tales like that."

Wyatt didn't touch the paper and didn't comment. He just sat quietly in the worn leather executive chair. The mayor's conference room furniture was a lot like the mayor himself. Over fifty years old, polished and yet rough at the same time, and for the most part, welcoming.

Finally, Billy looked up at him from under his brows. "Did she say she had proof?"

Wyatt stayed still.

"Because if she did, I'd like to see it. I can refute it. I didn't do anything." His upper lip glistened with sweat. "Somebody's trying to frame me."

Wyatt sat up, feigning interest. "Yeah? Who would that be?"

"I don't know. I don't have any enemies."

Wyatt sincerely doubted that. "Marcie also said you threatened her."

"Now, you listen to me. Ask anyone in town. Marcie was flighty…" Billy actually looked around, as if someone might be listening. "Know what I mean?"

"No. Actually I don't. Explain it to me."

"I was her boss. So naturally, if she did something wrong, I had to let her know, right? Well, she didn't take that too well. She'd cry if I asked her to retype something or find a misfiled deed." He shifted in his chair. "Why, one time she…" He stopped, looked nervous.

"She what?"

"Nothing."

"Who else has access to the documents in your office?"

"Now, see, there's what I don't understand. You keep accusing me of altering documents, but I haven't seen anything. You got the documents?"

He had Wyatt there. All Wyatt had was Marcie's deposition. She'd claimed she made copies of the altered documents and put them in a safe-deposit box, but after she disappeared, the documents were nowhere to be found.

"That's all for now, Mr. Whitley. Don't leave town without notifying me. We're not done here."

Billy shot up out of the chair as if it had burned him.

"Hold it." Wyatt stood, too. He pressed the intercom button for Mayor Sadler's assistant.

"Yes?"

It was Charla Whitley. Billy's wife. Wyatt had been dismayed to find out that she was an administrative assistant to the mayor. This case was definitely a tangled web.

"Where's Helen?" Wyatt asked.

"She went for coffee." Charla's voice was hostile, even over the intercom. "Anything I can do for you?"

"Yes. Please come in here," said Wyatt.

"But…Billy hasn't come out yet," Charla hedged.

At that instant, Billy turned and headed for the door.

Chapter Fourteen

"I said hold it, Whitley."

Billy froze.

"That's right, Mrs. Whitley. He hasn't come out yet. Please come in."

Within about seven seconds the door opened, and Charla Whitley stomped in, glaring at Billy. They'd obviously made plans to talk between interviews, to keep their answers consistent. But Wyatt wasn't about to give them even one second alone together.

"Please have a seat, Mrs. Whitley," said Wyatt. He turned to Billy. "You can leave."

Charla huffed, but she sat.

Billy stared at the back of her head for a few seconds, then walked out the door.

"Close it," Wyatt called.

The door slammed.

"You're not making any friends here," Charla commented, aiming her glare at him.

"Not my intent," he said. "My job is to figure out whose remains are in that shallow grave and who put them there."

Charla crossed her arms.

"How long have you worked for the mayor?"

"About five years."

"Did you know Mason Lattimer and Ray Phillips?"

She didn't react, but he saw her dark eyes flicker.

"Lattimer was an antiques broker who was rumored to be buying up Native American artifacts from Trace Becker. Phillips was—"

"I know Ray."

"You *know* him? When was the last time you talked to him?"

"I don't remember. Maybe last year."

Wyatt's brows rose. "Yeah? Can you prove it?"

A smirk lit her face. "Why should I have to?"

"It would save us a lot of time if we could rule him out as one of the bodies at the crime scene."

Charla grimaced. "What makes you think he might be dead?"

Wyatt shuffled through the thick folder in front of him. It was all the evidence and papers connected with the land fraud deal and Marcie's disappearance. "The last record of anyone seeing him alive was over three years ago. And it's been that long since any of his credit cards were used. He also hasn't paid taxes, and his disability checks have been stacking up at his post office box."

As he listed the reasons, Charla's mouth seemed to grow tighter and tighter.

"Something wrong?" he asked.

She shook her head stiffly. "Ray was…a friend of mine. A *good* friend."

"So now you're saying *was?* Has it really been only a year since you talked to him? Where was he? What was he doing?"

"Maybe it was longer." She met his gaze, and her black eyes narrowed. "Time flies."

He asked her a few more questions, mostly about Billy and his dealings on the city council, but she was as indignant as her husband had been that anyone would accuse him of wrongdoing. So he dismissed her.

He'd expected her reaction to his questions about her husband. But she'd surprised him about Ray Phillips. She'd seemed really upset when she heard the news that he hadn't used his cards and hadn't cashed his checks in over three years. Wyatt was glad he'd already seized the contents of Phillips's post office box.

The intercom buzzed. "Lieutenant, Sheriff Hardin is on line one. Will you be interviewing anyone else this afternoon? Charla was the last interview I have on my schedule."

"No. No one else. Thanks, Helen." He picked up the phone. "Hardin? What's up?"

"I've got a boy in my office who says he saw someone heading out toward Daniel's house around the time we figure the hatchet and bone were planted," Hardin said. "You want to be here while I question him? He's about twelve and so scared he's about to…you know."

"I'll be right there."

As he hung up, Wyatt glanced at his watch. *After four. Damn. He'd promised Nina he'd be at the lab by now.* He called her as he headed next door to the sheriff's office. The phone rang four times.

"Yes?" Her voice sounded irritated and preoccupied at the same time.

"Busy?" Wyatt couldn't suppress a smile at her tone.

"Very."

"I'm not going to make it by four o'clock."

"That's fine, because I'm not nearly finished."

"I'm headed over to the sheriff's office to talk to

a kid who might have seen something at Taabe's house."

"Who? One of the kids who was helping Daniel in his stables?"

"No idea. Hardin didn't give me a name. Are your students there?"

"They're washing bones as we speak."

"Well, make sure they stick around until I get there. I'm sure this won't take more than an hour, hour and a half at the most."

"Uh-huh," she replied absently.

"Those must be some interesting bones you're looking at."

She laughed, and the sound of it shot straight through him right down to his groin. "You have no idea."

"Okay, I'll see you around five-thirty or six. Nina, stay there. Lock the doors. And make the students stay there with you." He started to say goodbye and then thought of one more safety measure. "In fact, let me talk to Todd. I'll tell him to stay—"

But Nina had already hung up.

As he entered the sheriff's office, Wyatt dialed the Ranger lab. "Lizzie, what's going on up there with that print I sent you? I thought I'd hear back from you hours ago. And the courier delivered the bone scrapings, right?"

"We got them. Sorry, Wyatt. The computer's been down. The IT guys kept promising *one more hour.* That fingerprint you sent came up around two-thirty, so the prints are running now. I'll call you as soon as I get a match. The scrapings will probably be tomorrow at the earliest. You can't imagine how backed up we are."

"Can you check with the captain? I need that info ASAP."

"He already told us to make it a priority."

"You're the best, Liz."

"I know," she answered with a smile in her voice.

When he got to Hardin's office, the sheriff waved him in. On the other side of the desk, in a straight-backed chair, with his hands clasped in his lap and his bare feet barely touching the floor, was a Native American boy of about thirteen.

His complexion was as ruddy as Taabe's, and his hair and eyes as black. He was holding an MP3 player. The white wire led up to the earbuds in his ears.

Choosing a side chair where he had a good view of both of them, Wyatt sat. He was close enough to the kid that he could intimidate him if he leaned forward. He doubted he'd have to, though. For all his posturing with the music player, the boy looked terrified.

"Kirk, we're ready to get started now," Hardin said.

Kirk ducked his head and took the earbuds out. As he wrapped the wire around the player, his hands shook.

"This is Lieutenant Wyatt Colter. He's a Texas Ranger," said Hardin.

Wide black eyes met Wyatt's gaze. "A Texas Ranger? Seriously?"

Wyatt nodded and allowed himself a tiny smile. "Seriously." He flicked a prong of his badge with his index finger.

"Wow," Kirk breathed.

"Now, Kirk, tell the lieutenant what you told me," Hardin urged.

The boy nodded and licked his lips. "Yesterday I saw a big white pickup driving out toward Daniel's house."

"A big white pickup," Wyatt repeated. He glanced at Hardin, who shook his head once. "What kind of pickup?"

Kirk licked his lips again and looked down at the MP3 player he held. "I don't know. Big."

"Did you see who was driving?" asked Wyatt.

"No, sir."

"Was it Ellie Penateka?" Wyatt quizzed.

Kirk shook his head. "No, sir."

Wyatt looked the boy in the eye. "Are you sure?"

"Yes, sir."

Hardin's chair creaked as he shifted. "Kirk, why'd you come here to tell us this?"

"Daniel asked me and Tim and Andy if we saw anything after we left yesterday." Kirk shrugged. "I told Daniel I saw that pickup, and he said I had to come and tell you."

"Were Tim and Andy with you when you saw it?" Hardin asked.

"No, sir. They left earlier. I stayed to help Daniel put away the tools," replied Kirk.

Wyatt studied the boy. Could he believe him? Taabe hadn't mentioned that one of the boys had stayed longer than the other two. Based on what Wyatt had seen—and what Nina had said—last night, Ellie might well have driven out to Taabe's more than once yesterday.

But Taabe wouldn't have sent Kirk to Sheriff Hardin if the driver of the white pickup had been Ellie.

"Deputy Tolbert drives a white pickup. Was it his?" Wyatt asked, watching Hardin's reaction. The sheriff's jaw flexed.

Kirk shrugged.

"Sheriff, who else drives a big white pickup?" asked Wyatt. He was certain that Kirk knew who the driver was. A glance at the sheriff assured him that he thought the same thing.

"White pickups are pretty common around here. Let's see. Charla Whitley drives one. Reverend Lewis, but his is about twenty years old. And I'm pretty sure one of Jonah Becker's trucks is white." Hardin propped his elbows on his desk. "Kirk, I gotta say it's kind of hard to believe that you saw it but you can't say whose it was."

"The sun was in my eyes, and I didn't think nothing of it. Miss Ellie drives out there all the time," Kirk replied.

"You said it wasn't Ellie," Wyatt reminded him.

"It wasn't," Kirk mumbled.

"How come you're so sure?" Hardin asked. "Didn't you say the sun was in your eyes?"

Kirk frowned and shrugged. "I just know."

"You like Ellie, don't you? Because she's Daniel's friend?"

Kirk nodded. "I guess so. I mean, I like her and all, but it still wasn't her truck."

Hardin stood. "Okay, Kirk, you did the right thing, coming to us. Now I want you to sit in there." He pointed toward a small conference room.

"Are you arresting me?" Kirk gasped.

"No. But I need you to think about that pickup, and why you're so sure it wasn't Ellie," said Hardin.

Kirk shrugged. "I told you, I don't know. It just didn't look like her truck."

Hardin sighed. "What did Daniel say when you told him about the truck?"

Kirk ducked his head.

"Did he *tell* you to say it wasn't Ellie?"

"No, sir. He told me to tell the truth."

"Okay, son. Why don't you draw me a picture of the pickup. I'll let you work on it a few minutes." Hardin gave Kirk a few sheets of paper and a pencil, then let the boy into the conference room and closed the door behind him.

When Hardin came back into his office, Wyatt asked him, "Do you think Taabe told the boy to lie?"

Hardin shook his head. "I've been thinking about that. I don't think so. He wouldn't trust a lie like that to a twelve-year-old. I'm guessing we can eliminate Ellie from the list. As well as the preacher. My guess is Trace Becker. I don't trust him as far as I can throw him. Of course, Charla's a good candidate, too."

"But not Tolbert? You know he told Marcie that if he ever caught her with another man, he'd kill them both."

"Right. So, you going to arrest every guy who's ever said that to his ex-girlfriend?"

"Nope. Just the ones who actually do it." Wyatt sighed. "I guess we've got to search all the white pickups. See if we can pull any mud or other trace evidence that might tell us who planted the hatchet and bone in Daniel's truck."

"And check their alibis," Hardin added. "But right now I'm hungry. I didn't get lunch, and I've got to take a shift out at the site tonight. Kirby and Shane are beat."

"You know, Taabe offered some of his men to help guard the site. I didn't take him up on it, although I was tempted. But what I can do is call on Sentron. They're a security agency we use sometimes. They can send a couple of temporary security guards to help. We've got the resources. They could take one shift."

Wyatt heard a tentative knock.

It was Kirk, holding a sheet of paper. "Uh, Sheriff? I know why it couldn't have been Miss Ellie's truck," he said.

Hardin took the drawing. "Why's that?" he asked.

"'Cause the truck had mud all over the underside, and Miss Ellie's truck ain't ever dirty."

"Good job, son. This is the truck you saw?" asked Hardin.

"Yes, sir. Best I can remember."

The sheriff nodded. "Is that a truck box on the back?"

"Yes, sir. One of those silver ones," Kirk confirmed.

Hardin sighed. "Okay, Kirk. You can go."

"What should I tell my mom? She'll want to know why I'm late."

"Tell her you were helping with an investigation," Hardin replied.

"Yes, sir."

After Kirk left, Wyatt took a look at the drawing. "Tolbert's got a truck box on his truck," he commented.

"So does Charla," Hardin countered.

"And Ellie's?"

"Nope. Not that I recall."

"Well, at least that narrows the number of trucks we have to process. What'd you decide about the security guards?"

"If the Rangers are offering, I'll take 'em. Probably ought to keep the deputies and me on the night shift for now. But maybe the guards could take the early shift so my guys can get some sleep."

"I'll arrange it. They won't be able to start tomorrow, but I might be able to get them for the next morning shift. I'll have the head of the security company call you with their names and credentials."

"Great." Hardin rubbed his eyes. "So where are you headed now?"

Wyatt looked at his watch and grimaced. "I need to get back to the lab. Nina's working over there, and I don't want to take a chance on her being there alone, not even for a few minutes."

Chapter Fifteen

After Nina uploaded the photos of the skull fragments and e-mailed them to the Ranger lab, she set the camera aside and stared at the fragments and the one partially intact skull for a moment.

Her fingers itched to touch them, inspect them, get them under a microscope, but she'd promised herself she'd unload the last box of remains Todd had brought in and get the important pieces into the sink to soak first.

Todd and Julie had wanted to stay and help her examine the skull fragments. In fact they'd begged her, but she'd told them no. They were muddy and exhausted from their days' work. They deserved a night off.

That was one reason she'd sent them away. The other—the most important reason—was that she wanted to be alone when she examined the skull fragments.

In case one of them was Marcie's.

With stoic resolve, she turned her back on the skull bones, pulled on thick work gloves and dug into the box.

Most of the contents were tiny splinters and fragments that had been pulverized by the bulldozer. But there was one large piece in the box. She pulled it out, her pulse skittering.

It was a pelvic bone. Male, unlike the one that sat on the lab table. She brushed at it, but it was caked with dried mud. So she lowered it into the lab sink to let it soak for a few minutes.

Dusting her hands together, she glanced around. It was getting late. The big clock over the front door read six, the time Wyatt had told her he'd be back. A thrill skittered through her.

Wyatt. He'd have the test results they'd been waiting for, but that wasn't the only reason for her quickened heartbeat.

She missed his calm, low voice, the whiff of the mint on his breath, the tingling sensation that filled her whenever he was close to her.

Dear heavens, she was in deeper than she'd realized. Resolutely, she took a deep breath, trying to quell the sense of anticipation.

Reminding herself that it hadn't taken him any time to realize he'd made a mistake in taking her to bed. Otherwise, why would he have rejected her apology so abruptly?

Come on, she berated herself. *Don't fall for the sexy Ranger.*

Deliberately, she turned her attention back to the skull fragments and the partially intact skull. She'd intended to have some information for Wyatt about them. As soon as he got here, he'd be pestering her to stop for the night, and she didn't want to quit until she'd determined whether one of the fragments or the intact skull had belonged to a female.

She'd already tentatively matched the partially intact

skull with the shorter thigh bone, and she couldn't wait to tell Wyatt what she'd found.

Based on the state of the teeth and the skull's age as indicated by the sutures, she was about seventy percent certain it had belonged to Mason Lattimer, the missing antiques broker. On the other hand, no matter whose it was, she was a hundred percent certain he'd been murdered. A couple of matching bone fragments had been splintered by a blow.

The remaining pieces were in two piles, based on their appearance. On casual examination as Todd and Julie were cleaning them, she'd concluded they had belonged to a male, but most of the fragments were small, so she wanted to double-check.

She changed to exam gloves and picked up a piece of skull about two inches in diameter. Its general architecture was rugged, which indicated a male, but there was an odd texture to the surface. It reminded her of the surface of the female pelvic bone from Daniel Taabe's truck.

She fetched the pelvic bone and looked at it and the skull fragment side by side under the lighted magnifying lamp.

Her first impression was right. The two bones had similar markings. Their surfaces appeared to have been etched. Nina frowned and adjusted the light and magnification.

Definitely etched. And not just the outside. The inside, as well. As if with acid. That couldn't have happened in the ground. The soil in this area was alkaline, due to the high limestone content.

She stared at the two pieces. There was another problem, too. The pelvic bone was female. But the skull fragment was definitely male. They matched—and yet they didn't match.

It didn't make sense.

She took close-up photos of them both, hoping the flash would heighten the contrast enough to show the etching in more detail. Then she reached for a scalpel to take scrapings. Using the chemicals here in the lab, she could identify any lingering traces of acid.

She straightened, rubbing the back of her neck. She'd been bent over too long. As soon as she finished with this one test, she would let Wyatt talk her into going back to the inn.

She was looking forward to a long hot bath and...

Her brain flashed on the luxurious pleasure of climbing into a warm, comfortable bed, but in the next nanosecond, her fantasy changed from a bed alone to a bed filled with Wyatt's big, hot, sexy body.

She'd never been completely comfortable waking up next to someone. Even though she'd dated two guys seriously and long enough that she should have.

But this morning had changed everything. Waking up next to Wyatt had felt natural. Right.

Like a really good thing.

And that was a really bad thing.

It looked like they might get the case wrapped up soon. And that meant whatever this *thing* was between Wyatt and her, even though it was brand-new, it had a rapidly approaching expiration date.

That meant she had to rein in her imagination bigtime. No more thinking about how nice it felt to wake up next to him. Or how his slightest touch had awakened her sexuality to a degree she'd never imagined possible.

No. The best thing she could do was to focus all her imagination, all her knowledge, all her energy, on identifying the three sets of remains as quickly as possible.

She carefully scraped the surface of the skull fragment, collected the dust in a beaker and labeled it. Then she did the same with the pelvic bone and a second beaker. As she set the scalpel down, a noise startled her.

A dull metallic thud. She realized she'd heard it before—several times, in fact—since Todd and Julie had left. She squeezed her eyes shut and stretched, trying to loosen up her tense muscles.

She heard the noise again and recognized what it was.

It was the hollow sound of a metal door slamming shut. Probably the door to one of the classrooms or other labs in the building. People leaving for the day.

Wyatt would be here soon. She smiled as she stepped over to the wall shelf that held bottles and jars of common chemicals used in first- and second-year chemistry lab work.

She quickly spotted the substance she needed behind a jar of pure sodium. She carefully lifted the heavy jar and set it on the counter, then stood on tiptoe to reach the bottle labeled Sodium Carbonate. Once she mixed the white powder with the bone dust and added silver nitrate, the resulting reaction would tell her if there was any acid on the bone.

She heard another door slam, and Wyatt's handsome, angular face rose in her vision, setting her pulse to racing. She shook her head. Wyatt was here. *So what? No time to get all girly*.

She dipped a spatula into the sodium carbonate and sprinkled powder over the bone dust. She scanned the bottles on the shelf, looking for silver nitrate solution. Every chemistry lab at every college in the world had a bottle of silver nitrate.

Just as she spotted it, the lights went out.

She jumped, and the spatula hit the granite counter-top with a clatter.

"Wyatt?" she called. But nobody answered.

Her night blindness faded quickly, but the blue-and-purple sunset haze coming through the windows wasn't enough light to see by. Squinting, she scanned the room. Maybe it was a security guard who'd come in and thought the lab was empty.

"Hello?" Her throat spasmed.

The silence was ominous.

Her initial startled response catapulted into outright fear. Someone was in the lab with her.

Someone who wasn't identifying himself.

Stay calm, stay calm. It was probably students playing a prank. Maybe they'd popped in, hit the light switch and run.

Suddenly a flashlight came on, blinding her for an instant. It panned across the room. Nina ducked. Maybe it really was a security guard. She opened her mouth to identify herself. Then dread certainty closed her throat.

No. It wasn't a guard—or a student. Whoever was here with her was not harmless.

Her throat was so tight she couldn't breathe.

Run, her instincts said. *Try to make it to the other door*. But the fire exit was as far away as the front door from where she crouched.

At that instant the flashlight's beam passed over her—and paused.

She froze. Could he see the top of her head?

The harsh beam moved, sweeping the room. Then heavy footsteps echoed on the concrete floor, coming closer. He wasn't even trying to stay quiet. She could hear him breathing, even over the pounding of her heart.

Then an electric hum drowned out all other sounds, and with a dull thump, the emergency lights kicked on.

Adrenaline rushed through her like a cold chill. The lights were dim, but they were better than the pallid glow from the windows.

She stood carefully. The flashlight beam's source was near the door. The beam moved, giving her a view of a large figure clothed all in black. He held the flashlight in his left hand and what looked like a mallet or a large hammer in his right.

Right-handed. Over six feet. One hundred ninety to two hundred pounds. Male. Her brain ticked off the attributes so she could later describe him—assuming she lived.

The flashlight's beam stopped on the bones she'd left on the counter next to the lab sink.

With a satisfied grunt, he rushed toward them.

He was going to destroy her bones.

"No!" she shouted.

The beam pinned her and the man cursed. Brandishing the mallet, he started toward her.

Dear heavens, he hadn't known she was there. She should have stayed quiet. But he was going to destroy her bones.

He hesitated while she stood frozen, pinned like a rabbit under a hawk's piercing gaze. Then he turned and rushed toward the table, with the mallet raised over his head.

Nina knew she couldn't stop him. He was much bigger than she. Even if she had the courage to confront him, she had nothing to use for a weapon.

She watched, helpless, as he swung the mallet.

"No!" The protest was wrung involuntarily from her lips as she cast about for anything she could use to stop him.

But there was nothing, unless…

She reached behind her, feeling for the jar of sodium. Even a freshman lab student knew that pure sodium exploded in water.

Although the jar was heavy, the rock of sodium inside it weighed no more than a couple of ounces. It was suspended in mineral oil to keep it from reacting with moisture in the air. Even if she could toss it into the water-filled sink, it might be too insulated by the mineral oil to flash, much less explode.

Still, it was her only chance to save her evidence. *And her life.*

So she picked up the jar and held it over her head. "Hey!" she shouted. "Over here!" She prayed he'd take the bait and shine the light her way. At least enough so she could take aim at the edge of the sink, where she hoped to smash the jar.

He did.

She threw.

The jar swirled through the air in slow motion, spewing big, glistening drops of mineral oil in spirals.

The intruder ducked.

From somewhere, a voice shouted her name.

The jar hit the edge of the sink and shattered.

She heard a loud splash.

Then with a bright yellow flash, a huge fireball exploded straight up—like a volcano—and bright sparks rained down.

Nina dropped to the floor and covered her head.

DESPERATELY, HIS HEART in his throat, Wyatt slapped the tiled wall with his left hand, searching for a light switch. He clutched his weapon in his right hand, aimed at the blinding explosion. He couldn't see anything but the yellow light, and couldn't hear anything but the bang echoing in his ears.

"Nina!" he shouted, unable to hear even his own voice. *Dear God, don't let her be hurt.*

Then his fingers touched the switches and he flipped them, flooding the lab with light. When his eyes focused, he saw a figure flopping around comically. Each time the intruder tried to get a foothold, he slipped in the thick liquid that coated the floor.

Wyatt squinted, wondering if his eyes were playing tricks, but no, they weren't.

The intruder's hair was smoking.

Holstering his gun, Wyatt crossed the distance between them in two strides and grabbed the man's collar. He dragged him away from the sink, leaving streaks of thick liquid on the concrete floor. He dumped him next to an adjacent lab table and yanked a pair of handcuffs out of his jacket.

Once he'd cuffed the man's hands around the steel table leg, Wyatt straightened and scanned the room. He'd figure out who his perp was later.

Right now he had to find Nina.

The explosion had died as quickly as it had erupted, leaving the room thick with smoke and a distinctly vile and caustic odor, like rotten eggs.

"Nina!" he shouted. "Nina, damn it! Where are you?" He heard something—clothes rustling maybe— and whirled in that direction. "Nina?"

"Wyatt?"

He didn't see her. He wanted to sprint around the counters and tables, searching for her, but while his instincts told him that her voice sounded more relieved than scared, his training kept him from rushing headlong into a trap.

"Are you okay?" he asked, retrieving his gun and holding it at the ready.

She didn't answer. He heard a small sound, like a sob.

His pulse throbbed in his temple. Was there a second intruder? Was he holding Nina? "You've got to answer me, Professor. Tell me what's wrong. Should I call the doctor?"

"No…" Her voice caught. "I'm fine."

He tensed. Her voice sounded stronger, as if she was finally getting it together after a bad scare, but he still wasn't taking any chances. "Can you stand up? I need to see you."

More rustling of clothes. Then he saw the top of her head. He waited until she'd straightened completely and he'd had a good look at her before he lowered his weapon.

Her dark, dark eyes were wide as saucers. Her face looked impossibly pale, and she was shivering, but she was okay.

It took him two tries to slide his gun back into his holster. "Damn it, Professor," he growled. "What were you doing here alone?"

He held out his hand, and with a small cry, Nina ran straight into his arms. For a split second, he pressed his lips against her hair and held her as close as he could, wrapping his arms around her.

She didn't seem to mind. In fact, her arms slid around his waist and held on tight. After only a few seconds, her shivering stopped, and she took a long, shaky breath and sighed, warming the skin of his neck.

"Hey, help me over here!"

It was his perp, complaining.

Nina tensed, then pushed away.

"Help, damn it! My hair's on fire!" yelled the man.

Wyatt squeezed Nina's shoulder, then stalked over and looked down at the man's brown hair. "It's just smoking," he said. He eyed the lab table. Sure enough there was a sink with a sprayer attached to the faucet. "Here, I'll put it out." He jerked the sprayer to the length of its hose and squirted water on the guy's head.

A stream of curses, some in Spanish and some in English, spewed from the guy's mouth. "*Madre de Dios!* What the hell? I'll sue you!"

"Yeah? When? After you're convicted of breaking and entering and assault?" Wyatt barely restrained himself from kicking him in the ribs. He'd attacked Nina.

Luckily for the man, at that moment sirens screamed and blue lights flashed. Within seconds, Sheriff Hardin and three men in fire gear burst through the door.

And stopped in their tracks.

Hardin scowled at Wyatt. "What the…?"

Then two men whose shirts said Security came running in.

"Sheriff, I was just about to call you," Wyatt said. "Looks like this guy was trying to blow up the lab."

"The hell I was," the handcuffed guy said. "That was her!"

Her? Wyatt turned to stare at Nina.

"He was smashing my bones," she said. "I had to stop him."

Hardin cleared his throat. "What's going on here? I need some answers now!"

Wyatt ignored him and the firemen, who headed over to the sink to look at the damage from the explosion. He stepped over to Nina. "Professor? What the hell did you do?"

Nina scraped her teeth across her lower lip, a gesture that in another circumstance would have had him groaning with lust. But all he could do was wait, stunned, to hear how she'd caused the explosion.

"I just threw some sodium into the sink. It's a simple chemical reaction. Sodium oxidizes quickly upon exposure to air and violently when it's dropped into water—"

"Okay," Wyatt said. "I get it. You blew up the sink."

Her eyes widened and she whirled around. "Oh, no!" she cried.

Wyatt sprang toward her and wrapped his arm around her shoulders. "What is it? What's wrong?"

She pointed at the sink. "I destroyed my evidence!"

Chapter Sixteen

Wyatt quickly and efficiently patted down the intruder and found his wallet and car keys in his pants pocket. "Good idea," he muttered. "Carry your ID when you're planning an assault. Saves the law enforcement officers a lot of time. We appreciate it."

He handed the keys over to campus security and ordered them to find and search the car, then take it to Impound.

"Let's go," he said, jerking the perp up and cuffing his hands behind his back. "You're going to have a long night." Looking around, he saw Nina over by the sink, examining the smashed bones. "Nina, come on."

"I can't leave. What about my bones? He smashed one of my skull fragments, and I was in the middle of a test for acid residue."

"Leave it until tomorrow. I'll make sure campus security assigns someone to the lab for tonight."

"They'll be inside? But what if they touch something? I can't afford to have them—"

"Call Todd to spend the night. Can he do some of that testing?"

"Yes, but—"

"Professor, that first night Todd nearly passed out

from excitement just thinking one of the bodies might have been murdered. Let him guard the bones. He'll think he's Indiana Jones. Now come on."

Wyatt hauled his prisoner out of the building and to his Jeep. "Oh, by the way, Jeffrey Marquez," he said, holding the guy's driver's license up. "You have the right to remain silent. Anything you say…"

By the time Wyatt finished reciting Marquez's Miranda rights, they'd reached the Jeep. He shoved him into the backseat and propped a hip against the door to wait for Nina.

Within five minutes, she was walking toward him. Twice she looked back, as if to make sure the lab was locked.

He held up his keys, then tossed them to her.

"What's this?" she asked.

"You drive. I've got to keep an eye on your attacker."

Marquez shifted uncomfortably. Wyatt had the distinct impression that he'd never been in handcuffs before.

Interesting.

When they got to the sheriff's office, Kirby Spears was waiting. He wrangled the prisoner out of the backseat and took him inside.

Nina reached for the door handle.

"No," Wyatt said, laying a hand on her arm. "Take the Jeep. Go back to the inn, and relax. You've had a long day."

Nina's gaze snapped to his, and her dark eyes burned with irritation. "Relax? I'm not going anywhere, cowboy. Not until I find out who this man is and why he tried to destroy my bones."

Wyatt opened his mouth to protest, but he'd seen that look in her eyes before, and he was pretty darn sure she wasn't going to change her mind. So he shrugged, got out and headed inside. Behind him, he heard the driver's-side door slam.

NINA MADE IT INSIDE IN time to hear Wyatt give Deputy Spears an order. "Everything about him. Where he works, lives, hangs out. Where his parents live. Who he's dating. Everything."

When Spears got through writing everything down, he waited, pen poised above paper, but Wyatt didn't say anything else. "Uh, Lieutenant?" Spears said. "What about pulling his record?"

Wyatt nodded. "Right. We need to verify it, but I'll guarantee you, he hasn't got a record."

Nina stepped up beside Wyatt. "You can't know that. He was sneaking around like a pro."

Wyatt leveled his blue gaze at her. "There's no yardstick or calipers for measuring how an ex-con acts, Professor. It's experience and instinct."

"Okay, then. What in your experience makes you so sure about him?" she asked.

"Today's the first time he's ever had to sit or walk with his hands cuffed behind his back. I'm telling you, he's an amateur," Wyatt insisted. "Whatever he was doing in the lab, either it was to protect himself, or he did it for a friend."

Nina frowned at Wyatt as her brain raced.

"Hey, Professor. What is it?" Wyatt waved his hand in front of her eyes.

"I don't know," she whispered. "Something you said. I don't recognize his name, but I think I've seen him before."

"Where?"

"I can't remember. But I will."

"Lieutenant?" Spears interrupted. "I've got something."

Wyatt stepped around the desk so he could see Kirby's computer monitor. Nina followed him.

"His work ID was in his wallet. He's an emergency medical technician," Spears announced.

"Some EMTs are well versed in anatomy," Nina said.

Wyatt's brows shot up. "Oh, yeah?" He turned on his boot heel and headed into Sheriff Hardin's office.

"Wait," Nina called. But he was already halfway to the door, so she rushed to catch up.

"Hardin, I want to talk to Marquez now," Wyatt declared.

The sheriff didn't even look up. "He's waiting for you in the conference room."

"Okay, then. Thanks," said Wyatt.

Nina suppressed a smile. Wyatt was used to giving orders and taking control. The fact that he and Hardin were practically on equal footing had him off balance. He wasn't used to working alongside someone else. He was more comfortable being in charge of—and responsible for—the people who worked under him.

He stopped with his hand on the doorknob. "Where do you think you're going?"

She almost ran into him. "I want to hear what he has to say." She took a quick breath and continued before Wyatt had a chance to interrupt. "Listen to me, Wyatt. He's an EMT."

"Yeah, you said that."

"This is important. When he broke in, I was about to do a test for acid residue on one of the skull fragments."

Wyatt looked at her for a beat. "Okay, I'll bite. Why?"

"Because the bony surface of the skull was etched. That doesn't happen naturally. That skull was soaked, or at the least washed, in a strong acid. I'm guessing hydrochloric."

"Somebody poured acid on the bones?"

"Not exactly. Acid eats away at a bone's surface. I've seen it before, on skeletons that are used for display. They're cleaned with acid, then bleached before they're put into classrooms. I had to clean one up when I was an undergraduate, for basic anatomy class."

Wyatt's eyes narrowed, then widened. "You think our perp here—"

"He may have planted a skeleton. And was trying to destroy it, or maybe steal it back."

"Why?"

Nina had asked herself that question. The answer fit with what they knew and the clues they'd been given. She met Wyatt's gaze and saw that he'd come to the same conclusion.

She also knew that like her, he couldn't bring himself to state the obvious conclusion—that Marcie was alive and had faked her death.

"Good job, Professor," he said softly as he pushed open the door to the small room and went in.

Nina followed. Jeffrey Marquez was handcuffed by one hand to his chair. He glanced sidelong at them. His face was sullen and he looked tired.

"So what's your story, Jeffrey Marquez?" Wyatt asked.

Marquez didn't respond. He barely acknowledged hearing him. Wyatt glanced at Nina and gave his head an almost imperceptible shake.

She got the message. *Don't talk.*

He sat there, watching Marquez. Every so often, Marquez would give Wyatt a glance, then look back down at the table.

Nina surreptitiously watched the minute hand on her watch. Wyatt stayed quiet and still for a full five minutes. Then he stood abruptly, scraping the wooden chair legs across the hardwood floor with a screech.

Nina jumped, and so did Marquez.

"Okay, then. I've got all I need. We're done here." Wyatt gestured to Nina. "I think we'll go with breaking and entering, destruction of state property in further-ance of a crime, interfering with an ongoing investiga-tion and, of course—" he turned the doorknob and opened the door "—attempted murder."

As Nina walked past Wyatt and through the door, she heard him whisper, "Wait for it. One...two... three..."

"Hold it!" Marquez yelled, his face draining of color. "Wait a minute. Nobody said anything about at-tempted murder."

Wyatt turned casually. "While I was in here, nobody said anything, period."

"If anybody's guilty of attempted murder, it's her," Marquez accused. "She set off a huge explosion right next to me. Nearly blew me up!"

Wyatt turned back toward the door.

"No, wait." Marquez tried to stand, but with his wrist handcuffed to the chair arm, he couldn't. "I swear, I don't know anything about any murder!"

"I didn't say murder," Wyatt replied. "I said *at-tempted* murder. But first things first. What were you doing in the lab?"

"I was just looking for something that belonged to me. I was hoping to get it and get out before anyone saw me."

"Something? What?"

Marquez shook his head and laughed uneasily. "I can

promise you, it has nothing to do with the bodies you're looking for."

Wyatt leaned over the table. "Listen to me, Marquez. If you were dancing any faster around my questions, you'd screw your head right off your shoulders. Now, I'll be happy to help you with that, but I'd like to get a straight answer first." He sat down. "Now, does your breaking and entering and destruction of evidence have anything to do with the fact that you're an EMT, and one of our skeletons has been washed in acid?"

Marquez jerked in surprise. "How'd you…? I mean, what makes you say that?"

"Not me. Dr. Jacobson." Wyatt jerked his thumb in Nina's direction. "She's a forensic anthropologist. So she notices things like acid-etched skeletons."

Marquez turned to her. "Then you know that skeleton has nothing to do with your case."

But Wyatt didn't give Nina a chance to answer. He broke in. "Nothing to do with my case? It was right there in the middle of my crime scene, with the other bones."

The young man hesitated as sweat broke out on his forehead. After a few seconds, he shrugged. "Okay, look. The bones came from the medical school. They supplied skeletons to area schools. I'd sneak into the room where the students would clean the bones, and grab something whenever I had the chance." He grinned nervously. "For a prank. That's all."

Nina gasped, and her fingers flew to her mouth.

Both Wyatt and Marquez turned to stare at her.

"I know where I've seen you before," she said, her voice muffled by her fingers. "You dated Marcie."

"Lady, I've never met you. I don't know what you're talking about," Marquez replied.

She turned to Wyatt. "I recognize that grin. She e-mailed me a photo of the two of them. They were friends who dated off and on." Her heart was pounding, but her brain was racing even faster.

EMT. Marcie. Terrified.

"You kidnapped Marcie," Nina cried. "You pulled her hair out by the roots and stuck the necklace in it and planted it at the burial site with the remains, didn't you? Making sure we'd be able to find it."

Marquez looked panicked. He spread his hands. "I swear, I don't—"

Wyatt stood. "You're wasting my time here. If you don't start talking in the next fifteen seconds, I'm charging you with everything I listed, plus resisting arrest, plus anything else I can get away with. In fact, I *will* add murder. The murder of Marcie James."

Marquez's face turned a sickly pale. "No! No! You can't. Please. Marcie's not dead!"

Wyatt glanced at Nina. She was frozen in shock, her eyes wild and bright as she stared at Marquez.

"How do you know that? What did you have to do with Marcie James's kidnapping?" Wyatt quizzed.

"I was… I just did what Marcie wanted me to do," Marquez explained. "You don't get it. She planned the fake kidnapping. She wanted to escape. Needed to. She was sure somebody was trying to kill her."

Nina's heart nearly stopped. Marcie had faked her own kidnapping. She'd disappeared on purpose. She'd almost killed Wyatt.

Everything Nina had believed for the past two years was suddenly turned upside down. She'd blamed Wyatt for causing her best friend's death. But now she had to face the truth.

Her best friend had almost killed the man Nina loved.

Loved?

Dear heavens, did she love him? Her heart was beating again, so fast and so loudly she was sure Wyatt and Marquez could hear it. It wasn't possible. Not after three days.

Why couldn't she take a hint? His brusque dismissal of her apology this morning should have squelched any blossoming attraction caused by their night of lovemaking. But strangely, it hadn't.

One night, and she was already in too deep. Not only had the sex been the best she'd ever had, but lying next to him, protected by his strong body, had awakened feelings inside her that she'd long feared she would never experience again.

She'd spent her childhood surrounded by a shield of protection. Her father and her older brother had taken care of her. They'd been her knights in shining armor. But then her dad had died, and less than a year later, her older brother was gone, too, killed overseas in combat.

The feeling that nothing could harm her had died with them.

Until now.

Dear heavens, what was she going to do when this investigation was over? Now that Wyatt had made her love him?

His voice interrupted her thoughts. "Did Marcie's plans include trying to kill a Texas Ranger?" he thundered, his expression dark and ominous.

Marquez winced. "Hey, Marcie gave me that gun. I'd never shot a gun before in my life. Didn't you see how wild the shots were? It was a complete accident that I hit you. I'm sorry, man."

"You're sorry?" Nina burst out. To her surprise,

Wyatt leaned back in his chair and appeared to relax. It was a few seconds before he spoke.

"Where is she?" he muttered.

Marquez's eyes widened.

"Damn it!" Wyatt's fist came down on the table, bouncing the pens. "Where. Is. She?"

Marquez shrugged. "I—I don't know, man. She hid out with me for a few days. Then she said she had to disappear. Said she had a friend who would help her."

"Who?" asked Wyatt.

Marquez shrugged again. "I don't know—"

"Don't give me that. Male or female? Here in town?" Wyatt quizzed.

"I said I don't know."

Wyatt glared at him. "Listen, bud. Right now you are on the hook for a very serious crime that carries serious time. The only way I can help you is if you cooperate. So if you know anything about why Marcie felt she had to disappear, you'd better start talking."

"All I know is she was afraid of somebody. Terrified. And she wouldn't tell me who."

"You're going to have to do better than that."

"I swear, man. She said if I knew, I'd be in danger, too."

"So you lied, stole and nearly killed for her, and you didn't know why you were doing it?"

Marquez wiped the sweat off his face with his shirt-sleeve and then eyed Wyatt narrowly. "Just exactly what can you do for me? I mean, if I tell you who I *think* she might have been afraid of?"

Nina watched Wyatt's expression turn black and his fists clench. She held her breath, but to his credit, he didn't go across the table at Marquez.

"I'll consider recommending assault with intent, rather than attempted first-degree murder," Wyatt said.

Marquez swallowed visibly. "I think she was scared of her ex."

Wyatt's expression didn't change.

"I knew it!" Nina burst out. "I knew it! Marcie was afraid Shane would kill her."

Chapter Seventeen

It took another hour or so for Wyatt to wrap up the paperwork and call a Ranger from Austin to come and take Marquez into custody, but finally, by eleven, Wyatt and Nina were back at the Bluebonnet Inn. As they climbed the stairs, Wyatt saw how tired she was by the droop of her shoulders and the heaviness of her step.

At the top of the stairs, he put his hand on the small of her back and guided her toward her door. "You're exhausted. Get some sleep," he said gently. "I won't wake you up until the last possible moment tomorrow."

She started to shake her head.

"No arguments. You'll need it, trust me. We've still got a lot of work ahead."

"Wyatt—"

He bent and stole a quick kiss. "I won't let you miss any of the good stuff."

"Promise?"

"Promise. Now give me your key."

She sent him an odd look, but handed it over.

He opened her door for her, instructed her to sleep for at least eight hours, then unlocked his own door and went inside.

He knew exactly what the look she'd shot at him

meant. She didn't understand why he was acting as though nothing had happened between them.

He couldn't blame her. He didn't understand himself. All he knew was that until this case was over, he couldn't afford to let his guard down again. His strengths were his focus and determination. He had to pour all his energy and concentration into the job at hand. Saving the innocent and catching the guilty was his purpose. For him, anything that took his mind off the job had to be ignored. Anything like sexual attraction or falling in love.

As he showered, he tried to figure out why pouring every ounce of his energy into seeking justice wasn't satisfying. Not this time. For the first time in his life, he was having trouble compartmentalizing the separate parts of his life.

He dried off, pulled on sweatpants and lay down with a sigh. He was so tired, his body ached. But when he turned over, his nose picked up on the subtle scent of roses.

With a growl, he turned over the other way, trying to ignore the longing that filled his heart, the longing to have Nina lying next to him. Her soft, even breaths were more soothing and relaxing than anything he'd ever experienced.

How was he going to sleep without her next to him?

BY NINE O'CLOCK the next morning Wyatt and Nina were back at the sheriff's office. Nina wanted to read Marquez's statement, to see just exactly what he'd said about Marcie.

Wyatt hadn't heard back about the examination of the boot casts, so that was his first question for Hardin. "Yeah," the sheriff said. "I've got the results right here. Turns out the footprints from the crime scene are Shane's. The indentations on the heels were made by taps. Shane wears rubber taps on the heels of his boots."

"Damn it. Obviously his prints would be there. All the prints couldn't have been his, could they? Didn't your deputy take more than one casting?"

"He took seven. Three were too smeared to identify. The other four were consistent with Shane's boots."

"So we still don't know anything about who attacked him." A faint memory came to Wyatt. "You know what? I need to talk to the doctor. I've got Nina's photos of Tolbert's head wound. There was a faint redness in a similar shape next to the wound. Like a hesitation wound."

"Hesitation wound? What are you saying? That Shane hit *himself* over the head?"

Wyatt shrugged. "It's within the realm of possibility. That's why I want to show the pictures to the doctor. Get his opinion."

Hardin shook his head. "Fine. I can't stop you. But I'm telling you, I find it hard to believe that Shane would risk his job. He's worked really hard to get where he is."

"I've got to cover all the bases…" Wyatt was interrupted by the ringing of his cell phone. "This is Lieutenant Colter." He heard nothing but rapid, shaky breathing on the other end of the phone. "Hello? Who is this?"

"I need help! Daniel's been shot. At his house. Please hurry." The feminine voice was a whisper, but the words might as well have been a scream.

"Who is this?" Wyatt demanded, shooting up out of his chair. His hand rested briefly on the hilt of his weapon as he caught Hardin's eye. "Ellie?"

The sheriff got the message. He stood and grabbed his holster.

To Wyatt's right, Nina bounded up.

"Talk to me. Tell me where you are." Wyatt listened, but all he heard was the woman's quick, shallow breaths.

"Just hurry, or he's going to die," the woman gasped.

The phone went dead.

"Damn it," Wyatt spat.

Hardin was already headed out the door, with Nina right on his heels. "What's going on?" he threw back over his shoulder. "Who was that?"

"A woman. Said Daniel Taabe had been shot. At his house," Wyatt called.

Outside, Hardin headed for his truck, and Wyatt sprinted toward his Jeep.

Nina climbed in beside him.

As they pulled away, Mayor Sadler and Jerry Collier walked out of the courthouse. The mayor raised his hand to wave, then frowned. Collier looked shocked, and Wyatt could see his prominent Adam's apple bob from where he sat.

Wyatt checked the last call that came in and dialed the number. He listened to the rings until voice mail picked up. Sure enough, the voice was Taabe's. Wyatt cut the connection. "That call came from Daniel Taabe's house," Wyatt said as he followed Hardin's truck onto the road to Taabe's house.

"Did you give Ellie your cell number?" Nina asked Wyatt.

Wyatt muttered a curse. "I gave out my card to everybody I talked to. So yeah. She has it. Charla Whitley has it. And of course, I gave Daniel a card, too, so anyone at his house could find my number. The call could have come from just about anybody."

It took them less than five minutes to get to Taabe's

house. Wyatt pulled up beside Hardin's truck. "Stay here until we clear the house," he ordered Nina as he jumped out of the Jeep and hit the ground running, drawing his weapon.

The house looked dark, and the driveway was empty. He glanced around, wondering if Taabe had put his truck in the barn or behind the house. He slowed down and crept up to the front door, a few steps behind Hardin.

Hardin pounded on the front door. "Daniel Taabe. Police! Open up!"

Nothing.

"Police!" Hardin yelled again. "We're coming in!" He glanced back at Wyatt, who nodded, then kicked the door in.

Inside, a hallway separated the living area from the bedrooms. Wyatt took the right side, and Hardin the left.

Wyatt checked the living room, including the coat closet.

"Front bedroom clear," he heard Hardin say.

"Living room clear," he answered. He sidled along the wall to the door that led into a small dining room. He could see the kitchen beyond it.

"Second bedroom clear," called Hardin.

The tiny dining room couldn't have hidden a mouse. Wyatt stepped through it and into the kitchen. As soon as he rounded the door, he saw the blood and Daniel Taabe's black hair.

"Back bedroom clear."

"Hardin! In here!"

The sheriff appeared through a door on the left side of the kitchen. "Damn it," he said when he saw Taabe's body.

Wyatt leaned over and pressed his fingers against Taabe's carotid artery, although he knew it was futile. "He's dead. I'm going to get the professor."

He ran through the front of the house and outside and waved at Nina. To his relief, she waved back and then got out of the Jeep carrying her kit.

"I can tell by your face," she said when she reached his side. "Daniel's dead, isn't he?"

Wyatt nodded, wondering when he'd become so easy to read.

"How?"

"We haven't examined him yet."

When they got to the kitchen, Hardin was crouching beside Taabe's body. He spoke without looking up. "He hasn't been dead long. Blood hasn't had time to coagulate."

Nina snapped on a glove and knelt beside Taabe. She touched the edge of the pool of blood. "There's not even a demarcation line. What do you think, Reed? An hour?"

"Or less," said the sheriff.

"COD?" she asked.

"The cause of death is a gunshot wound to the upper chest," Hardin observed. "Through and through, judging by the amount of blood on the floor. Probably at close range."

"Through and through," Wyatt said. "Then we have a bullet."

Hardin nodded. "I haven't turned him over yet. Have you got your camera? I'll get started photographing the scene."

Nina took her camera out of her kit and handed it to Hardin. "Go ahead." She stood. "What do you think? Did he confront the person who planted the bone and hatchet in his truck?"

Wyatt shook his head. "I wish I knew. First thing I want to do is question Ellie Penateka. She may have been the last person to see him alive."

Nina looked at him questioningly.

"There, on the kitchen counter." Wyatt gestured with his head. "Two coffee cups. One with lipstick on the brim."

Nina looked where Wyatt had gestured. Sure enough, there were two large yellow coffee cups sitting on the counter, along with two crumpled paper napkins. She took in the rest of the kitchen. There were dishes that matched the cups on the drain board. She walked over to the sink. On the shelf above lay a woman's turquoise ring.

She was about to point it out to Wyatt when her phone rang. She glanced at the display. She didn't recognize the number. "Hello?"

"N-Nina? Oh, thank goodness I got you. I think my phone's about to go dead."

Nina almost dropped the phone. She knew that voice. It was a voice she had known for ten years but hadn't heard in more than two. A voice she'd thought she would never hear again. "Marcie?"

"Yes…" Marcie's voice broke.

"Dear heavens, Marcie. Where are you? What's going on?"

Wyatt, still crouched next to Daniel's body, twisted and sent her a shocked glance. She met his gaze, knowing her own expression was as stunned as his.

Marcie was talking to her on her phone.

Marcie was *alive*.

"You're there, aren't you? At Daniel's. He's dead, isn't he?" Marcie sobbed.

"I'm sorry, Marcie. Yes." It was hard to talk. Her lips felt numb. Her throat was constricted. "Where are you? What were you thinking?"

"Listen to me, Nina. I don't have time to explain. I'm at the cabin—the one above Dead Man's Road."

"Dead Man's Road?"

"It's the road out to the crime scene. The cabin is on the ridge above. Daniel told me to come here—"

"Daniel told you? Marcie, were you here? Did you see who shot Daniel?"

"I was…in the basement, taking a nap. I heard the shot, and then I heard a vehicle start up. When I came upstairs, Daniel was on the floor." Marcie took a shaky breath. "I swear, Nina, I wanted to call a doctor, but Daniel told me to take his truck and get to safety. I didn't want to leave him."

"Marcie, tell me what…" Nina suddenly found herself empty-handed. Wyatt had grabbed her phone.

"Marcie," he snapped. "It's Wyatt Colter. Where are you?" He listened for a second, then turned his head toward the sheriff, who had pulled out his cell phone and was about to dial. He shook his head violently and held up a hand. "Don't call anybody. Who's at the crime scene this morning?"

"Shane," Hardin replied.

Wyatt cursed. "Marcie, can you see the crime scene or the road? No? Well, Shane is on duty over there. You want us to call him?"

Nina heard Marcie's terrified voice through the phone. "No! Please. Not Shane."

"Okay, okay. I understand. We won't. You stay put. I'm on my way." Wyatt hung up and handed the phone back to Nina. "Damn it."

Hardin spoke up. "I'll get Kirby to head over there—"

"No. I'm going. Marcie knows I'm coming. Just be ready, in case I need backup." Wyatt already had his keys in his hand and was headed for the door.

Nina followed him.

At the door, he turned, pinning her with those intense blue eyes. "What the hell are you doing?"

She stood up to him, refusing to be intimidated by his expression or his attitude. "Marcie was dead. Now she's alive," she said. "I have to see her."

"There's no way I'm taking you into such a potentially dangerous situation," Wyatt replied.

She lifted her chin and gave him back stare for stare. "I will steal a car if I have to," she said. "But I *will* see my friend. The only way you're going to stop me is by arresting me or knocking me out."

His eyes glinted dangerously, and for a small space of time, she almost believed he might accept her challenge. But in the next split second his gaze wavered, and she knew she'd won.

She didn't have time to even sigh with relief, because Wyatt was out the door and loping to his Jeep. She barely made it into the passenger seat by the time he had the engine running and in reverse.

Neither one of them said anything on the way. Wyatt's Jeep ate up the roads, kicking up clouds of white dust. It hadn't rained since that first night.

Nina's seat belt strained against her midsection as Wyatt careered onto Dead Man's Road and immediately took an abrupt turn up a steep back road.

Several bumpy, dusty moments later, Nina saw a weathered cabin through a stand of trees.

Wyatt stopped the car. "Stay here."

"Fat chance, cowboy." Nina's heart was pounding in anticipation of seeing her friend. Marcie had lied, she'd broken the law, she'd pretended to be dead, but Nina still loved her.

Marcie was her friend.

Wyatt grunted but didn't say anything else until they were out of the Jeep and headed toward the front door. "You think you can stay by my side?"

"It would be my pleasure," she murmured.

Wyatt sent her an intense sidelong glance. An odd expression lit his face, but as soon as it had appeared, it was gone, and he was back to being the tough, brave Texas Ranger. He drew his weapon. "We'll go in on this side of the cabin. There's only one window, so there's less likelihood that they'll spot us."

"It's just Marcie. Why…?"

His hand went up, palm out. "Follow my orders or go back to the car."

Nina bit her lip. "Yes, sir."

"When I move, you move. *Not before*. If I do this—" he held up his fist at shoulder height "—you stop, and don't move until I wave you forward. Got it?"

"Got it."

Nina's answer was drowned out by the crack of a gunshot, which shattered the silent air around them. She heard a thud to her right. A puff of dust or smoke rose from the trunk of a tree not three feet away.

Before she could react, two more shots split the air. One of them came close enough that her heart jolted hard in her chest—so hard it could have been a blow.

Wyatt's hand wrapped around her wrist and pulled her down beside him. She hadn't even noticed him crouch down.

"That was close," she whispered, putting her hand over her heart. "I nearly jumped out of my…" She drew back her hand and looked at it. The fingertips were coated with red paint.

Then her eyes lost focus and she felt dizzy and faint.
What if it wasn't paint? she thought.

What if it was *blood?*

"Wyatt?" she whispered.

Chapter Eighteen

Wyatt looked in horror at Nina's stained fingers, then at her shirt, where dark red blood was spreading.

She'd been shot.

"Nina!" He shoved his gun into his shoulder holster and dove toward her. He ripped her shirt apart, popping the buttons.

Blood coated the area between her shoulder and neck, and dripped down around her left breast.

"Oh, God, Nina!" He took a piece of her shirt and used it to wipe away as much blood as he could. "I knew it," he groaned. "I knew something would happen to you."

He'd gotten her shot. The thing he'd most feared had come true. He'd sworn to protect her, and he'd failed.

He peered at the wound. It was her shoulder, in that sweet spot between the shoulder joint and the clavicle. Thank God, it hadn't pierced any organs or broken any bones. He folded the cloth and pressed it against the entry wound.

Mere inches above his head, a bullet whizzed by. And another. Whoever had shot Nina hadn't stopped. He was still shooting. Still aiming to kill.

"Hey, Professor," Wyatt muttered. "You're going to be fine. All I need to do is lift you up a little bit so I can see your back. It might hurt, but I promise you you're going to be okay."

"I trust you," she whispered.

His arms shook as he slid them around her back and lifted, giving her as much support as he could. He didn't feel any wetness. A good sign? Or a bad one?

She moaned as he shifted her slightly so he could see her back. No exit wound. That meant the bullet was still in there. He ran his palm along her skin.

There. The small lump he felt had to be the bullet. He needed to get her to a hospital now and get that bullet taken out.

But he couldn't. His priority, once he'd assured himself that Nina wasn't in mortal danger, was to stop the gunman and save Marcie.

This time.

Another shot rang out, too close. Wyatt ducked and covered Nina with his body. "Don't worry. I've got you," he whispered.

"I know." He heard the strain in her voice. She was in pain. A lot of pain, and there was nothing he could do about it.

"Listen to me," he whispered in her ear. "I need you to stay here. Stay hidden. Can you call Hardin for backup? Because whoever shot you is in there. And I've got to stop him."

Nina nodded. Her lips were pressed together and white at the edges. Her eyes were closed. But she held out her hand for the phone. "I'll call him. You save Marcie," she mumbled.

Wyatt pressed his lips to her forehead. "I'm going to save both of you."

"I know." When he gave her the phone, she grabbed his hand and squeezed it. "Wyatt, be careful."

Wyatt squeezed back. Then he moved carefully, staying low, until he was twenty feet away from Nina. He didn't want the shooter in the cabin to have any idea where she was. He needed to draw the fire away from her.

And he needed to get inside that cabin.

He raised himself up enough to aim and shoot at the open side window of the cabin. Then he ducked. The shooter responded with three quick rounds.

Wyatt stayed low, sneaking from one scrubby tangle of sagebrush to another. He fired at the window once, twice, three times. Then he took several shots at the front porch. He knew that, although the bang would sound in the same place, the bullets would hit or ricochet off the wood on the front corner of the cabin. The shooter's perception of where the sounds came from would be confused, unless he was very experienced.

Sure enough, the shots from inside the house stopped.

Wyatt used the lull to duck and roll, ending up next to the rear corner of the cabin. He pushed himself to his feet, his back against the rough plank wall. Then he sidled toward the back and peered around the corner.

Sure enough there was a rear door. Beyond it he saw the nose of a white pickup.

Damn. The shallow print of boots in the dust led from the pickup to the wooden stoop. Someone had used this door recently. Someone who'd driven a white pickup.

Wyatt crept over to the door and gingerly turned the knob. It turned easily and quietly. A little surprising for such a dilapidated cabin.

He could hear shots coming from the front of the

cabin. His stomach clenched. Nina wouldn't have stood up, would she? Not after he'd told her to stay down.

Surely not. Still, she was stubborn and bullheaded. Just about as bullheaded as he was. But she was wounded, damn it.

He suppressed the urge to yell out a warning to her. If he did that, he'd be handing the shooter a lot of valuable information on a silver platter. Where he was, and that there were two of them at least.

Not knowing what to expect, he pushed open the door and angled around it, leading with his weapon. He found himself in a mudroom, which led to the large main room. The interior of the cabin was bathed in shadow, the only light coming from two bare windows.

On one side of Wyatt was a short hallway. He started that way but stopped when he heard a muffled curse and the unmistakable sound of a magazine being ejected from a semiautomatic handgun.

The shooter was out of bullets. He stiffened and laid his back against the wall, preparing to round the corner with his weapon ready to shoot. Before he could make his move, he heard a magazine being slapped into place. The man had reloaded.

More shots rang out.

At least the guy didn't know Wyatt was behind him. After all, it hadn't been more than two minutes since he'd left Nina, and it was an understatement to say that he'd been sparing with his shots.

But if another minute passed without a response from outside, the shooter would suspect that something was up. So Wyatt had to move fast.

Fast and smart.

He decided to take a chance and peek around the door into the main room, to get an idea of where the shooter was. From the sounds, he figured the man had moved from the side window to the front, which meant his back should be to Wyatt.

Carefully and quickly, he took off his hat and peered around the corner. What he saw shocked and sickened him.

Sprawled on the floor near the fireplace was the body of a young woman with blond hair. Wyatt didn't need a long look to know the woman was Marcie James.

Or to know that she was dead. Her sightless eyes caught the light from the windows.

Standing beyond her, at the open front window, was Shane Tolbert, straining to peek through the heavy curtains, his weapon aimed at something Wyatt couldn't see.

At that instant, Wyatt's ears picked up the faint sound of a car engine. Without wasting precious time assessing whether Tolbert had heard it, he acted.

"Tolbert, don't move." He kept his voice low and steady.

Tolbert tensed, then started to turn.

"I said don't move."

"Lieutenant Colter?" The deputy raised his hands slowly and let his gun dangle from his index finger.

"Drop the gun."

"Thank God it's you," Tolbert said, lowering his arms.

"Slowly!"

Tolbert set the gun on the floor and straightened. His face was pale. His eyes were wide, and a trickle of blood ran down his neck.

"Did you catch whoever was shooting at me? I thought I was dead, too." His gaze dropped to Marcie's body, and he shook his head, as if he couldn't believe his eyes.

Wyatt frowned. Tolbert was acting like Wyatt had rescued him. Like they were on the same side. But Wyatt didn't have time to waste on questions. Nina was out there, wounded, hurting, possibly bleeding to death.

The vehicle's engine got louder, and Wyatt heard the crunch of tires on limestone rocks.

"Put your hands behind your back and turn around," Wyatt ordered.

"What? You think I did it? Are you nuts?"

Wyatt gestured with his gun barrel. "Don't push me, Tolbert. Do it! And spread your legs."

The deputy obeyed. "I understand how this looks. Believe me. But you've got to listen to me. Marcie called me. She wanted to meet me up here. I couldn't believe it was her—after all this time."

Wyatt snapped the cuffs shut around the deputy's wrists just as a second vehicle roared to a stop outside.

God, let it be the ambulance.

"Colter, you've got to believe me. Somebody hit me over the head as soon as I walked in the door. When I woke up, I saw Marcie lying there…" Tolbert's voice broke.

The door burst open, and Reed Hardin stepped in, brandishing his weapon.

"Sheriff! Tell him I loved Marcie," Tolbert yelled.

Hardin's surprised gaze took in the scene before him. "What the hell?"

"Why were you shooting at us?" Wyatt prodded.

Tolbert drew in a shaky breath. "I thought whoever killed Marcie was trying to kill me."

Wyatt had to hand it to the deputy. He was convincing. But was he innocent? "Save it, Tolbert. I'm taking you in for the murder of Marcie James. Shane Tolbert, you have the right to remain silent—"

The sound of an engine interrupted Wyatt. Red blinking lights glanced off the walls.

"Hardin, you got this?" Wyatt asked. "Because Nina's out there. Tolbert shot her."

"Sure. Go." The sheriff sounded slightly dazed.

"I shot Nina? Oh, no!" Tolbert moaned.

Wyatt shoved his gun into its holster as he rushed out the door. But he was too late. The ambulance, carrying its precious cargo, disappeared into a cloud of white dust down the steep back road.

WYATT RUSHED IN THROUGH the emergency room's automatic doors and headed straight toward the desk. "Nina Jacobson. Gunshot wound," he snapped.

The woman behind the desk recoiled. "What? Who?"

From the corner of his eye, Wyatt saw a hospital security guard start toward him.

"Lieutenant Colter, Texas Ranger. I need to check on Nina Jacobson."

The woman looked at his badge, the guard and then the computer screen in front of her. "Uh, cubicle eight," she said, pointing to Wyatt's left. "That way."

Wyatt took off, nearly running into a steel cart. He skirted the edge of the cart and skidded to a stop in front of the cubicle labeled eight. When he shoved the curtain aside, his heart skipped a beat.

Nina was lying on a hospital bed, seemingly surrounded by tubes and wires. Her face was impossibly pale against her ink-black hair. An oxygen tube was anchored to her nostrils, and the electronic display on the box beside her bed beeped in rhythm with her heartbeat.

A nurse finished injecting a yellow liquid into a port on the IV tubing that led from a huge bandage above her wrist to the bag of fluid hanging beside the bed. The nurse, whose multicolored jacket had puppies and kittens cavorting on it, frowned at him.

"I'm Lieutenant Wyatt Colter, Texas Ranger," he said defensively. "She's my…my…"

His throat tightened. His what? His colleague? His Professor? His *love?*

Nina opened her eyes and sent him a ghost of a smile. "Hey, cowboy. Still as eloquent as ever, I see."

"You forgot charming," he replied.

"No," she muttered, "I didn't forget." She licked her lips and lifted her left hand to adjust the oxygen tube.

He caught her hand in his. "Can she have some water?"

The nurse glowered at him. "No. She's about to go into surgery."

"Surgery?" Adrenaline sent Wyatt's heart pounding. He knew the bullet in her shoulder had to come out. But knowing it in his head and seeing her—pale and weak and being prepped to go under the knife were two very different things.

"I'll be right back, Ms. Jacobson." The nurse left the cubicle, yanking the curtain closed behind her.

Wyatt couldn't take his eyes off Nina.

She squeezed his hand. "Don't look at me like that," she said hoarsely.

He grimaced. The oxygen was already making her throat raw. "Like what?"

"Like I'm about to—"

He stopped her words with his fingers. "Don't even joke about that," he said gruffly.

"What happened?" she croaked.

"You don't need to worry about that right now."

"Wyatt, I need to know who was shooting at us. It was Shane, wasn't it?"

He nodded.

"Did he kill Daniel?"

"I don't know."

She coughed.

"Now, hush. You need to rest and stay calm." He bent forward and kissed her. Her lips were dry, so he ran his tongue along them to moisten them.

She laughed softly. "Thank you," she whispered. Then she kissed him back.

His heart leapt and stuck in his throat. The feel of her lips had sent signals that his body didn't want to ignore. Signals that were bound to cause him a lot of embarrassment when that nurse came back.

But far stronger than his physical need was the fierce protective urge that filled him.

"I was supposed to keep you safe," he said, pressing his forehead against hers. "And I didn't."

She stiffened. "Oh, Wyatt…"

He knew the leap her brain had made, because his had made the same instantaneous jump. She was thinking about Marcie.

God, he'd failed to protect her friend—twice.

"Wyatt, tell me about Marcie."

He pulled back and reluctantly met her gaze. But for the life of him, he couldn't think of the right words.

Or any words.

She touched his cheek with her left hand. "It's okay. I know she didn't make it. I heard the radio in the ambulance when Reed called for the ME. She was pronounced dead on the scene. Did Shane shoot her?"

He nodded. "He claims he found her like that, and somebody hit him on the head. I don't believe him. He had the gun in his hand."

"Could you tell anything about the blood spatter? Or the angle of entry?"

He couldn't help but smile. "No, Professor. I didn't have much time for that. I arrested him on the spot, though, and turned him over to Sheriff Hardin. I've already called Ranger Sergeant Olivia Hutton, my crime scene analyst. I've made sure she understands to check everything thoroughly—herself."

"Good." Nina's voice was hoarse and her eyes were filled with tears. "Poor Marcie."

Wyatt sat on the edge of the bed and laid his palm against her cheek. "God, Nina. I'm so sorry." He muttered as his heart wrenched in grief and regret. "I was too late—again."

Nina's fingers brushed his lips. "No," she said vehemently. "No you weren't. You did everything you could. Today and two years ago. It took me a while to realize what kind of man you are. It shouldn't have taken that long. I should have known the first time I met you."

Wyatt caught her hand in his and squeezed it. He couldn't look at her.

She went on. "I should have known that badge was more than just a piece of silver that gives you the authority to bring in the bad guys. That piece of silver represents you, down to your soul."

"Nina, I—"

"Shh. Marcie got Marcie killed. And I'm afraid she got Daniel killed, too. If she'd been truthful with you—if she had accepted your protection—then she might be alive today." She shook her head. "I lost my friend two years ago."

Wyatt's heart was still pounding, but now not with fear or lust. "God, I love you."

Nina blinked. She knew she was hazy from the drugs they'd given her, but was she hallucinating, too? Did she imagine him saying what she wanted so badly to hear? "What did you say?"

Wyatt's face had gone pale, which wasn't a good sign. "I said I love you—I think."

Those last two words wrenched the breath right out of her. It took her two tries to be able to speak. "You—you think?"

He shook his head and mumbled a curse. "No, I don't…I mean, I didn't…"

She bit her lips to keep from moaning aloud. She lay back against the pillows. "It's okay, cowboy."

He growled deep in his throat. "Look, none of this is coming out the way I wanted it to." He took a deep breath. "I love you. I want to marry you, damn it!"

A clatter of metal against metal announced the nurse's return. She stopped, an amused look on her face. "Wow! How romantic," she drawled. "Now if you're done with that lovely proposal, the bride needs to go to surgery."

To Nina's drowsy amusement, Wyatt's face turned red. He jumped up from his seat on the bed. "Right. Sure," he stammered. "I'll, uh—"

The nurse held up a syringe. "They're on their way from the operating room to get you now. After this shot, you'll be pretty sleepy. So if you've got anything to say, you'd better say it now."

Nina smiled at her flustered Texas Ranger. "My charming, eloquent hero. It's settled, then. I want to marry you, too, damn it."

"You do?" Wyatt's face was still red as a beet.

The nurse snorted as she injected the drug. "How could she pass up such a sweet proposal? You'd better kiss her fast. She's about to nod off to sleep."

Nina lifted her head for his kiss, which was the

sweetest, most tender kiss she'd ever experienced. "Are you running off to chase bad guys?" she murmured.

"Sheriff Hardin and Sergeant Hutton can handle the bad guys for now. I'm not going anywhere until you're all sewn up. I'll be right here when you wake up. You can count on it."

She could no longer keep her eyes open, but she knew that Wyatt Colter, Texas Ranger, was a man of his word. "I know," she whispered, smiling.

* * * * *

INTRIGUE...

2-IN-1 ANTHOLOGY

TWELVE-GAUGE GUARDIAN

by B.J. Daniels

Journalist Raine is on the run from a killer, but her luck
could be about to change when she catches the eye of
sexy cowboy Cordell Winchester.

SHOTGUN SHERIFF

by Delores Fossen

Texas Ranger Livvy's been sent to Comanche Creek as a
forensic expert, horning in on Sheriff Reed's investigation...
and getting him hot under the collar!

•••

2-IN-1 ANTHOLOGY

GUARDING GRACE

by Rebecca York

Grace was haunted by a sinister secret tied to her brooding
bodyguard Brady's brother's murder—a secret that
could tear them apart forever...

SAVING GRACE

by Patricia Rosemoor

Grace never thought she'd trust a man again...until she
met Declan, her gorgeous P.I. protector. He's duty bound
to safeguard her, but could she capture his heart?

**On sale from 17th June 2011
Don't miss out!**

Available at WHSmith, Tesco, ASDA, Eason
and all good bookshops

www.millsandboon.co.uk

0611/46a

INTRIGUE...

2-IN-1 ANTHOLOGY
MEDUSA'S SHEIKH
by Cindy Dees

Playboy Hakim lives life in a gilded cage, his family
blackmailed by terrorists...until exotic, mysterious
Cassandra enters his world.

HER SHEIKH PROTECTOR
by Linda Conrad

Caught in a war between two families, Rylie wants only to
bring her father's killer to justice. She not looking for love.
But the desire burning in Darin's eyes is irresistible!

•••

SINGLE TITLE
ROYAL CAPTIVE
by Dana Marton

Prince Istvan expected to inherit his crown, not lead a
death-defying chase to retrieve it. Until Lauryn stormed
into his life, set off sparks, and vanished—along
with his precious crown!

On sale from 1st July 2011
Don't miss out!

Available at WHSmith, Tesco, ASDA, Eason
and all good bookshops
www.millsandboon.co.uk

0611/46b

MILLS & BOON

are proud to present

June 2011
Ordinary Girl in a Tiara
by Jessica Hart
from Mills & Boon® Riva™

Caro Cartwright's had enough of romance – she's after a quiet life. Until an old school friend begs her to stage a gossip-worthy royal diversion! Reluctantly, Caro prepares to masquerade as a European prince's latest squeeze…

Available 3rd June 2011

July 2011
Lady Drusilla's Road to Ruin
by Christine Merrill
from Mills & Boon® Historical

Considered a spinster, Lady Drusilla Rudney has only one role in life: to chaperon her sister. So when her flighty sibling elopes, Dru employs the help of a fellow travelling companion, ex-army captain John Hendricks, who looks harmless enough…

Available 1st July 2011

Tell us what you think!

millsandboon.co.uk/community
facebook.com/romancehq
twitter.com/millsandboonuk

EB/M&B/RTL3

Discover Pure Reading Pleasure with

MILLS
BOON®

Visit the Mills & Boon website for all the latest in romance

Buy all the latest releases, backlist and eBooks

Find out more about our authors and their books

Join our community and chat to authors and other readers

Free online reads from your favourite authors

Win with our fantastic online competitions

Sign up for our free monthly eNewsletter

Tell us what you think by signing up to our reader panel

Rate and review books with our star system

www.millsandboon.co.uk

Follow us at twitter.com/millsandboonuk

 Become a fan at facebook.com/romancehq

2 FREE BOOKS
AND A SURPRISE GIFT

We would like to take this opportunity to thank you for reading this Mills & Boon® book by offering you the chance to take TWO more specially selected books from the Intrigue series absolutely FREE! We're also making this offer to introduce you to the benefits of the Mills & Boon® Book Club™—

- **FREE home delivery**
- **FREE gifts and competitions**
- **FREE monthly Newsletter**
- **Exclusive Mills & Boon Book Club offers**
- **Books available before they're in the shops**

Accepting these FREE books and gift places you under no obligation to buy, you may cancel at any time, even after receiving your free books. Simply complete your details below and return the entire page to the address below. You don't even need a stamp!

YES Please send me 2 free Intrigue books and a surprise gift. I understand that unless you hear from me, I will receive 5 superb new stories every month, including two 2-in-1 books priced at £5.30 each and a single book priced at £3.30, postage and packing free. I am under no obligation to purchase any books and may cancel my subscription at any time. The free books and gift will be mine to keep in any case.

Ms/Mrs/Miss/Mr _____ Initials _____

Surname _____

Address _____

_____ Postcode _____

E-mail _____

Send this whole page to: Mills & Boon Book Club, Free Book Offer, FREEPOST NAT 10298, Richmond, TW9 1BR

Offer valid in UK only and is not available to current Mills & Boon Book Club subscribers to this series. Overseas and Eire please write for details. We reserve the right to refuse an application and applicants must be aged 18 years or over. Only one application per household. Terms and prices subject to change without notice. Offer expires 31st August 2011. As a result of this application, you may receive offers from Harlequin (UK) and other carefully selected companies. If you would prefer not to share in this opportunity please write to The Data Manager, PO Box 676, Richmond, TW9 1WU.

Mills & Boon® is a registered trademark owned by Harlequin (UK) Limited.
The Mills & Boon® Book Club™ is being used as a trademark.